Once, a long time a
to never allow a m
for that way led
beauty with alluri
pregnable defenses a
The men who came to adore her, fought
to conquer her and learn her mysteries,
made her the toast of London, but none
were able to rouse her passions.

BEAUTY AWAKENS

But that hard-taught lesson is about to un-
ravel because of Sir James Stoker. Back in
England with a treasure of gold from his
adventures, newly knighted by Queen Victoria herself, and feted everywhere, the
handsome explorer has the world at his
feet. He's exactly the man Coco might have
dreamed about when she was young: a
tall, fair hero with a charming smile. Now
he's turned his energy toward winning
her, the most desirable and the least at-
tainable woman he knows; and Coco's
afraid James may just find his way past the
thorns that have so long protected her
from the world, and awaken her slumber-
ing heart . . . with just one kiss.

JUDITH IVORY

SLEEPING BEAUTY

An Avon Romantic Treasure

AVON BOOKS ◆ NEW YORK

AVON BOOKS, INC.
1350 Avenue of the Americas
New York, New York 10019

Copyright © 1998 by Judith Ivory
Published by arrangement with the author
Visit our website at **http://www.AvonBooks.com**
Library of Congress Catalog Card Number: 97-94766
ISBN: 0-380-78645-1

First Avon Books Printing: June 1998

AVON TRADEMARK REG. U.S. PAT. OFF. AND IN OTHER COUNTRIES, MARCA REGISTRADA, HECHO EN U.S.A.

Printed in the U.S.A.

WCD   10 9 8 7 6 5 4 3 2 1

Part 1

The Happy Kingdom

It must be remembered that Sleeping Beauty was a hundred years older than the prince. She was from another era entirely.

From the Preface to The Sleeping Beauty
DuJauc translation of Perrault's
La Belle au bois dormant
Pease Press, London, 1877

Chapter 1

London

James Stoker, or rather—he liked to remind himself—*Sir* James Stoker these days, dashed between horses and carriages, finally leaping a puddle to get himself across a busy London street. The street, Blenchy Road, actually, was a minor, quasi-residential thoroughfare just north of Mayfair. Scarcely had he stepped up onto the curb, however, than a passing coach wheeled through the puddle he had vaulted. The backs of his legs were sprayed with a small rooster tail of water, the bottom of his greatcoat and trousers instantly wet. James stomped once or twice, then began to walk, bouncing even a little on the balls of his feet. It was a cool enough spring day that he could have been uncomfortable for his legs being doused. Yet it was impossible to dampen his spirits.

They were unusually high. Or perhaps not so unusual. In the thirty-six days he had been back in England he had virtually awakened every morning and gone to sleep every night in the same sweet

3

state of buoyant grace. Around the clock lately, he was so cheerful, he hardly knew what to do with himself.

He was slightly amused with his state of mind. A fairly sophisticated man, he found it all but in poor taste to go around with a stupid grin on his face. The truth was, though, that his life was going unreasonably well—and it had gone so beastly rotten for so bloody long that he knew to appreciate good fortune when he stumbled into a little.

He had stumbled into quite a bit, in fact. For one, he was alive, something he would have bet money a month ago would not be the case. He had new living arrangements that were some of the most comfortable he had ever known, in an architectural marvel built by an English king four hundred years ago and rooted in more tradition and pure, solemn Englishness than just about anywhere else on earth. And nothing could be too English for James, who had never thought to see his beloved homeland again. Moreover, he had arrived in his country a hero, Queen Victoria herself knighting him three days ago. He had gleefully signed his name this very morning, Sir James Stoker, KB. The Order of the Bath, no minor or courtesy knighthood. The Queen had been quite sincere in her appreciation.

Beyond this honor, he had stepped into a host of more minor—and more remunerative—ones. Within the last month, he had been appointed to a generously endowed stipend, honored with three different prizes, and been voted in as the Vice-Provost of his college at Cambridge, making him the youngest Vice-Provost at All Souls College in more than a hundred years (which also accounted for his wonderful living arrangements). Best of all, James had been named chairman of the Council of the Senate's Financial Board *and* made Deputy Vice-Chancellor, both positions that functioned hand in hand with the Vice-Chancellor himself, who ruled de facto over the entire university. Either appointment would have said that James's star was rising; the two together made him dream of that star one day settling into the seat of the Vice-Chancellory itself.

For James was ambitious. He had left England for the sake of furthering himself. He had suffered for it, quite nearly died for it. And now, as seemed just, he was returned to find all his early aspirations met: a modest seat of power, undisputed renown, and, after all his stipends, salaries, prizes, fellowship dividends, and appointments were added up, enough money for pretty much anything he wanted, including a natty new wardrobe, a cook (he no longer had to suffer through his gyp's midday meals, the only thing English he despised), three first-rate horses, and the sportiest little calèche he had ever laid eyes on, one with red-hubbed, brass-spoked wheels.

James had landed in heaven. Or on earth with his soul bartered to his eyeteeth; he wasn't sure.

In any event, *carpe diem* didn't even begin to express his attitude. He spent his new wealth enthusiastically (and socked a little away). He imbibed his fame, blushing, basking in it. He lived off jubilation till, most days, he felt all but drunk from it.

Presently, James hummed lightly to himself as he scanned house numbers along Blenchy Road, looking for the address he'd been given. He stopped at the sign that read, "Mr. John Limpet, dental expert, gentleman's barber, and notary." Limpet's shingle hung from beneath the overhang of a simple two-story house. Here was the place. James went up the steps of what looked to be a two-story home in good care, freshly painted, clean windowpanes, flower boxes full of red geraniums beneath the windows. The door handle was bright, tended brass, as was the knocker with which he rapped.

A squat, squarish woman admitted him, conducting him to a "waiting area" with apologies. The good Mr. Limpet was with another client (victim, James thought, for he could hear the faint grind of a dental engine); the dentist's schedule was running late.

James found himself in a small anteroom, a former sun parlor, perhaps. He shrugged out of his coat—the room was warmed by afternoon sun, not stuffy, but clear and comfortable. He took a seat on the window bench. It was a congenial room with chairs along its circumference. One wall was covered with miniatures. There must have been fifty of them placed in a pleasing disorder, all of flowers. From a distance they didn't look too bad, possibly the result of talent.

It was then, as he came to the end of the wall display, that James saw he was not alone. He nodded to a woman sitting across from him in the far corner. She let out a soft hiccupping sob.

"Are you all right?" he asked.

She nodded, then waved a wrinkled handkerchief, shaking her head. It was nothing. Pay no mind.

He tried politely to ignore her, since that seemed

to be what she wanted, examining the wall of miniatures again, then a vase of carnations set into a
bookcase. But the woman's sniffles made him turn
back. She was overwrought. He realized she was
holding the side of her jaw.

"Your tooth?" he asked conversationally.

She nodded, then wiped at her nose.

"It hurts?"

Again she nodded.

"Well, you've come to the right place," he said.
The remark was intended as comfort.

Which it wasn't, apparently. She shook her head
again and began to weep silently. Her shoulders
shook from her trying to keep herself quiet. There
seemed nothing else for it. James got up, went over
to sit down beside her.

"Here." He offered his own dry handkerchief.
Hers was soggy. "Which tooth is it?" As if the
information would mean anything to him.

She gingerly rubbed two fingers over her left jaw,
a far back tooth.

"Oh, wait—" He suddenly realized. He reached
into his coat and drew out a snuff box he had been
carrying with him for a few months now. He opened
the silver lid to show what had nothing whatsoever
to do with snuff. "Cloves," he said. "I hit my tooth
a few months ago, chipped and loosened it. It gave
me fits, and I was far, far from anyone I would have
trusted to help. Some people I was with, though,
showed me a trick. I've lived off it: pack two or
three cloves around your tooth. The pain will sub-
side."

She looked at him skeptically. She had dark eyes,
thick, thick lashes, a pretty face, pretty even when

slightly puffy from crying. After a moment, she rather delicately reached out and plucked two cloves from his little storehouse. She put them in her mouth, then bent her head, hiding behind his handkerchief as she presumably arranged them with her tongue. She smiled up over of the handkerchief. From behind it, she murmured, ''Thank you.'' A slightly foreign sound, he thought.

In fact, she didn't look English. Or not typically English, at least. She was too fashionable. He judged her to be from the continent, one of those cosmopolitan women who had the money, time, and taste to put herself together with great care and to fabulous effect. Her hair was dark, in the present light almost black. It was swept up under a small fur hat. Her dress was made of dark green velvet, with dark, glossy brown fur at the collar and cuffs. In her lap lay suede gloves to match. Her clothes fit her as if they had been sewn onto her, not tightly, just perfectly conforming: round where her arms were round, curving exactly with her shoulders, her bosom, narrowing rib by rib to her waist, spreading across her lap.

She took a deep breath, then let it out as she took the handkerchief away from her face. She was *very* pretty, he realized. Slender and shapely. With the sweetest, gentlest visage. Delicate features. Almost fragile. The small bones of her face made her eyes look enormous. These eyes, also dark, met his. She murmured, ''It burns a little.'' Her English was so good it was hard to determine her exact origin; she was definitely foreign. He settled on French, though there was the off chance she was Italian.

"Clove oil," he explained. "It numbs. You'll be much better in a moment."

She looked down. Her dark lashes rimmed her eyes like kohl, large Cleopatra eyes that remained sheepishly downcast. "I wasn't really crying over the pain, though." She made a weak smile up at him. "The tooth is bad. Mr. Limpet has just told me that it has to come out."

James shrugged. These things happened. "Well, you will feel better then to have it over and done with."

She shook her head. "I dread it." She had the most lovely manner. Not bold, exactly, but unafraid, straightforward. Sure enough of herself to look a stranger in the eye and speak about her pain and fears.

"It won't hurt too much," he counseled. "He can give you laughing gas. You can chuckle your way through it; you'll hardly know it happens."

"It's not the pain of having it out—"

"What then?"

As if the next statement followed perfectly, she said, "I turn thirty-seven next week."

Seven years (and eight months) older than James himself. Though she didn't look it. Or yes, she did, in a way. There was a serenity to her, an ease that one seldom saw in young women, even as she sat there holding a soggy handkerchief wet from crying. A kind of maturity showed in her face most pleasantly—in faint lines at the corners of her eyes. From smiling too much, perhaps. And in a liveliness behind her eyes themselves. A kindness. Her regard lacked the demure casts and glancing diffidence that was so favored by the feminine upper class.

Her pretty, somehow welcoming eyes smiled, a really beautiful smile with a lot of small, white, perfectly fine teeth. "Yes!" she said quietly. "It's working better and better! Oh, thank you."

"My pleasure. In fact, my tooth has settled down. I am here today for Mr. Limpet to buff the chipped edge smooth. I should have done it a while ago. I keep cutting my mouth. Anyway, I get to keep my tooth for now, so here." James handed the silver snuff box full of cloves over to her. "Take this. Maybe your tooth will behave too, if you give it some time. Maybe it will fix itself. Lots of things do, you know."

Her fist closed around the gift. "Thank you, I appreciate it. I am glad to have your cloves, then." She continued, full of sincerity. "You see, I've never lost a tooth. It seems something that happens to—" She stopped, looked down again. "To toothless old crones." She laughed at her own foolishness.

James laughed, too. Her worry was so far removed from reality, it was ludicrous.

He listened to her laughter, a breathy sound that he wanted to hear again the moment it stopped.

Still smiling, she extended her arm straight out toward him, her hand dropped at the wrist, at the fur cuff of her narrow sleeve. It took several moments for James to understand that she was offering her fingertips. An unEnglish gesture. Not one he was used to, though he knew what to do. He took her fingers. They were cool. Soft and humid against his lips, when he kissed them.

"Mrs. Wild," she said. A most English name. She withdrew her hand with all the bearing of a duchess, a queen. "And, no," she continued with another soft laugh, "I don't normally introduce myself to men on mere seconds' acquaintance, but—" She laughed again, a woman who laughed a lot, this time a little self-consciously. "Well, since you have just saved my tooth—" She broke off once more, then her face opened with such a full and lovely smile, and she spoke with such earnestness, James was taken aback. She said, "Oh, I am so grateful." She reached over and squeezed his hand, a quick movement, then gone. "The ache is so much less. How very ingenious and good of you."

Her eyes held his with perfect candor, an undisguised warmth.

James asked, "And Mr. Wild?" He had already glanced at her hand, checking for a wedding ring. He knew there was none. "Is he English then? I believe you are not."

"Mr. Wild *was* English. But he passed on about two years ago."

"Aah." He tried not to look too pleased by the news.

"I am French by birth. My husband and I lived abroad. I have only been here a few months."

James made a nod of his head, a kind of bow. "Sir James Stoker," he said, trying to hid the smugness he felt. If she read the newspapers at all, she would know the name.

He met with disappointment, however, for her face remained politely blank.

"And what are you up to in England, Mr. Stoker?" she asked. "Why are you so happy?"

"Happy?"

"Yes. You are quite obviously joyous today. Let

me see." She teased. "I think you must have just proposed to the girl of your dreams, and she has said yes."

He quirked one brow, laughing. He was being courted by far too many families. If he had his way, he wouldn't find the girl of his dreams for years. It was too much fun choosing—and being wooed himself.

She tsked. "Aha, I'm wrong, I see." Again her light flurry of laughter. He was getting used to the way the sound punctuated her speech. "In that case," she ventured, "it must be that a woman you desperately wanted free of has at last let you go: honorably."

James let out a hoot. "Now, you're closer. I am just returned from Africa, and I never, never have to go back. Africa has let me go. And let me tell you, I am glad." He paused a moment, surprised to hear these words himself. They were not the ones he usually chose to define his current good fortune.

Then he knew why he had put it in such terms. She shook her head sagely, her brow furrowing into a serious expression. "Indeed," she said. "That is no continent for me either. I hear there are tribes down there that will eat you. Though these people have to beat the lions and leopards to you first."

They both chuckled over this romantic half-truth, the romantic horror. But James ascended into a kind of plane of relief. At last. Someone to sympathize, someone who didn't make his whole three-plus years in Africa into a noble, manly adventure. Which it categorically was not. He said, "Yes. I can't tell you how happy I am to sleep each night far, far away from shallow rivers with leeches and deserts with camels that spit. And I am relieved beyond measure to be well removed from swarms of mosquitoes and bats.''

Bats. God above. Yes. How good to be out of reach from flying, bony masses of fur that squealed like dying children and stank up everything about. He had never mentioned them aloud before and couldn't now speak, beyond passing remark, of bats so abundant they hung from trees like clustered fruit.

The light in the room grew hazy with the passing of a cloud outside. The incoming sunlight became muted, dust motes dancing visibly in the beam that poured through the windowpanes. Mrs. Wild turned toward him slightly, sitting crookedly in her chair, raising one elbow leisurely up onto her chair back. She sat on her discarded coat.

James meant to bring the conversation back to where it belonged, into the realm of inane chatter, niceties, all unpleasantness minimized.

But she said, ''I think the Burtons and Livingstons of the world quite mad to pursue so much danger, let alone discomfort.''

Exactly. James felt a little zing of rage, injustice. He found himself adding, ''It's almost galling, you know.'' A kind of confession poured out. As if *he* were under the influence of laughing gas, giddily telling a stranger the truth. ''A chipped tooth. It hardly seems worthy enough damage, considering I was at wit's end, lost, sick, and sure of dying in the midst of people to whom I could barely speak. I mean, I should be missing a leg, an arm, be wearing an eye patch. But no. Not even a scar. I am healthier and stronger than the day I left England. With nothing to show for three and a half years of hell but a tooth I banged on something or other on one of the numerous occasions when I blacked out and fell flat on my face.'' He let out a snort of disgust. ''And within the hour, even that will be fixed—'' He took a breath.

God, give him enough time and he would tell Mrs. Wild here his life's story.

His mouthful was hardly the heroic tack, hardly the vein in which he, the Queen, and the Vice-Chancellor spoke of these things. James had not told his true feelings to a soul. Not even himself, apparently. For he was mildly appalled to hear these words—and feel the extreme satisfaction of saying them. They were so true. And here he was, pouring himself out to an unknown woman in a dentist's waiting room, just because she seemed to recognize the truth when she heard it and have some sympathy for it. Just because she had a pretty face and an understanding mien.

He pressed his lips together, not sure what he had done—other than discomfit himself considerably.

She smiled at him and leaned forward. Again the light touch of her hand over his, again quickly withdrawn. ''Don't worry,'' she said. As if she could read his mind now as well. ''I won't mention it. I can see that you have embarrassed yourself by speaking so openly. But believe me, there is nothing wrong with being open. Everything right with it, in fact.'' She waved her hand as if she could wave away his concern. ''And your secrets are safe with me. Honestly. I *have* no one to share them with. And even if I did, I never tell tales. It's unseemly, don't you think? To go around telling one person what another one told you? I mean, if a person had wanted someone to know, he could have said himself, no?''

James said quickly, ''You are so right. Thank you.''

She nodded, her mouth pulling into a smiling line, just the faintest humor. Then she held up her new silver case of cloves. ''My pleasure,'' she said, repeating his words, indicating an exchange.

Rightly or wrongly, James felt his distress ease. Apparently, a cozy dentist's parlor could be a haven for a few minutes, a place to babble in safety. For that was certainly how it seemed.

The strangely charming Mrs. Wild stood. From her chair James picked up her coat, a loose, silky bundle of dense fur. He held it for her. It was not bulky, but rather the well-trimmed, feather-soft undercoat of a winter animal. The label sewn into the satin lining bore a name: Worth. And a city: Paris. The coat perfectly matched the fur at her cuffs and collar and the small hat that sat back on her head. The hat's netting—studded at each juncture with tiny bits of cut jet—had been folded back, presumably so she could have her good, eye-mopping cry. The net sparkled with these bits.

James stared down at it as he helped her, an arm at a time, into her coat. A coat sublimely soft in his hands, the lovely weight of smooth, glistening fur that poured all the way to the floor. It was really a gorgeous piece.

As was the woman who smoothed her gloved hands down the front of it, then pulled the coat's collar to her throat, her fists tight about its edge.

On a whim, James said suddenly, ''I have a party

to go to tonight. In my honor, actually. I would be delighted if you would accompany me.''

She glanced up, lifting one eyebrow. Her gentle smile became arch, faintly amused, faintly skeptical. She said, ''You are a lovely young man.''

The operative word was *young*.

''A dear,'' she added. She smiled again, less kindly.

All right, he had overstepped. It had been overly familiar for him to ask such a thing. As if he could pick her up off the street. But James found himself, since returned to England, not always in harmony with the rules of protocol and society. The same rules he had lived by four years ago occasionally struck him now as stupid, arbitrary. Why not? Why couldn't he ask a charming woman to go to an enjoyable celebration, and thus make it more enjoyable?

She said, ''You must find yourself a nice young woman to go with you to your parties.''

She reached above her head and lowered the netting of her hat over her face. For an instant—from behind the bobbinet, as her eyes held his—it seemed to be something more, something beneath all her chic and polite smiling: a flicker of indefinable sadness. Then it was gone.

''Thank you,'' she said again. Whatever James had seen, if he'd seen anything at all, she recovered quickly. ''Please tell Mr. Limpet that I have decided to keep my terrible tooth a while longer.'' She laughed—once more the treat of that whisper-like sound. ''I am just too attached to it, tell him. I can't give it up just yet. Maybe tomorrow. Maybe never. Thank you again, Mr. Stoker.''

And, with a sway of sliding fur, the lovely Mrs. Wild turned and disappeared through the haze of motes and sun out the door into a bright spring afternoon.

Chapter 2

The earliest known version of The Sleeping Beauty *is probably the legend of the valkyrie Brynhild. Interestingly enough, in this tale the princess sleeps in full armor—a warrior-maiden all alone on a deserted island surrounded by a wall of fire.*

From the Preface to The Sleeping Beauty
DuJauc translation
Pease Press, London, 1877

London
29 March 1876

Dearest David,

I'm so happy to hear you are settled in at last. The house sounds wonderful (though the bees are a little worrisome). I can't wait to see

18

what you have done with it. I will check the train schedules and be there before the end of the week.

Yes, indeed, I have heard from the publisher here in London. There was a letter in today's afternoon post. He liked the drawings I did for the Paris imprint, but he wants me to do new ones. He wants them to be "more English." Ha ha ha. So why doesn't he hire an English illustrator? you ask. I know the answer: He tells me the translator, some English ladyship or other, likes my drawings best. She likes all my "curlicues and squiggly things." Prized for squiggly things, but prized at least. At any rate Perrault's La Belle au bois dormant *is to become* The Sleeping Beauty *for Pease Press here in London, and none other than myself will be doing all the illustrations. I am very happy. Mr. Pease says it is to be a lovely book with gold edges and color plates—which alas means he wants a dozen sketches by the end of the summer in order to pick and choose which ones they will want in color. I have my work cut out for me.*

And, yes, thank you, I am better. Much better. Terrible of me to have felt so sorry for myself in my last letter. The above brought my spirits up considerably. But there is another reason I am feeling less woebegone. Don't laugh. I still have my awful tooth. At the dentist's today, the nicest young gentleman showed me how to ease the ache by sucking on clove buds. So now I intend to numb my pain with his tasty cure till the tooth either stops hurting or falls out!

The gentleman today had been to Africa, by the way. Stoker. Sir James Stoker, I think. Have you heard of him? He acted as if I should have, though in fact I know so little of England. (I laugh when I think that Mr. Pease wants my drawings to be more English. Does he want them to be grayer perhaps? Or wetter? Or more unfriendly, do you think? Don't answer that.) You are right, of course: I know little of London and elsewhere because I keep too much to myself. Just to show you I am taking your advice, I am going out to dinner tonight with three rich, calculating friends. I will spend all evening listening to jokes about things like dividends, interest rates, and negotiable securities.

Nothing like what I spoke of to my gallant hero in the dentist's parlor. He was so impetuous. And young. He made me laugh with all his cheeky, flirtatious antics. All quite good for my conceit. Still, it would never do, would it, to be chummy with a stranger just because he pleased one's vanity? And imagine the damage I could do a knight of Her Majesty Queen Victoria. In the end I was abrupt with him. For his own good. I am old enough and wise enough to know how to protect a man from his own imprudent gallantry.

Which I must now do a little with you, too, my dear: No, I do not think you should call me "Maman" nor address your letters thus. Please stop. No, people would not think it "only natural." "People" do not care that you are Horace Wild's heir, that I am his widow, that you love and appreciate my "unconditional maternal support" of you (which is my pleasure, all my pleasure, dear heart), and that you wish to honor me before the eyes of the world. Bare in mind you are in England, which is not the "world" at large. If someone caught wind of this Maman-business, the dust of my past could rise up— it could blacken your future. No. I say this firmly. I will hear no more of the matter.

Oh, England, silly old cow that she is. I despair of ever making friends here. I envy you the way you slide into your English skin. I laugh when I see how British you've become again—in only two short weeks. (And, yes, you may take me to your "hole-in-the-wall tea house" for clotted cream, whatever that is. It sounds ghastly.)

I dreamed last night of Italy. Of our beautiful time there in a pretty house by the sea. How lucky we were. Not that we aren't lucky now. We are, of course. Luckiest of all, I will see you soon. I delight in your enthusiasm for this new country. I bask in your affection and the private honor you do me daily.

A thousand kisses,
Coco

Chapter 3

◦—⟨○⟩○◦

I am finally able to write. I have been sick for untold numbers of days, weeks, months, perhaps years. Only God knows. As I staggered out of my hammock today, an equally disheartening fact greeted me: the chief of these people wears two of the micrometer microscopes of my altazimuth theodolite from his belt. I have no idea where the third has gone. It hardly matters. Two boys were given the wheels that determine the instrument's horizontal and vertical axes, which they played with and lost. It is almost redundant to add that my sextant is missing or that its lens seems to have been fashionably affixed somehow into the chief's wife's ear. Children. I owe my life to children with Lilliputian minds.

From the diaries of James Stoker
Principle Geologist to the 1872–1876
Royal Geographical Society expedition
from Transval north into the Congo Basin

The party to which James had invited Mrs. Wild was, in fact, at Buckingham Palace, in the largest state ballroom—the only space of sufficient size to hold the public exhibit of what he'd brought back with him from Africa while also holding all the people in attendance at tonight's opening of the exhibit. Half an hour ago, the Queen herself had come down from her rooms to pay a visit of fifteen unprecedented minutes. The Prince of Wales, the royal who usually saw to Her Majesty's public duties since his father's death, was due any moment.

Neither the Queen nor her son, however, was hosting the party; they were simply its most illustrious guests. The celebration was being given by the unlikely trio: the Royal Geographical Society, the University of Cambridge, and the Episcopate of England in the form of none other than the Most Reverend Father in God himself, the Archbishop of Canterbury, aided here in London by the good ladies of Mayfair and Belgravia, who had contributed what they contributed best: not cakes and pies, but rather money with which to buy the finest catering available. In a very high-society way, the gathering was a kind of church-supper-cum-gallery-opening-cum-hero's-reception.

The party was ostensibly in James's honor, a homecoming welcome of huge proportion—that is to say, in proportion to the monetary value of tonight's exhibit, the figure (according to Lloyd's of London, who'd insured it) being upward from four hundred fifty thousand pounds sterling. James had returned from a southern river basin, that of the Zubtzee River, with offerings from a remote and previously unknown Bantu people who called themselves the Wakua. They had sent the "reigning chief of James Stoker's tribe" gold implements and adornments hammered and worked with remarkable skill. Tonight, displayed along a hundred-foot dais against the ballroom's east wall, sat twenty-four-carat gold platters, thick and heavy, soft and brilliant-yellow. Beside these, behind them, around them lay masses of bracelets and anklets and rings and breastplates, beautifully worked, exotically creative. The long gold-piled dais looked like something out of Burton's Ali Baba tale—more like the open coffers of forty thieves than a gift from a simple, primitive tribe.

James stood at the far end of this display, momentarily free after two hours of all but uninterrupted congratulations. He glanced at the long run of Wakua gold, then averted his eyes. The sight vaguely unsettled him tonight. Set out in one place, all the shining yellow was a monstrous congeries. James had not realized it was so much.

The music had become a swaying blur an hour ago, one long, interchangeable waltz—at about the same time that all the ladies with whom James had been dancing had become an embarrassing muddle; he could no longer keep their names straight. Presently, he let the room swirl, content to watch the prisms of light from the chandeliers move through the crowd and over the gilt walls. His sense of movement was, he hoped, more the affect of four hundred or so people's spinning and turning in a mass before him than the result of his consuming an imprecise number of glasses of champagne. There had been a lot of toasting when he had first come into the room, then some smaller private rounds as he'd paid his respects to the university's Chancellor and Vice-Chancellor, various chairs and heads of college, the president of the geographical society, and ultimately, the Queen of England.

"Dr. Stoker—" A gruff voice interrupted his peace as an elbow jostled into his arm. Champagne spilled over the rim of James's glass onto his hand. "You brought all this back single-handedly?"

James turned to find the only guest of any importance to whom he had not yet spoken tonight, Nigel Athers, the Bishop of Swansbridge. The Archbishop of Canterbury, Athers's immediate and only superior in ecclesiastical government, had sent him in his stead to represent the Church of England tonight.

James smiled benignly. "Well, not exactly alone, Bishop," he said. "I had the help of almost four hundred carriers and twenty native scouts." Not to mention the entire Wakua tribe as far as the Zambezi, eventually a caravan of several thousand camels, and finally Captain Layton and his crew of the British Royal Navy.

"But of your expedition party, you alone survived."

James glanced down into his glass of champagne. "Yes," he murmured.

"Amazing," Athers said. Though he didn't sound amazed. He sounded like what he was, an energetic and highly placed member of a large and powerful organization, a man who, until a week ago, had held to the position that all the gold before them belonged to the Church of England, saying God, as reigning chiefs went, superceded the Queen.

Last week, the Vice-Chancellor and the Bishop

had taken the joint position that the Crown was entitled to the golden tribute that had cost their people their lives—though "certain compensations" would have to be negotiated. This shared stand went on to propose that the "compensations" should be shared out "publically," that is, that the university and church represented larger moral interests than "mere adventurers."

James tried to stand clear of the fray, but he knew where his loyalties lay—with the Vice-Chancellor and the university, which alas meant that for the moment they must also lay with the contentious Bishop who stood beside him.

As if aside, Athers added, "Father Menlow informed me today that Ishmael Rogers of your expedition was supposed to have gotten twenty-eight pounds, two shillings with which he was to buy bibles in Cape Town."

"Really?" James thought it impolitic to mention he didn't care about how many blooming Bibles came along on a geological expedition.

"Yes. But, you see, Ishmael wired us from Capetown. He never mentioned Bibles. Never even mentioned the money. What I want to know is, Did he get the money, and where is it now?"

"Money?"

"The Bible Fund. What became of it?"

"I was not aware there was a Bible Fund."

"There was. Rogers apparently expected to take three boxes of Bibles into the interior, Bibles that a monk had translated into Arabic."

"Arabic," James repeated flatly. He frowned at the Bishop. The thirty-some Bantu tribes in the southern regions of Africa had their own language and dialects, all as far removed from Arabic as they were from English.

Athers continued. "What happened to the money Rogers was supposed to get?"

"I couldn't begin to say. I know nothing about it."

"It was your expedition."

James had to hold back an indignant snort. "Dr. Athers, I only headed up the geological portion. I have no idea what went on in any number of other parts of the expedition. We divided up and were often separated, one group from the other, for months." Seeing this was not going to appease his ecclesiastical sense of injustice, James offered, "But, if you are asking me to guess, I'd say any money Rogers had was buried with him. The people who found us had no clear notion of pounds sterling."

Without missing a beat, Athers said, "Well, you are the only one remaining now, so I advise you not to guess. You'd best find out and prepare an official statement."

James laughed. "For twenty-eight and two? You're joking." But Athers eyed him as seriously as if he were conducting a mass for the dead. James lifted one brow and said, "I won't. Tell Menlow I'll write him a bank draft for twenty-nine pounds out of my own account. That should suit him. I would think, Nigel"—James used the Bishop's first name, an intentional leveling of the playing field—"you wouldn't allow your subordinates to burden you or anyone else with trivia. My God, men died there."

"It's not the amount, it's the principle."

"Precisely."

"The principle of the Church's interests and investments being treated lightly from the start—"

But before James could hear, the conversation was sidetracked as someone clasped James round the shoulders.

A friendly voice broke in. "By God, Jamie, what a good show! What a bloody, splendid good show! Ai—Oh—Sorry, my lord Bishop—" It was Teddy Lamott, a fellow from All Souls, who continued with the cheerful nonchalance of a man well corked. "But what a dashed good show, all the same, what? All that glittery stuff taken into the proper care of an upstanding Englishman. God, Queen, and country, all that. Then carried up the whole bleeding— er, 'scuse me, blooming Continent and across the Med home. What a job, Jamie. Egad, *Sir* Jamie. Fine show, aye, old man. . . ."

Teddy blathered on, with James stepping between his tipsy friend and Athers, separating the young man from a clergyman reputed to be a teetotaler.

Happily, something across the room distracted the Bishop momentarily.

James took the opportunity to murmur, "Teddy, you're foxed. This is no place to make a fool of yourself."

"Never mind. Guess who I just met?" Teddy didn't wait for an answer but leaned toward James, saying in gleeful sotto voce, "Nicole Villars is who."

"Who?"

"You know." Teddy nodded in the direction of the orchestra, widening his eyes and wiggling his brow in a lusty manner. "That woman who reput-

edly took a bath in champagne for the private ben-
efit of Prince Napoleon back when, you know,
France still had a shred of dignity. The one with the
house on the Bois in Paris. She's over there. We
spoke. I'm sure it's she.''

What the devil was Teddy talking about? James
shook his head. "Lord," he muttered. He took his
friend's arm. "Let me get you a hansom, before you
ruin yourself here.''

Teddy lifted his arm up and away, however, as
oblivious as an overexcited child. "No, no," he insisted. "You have to meet her, James. Or at least
see her. God, she's gorgeous. And so nice. You just
wouldn't imagine. Look.''

Teddy pointed, none too politely, toward the
other end of the ballroom again. "Over there, just
past Lady Motmarche and the Bishop's wife.'' He
apparently saw his target, because he crooned a soft
sigh. "Jesus, she's mythic. I'm in love. Look.''

James tried to. Briefly. There were about a hundred women standing or dancing between him and
the far end of the room.

Teddy continued. "She's not like those others,
not like that bloody tightrope walker who wiggles
her hips or those two actresses who pretend to have
a career on the stage. Nothing so vulgar. She's intelligent and cultured. You should hear her talk.
Like that Madame Valtess de la Bigne with the
mansion on the Boulevard Males-herbes. *Une
grande cocotte.* From Paris, James. About the class-
iest bit of skirt you're ever likely to meet. Jesus,
how much do you think she is? Do you think she
has a nightly rate, or do you suppose you can only

. . . you know, if you buy her a house and keep her for a while?''

Now James *was* curious. After casting a glance at the preoccupied Bishop, he took an earnest look toward where Teddy pointed. He shifted once, twice to see between heads. On the far side of the room, between waltzing couples, he caught a glimpse of an attractive woman just getting up to dance, then another sitting in a flowing red gown that spread up and over the arms of her chair.

"No, no, not either of those," Teddy said. "To the right a little. The woman standing with her back to us. There! See? The one in the white, well, not white exactly, the steel-colored satin. Silver-white. Ooh, I bet there are some men feeling a bit hot in their shirt studs tonight. Her door in Paris was said to be the one most likely to see enter a misbehaving Englishman who wanted, above all, discretion. And some of those weren't so discreet. Rumor has it that when Prince Edward turned sixteen, some of his cronies got together: she was his present.''

James's curiosity increased. He stared between heads, hoping for a better look at the woman in silver-white, when quite suddenly, people moved and momentarily, he had a clear view.

He laughed. "No." He shook his head. "You are quite drunk, my friend.''

"Isn't she gorgeous?''

She was that. James adjusted his stance now, keeping sight of her as much as possible: it was Mrs. Wild from the dentist's office. "Yes, she is. And I know that woman. You are quite wrong: she's delightful.''

Teddy said nothing. When James looked at him,

his friend was giving him his full inquisitive attention. "You *know* her? How, Jamie? Where? Oh, do
tell, old man. 'Cuz, I'm not wrong. Jamie, Jamie,
Jamie. I say, still waters and all that. Don't you have
a surprise or two the Vice-Chancellor doesn't suspect—"

"You're mistaken. That woman is the widow of
an Englishman. Her name is Wild, Mrs. Wild."

"Ha-*ha!*" Teddy exclaimed, as if this proved his
point. "Right-o. Nicole Villars Wild. Married a
doddering old retired admiral of the Royal Navy
when Louis-Napoleon's empire collapsed, lots of
money. Lived with her admiral in Italy somewhere
till the fellow died and left her even more filthy rich
than before. That's the one, James. Coco Wild to
her friends. The one. The only."

James glanced at Teddy, who, even sober, frequently got his facts confused. He stared back at
Mrs. Wild. She was lovely; there was no doubt. Petite, feminine; stylish, smiling. That she should be
. . . well, anything other than what she seemed was
impossible. Unthinkable. "You're wrong," he said
flatly.

"All right. Explain all her money. And why men
give her houses."

Across the room, Mrs. Wild accepted a champagne glass from a barrel-chested man in a natty
evening suit, his white silk scarf still over his shoulders. Their party must have just arrived.

Teddy slouched toward James, reaching up to
sling his arm around James's shoulder. "Here's
what I've heard." His voice dropped to the whisper
of shared, delectable secrets. "Prince Napoleon, the
emperor's cousin, built her an astonishing house.

Huge. Marble staircases, an onyx tub the size of a small pond, with jeweled faucets. Legend has it he filled it with champagne and she bathed in it nude for him. Then later some eastern shah or other filled it with orchids and had her picture painted in it, up to her naked shoulders in fat purple orchids. She has another house here. No one is willing to speculate who paid for it. The money came through a small private banking house. She's terribly discreet. And has a bevy of smaller properties in England and on the Continent, a regular real estate tycoon over the last decade.''

James tried to imagine what a woman could do to merit such gifts. A woman other than one's wife.

A wicked woman.

Wicked. He ran his mind around the word, caressing it. While he stared at the very nice woman from the dentist's office. From across the room, he watched her wide, mobile mouth, red and smiling. She didn't look wicked. She looked human, warm in her demeanor. And genuine. There was no pretense to her interest in those around her, in her easy composure. She chatted, laughed with her companions—three men and two women of whom James knew only one, a showy, abrasive American he'd met once and didn't much like; he couldn't remember his name.

"Who is her 'protector' now?" James asked.

Teddy shrugged, his slung arm sliding along James's shoulder. "No one, I suppose. That's the rub. Giving a woman all that money, so many things. Well, she simply doesn't need a man any longer, does she?"

The question went unanswered, for Athers suddenly cut between James and Teddy and the rest of the room. The man was moving at a clip, on a mission.

James watched him head through the crowd directly toward Phillip Dunne, the Vice-Chancellor. Phillip would soothe whatever was wrong, James didn't doubt. But James was fascinated to understand so clearly that soothing was necessary. Athers spoke heatedly to the Vice-Chancellor for perhaps a minute. Phillip nodded. The Bishop spoke some more. More nodding, an exchange, then some sort of agreement. The two of them signaled someone across the room. The majordomo. Before the chief steward could get over to the men, however, Athers's wife had joined the group. She spoke intently, mostly to her husband, all the while smoothing the front of her gown, one gloved hand down her skirt, once, twice, and again. As if she could smooth out her own agitation: she too displayed an inappropriate choler.

The majordomo arrived, after which a quiet, though heated, discussion ensued.

James frowned at the foursome. Phillip, he imagined, was constrained to accommodate his new and temperamental ally, who, in turn, seemed to be trying to calm his wife. Mrs. Athers gesticulated, arm extended, finger pointing—in the direction of the hapless Mrs. Wild. A little stab of fear ran through James.

"They're going to throw her out," he murmured more to himself than his friend.

Without thinking further, he set off straight across the dance floor, weaving his way through the crowd. As he walked purposefully, Mrs. Wild—Nicole, he reminded himself, Coco—bobbed in and out of view, between heads and swirling bodies.

He glimpsed her speaking to her companions, her dark eyes animated. The group laughed as she spoke. She looked intelligent, interested and involved in the conversation. If she were a trifle too vivacious, too flirtatious, well, she was French after all. Her mien was continental, her energy Parisian. She had the air of a hostess of a literary salon—

Or a Greek hetaera, he told himself as he watched her. Aspasia among the friends of Pericles. She could be. . . . It seemed possible for a moment. Then not possible.

Still surely such things existed as courtesans bred to cater to the powerful, the educated, men who had the taste and money for something better than what was found at Piccadilly or Pigalle.

No. No, no. As James navigated closer, it seemed more and more unlikely that this lovely woman could be, well . . . She was too . . . beautiful. More than beautiful. Gracious. Her manner was kind and inviting. There was a high style to her that was both marvelously elegant and totally unintimidating. Perfectly lovely. The way a well-stocked, well-laid-out library invited you to take down and use its embossed, illuminated, gilt-edged books, to slouch into its soft crushed leather chairs—

James collided into a dancing couple, then watched spinning feet as he sorted himself out again, lost in the in-and-out movement, having disconcerted himself. That he should liken a decent woman to a library, a place where lots and lots of men could visit . . . use a book, put it back, then return and use it again. . . . How very ungentlemanly.

Yet, when he looked up and got another unobstructed view of Mrs. Wild, James couldn't help but think (loving good libraries as he did), Here stood a well-stocked, well-laid-out woman. She was slightly long-waisted, small yet willowy, narrow in the right places, full where she caught a man's eye, and divinely dressed tonight in silver satin that rose and dove in a kind of heartshaped neckline across her bosom, rounding over each breast, plunging between, yet somehow modest. Her shoulders themselves were all but bare, swathed in organdy so sheer it was like silver air. Her dress was proper, not too tight, not a moment's criticism, yet it left nothing to the imagination when it came to where and how the perfections of her figure lay.

She was stunning. Whether or not she had made a fortune off her charm, she *could* have.

Out the corner of his eye, James caught sight of the majordomo cutting his own path toward her, walking briskly. James sped up the last few yards, sure he could avert an embarrassment for everyone.

He came up to her group, behind her, with her in quarter profile. He touched her arm, and a thousand details seemed to assail him. Everything about her suddenly seemed erotic. Intentionally erotic. Her long gloves up her arms. The way she held her fan. Her dark, shining hair caught at her nape in a silvery net dotted with silvery beads. Her necklace of cut garnets, blood red, sparkling in a delicate display of bits and drops against her ivory throat. And her perfume, not heavy, hardly that of a trollop, but faint and fragrant in a way that invited you closer.

Breathing it was like wanting to stick your nose—
lose your face—down into the center of a flower.

His exchange with Teddy was suddenly vivid
again.

Who is her "protector"?

*No one, these days. Giving a woman all that
money, so many things . . . well, she simply doesn't
need a man any longer, does she?*

James's heart skipped, then raced into a hard
rhythm. "Mrs. Wild," he said.

And as the name came out his mouth, a reply to
Teddy's question sprang to mind, fully formed: *not
necessarily,* James thought. *That would depend on
what the woman wanted these days.*

Chapter 4

C oco Wild had arrived at Buckingham Palace that evening with Jay Levanthal, a witty, brash fellow out of San Francisco with a Harvard education he had parlayed into a bank charter and a number of prudent investments. He, Coco, and two of his visiting partners and their wives had dined out tonight, then come here. Levanthal had dragged her and the others along as a blind, so to speak, in order to get a clear shot at a duck whose money he wanted for his latest investment scheme. If the duck were smart, Coco thought, he'd give all his money over to the American. She herself had made a sizable piece of cash by investing with him.

"Mrs. Wild."

Coco turned, then laughed, astonished. "Why, what a surprise!" It was the young man from the dentist's parlor.

Mr. Stoker looked splendid in evening clothes— crisply pleated white against black. He was taller than she recalled, the set of his shoulders wider, his stance more square and straight. Perhaps it was the neat upperclass cut of his evening suit. In any event, his beaming smile was exactly as she remembered—as cocky as a new rooster in the yard. Something about him, possibly his energy, amused her afresh: he conveyed a vigor, an impetus she no longer possessed. A verve for life. He wanted things. And believed he could have them.

"Jay," she said, reaching back. "You have to meet—"

Jay wasn't immediately behind her where he'd been a moment ago. Coco let him be, since he seemed to be talking to a man who had just come up, an official of some sort. Good. He loved officials.

To Mr. Stoker, she said, "And this is your party?"

"Indeed."

The American's voice grew loud all at once, making both her and Mr. Stoker turn. "But I'm telling you," he said, "I *have* a damned invitation, and the lady is here as my evening's companion."

The official said, "Nonetheless, sir, you and the lady will have to leave."

The man blew angry air through his lips as he reached into his inside coat pocket. "I can show you the damned invitation—"

From behind her, Coco heard Mr. Stoker say, "I would like them to stay. As my guests."

Stay. Go. She frowned and looked from one man to the other.

The official scowled at Mr. Stoker. Jay glowered at both of them. While Mr. Stoker kept his eyes fixed on Coco. His smile was radiant. She stared for a moment into a handsome, young face so full of pure, guileless goodwill it was hard to look away.

Their gazes held for just a dash longer than seemed quite normal, till his interest seemed . . . complicated somehow, disconcertingly frank. Reflexively, Coco smiled, a warm, lively social mechanism. "Jay," she said, "this is the young man from this morning, the one I was telling you about."

Mr. Stoker nodded in acknowledgment, but his attention remained immovable—so insistently upon her that Coco began to feel as if . . . as if her dress were ripped or her hair coming down or her necklace come undone. Her smile wavered; she put her hand to her throat, raising her brow in bemused query: *What?*

His answer was to laugh as if they shared an inside joke.

She laughed too, her face warming—though the real joke was that she hadn't the slightest idea why she was laughing.

Behind she heard him say, "*This* is the man?"

She looked around. "Um. Yes—"

"But tonight's party is for him, Coco, my dear."

"Is it?" She faintly remembered Mr. Stoker saying something about a party being in his honor. But this affair, well, it was more than a "party."

"Indeed. And the Queen bestowed a knighthood on him last week. For bringing her all that gold over there." Jay offered Mr. Stoker his hand. "Glad to see you again, Stoker." His laughter was booming: *har har har.* "Sir James, that is. Good job, man."

Mr. Stoker blushed; he beamed. While his earnest regard remained on Coco, as if he might suddenly blurt out a truth about himself that might beg a reciprocity.

"Yes," she said quickly, "a regular Lancelot."

The official intruded again. He said, "I'm sorry, but you must go." He looked straight at Coco.

Jay turned on him. "You nincompoop, I'll have you know that we are here by invitation of Bernard Fitzwilliam of the Royal Geographical Society. He—"

The official, a steward of some sort, insisted, "Nonetheless, I have strict instructions that the lady must leave."

Coco stared. *She* was expected to leave? Why? She looked at her companion, frowning, offended, bewildered.

Mr. Stoker intervened again. "Now, see here, my good fellow. I am the guest of honor here tonight, Sir James Stoker, and I want her to stay, which, all things considered, I think should settle the matter."

The steward glanced briefly, nervously toward the far end of the room, but was already shaking his head. "Unfortunately, it doesn't, sir. I am expected to effect the immediate departure of Mrs. Nicole Wild." To Coco, he said, "Madam, I am most sorry, but you must go voluntarily or I shall take you in hand and escort you to the door personally."

Of all the insane things. She drew her wrap up around her. "Well, um—" She didn't know what to say, where to look. "I—well, of course, I—" Of course she must leave. Though she was at a loss to understand why or how to do so gracefully.

Angrily, Mr. Stoker told her, "You don't have to go anywhere." To the steward, "Now look here—"

She put her hand on his arm. "No, no. I wish to leave. Jay," she said, "you stay and don't think another thing of it. I'll speak to you tomorrow.'' The American began to object, but she made a small, brisk shake of her head, pressing her lips together. ''You have someone you must speak to. Go do it. I'm fine. I can perfectly well see myself home. I insist.''

She picked up a handful of her skirts, about to brave the long walk to the stairway that led up to the entry lobby. So public. She could not help but look around. Were there people who understood what was happening? A few curious looks, perhaps. It was hard to say.

A strong hand slipped around hers, stopping her. Mr. Stoker said to the steward, ''I'm going to dance with her one time around the room. When we get to the stairs, we'll leave.''

The fellow jabbered a few syllables of dispute.

To which Mr. Stoker responded, ''If you interfere, I'm willing to hit you—''

Coco blinked, giggled. ''Oh, no. Honestly, Mr. Stoker—''

''—champion pugilist, Queensberry Rules.''

She shook her head vehemently. ''No, no, no—''

He squeezed her hand as he braced his stance and drew himself up, a man with a calling: her salvation. Lancelot indeed; her hero again. She giggled once more, a laugh so unlike herself she barely recognized the sound as her own.

As she was drawn forward by the tips of her fingers, she let out a single burst of giddiness. Then the movement of the room came up around her. It embraced her as surely as the arm that took hold of her waist, and she was pulled into the swirl of couples, out onto a crowded, spinning dance floor. Almost straightaway, she was chasing her own breath to keep up.

Absurd, absurd, she kept saying to herself. Yet despite everything, a joyfulness took hold. James Stoker guided her backward through a quick-turning waltz, both he and the music moving to a glorious swoop and turn of rhythm. Dancing with him was like riding high on a long-roped swing—natural, kinetic, exhilarating. It was both effortless yet too consuming of energy to allow speech. Which was all well enough, since Coco wouldn't have known what to say anyway to a young man who indeed looked as if he were the champion of everything he attempted.

James Stoker was English public school handsome, with his fair hair and Anglo-Saxon good looks. Coco let herself acknowledge the fact: He was quite striking. The sort of young man who dressed in cream-colored trousers (with grass-stained knees) and played cricket endlessly; the team's bowler, the president of the boat club, every young lady's first choice for the first dance of the Season.

This amazing young man pivoted her around, while staring down at her with such unbroken interest she could ónly imagine what he must be thinking.

Yes, she *could* imagine, come to think of it, because his regard suddenly did not seem so straightforward or wholesome. Oh, my Lord. She laughed again—a laugh that in her own ears was coming to sound slightly hysterical—as she spun backward round and round in three-quarter time, feeling positively vertiginous in the arms of a young swain she might have dreamed about when she was too young to have known any better.

"What?" Mr. Stoker asked.

She had to tilt her head back to look up at him. She came only to his chin—he was easily over six feet. "Pardon?" she asked. His hair was slicked back with some sort of pomade, darkened by it. Yet she could see it was quite fair—the color of sand made silvery gold in streaks by the sun. Gilded hair.

"You laughed." He smiled down at her. A melting smile that undoubtedly had every eighteen-year-old girl here faint with yearning. "What are you laughing at?"

Coco shook her head, incapable of speaking for any number of reasons. She could not fathom how he spoke and danced and still concentrated on her the way he did. And the way he concentrated—it made her face hot. She stifled her own excessive laughter, waves of it that she swallowed till her throat was tight. Flattered laughter. She couldn't help herself. She cast her eyes down. It was all she could do to focus on the dewy white stephanotis in his buttonhole. Her savior for the second time today. Who, darling that he was, had the priceless conceit to leap to the notion that his wanting her made the having possible.

The room revolved. She tried to give herself over into the spinning progress of the dance, the music. When she accidentally met her partner's eyes again, though—which, the instant before, had been watching her mouth—she felt her skin flush, her face, her neck, her shoulders. She could barely credit it. She hardly ever blushed, yet for the past five minutes she'd done little else. Meanwhile, her young man's smile broke across his face till it creased his cheeks in dimples, indentations so deep they were inch-long lines. His teeth were even, white, and straight. The dentist had done an excellent job with the chipped tooth.

Their gazes held. His eyes were arresting. They were light in color—not a true hazel, but rather a very light shade of brown that could catch a greenish glint; golden. Amber, perhaps. He had the eyes of a timber wolf.

A handsome, innocent-faced man with dangerous eyes.

And not a tooth in his head aching. He seemed so gallingly perfect all at once—so vigorously healthy and optimistic that she could have smacked him for it. (Her tooth, in fact, had begun to bother her again.)

They danced the circumference of the room, to the wide entry stairs that led to the lobby above. There he stopped, lifted her hand through his arm, and as natural as you please, led her up the staircase and out of the ballroom.

Just into the overhead lobby, she paused to open her reticule. He waited while she dug through the small, silver-beaded bag—looking for her composure there as well. From a satin pocket she removed the tiny silver case. It was engraved, she only now noticed. She opened a snuff box with the initials JPS on it. She took two cloves, slipped them into her mouth, then closed the little box with a click. She sucked on the cloves a moment, wetting them, then put them with her tongue into the right spots. She felt herself relax a little as the sweet, slightly sting-

ing taste spread through her mouth, the taste of im-
minent relief.

She smiled. Then knew immediately that she had
smiled too much. She was encouraging Mr. Stoker's
nonsense. She turned away—and found herself
looking down into a ballroom where she wasn't allowed.

She shook her head. "I'm flabbergasted. I have
never been thrown out of anywhere before."

Behind her, Mr. Stoker murmured, "They had no
right—"

"But they did. They had the right and ability,
apparently. For here I am, up the stairs and out."

"No—" he started to protest.

She glanced over her shoulder, lifting one eyebrow.

He laughed again, shrugging. "All right, yes. It
looks as though they have. And me as well." His
laughter was deep, genuine. "So much for being the
guest of honor."

She turned fully to face him. "What a foolish
thing," she chided. She had to push him back to
walk past him—poke the top of her folded fan into
his chest to make him step back. She laughed at his
persistence, saying, "I suspect that everyone who
matters to you is in that room, and here you are
with a woman they removed from their midst."

"Which makes us comrades of sorts, since no
one gave a rat's tail if, by removing you, they removed me as well."

She shook her head. He would try to pair them,
but she would not allow it; she kept walking.

The lobby was large and relatively vacant. A man
and woman sat on one of the far sofas; they were

deep in conversation. Two fellows smoked cigars by a potted palm. The coat-check, the doorman. Hardly anyone else. Most everyone was downstairs, awaiting the Prince of Wales. Up here the most pervasive presence was, oddly enough, the sound of rain. It spattered irregularly against a long run of window glass. A typical London spring night. Pouring. It occurred to Coco that it might take some time to rouse a cab.

All the more important that she leave Mr. Stoker here. "Thank you," she said, nodding toward him. "I'm fine now. You go back in." She walked in the direction of the doorman, trying to get his attention.

"I don't want to."

She glanced at him. "Don't be naïve."

"I'm not naïve." He followed.

"You are." She laughed again; she just couldn't seem to keep from it.

Behind her he said, "God, I love the sound of that, the breathy, musical way you make everything seem funny."

"Oh, do stop." She turned on him, bringing him up short. "One of us had best be sensible. You're wasting your effort."

But he continued in his smooth Cambridge syllables. "They had no right. You did nothing to deserve—"

"You barely know me. You have no idea what I have done or not done." They remained eye to eye for a moment, almost chest to chest. Until she let out an exasperated breath. "Just for the record, so you don't waste a lot of time and possibly your very valuable reputation: I associate with men much older than yourself. Much older than myself, come to think of it. Seasoned men." World-weary men, she thought. Never a man like the one before her. "Go back in, Mr. Stoker. Go use all this charm to bowl over some sweet, nice—"

"It's Dr. Stoker."

It took a moment for her to realize he'd corrected her. Then another moment to realize he'd embarrassed himself.

He looked first sheepish, then annoyed. He made a quick shake of his head. "Sorry." He frowned. "I never insist on the title. But I'm a little desperate, I suppose, for you to see me with all the stature and authority I possess. Truly, I'm hardly a child." He made a crooked grin. "More than manly, in fact: I'm an African explorer, remember?"

She compressed her lips, but a smile came out anyway. "And hated every moment of it."

"I should never have told you that." He rolled his eyes.

And, God help her, they both laughed. Their gazes held. Till their smiles faded—and still they didn't break eye contact.

She looked away finally, not sure whether to laugh or cry. Dear God. At least seven, perhaps more, years her junior. A proper knight and blessed hero of the realm, for goodnessakes. Who hadn't an ounce of reason in his head . . . chasing after her, of all people.

Coco shook her head. If he wouldn't consider his own best interests, she would.

"Mr. Stoker," she said, "Or even 'Dr. Stoker,' I am most comfortable with men who have lived a little. Mature, experienced men who have already accomplished a great deal." Coco thought, Better Sir Knight here lose a few drops of pride now than march into the thick, thorny tangle of her life that could bleed him to death in the end. So she aligned herself with what most people thought of her anyway. "Not to mince words," she told him, "I enjoy power in men. And money. And a cheerful, generous spirit when it comes to both. You couldn't even begin with me. I am far too expensive for both your pocket and your soul."

The word *expensive* made him blink. He lost his smile, opened his mouth, then couldn't speak. He cleared his throat.

When he finally found words, he seemed disconcerted but also a little annoyed. He said, "Mrs. Wild. I brought back every bloody piece of gold down in that room, not to mention new maps, notes, diaries, and three thousand of the best geological bore samples anyone has ever taken out of the African continent. To bring these things back, I had to outlive not only dysentery: I survived warring tribes, overly friendly tribes, snakes bigger than you are, dampness till my skin molded, dryness till my throat was sand, not to mention lethal insects, and trees full of bats—"

He took a breath, narrowing his eyes, He had to compose himself for a moment.

But he continued. "I was lost, sick, starved, halfkilled, tortured. The Wakua didn't just give me all that gold because I was a pretty young man." His crooked smile materialized again. "Though that was part of it perhaps." Then there was more in his expression than smiling. Determination took over.

"Mostly, though, they made a present of the gold because I held my own, no matter what they threw at me. And they threw a lot.

"And since I've been back, I haven't been very different to the English. I've been sized up, attacked, wooed, and feted by governments, social groups, and the bloody Church of England." He took a breath. "I don't know what you mean by experience or maturity exactly. But I know what it feels like to be so intent on surviving that your skin won't be still, that it ripples and stands your hair on end while a watchfulness breathes inside you so sharp it makes your nerves feel like pins in your veins. I've had more experience than most men twice my age, more experience than I'd like." He laughed without humor. "Maturity and experience? The words are almost silly to me. But for your sake, I'll tell you: You are probably staring at more 'experience' and 'maturity' than you have seen in a long time."

Coco said nothing, fighting an urge to be impressed—if nothing else with his impassioned desire to speak up for himself. She nodded in acknowledgment. "All right, Mr. Stoker," she said. "You are manly, a sterling specimen—"

"Who wants to see you home tonight. And call on you tomorrow."

She laughed, taken aback; charmed, exasperated. "No." She smiled wanly, shaking her head. "Manly or not, I still don't want to deal with you. And if you were smart, you would understand *I* am bad for *you*. I'm too old for you. And too questionable in any social context." She threw a distracted frown in the direction of the ballroom. "Though I had no idea I was *that* questionable." To him, she said, "Still, it is true. I have no proper English connections. A rich foreign woman with no visible means of support. I am . . . suspicious to the English, at best. I am not a valuable person for you to know."

Coco pulled her organdy wrap up around her shoulders, then, looking down, said what shouldn't have needed to be said: "You are a worthy gentleman, who—if you don't make any horrible missteps—will come into every advantage. You will see many lovely young women home, I'm sure."

She heaved a sigh. She felt tired all at once. "So thank you again, Mr. Stoker." She corrected, "Dr. Stoker. I don't want to appear ungrateful. You were very kind to me tonight. And this morning. Thank you for both. Now you must return to your party."

She raised her hand, looking around him to capture the doorman's attention. When the man came over, she asked, "Could you flag me a hansom, please?" He nodded and went off, presumably to do as she bid.

The bemused man beside her frowned, opened his mouth, halted, then furrowed his brow deeply. "You mustn't get into a cab," he said.

"Oh, do stop—"

"You misunderstand me. I am only telling you that in London a lady doesn't ride home alone in a hansom cab." Almost apologetically, he offered, "They are considered quite dashing transportation for men. But perhaps because of this, they are deemed inappropriate transportation for a woman alone at night. Assumptions would be made that would harm your reputation."

Coco was surprised by this. But not much moved. "Well. Appearances are not always the best thing on which to gauge one's behavior. Don't worry. I'll be fine. Good night, Dr. Stoker."

His amber-colored eyes held her attention a moment longer—his expression was puzzled, like that of a man thrown from one of his "dashing" hansoms, left out in the middle of nowhere.

Coco was temporarily lost herself. What a beautiful face he had, even puzzled or insulted. Its bones were lovely, but it was more than bones, more than his angular jaw, his straight nose, his alert, remarkable eyes. Except for the darkened promise of a dense beard, his clean-shaven face was smooth. It was still faintly tanned from his living out of doors so long, lined slightly from the sun; there was a single pockmark by his ear. But his skin . . . Never had she thought of a man as having fine skin, but she imagined that if a woman lay her palm against his jaw, it would feel satiny. The plane of his cheek was as golden-smooth as light, polished teak.

With a sigh—at herself for such pointless speculation—she went toward the door. While her undeterrable suitor followed right behind, murmuring to her, " 'James.' Please call me 'James.' "

The doorman brought her coat. Mr. Stoker, Dr. Stoker, James—the handsome young man with no good sense—tried to help her with it. She simply cooperated with the doorman, whom she tipped, then plunged her hands deep into the pockets of her coat, drawing it up around her. Despite herself, she threw another glance at James Stoker.

He stood not a foot away, restrained, stymied, full of indefatigable energy—and romantic idiocy. She

couldn't explain it, but looking at him shot her
through suddenly with a terrible sadness. Like an
old wound remembered, a ghost-feeling as of an old
grief, neither the exact nature nor cause of which
she could name.

She pulled the soft collar of her coat up against
her neck and said, "Yes. Well. Good-bye then, Dr.
Stoker." She realized she was repeating herself.
Good-bye, good-bye, good-bye. Enough.

The doorman held the door. She made it a point
not to look back.

When James returned to the ballroom, any pleasure he had taken in the evening was lost. The gran-
deur and glamour that waltzed around him no
longer even felt festive. His mind converged only
toward one notion: Coco Wild. Who was she, really? *What* was she? Where did she come from?

Certainly, her money and property gave her an
unusual autonomy for a woman. She could be as
free-living as she chose. Perhaps she was fast and
loose, as Teddy implied. A relic of a lost regime.

Perhaps she wasn't. A more likely explanation for
her questionable reputation occurred to James: that
the lovely Mrs. Wild (even her name—*Wild*—
added an unfair argument against her) was a
stranger, a gregarious foreigner in the midst of the
English upper class, inexperienced with its customs
and judgments. The hansom cab, for instance.
Someone should instruct her, really, explain, he
thought, become her guide of sorts.

Someone at the very least should tell her why she
shouldn't arrive with the likes of Jay Levanthal at

a party where the Queen herself had been in attendance.

For James had remembered who the American was. A rich investment banker with a minor position on the fringe of New York society and a major interest in variety show girls. James told himself that the main reason he didn't like for Coco Wild to take Levanthal's arm when offered or get into *his* carriage was that the association was the worst possible one for her reputation. Levanthal's flamboyant manner and predilection for flashy women could only cast further aspersions upon her social standing in London.

Then, too, James hated for her to take the man's arm, because as of tonight, he was horribly jealous of the American.

A state that felt particularly acute when Jay Levanthal walked out of the crowd and up to the Vice-Chancellor. James, on his way over to speak to Phillip, stopped. Annoyed, he redirected himself toward the punch table. There he poured himself a glass of water, then over its rim looked back at his friend and superior.

James liked Phillip Dunne. No, he had trusted and admired him for years, since well before Africa. Phillip had taken him under his wing long ago, well before Cambridge. Their interests, professional goals and beliefs had always been similar. Their personalities meshed. Between the two men lay years of sincere mutual regard. Though many, he knew, neither liked nor trusted the man.

The Vice-Chancellor put on a sage expression at something Levanthal said now, a look that was supposed to pass for accord. And profundity. Phillip's expression always made him look as if he were deep in important thought. It had to do as much with his facial features—his high, wide brow, the square set of his jaw—as with any mental preoccupation. He always appeared pensive and intelligent, even when he was tying his shoes. Presently, James knew Phillip well enough to recognize a tightness in his ascetic face, a struggle to maintain polite interest.

James should have felt sympathetic. Yet all he could think was, *You kowtow to men who are questionable allies at best (even if it means you must oust a woman who deserves your protection).*

Alas, Phillip looked like a man who needed allies tonight. He looked worn. His evening suit fit more tightly than it should. It made him seem soft and overweight, a middle-aged man beginning to show an erosion from too much success. Too many friends, too many rich dinners and jovial toasts. For James—dissatisfied with everyone and everything at the moment, if he were honest—the Vice-Chancellor tonight had all the smiling charm of a quack hawking nostrums from the back of his wagon.

"So what's she like?"

"What?" James turned to find Teddy Lamott standing beside him again. The fellow looked more sober, though he offered James a champagne glass; he was carrying two. James took one, gulping a swallow of champagne. It was cold and effervescent all the way down his throat. Then he asked, "Who?" Of course, he knew whom Teddy referred to. James asked from the perverse desire to hear Coco Wild's name spoken again aloud.

A pleasure he didn't get. Teddy said, "The highest priced female on the Paris market seven years ago. You know damned well who. I saw you dancing with her."

James scowled down into his champagne glass. "I'm not sure you should believe, or spread, the rumors you think you know about the woman." He didn't know why he defended the lovely Mrs. Wild. He hadn't known her twenty-four hours—and Teddy's rumors could as easily be true as not. Still, he added, "She's quite nice, you know."

His friend's laughter had a lewd edge to it. "Right-o, Jamie," he said as he thumped James on the back. "Anyone with eyes could bloody well see you think she's nice."

James threw Ted an exasperated look, then sighed and gave up.

There was nothing wrong with Lamott, he told himself. His friend thought as did most of his peers—as James himself had three years ago. He saw anyone who wasn't male, English, and upper class as either a misguided child or an exploitable object.

James asked, "What do you know about this fellow Levanthal?" He nodded in the man's direction. "What's his interest in Mrs. Wild?"

"What do you think his interest is in her? Same as yours." Teddy laughed. "Same as mine, as a matter of fact."

James felt a jolt of resentment this time that went beyond exasperation, surprisingly sharp. He hid it in the bottom of his glass, swilling the last of the champagne before he asked, "Is he successful, you think?"

Teddy snorted. "As I said before, rumor has it

that *no one* is successful anymore. She does as she pleases.'' He laughed crudely. "So long as she doesn't please to attend gatherings where the Prince of Wales is expected at any moment. Impolitic to embarrass our future monarch.''

James dropped the subject altogether. It was becoming too difficult to keep his face impassive and say nothing. Teddy soon rambled forward into other subjects.

The orchestra started up again, the opening, sedately misleading strains of "The Beautiful Blue Danube.'' The same waltz that had put Coco Wild into his arms, the two of them spinning dizzily across the dance floor by the end. He remembered holding her. How light and solid and strangely right she had felt. How easily she moved, how easily they moved together.

Romantic blather, he told himself.

Yet her departure stayed with him. He kept seeing again in his mind her disappearing into the rain, her small bounce up as she climbed into the cab, the rainy shimmers of spray from the wheels just before the dark swallowed her up.

Likewise, he couldn't shake the blankness he'd felt immediately after she'd gone—like the empty street itself. Cold, wet, dark.

For the rest of the evening, he managed to smile and talk, even to dance two or three times. He socialized, yet he felt remote. Alone. Not that he wasn't grateful for the attention. (The Prince arrived and thumped him on the back. James was barely alone, in fact, for a moment.) But the notice and high regard, as fine as it was, did nothing for his strange mood. Tonight's pats and congratulations from these people—these strangers he used to call countrymen—were like the lights of passing coaches, illuminating his aloneness in a way that surprised him. Like the sight of rain, silver slashes, that materialized in bursts out of the dark of his soul.

That night, James dreamed of Africa, of damp jungles curtained in darkness, lush, clicking, pulsing with life. Of ancient rivers. The names themselves mysterious, eternal. The Zambezi. The Nile. Of dark-skinned women painted with vegetable dyes, women who wore no tops, their breasts exposed. Dancing breasts. Smiling women. Females who cheerfully stroked him, pressing their hands, their bodies along his penis, till he—with only the greatest trepidation—let go of his English ways and followed instincts he hadn't known that he possessed.

Chapter 5

◇◯◯◇

*Whether by means of a thorny forest or
a wall of fire, a primary concern in all
versions of the Sleeping Beauty legend
seems to be to protect the sleeping princess from the mischief of cowards—
though neither thorns nor fire does her
much good when it comes to the mischief
of a brave man: In all versions, other
than that of the Brothers Grimm, the
prince takes considerable more advantage of her sleep-enchanted state than
that of a mere kiss.*

From the Preface to The Sleeping Beauty
DuJauc translation
Pease Press, London, 1877

The dentist had her address. James had only to
produce the smallest lie, about wishing to re-

turn a found glove, for Mr. Limpet to give "a gentleman such as yerself, sir" the lady's street and house number. Thus, that next morning, James stepped down onto Havers Square Road, the quiet, tree-lined street on which Nicole Villars Wild lived.

In front of him stood a row of tall, posh townhouses that overlooked, across the street, a rolling, grassy park. Along the sidewalk, a high iron fence protected Coco Wild's particular property, the barrier's black spear-point pickets overrun with wild roses. A man approaching along the sidewalk had to push their riot of flowers and shoots out of the way or else walk along the curb. Other than these wayward roses, Mrs. Wild's rather prime piece of London real estate was neat and well kept. Fifty yards beyond the iron gate, the townhouse ascended into three high stories of white brick inset with tall, arching windows. A very proper façade, right down to the black-lacquered front door with its polished brass mail slot. The whole was nestled into manicured lawns with stands of ivy banked and climbing against the house, a single pear tree to the side. Very respectable.

And vaguely disappointing. As James closed the front gate behind him, he admitted to himself that he had not traveled to the dentist's and back across London this morning because he dreamed of Coco Wild's being respectable, but rather on the titillating possibility that she was not. Alas, reality disputed fond hope, though, stone by stone, brick by brick.

A uniformed maid answered the door, but almost immediately another voice rang distinct. "*Chi è là?*" asked the invisible Mrs. Wild from the dark recesses behind the maid. *Who is it?* she asked in

Italian that sounded both offhand and natural.

"James," he said, "James Stoker," as he tried to see around the servant to the woman who went with the voice.

Out of the dimness behind the maid's shoulder, Coco Wild materialized, looking fresh and perfect. The morning sun caught the dark crown of her head; it gave her hair, tied up loosely, a high luster—thick, silky-looking hair as shiny as glass.

"Why, Mr. Stoker—" Surprise registered on her face, followed by a degree of reluctant delight. "And here you are again. Heedless of my advice."

James smiled. "Yes. We neither one paid much attention to the other's advice last night: I came to be sure that the hansom got you home safely."

"As you can see, it did."

He waited. When she offered nothing further, he said, "That's wonderful. May I come in? You could tell me how the trip went."

She laughed and shook her head. Which could have meant, No, he could not come in. Or she was perhaps shaking her head at the foolishness of his standing at her doorstep on so little pretext. She said finally, "You're hopeless."

He grinned. "Actually, I'm full of hope. May I come in?"

"I can't think why I should entertain an uninvited visitor who—"

"Because you like me."

Their eyes held till her smile admitted ruefully that she did. She said something more to the maid, who then stepped forward and took his hat. Coco pressed herself back to let the maid pass. (*Coco, Coco, Coco.* James took possession of the name, turning it over and over in his mind like a dissolving sweet in his mouth.) "Come in then, Mr.—that is, Dr. Stoker."

The sun shone briefly down the length of her—down beige-white satin that fit snugly from her neck to her wrists, down her ribs, to pull tight across her abdomen before it belled into skirts. He could see the faint rise and fall of her belly, her rib cage. Then she turned to lead the way, and the view became that of heavy satin tied up in back into loose bundles that shimmered beneath a lot of limp, tea-colored lace—less bustle than mounds of fabric, tucked and layered into drapes and tiers. He followed this blessed sight down the dim hallway.

Inside, his high spirits translated into a sharp though agreeable agitation, a kind of exuberant nervousness. It thrilled him simply to watch her. She was carrying something, he realized. A fat, pale pink rose, very different from the ones along her fence. Its long stem extended into her skirts.

The foyer opened up on one side into a gracious sitting room. She motioned him toward a tufted sofa, while she herself paused by a small half-table beneath a mirrored hat rack. There, she bent over a bouquet of more flowers exactly like the one she carried—hothouse roses—at least two dozen, all unnaturally large, the substance of their pale pink petals as thick and glistening as the satin of her dress.

She inserted the stem of her flower down into the vase as she said, "I hope the rest of your evening went better, once I was gone."

"It was boring after you left."

"Well, yes. My departure was anything but boring.'' She glanced over her shoulder, sending him a wry smile, the one from last night that was coming to make the hair on his arms stand on end. It was lovely; it was sad somehow, resigned. It did things to him, made him want to know her, protect her, swoop her up into his arms.

As she reached for another rose, James realized that the flowers came from a pile of tissue paper by the vase, in front of which sat a card, a note: they were from a man. James stared fixedly at this evidence of competition.

He sat frowning at her back, crossing, recrossing his legs. Finally he released some tension by extending his arms out along the top of the sofa back and asking, ''Mr. Levanthal?'' The question didn't nearly sound as casual as he'd intended.

She merely glanced again over her shoulder.

He clarified, ''Mr. Levanthal sent you the flowers?''

She poked the last stem, saberlike, down into the vaseful of water, then turned. Ignoring his question, she smiled more fully, a radiant look, and said, ''Now. What can I do for you?''

The sheer beauty of her smile washed over him, counteracting to some extent his sense of being cut loose, being left adrift. James grappled with the strangely ambiguous sensation as he spoke his reason for coming, the one he'd been telling himself all morning: ''I, ah—I came to say that I could help you, if you'd let me.'' He cleared his throat. ''I have, um, considerable influence of late. If you would allow me to advise you, I could see to it that you were better accepted into social circles such as—''

She made a wave of her hand as she came forward. "Oh, that." She smiled again, a social smile that seemed this time more beautiful distraction than sincere pleasure. She sat into a chair that shared a corner tea table with James's sofa. They sat knee to knee. "Well, there's nothing to be done for it," she said. "Mostly, I just keep thinking, How embarrassing for Jay—for Mr. Levanthal, that is. If I had realized. . . ." She let the sentence trail off, too difficult to complete. If she had known she was some sort of pariah here, then what? She said, "Well, I would have spared him and the other people I was with from being associated with the incident. I wouldn't have gone with them in the first place."

James shifted back, nodded, trying to look worldly. Bloody hell, he *was* worldly. Why did she make him so nervous? "Nonetheless, I do have connections who—"

"I'm sure you have brilliant social connections, Dr. Stoker. Queen Victoria among them." The maid arrived with tea. "Ah," Coco said, "exactly what we need. Now, no more talk of this unfortunate incident."

He blinked, left hanging again. At least she wasn't throwing him out. Tea. All right, he'd have tea with her then.

To set the tea service on the table, the maid had to ease aside some knickknacks and papers, including a flat crystal box and a collection of envelopes, the morning's post.

The crystal box was a cigar humidor, James realized. He stared at it, trying to figure out what a humidor full of cigars was doing in the house of a woman who lived alone.

"When was the last time you had a good cigar?"

He glanced up. Coco Wild was settled back into her chair, a gracious smile on her face. "I can't remember," he said. "Before Africa."

She tilted her head sideways, the faintest movement, indicating the humidor. "Go ahead, if you wish."

More for something to do than anything else, James leaned forward and opened the crystal box.

He took a cigar. It was fresh; it rolled smoothly without a crackle of sound. Then, as he closed the lid again, he felt the tobacco ease from his fingers.

Mrs. Wild took possession of his cigar. She clipped the end with a silver cigar snip, then offered back the roll of tobacco. Taking it, James frowned, then was further undone when she leaned forward to look at him through a two-inch flame that rose from a large silver lighter, a raven with its beak on fire. The lighter was heavy; it took both her hands.

Cigar in his teeth, James leaned forward. The blunt tip of the tobacco in the flame, he drew in short, strong puffs. It lit evenly, the luxurious smoke filling his nose and mouth. He closed his eyes as he let the smoke drift up his face, smelling it, feeling it, tasting it as he leaned back into an overstuffed sofa.

He drew smoke in again and blew out, narrowing one eye to watch this accommodating woman. The lovely Mrs. Wild relaxed back into her chair, leaning in a manner that was coming to be characteristic in James's mind: slightly askew—canted sideways, one elbow raised, bent to rest atop the low chair back. She leaned thus, her head tilted to level her regard, relaxed, attentive.

James closed his lips round the cigar and drew smoke into his mouth as he stared. His heart skipped a beat, then thudded into a hard rhythm against the wall of his chest. She was. She really was one. She was telling him so. A *demi-mondaine*. A courtesan with a reputation beyond repair, beyond his social affiliations. A *grande cocotte*. Or whatever one called a woman who became wealthy and powerful off rich men's sexual desires. It seemed so plausible all at once. Not in all the stereotypical ways he'd dreamed, yet in a real, earthly way it could be true, absolutely true.

He turned the whole story over in his mind a moment, that she *might* have been a bedfellow to ministers and diplomats, even the Bishop of Swansbridge. Incredible to contemplate. And a French prince as well as an English one. He was helpless against his own imagination: All at once, this tiny, well-dressed woman seemed the wickedest, naughtiest piece of femininity he had heretofore ever contemplated.

He wished he could say he was offended or repelled. In fact, he was so entranced he embarrassed himself.

Oh, to think. The lovely, laughing woman from last night, a woman of doubtful virtue. No, if rumor were right: of no virtue. Perfect. The exact amount of virtue in a woman he wanted.

As the idea settled into his brain, it became charming, somehow. No virtue whatsoever. Yet allowed, cultured, and entertaining. So perfectly polite and sociable. For one silly moment, he thought, why couldn't all the ladies in London be like this. Without any virtue at all. Rather like the men. Only softer and layered in ruffles and silk, with their feminine points of view. But without their feminine ignorance—schooled ignorance—or worse, schooled disgust. Everyone would dance and talk and laugh, then go off somewhere private afterward and copulate like rabbits, rather like the Wakua after a nice feast. And all would be very happy and unconcerned about propriety, because this would be propriety—

He didn't know what to say, how to phrase what was in his mind: obviously she didn't need money. She didn't desire a social entrée. Then what was it she wanted? What was the price now of "the highest priced female seven years ago on the Paris market"? What did one *pay* for a sexual object par excellence? Or at least, for one of the more erotically straightforward and knowledgeable women in the civilized world?

For surely she was this. Oh, his fancies. How impossible. This little woman. This delicate, underfed French person. She couldn't *possibly* be as wild and salacious as he imagined. But French. . . . Oh, even this stirred him up. Trite. Silly. So ridiculously predictable. As with the most sensational of pornography, her faintly Frenchified air titillated his poor English mind.

As demure as you please, she poured tea, moving things aside on the tea table to make room for his teacup. When she shoved her mail, a piece of paper came partway out of an opened envelope. A bank draft. He couldn't see the amount, but he could see the signature: Julius J. Levanthal.

James felt his stomach roll over; his eyes grew hot. He couldn't help himself. He glanced at the roses again, then back at the check that peeked out, rebuking him. Only this time she caught him: when his eyes met hers again, she was laughing—that hair-raisingly quiet, unvoiced laughter of hers.

"Oh, Dr. Stoker." She bowed her head, but her laughter increased. She took the bank draft and envelope from the table, folding them together, and put them into her pocket. "Jay wrote it to me, of course." She was teasing him.

Though James resisted seeing any joke. He stared at her, utterly humorless.

More laughter. "Oh, the priceless look on your face," she said, then sighed, as if reluctant to be humane. She explained, "You see, I invest with him. These are my dividends this quarter. He manages some of my money, as a kind of financial advisor. He's very smart about such matters. There is nothing untoward." She paused, then gave way to more laughter. "No matter how much you or anyone else might like to believe there is."

"Levanthal, you should know, is tolerated here only for his financial connections. He is the worst possible sort of choice for you as a social companion, at least in London society."

"I didn't realize there *was* a bad choice for me." She looked annoyed momentarily, then cast her eyes down. She added, "Until last night of course." As if in explanation, she murmured, "People in Paris *like* me. I go wherever I wish. I've had the emperor's cousin to dinner at my home, sat him down at my left with a duke at my right. I have entertained Russian princes and American senators. I married an English admiral who loved me. Yet last night, I was someone to despise. It never occurred to me that"—her fine, intelligent eyes met his with genuine surprise—"London society would find me reprehensible."

He shouldn't have said it, but he wanted to see if it would shock her. He wanted to hear her deny it: "London society whispers of you as their future monarch's sixteenth birthday present." He laughed as if he found this droll.

Her lips pushed out, a quintessentially French moue of disdain, while her eyes came up to meet his, her scandalously beautiful eyes. She looked truly angry for a moment. Then she said, "Where the Prince of Wales puts his cock is no one's business but his own, especially where he put it well over a decade ago."

James felt his face run cold. His mouth went dry. He tried not to be too obvious as he attempted to draw breath. He put the cigar into his open mouth, puffed and blew smoke—a screen—into the air before his face. He hoped it hid his expression.

Apparently not. She said, "Oh, dear." She bowed her head, smiling her fey, not entirely ingenuous smile. A smile that continued to make fun a little. "I'm sorry. It's just that, when such things are said of me, I get . . . oh, I don't know. Something ferocious in me rises up. I want to knock someone down." She blushed slightly—and most attractively. "Or floor them figuratively." She murmured, "I'm sorry." Then, "I just feel especially misused when the gossip is based on ill-bred, unimaginative public speculation. As in Bertie's case. As if anyone would conduct something as touchy as an assignation with a future monarch by letting him and his friends sit with her in her balcony box at the opera.''

James blinked, frowned, and tried to decipher her comment. Good, he thought at first, she was denying the liaison. Then, no. What was wrong here? She *was* denying it. But *Bertie*. . . . James realized she referred to the Prince of Wales—using the name by which only his close friends and family addressed him.

She continued, ''Why do people persist in wanting to know other people's private business?'' She looked at James squarely, contemplatively, for a moment, then laughed. ''And, no, I won't deny my association with Bertie any further than that, nor any other rumors you present. So don't bother going down the list you have made in your mind. I won't be put in the position of denying one rumor or another, while by not denying some, I seem to admit too much.''

A list. James blinked. He wanted to say, A list? You can envision a list?

She pressed her lips together as if she could make herself contrite. ''In any event, I didn't mean to shock you. That wasn't what I was trying to do.'' A pause, then a slight smile: an earnest one. ''I don't think,'' she added. At which point she laughed outright. Peals and peals, like soft, clear-ringing bells.

The sound just about undid James. Coco Wild's laughter, in all its variety, so appealed to him, he would like to have inhaled it, put his nose down inside it, smelled it like a flower. Then eaten it out of her mouth.

Yes, he would like to be on her list. At the top.

With all the others crossed out. He wanted her. He was here to negotiate having her, he admitted to himself. Just as others had. How marvelously straightforward. Here was how matters should be done.

Yet the precise nature of the "how," the way to phrase it, to conduct himself, eluded him. How did one approach the subject? James had not the first idea how to approach a regular woman-of-the-profession, let alone—what? What was she?

Oh, gad, the idea made his skin prickle. With horrid delight. With blessed relief. A professional. A woman who sought to please a man, skillfully, purposefully. Sexually. No faints or flutters or pretense or disgust.

James reached forward and stubbed his cigar out in a dish. Stupid. All this circling. He was about to tell her that it was *he* who was sorry, who was being circuitous and difficult.

Yet before he could say anything further, she stood. "Well," she said. James was half-risen when she announced, "I have an appointment in half an hour. It was kind of you to stop by." She smiled cordially as she offered her fingertips—that friendly, arm's-length gesture from the Continent she embraced so easily, bestowing yet withholding herself.

He took her hand, from simply not knowing what else to do, kissing smooth, cool knuckles, her fingers dewy soft as they slid through his. The maid appeared out of nowhere with his hat. James took it, again more out of a loss for any other immediate alternative. He tapped the brim twice on his leg before he could think to say, "When may I see you again?"

Coco, turning to lead him out, paused halfway around. She said, "I'm afraid I shall be out of town for a while." She seemed wistful for an instant, then shrugged helplessly. "I leave day after tomorrow."

"Ah." He nodded. In fact, he himself had to be back at Cambridge for Easter term, which began in a fortnight. "When do you return to London?"

"In three weeks."

"I see." He couldn't keep the disappointment from his voice.

He followed, mulling, churning over how to stop his being thrown out—while she led him down the entry hall toward the front door again.

What he wanted, when she stopped before the front door, was to say, Tell me more about this ferocious thing that rises up inside you. Who are you? This gaiety of yours, how much is real? How much is well-rehearsed pretense—a metaphorical black-iron gate with wild thorny roses defending where pointed pickets don't suffice?

What he blurted, though, was, "I would like to suggest we meet regularly. As man and woman. I am not poor. I have—"

"Dr. Stoker. Please." She lowered her eyes there in the dimness of the hallway. "I don't walk the streets. I never have."

A misstep. James's heart raced. He'd leaped somehow, somewhere to a horribly wrong conclusion. Yet he hadn't. He couldn't get his bearings. She was the classic confusion to the male mind: a woman who could drop terms like *cock* into a sentence while still holding on to a self-possessed—

lady-like—poise. The lady. The whore—the word itself so beyond the pale of decorum, one never said it in public. Which left him somehow the idiot. He couldn't form a coherent sentence, let alone an appropriate apology. "I'm so sorry," he stammered, "mortified. I can't tell you how—"

She put her hand up over his mouth. Her small, cool hand. He quieted instantly.

They stood there in the shadows of the hallway, with James breathing in the fragrance of her fingers. They were unperfumed. She smelled simply sweet, naturally so, the curve of her hand almost waxy in its smoothness, soft, moist—redolent of vanilla orchids, the sort that vined their way up through the canopies of treetops. He counted the heartbeats of the duration of her touch, her hand against his lips.

When he could stand it no longer, he took hold of the back of her hand, pressing her palm to his mouth, kissing it.

She let out a sound, consternation, went to pull back. He wrapped two fingers round her wrist. Her arm went rigid. She wet her lips, stared at him. With her hand cupped in his, hovering at his mouth, she shifted her weight, the shushy-silk of her dress rustling, echoing in the narrow corridor.

He murmured, "You are sad, somehow. I want to help."

"That's not why you came."

"No," he admitted. "I came because you are the most lively, most interesting, cultured, lovely woman I have ever met. You please me a thousand ways. Tell me what to do, how to court you—"

She laughed again, a light, slightly nervous sound. "Oh, you are dangerous. So honest and romantic''—more faintly anxious laughter—''and cheeky.''

''What do you want?'' he asked. ''Tell me.''

She bit her lips together, frowning up at him, her upturned regard lingering over his features in a way that made his whole body warm. She said, ''You mean, What is my price?''

''All right. What is your price?''

She let out a burst, more edgy laughter, then stammered, ''I, um—ah—'' She blinked, shook her head. ''I don't have a price.'' She extricated her hand, then couched her face in the shadows of the hall. She took a breath, then heaved air out in a long sigh. ''Dr. Stoker—''

''James,'' he murmured.

''James, then. Don't judge me. I've made choices in my life. I would make them again. They were the right choices—''

There was an unexpected sadness in her posture, to her words—an unveiled moment that drew him, held him. He murmured, ''Choose me.''

She shook her head vehemently. No, no, no; he had it all wrong somehow. She said, ''Honestly, just for argument's sake, I ask you: How? Can you imagine how you could begin to court''—she let out an indignant snort—''the Prince of Wales's birthday present? Without causing yourself all manner of embarrassment, even injury to your career? Important people don't like me—''

''*I* like you. And I wouldn't be embarrassed. Moreover, those few people who did know would think me bold and worldly. If anything, debonair.'' He laughed.

''Oh, dear,'' she said. She looked away, but he

caught a sideways glimpse of her expression—the slightest curve of a smile, amused and full of a cynicism he was perhaps not meant to see. "*That* kind of courting," she said, then expelled a vocalized huff of dissent. "I'm finished with half-attentions and dark stolen moments, Dr. Stoker. I'm done with being someone's unadmitted guilt. What I loved about my husband—the reason I married him—was that he loved me in the light of day, in front of everyone. I deserve that."

She kept her face turned, her expression hidden, though her voice contained an unhidable malaise. She said, "Do you know, I have been in London three months and only last night did I understand that people here think I'm dreadful." She paused. "You think I'm vulgar. You think you can walk in here and buy me like a sporty new horse for your carriage."

"No, I—"

"Yes," she said. But added benevolently, "Though you're young. You don't understand. You are too innocent even to know how mean you are to stand here like this. Now good day, Dr. Stoker."

"I'm sorry—I just—"

"It's all right. You make me feel foolish." She laughed. "Innocent myself." She tilted her head sideways, looking up at him—letting him see her moodiness in all its glory for a moment. She laughed again, skeptically. "Which is saying something." The door opened a crack, her hand resting on the knob. She'd let a thin beam of light into their sheltered conversation.

"When will I see you again?" Don't make me leave, James kept thinking. She was so delicate, yet beautiful; formidable, yet wounded. He was amazed to discover a fragile piece to her. Amazed and fascinated.

"I have things to do. I won't be in London again till Michaelmas—"

"Perfect. There is a university break then. I could come to London—"

"But I am only here a day before I leave for France again, where I'll live till June. Then I always spend the summer in Italy."

James didn't know what to say. She was telling him that she wouldn't alight long enough for him to catch up with her.

She offered a wide, bright smile—that gregarious display of goodwill she could call up in an instant that could so completely, and dishonestly, mask the distress she'd let him see just moments before. "So," she said. "If we meet again, we'll be friends, all right?"

It was a boundary, not an invitation.

James felt a jolt of chagrin—even as he knew she behaved somehow from motives of self-interest, self-preservation.

Her charm and cordiality were more impediments than the niceties they pretended to be, ways to keep others out. Particularly him at the moment. Coming up against them was like trying to find a way through a thicket of politeness, a bramble of good cheer.

Fine. Since he understood what was happening here so well, there was no reason for a mature man to take offense. Not a mature man with mature attitudes—which was what she adored, after all, and what he was without a doubt. He was absolutely in the same league as all her rumored lovers—as good as any defunct prince or effete Napoleon. Or fat old Prince Bertie, for that matter, who laughed too hard and ogled actresses. Or the Bishop of Swansbridge, for godssake. Nigel Athers. His Grace the Bishop. Now *this* astounded James. Nigel. The idea of her and Nigel nose to nose was roughly as appealing as Nigel trying on James's trousers or taking his new carriage out for a spin.

And another burr, another thorn: if she had had a full-fledged affair with Athers, why wouldn't she favor James with more than ten minutes' of her time and a cup of tea? Why not? What was wrong with him? Why not *him*?

But *no* was *no*. And being mature, James would just dust off his pride and leave.

In a minute.

He put his hand up, meaning to stop the opening of the door—a man wanting a halt, time out, a moment to think about maturity and wanting a woman just because his rival appeared to have had her. The notion bore consideration. It was something a man should understand.

From here, the rest just happened. He pushed his hand out quickly—afraid she would have him out into the street before he'd had a moment to gather himself—and the heel of his palm hit the door's edge harder than he'd meant. The door shut with a small, firm, surprisingly loud, well . . . *slam*.

Her eyes opened widely. Her head leaned back. If James hadn't seen a brightness, a little thrill, in her eyes, or thought he had, he wouldn't have proceeded. But the light in her eyes seemed there, and it lit something inside him. The next he knew, he'd slipped his arm round her waist, turned her, pressed her to the door, and kissed her.

She scuffled immediately, unsurprised—no stranger to the mad, frenetic grope. He tried to make it sweeter than that. It was damn sweet for him. Her lips were smooth and springy, as youthful to the touch as to the sight. They were full, yet small and well defined. He could feel the neat ridge of her philtrum curving up, then down, then up, making a chiseled bow of her top lip, while her bottom lip was plump, pink, and soft.

She shoved him in the chest, while he kissed this very female mouth, thinking, *Oh, yes, this is romantic.* Except it almost was. Her lips didn't pull away exactly. Not immediately. The pressure of her hands against his chest was businesslike, angry. But the sweet-plump mouth clung to his for two or three heartbeats that made his head swim, made him forget whatever it was he thought he was doing.

Which was as far as it got. She broke away, turning her head, breathing hard, audibly, there in the hall. He kept hold of her, though he cranked back his head a degree, mostly for fear that if he stayed too close, this reversal of hers would see him bit or spit upon or something equally unpleasant. He stared; she looked up at him. Neither spoke.

It became a game of who would look away first. Not him. Not so long as he could watch the incredible, mythic eyes of La Belle Coco. That's what they'd called her; how could he have forgotten?

She looked up at him from beneath black lashes, her regard reminding him of the silent inscrutable wariness of Muslim women he'd seen in Africa. Women swathed in black from head to toe, veiled;

all eyes. Constrained women. Women who'd made him afraid to think what mutinies might boil inside them.

"Turn me loose," she said.

God bless, he was loath to. But the look in her eyes said he'd best comply. When he did, she stepped away, brushing at herself, straightening her sleeve where it had pushed up her arm.

He was going to apologize. He certainly should have. He said, "I—ah—I got carried away."

"I'd say so."

Further contrition would not arrive. Regret, yes. He regretted that he had missed the way into her good graces. He regretted that he was so inexperienced with such matters as to be awkward and not able to gauge anything properly, because there was an inroad here somewhere. He just couldn't find it. Moreover, she needed someone and it should be him, but he didn't know what to do to make it so.

She was vulnerable, fragile, yet afraid to be soft.

Who'd said no once and now was being quite emphatic about it. Her eyes said no. Her pink, dumpling-soft mouth had become a tight, compressed line that said no. No.

So, mature man that he was, he slapped his hat onto his head, nodding curtly. "Right," he said. Ruddy hell, he thought. He twisted the doorknob, then—annoyed with her and himself both—he added, "My dear Mrs. Wild." He said in a rush of earnestness, "If you ever do need a friend, I hope you will call on me."

It was, of course, most unlikely that she would call on a masher for any reason.

James swung the door wide, half-blinded by direct sunlight, but stepped through anyway, clapping the door shut with strength. His exit quaked the doorframe. The brass mail slot bounced, then clattered, a rickety rhythm that followed him down the steps onto her front walk and—or seemed to, at least—out her brambly overgrown gate.

Coco stood inside leaning back against her front door, dismayed, trying to regain her balance. All right, she shouldn't have played with him. She shouldn't have made a game of watching his sweet-innocent expression when she'd lit his cigar or enjoyed the fun of muttering a dirty word in his face. He had proven his point: a little innocence and curiosity could be dangerous. She had always known it. What a fool to dally with the notion now. At her age. A good thing she had gotten rid of him. What a relief he was gone.

Then why was she standing here against the door, fighting the urge to open it and run after her wounded young swain, to offer *him* an apology? An apology for being reasonable? Someone had to be. For being kissed like a tart? Which he had done rather nicely, if she were honest. Coco realized her hand remained over her mouth, touching where his lips had been.

My goodness, she thought, when had a man ever kissed her like that? Then she laughed at herself. It would be a longer time still before one did so again. (Though wasn't that interesting? She'd enjoyed it. The feel of it. The way he'd done it. The imagination and resolve behind it.) In any regard, the last person on earth who needed her apologies or reassurance was Sir James Stoker. He had the assurance of the world that he was an extraordinary young man. Let it be. Let him go.

"*Signora?*"

Lucia, her maid. She wanted to know, Would the beautiful young Englishman be back again soon?

Coco heaved herself off the door, frowning. "No, he won't be back at all." She walked down the foyer and into the parlor. "And he's not that beautiful. His feet are big. Did you see the size of his shoes?"

From the tea table, Coco picked up her mail, tapping it together distractedly, while behind her Lucia babbled in Italian about Dr. Stoker: his clothes, his manners, his carriage, which apparently had wheels that were red-rimmed and brass-spoked.

"In English," Coco said finally. She didn't like the tone of her own voice, but couldn't seem to make it otherwise. She added, trying to make her rebuke into something logical, "You must use English if you intend to learn it."

The girl tried. As she clattered tea items onto the tray, she said, "You look. Heese—cahr-rich—eese, how you say . . . *elegante, vivace?*" His carriage was stylish and jaunty.

Coco took the tray out of the girl's hands. "I'll get the rest. You go upstairs and finish with the trunks we're sending to San Remo."

Lucia stood, her hands out, open; confused. "*Prego?*"

"Upstairs. Go upstairs." In Italian, Coco told her, "Go pack the trunks."

Lucia's face took on a plaintive expression. "I only say," she explained, "he eese nice. A gentleman."

Coco lost patience. "For goodnessake, Lucia: a girl like you might ride in that jaunty carriage of his once or twice, or ride under him, if he can get past the guilt, but English gentleman don't take up with women of the serving class, or not seriously, at least. Stop being such a ninny, will you?"

Lucia frowned, hurt. "Me? No, no, not me. I think of you, *signora*. He like *you*." Her expression was one of offended good intentions.

Coco stared at her for a moment. Then, deflated, she said gently, "Nor me, Lucia. I am no different." She sighed, offering the tray back. "Here. Go on. Take this into the kitchen." She collapsed onto the edge of the sofa, then flopped back, rubbing her forehead. "I'm sorry," she said to Lucia. "I'm annoyed with myself. And with life."

She felt awful. Drained. The party last night had taken more of a toll than she'd imagined. In addition, her tooth had begun to hurt.

"No matter, *signora*. I take this, too?"

"What?" Lucia was pointing to James Stoker's teacup. "Yes. Then I can get the rest. Just take the tray into the scullery. I'll meet you upstairs in a bit."

Lucia disappeared with the tea tray. It took a moment for Coco to mobilize herself. But eventually she stood, picking up the cigar dish containing James Stoker's unfinished cigar.

Looking at it, she smiled wryly. She doubted that the "beautiful young Englishman" had ever propositioned a woman before. He was bad at it. He embarrassed himself easily. Yet bold—Lord, he was that. Bold and artless. What a combination. What a contradiction James Stoker was to her.

Innocent yet, she was sure, a quick study. He'd get better at rolling out inviting propositions. He was sweet. Gallant. Lucia was right, a gentleman. Lancelot dying to embrace the illicit, even though he didn't understand how to do it yet. Or, God knew, the consequences.

It was he she wanted to warn, not Lucia. Yet James Stoker, purveyor of cloves and other offers of help, had already denied he was heroic in the first place. She would not have known where to begin.

Moreover, he had the power to make kindness and generosity of spirit seem normal, to make romantic altruism plausible.

With a soft snort, Coco walked over and dumped the contents of the cigar dish into the empty rose box on the table under the mirror. Then, taking the box, she scraped dropped leaves and snipped stems into it.

Indeed, once she herself had indulged in romantic fantasies. She had dreamed things like, If I were the daughter of a great house—instead of the daughter of a papermill worker. . . . Then Sir James Stoker would have been exactly the sort of gentleman she'd have wanted to call on her. She'd have been in thrall to his fine manners, intelligence, and enthusiasm. Oh, these things—so *vivace*, indeed—they radiated from him like heat from the sun. While an implicit integrity in his gold-brown eyes made a person want to meet his gaze and believe every word he said.

Coco groaned inwardly. He *did* mean every word

he said, and that was the pity of it. She could have shaken him. But she only swept the last bits of flowers and leaves off the table, then picked up the card that had come with the roses, looking at it again. It was unsigned, though she had known the handwriting immediately even though she hadn't seen it in more than a dozen years. She had known it in only the slant of the letters in one repeated word: *Sorry, sorry, sorry.*

She crumpled the card and tossed it into the rest of the debris, shaking her head. Yes, she had been foolish once. But no longer.

That evening James was packing when a telegram arrived from Phillip Dunne, already in Cambridge. James opened the telegram, then had to sit down and read it twice:

DID NOT WANT TO MENTION TILL WAS CERTAIN STOP YOUR NAME TO GO ONTO HONORS LIST FOR JUNE STOP SUBMITTED IT THOUGH REAL CREDIT GOES TO YOUR MAGNIFICENT ACHIEVEMENTS STOP AM SURE HER MAJESTY WILL BE MOST GENEROUS STOP A FINE FINE THING CONGRATULATIONS STOP PHILLIP

James stared at the words, purely shocked. The Honors List was the list of suggested names given to the Queen by various counselors and authorities, the list from which, twice a year, at New Year and her birthday, she selected and bestowed hereditary titles.

As large as his plans were for himself, James's

aspirations had never included seeing his name on this list.

What business did he have with land holdings or a title of nobility? He had no experience in running an estate. He had little experience in the official protocol of rank—except near the bottom, of course, which wasn't very demanding.

His only formal experience with *noblesse* was actually with the Queen. Since his return, he had been commanded into Her Majesty's presence twice, on the two occasions this month when she had been in brief residence at Buckingham Palace. They'd been private audiences. He still didn't know what to make of the fact of having spent two strange afternoons, just himself and the Queen of England, with her asking questions, then listening raptly as he'd recited his exploits.

What a stunning notion to leap from here to becoming part of English nobility. How cynical the leap made him. He did not feel he had accomplished anything yet in life that could be termed a "magnificent achievement." What did his name on the Honors List mean? Other than that a man who brought back a lot of exotic riches from far away— and who possibly knew where there was more of the same to be found—appealed very strongly to Her Majesty's sense of manly daring?

Chapter 6

London
31 March 1876

My dearest David,

I wish you could see the bouquet of flowers I am looking at right now. It seems a shame that I must give them away or let them fade, but my tickets are in order: I am on the train to you tomorrow. If only these extraordinary flowers would travel. You would adore them. Big, fat alba Célestes. Tiny, fragrant noisettes. Bracts of simple musk roses. The cultivated and wild together. It is a raucous bouquet, as if from a vast, sunny garden. With tulips, violets, snapdragons intermingled with spikes of the prettiest little orchids, all with curling ferns and some lush green, tiny-leafed stuff I can't even name.

I thought perhaps if I described all these to you, then you might enjoy them a little before I deposit them with the cook who is taking them to her daughter—never to be seen again by the likes of us, my dear. Anyway, it is a once-and-never-again armload of flowers. I have never seen the match for it.

They arrived today from that fellow James Stoker (who himself arrived on my doorstep yesterday). Yes, the one from the dentist's parlor whom you think you know from Cambridge. Though I wonder if you are correct, since your Dr. Stoker is a don, and this man seems rather young for such a learned position. Tall, blondish hair? Unfashionably tan still from his travels (a much healthier color, in my opinion, than that of most Englishmen)? Does this sound like the gentleman you met three weeks ago?

I must say, I am curious about him. He strikes me as a little flashy for a scholar, while he seems too aboveboard for the political intrigue of a successful academician. How is it that he is both? He seems forthright, generous, kind, yet an image of him sitting in my front parlor yesterday stays with me: his arms along the back of my sofa, a clamped-down bite on one of Bertie's cigars, his lips pulled back, smoke roiling from between his teeth. He looked like a bloody czar.

Look how I ramble! You say I keep to my own council too much, but, look, I am a regular magpie with you. I took the contract to Mr. Pease, by the way, signed and sealed. He is toying with the idea of "doing a Brothers Grimm" on the fairy tale, that is to say, cutting the last half off. No Ogress Queen. No child-eating. A shame. I could do such a nice, horrific job on these. But, ah, well. I shall spin my "curlicues" into a pretty sleeping princess and a spiraling rococo woods. I shall make the forest fierce. It will all but swallow the handsome prince who comes along and, with a kiss, gives Beauty's life meaning again.

Ha. What a foolish tale this is at heart, don't you think? I say, wake up there, Beauty. Who better to make your life count than yourself?

And no, I am not too independent. Not too content, not too peaceful. Not, not, not complacently withdrawn from life. I've had my parties, darling. I no longer find swarms of people as amusing as I once did. Just give me a few friends—I hear from Marie-Louise and Denise from time to time. Lucia is with me; she plays a vicious game of cribbage. Oh, and I saw Margaret Drexel the other night, who is ill; I fear for her. Other than this, though, well, Jay does a first-rate job with my accounts; he does far more than he should for me. And Nigel, ever so carefully, makes certain that I'm all right. Always good when you have a bishop saying masses for your soul. Life is fine.

Besides, I have your regular letters, which are worth the world to me. And our occasional visit. Hurray! I can't wait to see you and hear more about the Battle of the Bees as well as your other chemical dilemmas. I miss your shining face. Thank you for reassuring me that Cambridge is deserted between terms. I would come anyway, though; now and then I simply *must. Still, it is best that even you are not seen with me too much, my sweet dear. Alas, all the more so in England, it seems. Take care, my darling. Remember to be kind to yourself. I embrace you, my love, my sweet cabbage in cream.*

> *I send you big, smacking kisses,*
> *Coco*

New York
February 3, 1876

Dear Mrs. Wild,

Enclosed please find a bank draft and statement reflecting dividends in the amount of $2,893.44. These represent your dividends from the last quarter of 1875 in Levanthal Preferred Investments. We thank you, a valued investor, for your faith in us and look forward to continuing to serve your financial planning and investment needs.

> *Most sincerely,*
> *Julius J. Levanthal*
> *signed in his absence by*
> *H.I. Raddison, Vice President*
> *Levanthal, Drexel, Raddison & Company*

Mar 29, 1876

Coco,

I here return to you L.D.R.& Co.'s letter, statement, and a new bank draft in the amount of 14,785 French francs, the result of my converting your check of $2,893.44 at the rate of 5.11 French francs to the U.S. dollar. Happy to help.

Jay

Part 2

Curses and Spinning Wheels

For the beauty Brynhild, sleep is a reprieve. Brave to the point of being defiant, she contradicts the wishes of her father, Odin—who punishes her by decreeing that she must marry a mortal. Odin tempers his edict when his daughter begs him to prevent somehow that this mean she marry a coward. Thus, he casts her under a spell of sleep and puts her in a deserted castle surrounded by a fire so fierce that only a man of great valor might pass through it. There, within her circle of flames, the beautiful valkyrie sleeps in full armor. When at last a mortal, Sigurd, comes through the fire, he removes the armor from her insensible body—literally removing her defenses and disarming her. By this, he awakens the beautiful maiden to the trust and intimacy of love.

From the Preface to The Sleeping Beauty
DuJauc translation
Pease Press, London, 1877

Chapter 7

~~~~~~∽⊙⊙⌣~~~~~~

Coco did not expect to see James Stoker again, least of all during her brief visit to Cambridge. For one thing, she had thought she would be in town only ten days, not one of which fell during regular term. Moreover, she had originally intended to stay several miles outside of town and thus the environs of the university. There should never have been cause for their paths to cross.

Except that a series of events put Coco in Cambridge longer than she'd expected, in residence off Chesterton Road at the very edge of the university, and on the north edge of Jesus Green at the precise instant James Stoker stepped off the sidewalk at the south edge and—unknowingly—began making his way toward her.

She watched him walk from between trees out onto the green and expansive sunny common, recognizing him instantly in spite of his attire: he was in informal dress, no hood or bands or doctoral scarlet, just a black academic gown billowing out and behind him as he strode across the grass. He walked with a slight bounce on the balls of his feet; she knew him by his long-legged gait—by, alas, the *vivace* spirit he put into each step.

Coco smiled and stood watching from her far border of trees. She had more than enough time to turn away, to pretend she didn't see him. Yet she couldn't resist the sight of him in his somber, bookish clothes.

If one could call a flowing, open silk-faced robe over an umber tweedy-looking suit "somber." She herself had always found scholarly gowns and adornments fascinating, from the simple black to the red robes and colorful hoods. Like the surplices and chasubles of priests. In any event, James Stoker certainly brought a stylishness to what one might have normally called respectably dull. It was not just his dapper suit, but also in the way he moved, in the square of his shoulders, in the way his hair glinted gold in the sun. He looked boyishly relaxed, yet delighted somehow—as if costumed, in gleeful disguise. She had the impression of a man granted permission—wearing it—to play, childlike, all day in a subject field he loved.

As he came closer, this impression was reinforced: he was humming. Oh, it was too much. Coco stepped out from the trees and walked toward him. She shouldn't have, she told herself. How awful to encourage him even a little. How awful to enjoy looking at him, to anticipate meeting him, speaking to him again.

And how truly horrid of her to enjoy the astonished look on his face as he recognized her ten yards off and stopped.

Coco laughed to herself—and, alas, smiled widely at him. Oh, hang all self-reproach. Sir James

Stoker, knight, scholar, and hero to the Queen, was
an impressive young man. Why blame herself for
being impressed?

As she came toward him, he looked down, shook
his head, looked up again, smiling in confusion, disbelief, and—his smile growing by the moment—
pure delight. Something leaped in Coco's chest. It
felt good to please him. Too good, perhaps.

As she approached, he seemed to search for
words, a man unsure where to begin. His smile became sheepish. He offered, "Friends, then?"

She nodded, herself with no appropriate response,
only smiles. Too idiots grinning at each other.

He asked, "You received the flowers?"

"Oh, yes. They were marvelous. Thank you."

"They went with my profuse apologies."

"Accepted."

He nodded. His hands went out, a man whose
wonder measured the width of his arms, as he said,
"But why are you here—how did you—oh, I hate
what I did in London—just terrible—so sorry—oh,
God—" He let out air between his lips, exasperation. "I'm making no sense—"

"I know what you mean. It's all right."

Which made him smile more broadly still and
shake his head, while she laughed at his confusion.
He said, "It's all right that I slammed your door
and stomped off, after . . . well, let us say I insulted
you roundly." He rolled his eyes, shook his head
some more—no, it was not all right—all with an
engaging self-deprecation. He said, "I don't know
if you'll believe me, but I have never done anything
as untoward as I did that day in the entirety of my
life. I have lost sleep over it."

She nodded soberly, squelching laughter. "Oh, yes, I believe you."

His smile looked briefly taken aback, a would-be rake whose credibility came a shade too quickly. He insisted, "It was inexcusable. Let me make it up to you—"

"No, no, it's fine. Really. Don't worry—"

"God, I'm so absolutely undone to see you here. And delighted, make no mistake. Where are you going? What can I do for you? Will you have dinner with me?"

"No." She blinked. No, no, no. She shook her head vehemently.

He just kept smiling, his amber eyes focused on her with his rare and inquisitive intelligence. "But why, how are you here?" he asked. "What are you doing in Cambridge?"

"Visiting a friend."

"A friend?"

"Oh, my." She realized, "In fact, I'm late." She was flustered, more flustered than she could account for. She shook her head again. "I'm sorry." She moved past him, then couldn't resist pivoting to walk backward, maintaining eye contact—while maintaining the helplessly broad smile that had taken over her face. She couldn't seem to stop beaming at him. It felt so good to see him, to stand in the fine, honest warmth of his fixed stare. How awful to feel this way. How wonderful. A friend, she told herself. That he was. A real friend. "I'm sorry," she said. "I have to go. I have an appointment in ten minutes."

"An appointment?" As she moved away, he began to follow.

She shook her head no. He halted.

To James, she seemed a mirage, a hallucination. He was afraid she would evaporate—or, more realistically, run—if he didn't do as she said. Oh, he was going to be so well behaved this time. Yet as she backed away, he was seized with panic. He still had no idea where she was staying or how to get in touch with her.

Under her parasol, held so charmingly in her gloved hands, she made another French shrug, powerless against her "appointment."

"Please," he said, "let me make up for my rudeness." As if a brilliant concept had been eluding him, he said, "If not dinner, then afternoon tea."

"No." She laughed, a slightly giddy sound that made his skin rise in goosebumps. Lord, she was lovely to his ears, to his eyes. Small and perfect, like a pretty flower at the peak of its bloom—so bright today, without a trace of melancholy. A happy woman. Who backed away from him, getting farther off by the second.

"A light supper then," he suggested facetiously. God, how to keep her attention?

"No."

"Elvenses." Morning tea.

She laughed. "No."

"Breakfast."

"All right."

James startled, then laughed heartily himself, with deep, full pleasure. "All right?" he repeated.

"Yes. I'll meet you in the basement of Tolly's across from King's tomorrow morning at seven."

He didn't lecture till noon. "Seven?" Breakfast. At Tolly's. In the midst of students clanging their coffee spoons, rattling their newspapers. "Seven in the morning?"

She teased him. "Aren't scholars always up early?"

"Not this one."

She raised one eyebrow, laughing, tormenting him now openly. Still moving, she called, "Well, if you can't come—"

"No—" He smiled. He frowned. He smiled again. Outmaneuvered. He told her, "All right. I'll be there." She was fifty feet away by then. He thought to ask, "Where are you staying while you're here? I could come fetch you." And why the devil was she here to begin with? he wanted to know. What sort of friend did she have in Cambridge?

But she only made another of her disarming shrugs. "I'll be out walking," she explained. No need to fetch her. Or know where she lived. "I'll meet you in Tolly's Cellar, then. Do you know where it is?"

"Yes. It's tiny, crowded, and loud."

Before he could suggest somewhere better, though, she had waved goodbye and turned—making Tolly's Cellar their unchallengeable rendezvous point.

He watched Coco Wild saunter off, her hair shining like polished jet. She had the blackest, glossiest hair he'd seen this side of Egypt. Egypt, yes. She had that kind of power. A tiny Cleopatra with charm enough to bow down nations and all the great men within them.

He watched her go, watched her parasol bob over the flounce at the back of her dress. James couldn't look away. With each step, the bouffant of silk atop her bustle wobbled precariously, the taffeta itself taking on a sheen in the sun. Her dress was pale, pale pink—like the roses, he remembered—a blushing dress. As she walked into the distance, the pale color took on a silver luster, becoming a luminous counterpoint to her vivid black hair.

James followed the sight of her all the way across the bright spring grass of Jesus Green. But she had no sooner stepped through the trees on the far side, crossing the lane, than it occurred to him that he could follow her literally. She wouldn't see him. He knew the back ways and alleys. Almost certainly, she had struck out for the main street. He hesitated a split second. Then he became the man of science that he was. He needed more data, the first available piece of information being, What sort of appointment did she keep at—he consulted his watch—three-thirty on a Tuesday afternoon?

He took off. As he headed for the border of trees, he shucked his telltale gown, wadded it up, and tucked it under his coat. He stayed behind the trees till he caught sight of her again. She crossed another lane, then a small square, then turned onto Bridge Street.

She went a good distance, Bridge Street becoming St. John's (with James using buildings for cover, darting covertly like some melodrama villain); St. John's Street became Trinity, which in turn became King's Parade, the center of town. There she crossed Market Square to Miss Anabel's Tea House, where—to James's great surprise and chagrin—a young man was waiting for her.

He was tall and thin, dark-haired, a good-looking fellow in his twenties, James would guess, very well dressed. He greeted her with enthusiasm, embracing her, kissing her cheek, pulling her to his chest. James felt strange emotions skip across his heart, like pebbles across a dark pool into which he wasn't certain he wished to dive.

She felt about the young man differently from the way she felt, for instance, about Levanthal. James knew a fearful yet near-rabid curiosity. Who was he, this young man? What was he to her? Who was the puzzling woman who called James himself too young, then went gaily off to meet a man who appeared even younger? Yet James's questions and observations floated over murkier motives in himself as he stared at the two of them: envy, an obscure neediness, a longing that was unplumbed.

James heard the wisps of her laughter. She stroked her hand up the fellow's arm once. Her young man made her laugh in a different way from that which James did. The sound was more intimate. More relaxed, James fancied, than when she greeted him.

He couldn't help himself. He bristled. He stepped back beneath an archway, looking at them across the distance of the Senate House Yard. How easily and forcefully jealousy came upon him with regard to Coco Wild. He had to stem it consciously, tell himself, No, no, you hated yourself for drawing poorly informed conclusions once before now. You will not do it again, James, old boy.

Don't be a raving lunatic in the face of any person—all right, any *man*—who happens to know her more than in passing. She is entitled to close aquaintances, warm associations, confidants.

Coco and her young man took tea outside at a little umbrellaed table on the edge of the square. They never stopped talking. She patted the infant's shoulder; she patted his hand. At one point, the young man brought forth something from his pocket, showing it to her. She was thrilled with it. As if she were his mother.

His mother. James frowned, letting his shoulder, his weight fall against the stone wall of the Senate front gate as he tried out his hypothesis: The young man was her son. No, there was not a shred of gossip regarding any offspring; and gossip was the by-word, the middle name, of Coco Wild. Besides, she would have to have conceived him when she was a child herself. Perhaps she sponsored the lad or was friends with his mother. Or his father.

Or—ugly thought—perhaps the fellow was another prince whose cronies had arranged an assignation. He dressed richly. He had a confident way about him, self-assured.

James tortured himself for a time with the sight of them and such ruminations. Ultimately, though, he left with no answer: only the abiding image of Coco Wild and her young man, the two of them sitting there, chatting, animated, familiar, easy in each other's company.

Chapter 8

Tolly's was a hole-in-the-wall basement establishment down a set of narrow steps just off King's Parade. As Coco descended into its small whitewashed brick room, she was immediately immersed in a congestion of undergraduates. They jostled her as they came up the steps, taking away tea and ploughboys—bread baked around hard-boiled eggs. They blocked her way in a bottleneck at the front counter where they placed orders for full English breakfasts—aside from an older man and woman eating at a far table, the rest all appeared to be young men escaping the morning's plain bread-and-butter commons found at most colleges.

Beyond the competitive front counter, the tiny dining common had a leisurely if slightly crowded milieu: half a dozen tables, most with students clustered around them, young men reading newspapers or books or chatting in the quiet intonations, the round vowels, of young, well-off gentlemen. She spotted James Stoker at the back. He stood; he'd been holding a table, one under the place's only window, the outward view being that of passing feet on the sidewalk outside.

Coco made her way to him, laughing at how out of place he looked. For once, he didn't look young. In fact, the students gave him a wary berth—a professor in their midst. She, though one of only two women in the room, they made way for without fuss. The regulars were apparently used to her—she had eaten here everyday for almost two weeks.

At the table, Mr. Stoker and she exchanged hellos, then places. She sat, holding their table, while he gave their orders at the counter, then waited.

He returned a few minutes later. As he jockeyed a tray over the head of a curly-haired fellow at the next table, he said, "So where are you staying and who are you visiting in Cambridge?"

"I'm staying with my aunt."

"And who, pray tell, is your aunt?" From the tray he unloaded her tea with cream, her eggs and fried toast, tomatoes, mushrooms, bangers; breakfast was Coco's favorite meal this side of the Channel. He set his own toast and—amazing he ordered it, amazing they had it—a cup of coffee onto the table, then put the tray into the window ledge overhead and sat.

Unfolding her napkin, Coco told him, "You wouldn't know her. And I didn't mean to stay with her." When he looked far too interested, she waved away query. "Oh, it's a boring story, honestly. Tell me: Where were you coming from yesterday? Do you lecture here?"

"Yes. But yesterday was a Senate meeting." He shoveled one, two, three spoonfuls of sugar into his coffee, then stirred as he flashed one of his dental-perfect smiles at her. "And I have all morning. Let's hear your boring story."

"I'd rather hear about you. You're part of the governing body of the university?"

He left a rueful pause, then allowed himself to be distracted. "The new Chairman of the Financial Board, I'm afraid. Appointed by the Vice-Chancellor. And on more ruddy committees lately than there are camels in Timbuktu."

"Which committees? Tell me about them."

"Not much to tell. A lot of stuffy old men. I'm the youngest on all the committees, the youngest deputy head of a college, and they don't let me forget it. I'm called bumptious or headlong at least once a week." He laughed with cheerful menace. "Which doesn't stop me from saying what I wish to say anyway and getting what I want most of the time."

"And what do you want?"

He slathered butter onto his muffin. "Besides money for more geological digs and research equipment?" He took her interested silence to mean yes. "Common sense, mostly. For instance, the two women's colleges wanting admittance to the university should get it, and they and Girton should be allowed to grant degrees." He laughed. "Which I'm not just saying to impress you with how forward-thinking I am." Then he slid her a grin, wiggling his eyebrows in that blatantly self-delighted way he had. "All the same, are you impressed?"

She laughed. "Oh, yes." She said in half-sincerity, "The vanguard of women's rights. And an important man. Are you really Head of College?"

"No, no. Deputy head. Vice-Provost."

"Which one?"

"All Souls."

She frowned, smiled, then furrowed her brow as she smiled down into her eggs. He was having her on. "All Souls? Really?" All Souls College at Cambridge was the largest, both in land and enrollment, the richest and most well endowed. One didn't just become second-in-command there. One campaigned for the position, then used it as a seat of power.

"Yes. Are you familiar with the college?"

"Somewhat." She eyed him in this new light. It had only just registered: "And the Financial Board of the Council of the Senate. You manage the money for the entire university. After only being back a month. Isn't that a little . . . much?"

"It's a lot of work. But"—he shrugged—"Phillip, that is, the Vice-Chancellor—wanted it. He has to show me everything. I'm a real novice. But then, he's always been a good teacher. I suppose I'm coming along."

"*And* the Vice-Provost of All Souls. Well, I'm in awe."

His face liked the idea of awing her, even in a teasing way. He looked down, his smile pleasurably self-conscious. "It's really not much. I was active at All Souls before I left, and all the voting fellows like me. So when the old Vice-Provost stepped down last month for health reasons, well, I think they were just excited to see me again after thinking I was dead. The rest are all appointments, mostly by the Vice-Chancellor who loves me—and who is also the Provost at All Souls. We work well together: I save him time and bring in money."

He shrugged, playing with his coffee spoon till it was better aligned to his napkin on the table, then said, "But I do have news that awes *me.*" His eyes down, his voice enriched with wonder and a sense of glory, he said, "I learned a week ago that my name has gone onto the Honors List. Do you know what that is?"

"Yes."

He glanced over at her, meditative for a moment.

It occurred to Coco that she was too knowledgeable. Too much understanding and details at her fingertips would raise questions. She amended, "Vaguely, anyway. It means a title, no?"

"A title, yes. An earldom, in this case, I'm told, courtesy of the good Queen Victoria. It's mine, so long as I mind my Ps and Qs till June, when she signs the patent letters at the official royal birthday celebration."

"My." Coco could only stare.

And he couldn't be thirty, she thought. What a future James Stoker had.

"An earldom," she repeated, feeling enthusiastically happy for him. And not just because he wanted the recognition (and by the look on his face there was no doubt), but because he seemed one of those rare cases: a deserving man. "How very nice for you. Congratulations."

He nodded, reddening slightly, a man who could blush.

She found the ability quite charming.

"Thank you," he said. After a few beats of basking in her goodwill, he broke the mood by drumming his fingers once on the table, then reaching for the jam. He smiled at her over twisting its lid.

"Well," he said, "where *did* you intend to stay, if not with your aunt?"

"Pardon?"

"You were telling me you hadn't intended to stay at your aunt's."

"Ah. No. I was going to stay at a boardinghouse, but I ran into some trouble."

"Trouble? What kind? Perhaps I can help."

She smiled, shaking her head. "Perfect. I was chased out by dragons. Shall I go ready your stead then, Sir James?"

He didn't know how to take this, whether it was meant kindly or not.

Coco looked down, feeling a little contrite as she scooped eggs onto her fork with her toast. "Teasing you. You make me nervous wanting to save me all the time."

"It's not really a matter of wanting to save you. I keep thinking if I hold my arms out often enough, you might drop into them. And if you did, believe me, saving you would be the last thing I'd be thinking about."

She blinked over the forkful of eggs halfway to her mouth.

He smiled sweetly across the table, his handsome face looking for all the world as if it were off some Italian ceiling, the face of an angel, an archangel, while his amber-brown eyes remained fixed on her with something less than angelic regard.

Plates clattered. A boy in an apron cleared the table to the side.

"Which committees are you on?" Coco asked.

"I want to talk about you."

She scowled. "Why?" Then threw him her best

smile. "When your life is so much more interesting than mine? With your academic politics and African adventures."

He rolled his eyes. It was becoming a game of who could outcharm the other; she wanted to laugh. "Oh, yes, now, there's something interesting. A lot of crusty dons. Or a continent as hot as Hades, damp heat, blistering dry heat. With bats. Bats as big monkeys."

"You've mentioned bats before."

Consternation passed over his face. "Have I?" He drank a sip of coffee, then sat back, still holding the cup, looking down into it.

"You hate them."

"Indeed." He paused, reflective, as if he didn't intend to say anything more. Then he leaned forward again, lowering his voice, and spoke in an appealing, quasi-confidential tone. "In Africa, there are bats that hang from the trees; they fold themselves up and hang there as big as cantaloupe. Flying, their wingspan is wider than my arms. One evening, just before sunset, I came into some trees at the edge of an open plain. I thought the things hanging all around were, oh, I don't know, grapefruit, large pomegranates, anything but bats. Then I shot at a hare, and, *whoa,* the fruit took off. I'd unsettled a battalion of the devils. They unfolded out of the trees, helter-skelter, flapping everywhere. The air was thick with them. They swooped at my head, my back, my shoulders, my face. They were everywhere. Warm, furry, bony things, like giant, winged rats. Hundreds of them." He shook his head, then shivered down his arms. "Ho, Lord, I thought I would die from fright."

"Did they bite you?"

He laughed, the sound of release. "No."

"What did they do?"

"Nothing. Except flap and call and drop a lot of *guano* on me." *Guano*. Bat feces. He'd embarrassed himself by discussing it. "Sorry. The point is, I'm a terrible coward when it comes to bats. Had one come down a chimney once here, fly into the geology lab. Had to have someone else come get it. It petrified me even to imagine trying to catch it or kill it. Can't stand them."

"Everyone is afraid of something."

"Well, yes. Thank you. Confessed and absolved. Though I still feel a little foolish."

"You shouldn't."

"You've never seen how insane I get around them."

"Batty over bats."

"*Blech.*" He made a face. "Do we have to talk about them?" He was kidding, but serious, too.

She laughed. Again. Talking with him, being around him made her burst out continually. She wasn't herself. No, she was better than herself: she felt happier.

The group one table over finished, everyone standing in unison, their chairs scraping the floor. The boy in the apron moved over to clear the finished table, slinging cups and plates and utensils onto his tray.

When Coco looked back, James Stoker was watching her. In that same intimate tone, he said, "Stop all this coy directing of the conversation toward me and tell me what dragons chased you out of the boarding house, where the boarding house is, where you are staying now, and who your aunt is."

She speared the last of her sausage. "Not dragons. Bees." She ate the sausage in one large bite.

"Details, where are the details?" He smiled affably through the nearby cacophony of dinnerware falling onto a tray.

She couldn't talk for a moment, her mouth full of food.

He pulled a face. "Oh, do stop all this infernal eating and tell me all about your visit here. I am dying to understand what great, wonderful coincidence brought you all but to my door."

She dabbed her napkin at her mouth and tried to talk through it. "Fine. But I warned you." She had to swallow, wait. "It's fairly silly. Some bees got into the roof of a boarding house I own here—"

"You *own* the boarding house?"

"Yes—"

"A licensed boarding house?"

"Yes." Already more than she wanted him to know. She continued quickly, "Anyway, they built a nest under the shingles. My tenants began to fret. One or two were stung—the nest was right by the back door. The young man who takes care of the house wrote to me. I suggested he call on an apiary, but he thought it a lot of bother for the sake of some trespassing bees. So he brought home some chemicals from the chem lab, mixed them up, and, voilà, he gassed the bees, with homemade chlorine gas, I think. He nearly asphyxiated himself in the bargain. At any rate, when I first arrived, all seemed well. The bees were gone.

"But then—oh, my. The May sun set about its work, and about six days ago honey started dripping in through the rafters onto everything in the upper east side of the house. Into my bed, my bags, onto my dresser.''

''Honey,'' James said disbelievingly, but he was transfixed. He chuckled.

Which only encouraged her; so did she. ''It's funny, isn't it? It's funny!'' Coco sat back, shaking her head. ''Lord, it wasn't funny when it first happened. And it remains an onerous problem. I've had to call in a roofer, and a carpenter, and get some people to come in and clean everything. But it's still—'' Her laughter became hearty. She had to put her hand over her mouth to keep deep, unladylike guffaws from coming out. ''It's hilarious, isn't it? Honey pouring from the rafters, over everything! So predictable, yet we just didn't think of it. Who would imagine?''

The two of them sat there laughing over the poetic revenge of wronged honeybees as Coco tried to get the rest of the story out. ''I—I had to find''— she covered her mouth with her napkin—''find a place to stay. Then, worse, it turns out there's an international colloquium on something or other right now—''

''Geology,'' he said. ''Geology—I'm part of it.'' More laughter.

''Yes! And there is not a free room anywhere, so I moved in with my aunt. End of story.'' She set her hands on the table and simply let her laughter go.

When she had calmed down enough, she let herself look at him. He was watching her in an embarrassingly attentive way. He murmured, ''A long way from boring.'' Then, with hardly a pause, he added, ''I love that you can do that.''

''Do what?''

''Laugh so much. At everything.''

She wasn't sure what to say. She stared at him, then said, ''Only with you. And there are those who might think that to laugh so much is shallow.''

He shook his head. ''The Wakua laugh all the time, over everything—''

''The Wakua?''

''The tribe who entrusted me with their gold.'' He continued, ''The Englishmen that met us at the river thought Mtzuba and his friends—''

''Mtzuba?''

''A Wakua friend of mine. They thought the Wakua were fools because of their laughter. Children. But I have seen them laugh over death and blight and fear and war. They see the ironies of life; they live its absurdity: when you think about it, everything *is* funny.''

Coco laughed—self-consciously this time—at his odd, flattering turn of mind.

He let her humor die off, his lambent eyes watching her the whole while. Then, as if it were part of the same conversation, he said, ''And your aunt is—?''

He wanted a name. She was thrown, bumbling out, ''You won't know her.'' He waited. She snorted, then said, ''All right, I'll tell you. My aunt is the head cook for one of the larger households here. I am living downstairs with the serving staff.''

''You're joking.''

''No, but it's quite all right. Nothing I haven't done before.''

He paused over the rim of his raised coffee cup. "You have lived below stairs?"

Coco smiled at the euphemism *hired help* and sat back. "I worked 'below stairs,' as you call it, for four months when I first came to this country." She raised her eyebrows, mildly tormented again. "Then I found more suitable work. One that pleased my inclinations."

He blinked, jerked slightly. She really had to stop playing with him like this, she thought. But then he didn't glide his eyes away as she expected; and after a moment she had to drop hers. Because James Stoker had somehow gotten beyond her vague joking references to her "profession." It didn't bother him anymore.

Staring speculatively at her, without lifting his eyes away for a minute, he said, "We have yet more in common: you're the niece of a cook. I'm the son of a coachman."

"Really?" She suppressed a giggle just as it was about to come out. Lord. The urge to laugh again. And it was not wisdom, as he said, but pure, simple nervous reaction by now. He unsettled her horribly, though she couldn't say why.

"Really. So you have me: we weren't even indoor servants. We lived over the carriage house."

"Now I *am* impressed. You sound as if you were educated at—oh, Harrow or Eton."

"Close. Tutored by an Etonian-Cantabrigian."

"Well, you *have* come a distance, haven't you?" A social distance that was purely astounding. She shook her head in wonder. "The son of a coachman: soon to be an earl."

He smiled at her. Really at her, not at what she'd

meant as a compliment. He said, "Sitting across from a beautiful former—what?—assistant to the cook?—who became the most independent woman I have ever met, save perhaps the Queen."

They sat there, each offering the other a kind of admiration, each watching from their new, extraordinarily rare, common perspective.

He asked finally, "Is the rest of your family in France, then?"

"One sister. The other here."

"Parents?"

"Both dead, years ago now."

"Do you see your sisters?"

"No." Coco frowned at all these questions. It was usually easy to keep a man talking about himself. Not so with James Stoker.

She pondered him, while she used her fork to move bits of her breakfast about on her plate.

"Which household? Where does your aunt work?"

She looked up, prepared to be annoyed. But his candor took her aback. He wore his deep, deep interest in her right there on his face for her to see. Along with an understanding—she had the uneasy feeling that he understood her far better than she wished. And patience. A profound patience lay in his feature, a tolerance for waiting, watching.

Which set off an alarm. For Coco knew herself to be a woman who lived by secrets. To share them at one point in her life would have meant her career, her ruin, all trust in her gone. To share them now would simply mean her best associations betrayed, her self-respect pierced, her dignity damaged or lost. No, she would not let him disarm her, though God knew that was his intention.

"I need more tea," she said. She started to get up, thinking to go to the front counter.

Dr. Stoker stood faster, taking her cup. "I'll get it." He picked up his own cup as well.

She watched him weave his way through the now mostly empty tables—only one other one at the front still occupied; the morning crush for breakfast had abated. At the counter, he gave over the cups, then waited, one hand in his trouser pocket. He stood there, relaxed, slender, more natty in attire than any donnish Council of the Senate's Chairman of the Financial Board had a right to be.

No academic gown today. His trousers were well tailored; they hung with the weight of expensive worsted—a warm reddish-brown herringbone pattern. His jacket matched; his waistcoat was the color of English cream, decorated only by a dangling gold watch chain that swung when he walked.

The girl behind the counter struck up a conversation with him. He responded in a friendly manner, laughing in that easy way he had. He was the one who laughed effortlessly at most of what life brought him. A happy man. He was happy, Coco realized with some amazement. It was not a quality she would attribute to many.

There was no snobbery to him. None. Which Coco found unusual. She had never known an Englishman of his class, his education and background, who didn't possess a grain of it—then she paused, remembering his background. A coachman's son. Like herself, he was not true gentry.

Or, no. That was the thing about James Stoker.

He *was* a gentleman. There was nothing false about him. His kindness, generosity, and awareness of others were real, intrinsic to him. He treated everyone with consideration. James Stoker was a gentleman at his core, at his heart.

It came as no surprise to Coco that the Queen should wish to honor this quality in him, make it official. Indeed, why should Victoria be immune to what any number of women must feel when they looked upon him? The desire to favor him, grant him privileges—and make him obliged.

Coco lowered her eyes to stare at the tabletop. Good Lord, where had *this* thought come from?

When he came back with the tea, coffee for himself, she asked flippantly, "So how is old Queen Victoria?"

"Queen Victoria?" James looked surprised as he sat, sliding Coco's tea across the table to her. But he answered anyway, "Her Majesty is stiff, no nonsense, but nice. With a lot of questions."

"Questions? You've talked to her?"

"Twice."

"You've had audiences with the Queen?"

"Yes."

"Private audiences?"

"Yes. Why?"

"And you think of it like that: 'Yes. Why?' Do you realize there is a line of people, powerful people, waiting, scrambling to meet with her?"

"I suppose."

Coco shook her head. This brash young fellow knew he was successful, enough that he could swagger and grin. But he had no real idea *how* successful. It was charming. It was maddening. It made her want to shake him and wring her hands.

She wondered if she should mention that she herself had had contact with the Queen years ago and that it had not gone well—that she was not Bertie's mother's favorite person.

She looked about instead. Tolly's was all but empty. Even the girl at the counter had retreated to the kitchen.

Coco heard her own voice echo softly against the bricks of cellar-cum–dining room as she asked Sir Knight, "What do you and the Queen speak of, when you go for a visit?"

He scooped sugar into his coffee. "Africa, mostly." He let out a single-syllabled guffaw: *Har.* "My manly adventures."

"Tell me." She watched him. Yes. Oh, dear. Manly, indeed. He was. Her Majesty's knight was slender but solid. Strong, tan-skinned, sun-streaked: reeking of health. His intelligence had a quirky, humorous aspect to it. It made him calm; it gave him a lively awareness of everything around him. *Vivace*, she thought.

"Tell you what?" he asked.

"Tell me whatever it is you've told her."

He frowned down at the wood table top. "I told her how and where the others died: why I didn't."

She waited, pondering him—as she felt his trust spread out to reach her, all but tangible. She was aware of it like the smell of something cooking in a closed kitchen, drifting under the door down the hall. Secrets. Coco knew when one was coming.

He was at pains for a moment, trying to avoid being pressed into account. Then he began. "We

were there for a year, then got lost coming
home. . . ."

She sat back. She didn't know where it would
come or when it would come. But she knew she
would hear something no one else ever had.

Chapter 9

◦◦◦

The Princess awaked, and said she to him, you have waited a great while. The Prince, charm'd with these words, and much more with the manner they were spoken in, knew not how to shew his joy. Their discourse was not well conn-ected, little eloquence, a great deal of love. He was more at a loss than she. In short, they spoke four hours together, and yet they did not say half the things they had to say.

Charles Perrault
"The Sleeping Beauty of the Woods"
Tales of Past Times
Samber translation, London, 1729

"We were deep in the jungle, on a native footpath," James told the lovely, sympathetic woman across from him. He prepared to tell her a story he had told a dozen times now, the story of how men had died—and how he himself, miraculously alive, had come to step off a boat onto English soil again. "It was the only way north. The African rivers, other than the middle Congo, are not navigable by any conveyance larger than canoe. No roads, no communication."

He was quiet a moment, finding it all too easy to be again in that dark place. Sitting back with his coffee, he let flow whatever wished to well up into his consciousness; he thought merely to indulge in a slightly more poetic version than he had given the Queen of England.

"It's hard to imagine," he told Coco Wild, "how completely adrift you are, how primitive. The savannahs are stark, wild. But the jungle . . . There, at night, the sounds are beautiful, eerie, and they rise up out of pitch black. Even moonlight doesn't much penetrate the densest part. You can't imagine such utter darkness.

"Anyway, after having taken a steamer round the Horn, landed at Cape Town, then been there a year, we were now traveling north through unmapped terrain, dense, remote: in a single file of porters on whose heads balanced all our earthly possessions in straw baskets, possessions that included our expedition's treasures, our samples and notes and records. I brought everything home, by the way. It will take me years to organize and decipher everything in those trunks. A year's work of one hundred forty-eight men." He paused. "With me the only survivor." He stared down into his black coffee, a drink he'd acquired a taste for from a Boer guide who had perished, a drink the color of skin everywhere he had looked at one point. "I wonder sometimes why I was spared. It doesn't seem right."

He couldn't talk for a few moments.

"Don't feel guilty for being alive," said the very civilized Coco. "What happened?"

It was logical enough to say, "They took all my instruments." But he didn't know where the next came from. "Then wanted my clothes."

He waited to see if she understood.

Of course, she didn't. Who would believe it?

"Your clothes?" she asked mildly. Then she raised her eyebrow, tilted her head, and followed him into his own private jungle. "What did they wear themselves?" she asked.

"Nothing." He let her absorb the word before he went further. "Though eventually various of them wore my trousers or vest or cravat."

She blinked, trying to make what he was saying into something else. She couldn't. "You went naked with them?"

It wasn't really a question. She knew full well what he had just said.

Adopting certain native ways was a horrible thing to European minds, and uncovering one's body was without doubt among the most horrible of all. No one he knew would comprehend his reasons.

"It was hot," he said inanely. And every other soul was naked and clothing grew to be an encumbrance and they had wanted his. So he had let them have his clothes, piece at a time, day at a time. It had just happened. "I never thought to be in England again," he added. Which, considering he sat here at an English table on the edge of an English university, seemed to say he'd been fairly soft in the head.

Indeed, his fellow Englishmen would think such behavior purely insane. King Lear running mad across the stage. An inmate of Bedlam who would not wear his pants.

He laughed. "What a private thing to tell you." He'd embarrassed himself. He looked off, self-conscious. "I had yet to share this particular information with anyone. I'd never intended to at all. I'm, ah—sorry. I shouldn't have said."

"No, no, it's all right." And oddly enough it was. Even though she widened her eyes and said, "Dear Lord. Well." He'd taken her breath away. Which, strangely enough, warmed him to the backs of his eyeballs.

He'd taken the breath away of a woman who was worldly in the most attractive way. Worldly enough not to mind the idea of him naked. And attractive, Lord God. He watched her smile and shake her head at him, thinking whom else in the world could he possibly have told this to? And who would have responded so benevolently?

While Coco sat there trying to imagine Mr. Stoker here shedding his shirt and vest out in the middle of nowhere, stripping down his trouser braces, stepping out of his trousers. Naked.

To a woman who wore layers of clothes—layers of self-protection—it was beyond thinking. Madness. Yet, equally crazy, the idea was momentarily beautiful to her: The tall, long-limbed James Stoker standing in the sun, his skin everywhere as tan as his face, the muscular smoothness of him, from one end to the other, smooth, brown, golden.

Then he tried to travel on the strangely intimate moment. Into their cozy quiet, he said softly, "That wasn't your aunt whom you met yesterday afternoon."

She bristled. "You followed me."

He lifted his shoulders as if to say: The temptation was too much, beyond his control or responsibility. How could she expect him to resist?

Well, she most certainly did. She puckered her mouth into a twist. Then said, "That was David. He maintains my property for me here. He's the one who killed the bees."

"Ah." He nodded. "That explains it. You were overjoyed to see a young man who'd ruined your roof."

David was none of his business, and she told him so with a quick, sour look.

He frowned down into his coffee, relenting a little. "You have a lot of men friends."

"Some."

"And do they all tell you their most intimate secrets, as I do?"

She frowned, conflicted, before she said, "Sometimes."

"Often," he asserted.

She lowered her eyes, running her finger along the foot of the sugar bowl. "Yes, often. I don't know why."

"How do you do it?"

"I don't do anything," she said quickly. She left a pause before saying, "Other than . . . well, I know how to make myself approachable."

He laughed humorlessly. "And how not to."

They were both silent. He had changed something

by pushing their conversation in this direction. She tried to hide the melancholy that had come over her, but couldn't quite manage it. Her defenses were down; she was unable to dissemble. And she deeply resented whatever part James Stoker had played in this. She said nothing. He drained his coffee cup. She stirred her tea, but didn't drink it.

"Well," she said at length, "a delicious breakfast. Thank you." She took her napkin from her lap and placed it on the tabletop. She glanced up, past his head, then, startled. The wall clock across the room said eleven thirty-three. Abruptly scooting back her chair, she said, "Lord, I was supposed to meet—" She broke off.

"David," he finished for her.

She stared at him.

He said, "You were to meet David. Where?"

She bit her lips together, as if she might clamp the answer in her mouth. Then released it combatively, a dare to disapprove: "In Grantchester three minutes ago."

James stood as well, reaching to pull her chair the rest of the way out. "Who is he?"

She slid from the chair, glancing over her shoulder as she picked up her parasol. "He is a good friend."

"I'll bet."

She stopped to glare at him. "Not that kind of friend."

"Then why do you avoid his mention as if he were a dirty secret?"

She felt a flash of pain, sharp enough to make her angry.

He must have seen her distress, for he took his

words back. "I—I'm sorry. I didn't—" His face held a kindness that was almost terrifying. A genuine compassion that made something quake deep inside her.

Damn it, no, she told herself. She found her smile, wide, direct, blithe. She made light of the whole issue. Turning away, she said over her shoulder, "Don't be naïve." She walked with premeditated ease, a saunter, toward the stairs. "He's a decent young man. I wouldn't want to . . . well, I want him to be allowed the right sort of associations here, to be happy—"

Outside, with James right behind her as they came up and out of Tolly's, he asked, "And you aren't the 'right sort'?"

She opened her parasol, a burst of pale yellow she arced up, then over her shoulder: hiding within it to say, "I'm a realist, Dr. Stoker. A realist who was thrown out of her last English ball."

Below ribbed and gored parasol silk, she could see his legs. Despite the parasol and her formal use of his name, meant to set him back, he followed. She walked quickly. He didn't even ask where they were going, merely refusing wordlessly to be left behind.

The day had clouded slightly. The sun shone, but the sky was gray. Rather like herself, she thought, trying to bear up under a cloudy mood. Why didn't he leave now? But, no: They walked together without speaking down King's Parade, then onto the grounds of King's College, its famous old chapel soaring to their right.

She took them along the sidewalks, then over spacious, green lawns, heading toward the Backs

and the river. She detoured toward King's Bridge—
the porter at Queens' would not have given her, or
any other woman, access. It was a good, long walk
without their saying a word. They crossed the river
Cam, then walked along its west bank, under trees,
over rolling grass, with gothic and Tudor colleges
limning the east horizon, architectural marvels from
centuries past.

As they started across Queens' Green, he said
suddenly, "Are you *walking* to Grantchester?"

"Yes."

"You know the way?"

"A footpath follows the river."

"Almost, not quite. And it's going to rain."

She tilted her parasol to look from under it at
him, about to argue. But, as if to prove his point, a
boom of thunder rumbled in the distance. She
waited for it to fade to silence, before she said, "I'll
be fine."

"I could show you a short-cut to the Grantchester
grind"—the path's colloquial name—"if you
like."

She tipped her parasol back, looking at the sky.
It was darker than she'd realized. Stiffly, she agreed,
"All right."

Beyond Silver Street, the grassy greens and
courts and Backs gave way to fenced pastureland.
A double-armed turnstile in the fence—sets of arms
that pivoted on a post—allowed people to cut
through, while keeping placid-faced cows confined
to their meadow.

He pointed. "From here, if you cut across this
field—" He stepped back to let her file into the
turnstile.

She wasn't sure if he planned it or it just happened. In all fairness, the idea seemed to take him as much by surprise as it did her. As if he thought it; he did it. She had no sooner entered the stile, one wooden arm across her belly, one at her knees, then it stopped. The rotating arms wouldn't move.

She twisted, peeping around the edge of her parasol to look back over her shoulder, puzzled, at first asking his help: till she realized he was the source of the problem. He held the rear wooden arm, immobilizing the whole contraption. She was trapped in the little wedge of space, unable to move forward, unable to step back.

Her heart began to thud, hard in her chest. Uncertainly, she offered a smile, a chance to be reasonable. Let go now and she'd dismiss what he was doing as a joke.

James Stoker met her eyes steadily, his knuckles moving in the silk bustle of her dress. He held firmly to the stile arm: no longer the sweet, predictable young man she thought he was. He looked confused, but buoyant—and absolutely determined—a man riding a kind of elation like wind under wing.

The moment became instantly and openly sexual. It said he wanted to hold her, even in this indirect way, more than either of them realized and that he might leap both their preconceived notions to do so.

The beat of her heart spread into her veins. She could feel her own pulse at her wrist, her neck, her stomach. Lord, he was so close and so much taller than she. Likewise, stopping the turnstile was a display of strength, not very subtle but effective. He'd made her aware of his physical vigor—a virility in him—that wasn't the least bit young. Just terribly,

terribly attractive all at once. Coco remained motionless, afraid to move, afraid she'd give herself away. He'd know. Then God help her. . . .

Turned partway around, she contemplated him from under her parasol, tilting her head to the side, glanced down at his hands, then up at his face again: trying to gauge his intentions.

His intentions. Dear God, James thought. What were they? he wondered. Here in full view of a pub, a row of shops, several fellows punting the river, and a herd of cows?

His eyes found the rise and fall of a glittering, malachite broach on her breast, the gentle pull and release of her breathing against darts and small mother-of-pearl buttons. He watched her breasts where they pressed one against the other, their fullness crushed together by her simply holding the parasol before her in both hands. Breasts . . . breasts so full, so globular, that naked, they could not help but brush the insides of her arms every time she reached, no matter how directly, in front of her. He wet his lips. His mouth was dry.

She reached out to the fence post, bracing herself. In a soft, fully cognizant voice, she murmured, "What are you doing?"

He slowly shook his head. He couldn't say; she probably knew better than he did. James only understood it felt marvelous when he lifted the parasol out of her hand. She grabbed once, but too late; she'd lost it before she'd realized what was happening. He collapsed it with a click of his thumb. "I want to see you," he said. "Don't hide."

He meant the words literally; he wanted the parasol out of the way. Of course, he wanted everything out of the way—her clothes, the turnstile, every creature, human and otherwise, within view. He wanted to be alone with her. He wanted close, deep, direct physical intimacy . . . emotional intimacy . . . intellectual, every kind of intimacy. . . . He wanted to be up against Coco Wild, as close as he could get, in every way possible. And with such a longing, it made him dizzy.

He tried belatedly for humor. "I do not think," he said, "that a few passing references to bees, a young fellow you've befriended, your aunt, and some sisters are in any way commensurate with my telling you I've run naked for the last year or so."

She made a dry grimace. "We're not children playing tattle-secret. I don't owe you a confidence."

"No, we're two adults, one of us being candid, one of us being evasive and self-protective. I'm not asking you to violate confidences or give me incriminating information. Although"—he laughed as it occurred to him—"you probably have some I would enjoy knowing." From nowhere, his enemy Nigel Athers sprung to mind. The thought that Athers might have something to fear here elated James for a moment, then disconcerted him. He had to reorient himself. "It's you I'm interested in," he said. "Just you. There must be more to your life than a boy and two sisters who, I gather, are not as nice to you as your aunt. Why? Why aren't they? Do you mind that they aren't? Tell me something, anything about your real life, what really matters to—"

"Concerts," she said, cutting him off. "Concerts matter to me. And the opera. And bouquets of flowers. And education. I believe in education for everyone, that it could be the salvation of the human race. I think every woman with any money should invest in real property for the highest returns. That's my present. That's what matters to me.''

''No. That's the surface—''

''Well, you aren't entitled to more than the surface, just because you decide to pin me in place till I answer—''

''Who is David? How is it that you own property here and—''

She shoved her hip into the front arm of the stile, very hard, so angry suddenly that, after one quick reflexive grip of the wood, James let it—and her— go. He made a show of raising his hands, one holding up a pale silk umbrella. An attempt to recapture his innocence.

She paid no notice, one way or the other. Released, she was off like a shot, out the turnstile before he could explain or soothe or undo whatever damage he'd done: marching out into the pasture as if a pack of wild boars were after her. James pushed through the stile. He had to trot to catch up.

She walked toward the storm in the distance, her small figure a contrast against a sky of dark, roiling clouds. Her dress, another in the light pastels she often favored, was pale-as-cream yellow today. The color delineated her against livid purple thunderheads that climbed the sky and dimmed the horizon. The rain was closer than he had imagined.

James came up on her, tugging her arm, thinking that they should find shelter. Yet when he felt the anger in the muscles of her arm, saw it in the stiff, defensive set of her spine, he quickly digressed. All, every one of these people, mattered to her. The boy, the sisters, the aunt, perhaps even the likes of Nigel Athers. It occurred to him: those whom she cared about she protected. She held them back from herself, letting no one too close, thereby making any exclusion from society strictly her own. Such a course seemed to James the loneliest of existences—a kind of ongoing, living sacrifice. It made him anxious for her; it made him angry on her behalf.

"So what," he asked, "is wrong with your two asinine sisters? Why don't they share their lives with someone as wise and gentle as you are?" He succeeded in turning her around.

Her face though was the essence of belligerence not capitulation. "Four," she said, "I had four." She sent a rush of words at him. "Two died, one as a result of an accident in the papermill where she worked—no, slaved; one in childbirth, having her ninth. The two still alive are married and living in poverty. Ninette's husband beats her. I have tried to send her and Chantelle money. They won't take it. They are poor, unhealthy, unhappy, uneducated—" She stopped herself, then laughed in that bitter, ironic way that could overtake her. "I'm the only one who made anything of myself, and look what I made of me: They call me a—"

Whore, she said. But the word was lost in a concatenation of thunder that boomed surprisingly close, then rumbled off for almost a full minute.

The word had been meant as a slap, a punishment. James would have had trouble pronouncing it aloud. It was vulgar, the concept unspeakable. Yet here it was spoken: *whore.* In what James was coming to think of as the labyrinth of English sexuality—that dark maze of dangerous turns, pits,

convolutions, and narrow ledges—the word itself
seemed a beacon. A light. A clear path out. Indeed,
it lit his mind like lightning; it boomed like thunder
in his chest. He was fascinated to hear her speak it.
He practiced saying it silently to himself.

Hearing it out of her own mouth, however, settled
a pall over Coco, dulling her anger. She did not
think of herself in despicable terms. Those who did
missed the point of her, she knew; they did her an
injustice. But she had long ago decided that getting
justice from this world was a herculean task, quite
beyond her. What she wanted was to live her life
peaceably. Peace: this was all she desired. So she
stood there, gathering as much as she could to her
as she watched the branches of a tree, a horse chest-
nut, bend in the wind, leaves shuddering. She felt
her skirt gust tightly against her legs.

She heard James Stoker murmur, "I'm so, so
sorry about your sisters."

"I'm sorry, too. Sorry that the living ones are as
gone from me as the dead. But I'm not sorry I'm
not one of them." When she glanced at him, he was
staring at her, a long, serious look of unwanted concern. She told him, "Make no mistake. I've done
the right thing with my life. Given all my choices,
I've picked the very best ones."

He nodded, a brief, single movement of his head.

This small thing—his look of bewildered agreement, the mere possibility that he understood—was
overwhelming for an instant. Too much for Coco to
bear. She began to walk again.

Together they headed back toward the nearest
college buildings, a silent, mutual decision, the wet
wind at their backs.

The man beside her said, "Whatever your sisters say or think, just make sure *you* aren't a snob. Let yourself in to your own good graces, Coco, your own good company." He cleared his throat, then added gently with great kindness in his voice, "A while ago, you spoke of your friend David. If David is really your friend, you *are* the right sort."

She looked across the field at the gray, gothic spires, towers, and cupolas, and said, "David is my son."

It didn't take a second for either one of them to recognize she had said something she did not normally tell people.

She continued, "He has been to the best schools, had everything a young man should, thanks to my efforts. He is clever, well liked. Make no mistake: I don't lie about being his mother, but I don't advertise it, either. I asked Horace to claim him, years ago, by the way, which he did. David is officially the son of the late Admiral Horace Wild of Her Majesty's Royal Navy. Most people assume David and I are on cordial terms because of Horace, his legal father. But I," she emphasized, "*I* have taken care of him. And I now have the supreme honor of sending him to university, where he thrives—something I could never have done for him as a cook's assistant or by cutting rags for the rag-boilers in a paper factory.

"Don't think I regret what I've done. I don't." She sent him a defiant look, then had to glance away for how churlish he made her feel: he watched her steadily—a patient attentiveness she found disquieting, his shrewd eyes attuned, responsive in a way she both distrusted and—God help her—craved.

She looked down at the ground. "In fact I've quite enjoyed it for the most part." She made a wry laugh. "And I wouldn't trade David for anything."

They had stopped in the middle of the meadow. When she let her gaze lift to James's face again, she found there only charity. No judgment. And perhaps something akin to . . . esteem. As if he found something in the unorthodox mishmash of her life praiseworthy, laudable.

Coco laughed again, more richly, more genuinely—leery of such a look, but enjoying it, oh, enjoying it on James Stoker's face . . . to an extent that was breathtaking, terrifying. Like enjoying a good, long stare into an oncoming train.

"And I think I *am* the 'right sort,' " she added, "for your information. Very much the right sort. But I am aware that such a conclusion is the result of fairly independent thinking, thinking that goes against the grain of, at the very least, English high society."

She didn't know what else he made of her disclosures and declarations, for at that precise moment a fat droplet of rain splatted onto her head. Then another pelted her shoulder. She looked up. Black clouds were rolling in overhead with dramatic speed. Another raindrop—as if ladled out of the sky—hit her cheek.

James said, "Come on!" as he opened her parasol and pulled her under it, up against him. As he herded her into a run, the sound of rain began to beat audibly behind them, coming across the field like the advancing roar of a crowd. "This way! Quick!"

He huddled her to him and took her across the

pasture at a dead run. At the fence, he lifted her up and dropped her on the other side as if she were no more bother than a wet cat—she was becoming drenched in expanding spots as the droplets came down faster and faster, more and more frequent, separate, generous dousings.

James himself had just cleared the fence, when the sky opened up.

Chapter 10

C oco and James ran the last thirty yards in a
full downpour, rain sifting through her parasol
in a heavy mist while pouring off its fabric so co-
piously she couldn't see where he was taking them
till she was inside the doorway.

They'd ducked under a stone archway in the side
of one of the monolithic college buildings, All
Souls' chapel on the west bank, if she weren't mistaken. As soon as they were under shelter, James
released her, then with an exasperated laugh began
to shake off water.

Coco carried on similarly and perhaps a bit too
gaily. Oh, this weather. What rain. How lucky to
find haven. What a disaster. She shivered, wiped
and shook her skirts. All the while, though, she was
aware that their mad run had left an indelible impression, the way staring at bright light can leave
an echo on the retina. No matter what she said, what
she did, superimposed over the cold and the wet was
the clear sensation, down her back and around her
waist, of the strength in his arm; against her shoulder and ribs, the pressure of a warm torso as solid
as the side of a mountain.

She glanced up, catching a glimpse of him as he pushed back his wet hair. His arms were long, like his body: lean-muscled. His build was limber rather than bulky, like that of a swimmer. He was an agile man, a man who could move quickly (and half-carry a small woman with him). His forearm, she remembered, broadened near the elbow, where she had gripped it for dear life; it was hard, corded, thewy. A lion in Africa who might have tried to eat him would have found him tough, all stringy muscle and gristle.

The handsomeness of his face came from the structure of bones, an angular, hollow-cheeked, broad-jawed masculinity. His slenderness made him look boyish; it made him appear younger than he was.

This handsome young man—going on thirty, yet looking for all the world about twenty at the moment—stopped his movement. His glistening-wet face smiled at her, a quizzical look.

Coco realized she was staring. She laughed and said, "You look dreadful, half-drowned." What a liar. He looked like Gabriel: as if he might sprout huge, snowy-white, magnificently tendinous, muscular wings strong enough to fly them both away from here. From the rain and the dark day that this one had become. From worldly reality altogether.

Gabriel, St. James, Lancelot—no, Galahad, she revised, since Lancelot in the end had proved to be somewhat less than saintly—reached into his pocket. Over the din of rain, his voice echoing against stone, he said in that perfectly mild, gentlemanly tone he had, "Here you go." He offered his dry handkerchief.

She took it. "Thank you."

It was freshly pressed, crisp, warm from having been against his body. Oh, wonderful, she thought sarcastically. But it *was* wonderful. As she ran it over her face, she caught whiffs of laundry soap mixed with sandalwood and spices. Odd spices, when she thought about it: cardamom and clove, citrus, perhaps, a faintly Eastern bent to the smell of a man's morning toilet. She wiped her eyes and eyelashes, her nose, cheeks, chin, then used the handkerchief to rub round the hairline at her face— her chignon had come down in part, leaving clinging, wet bits on her cheeks, at her ears and forehead, down her neck.

She began to realize the full extent of her own mess. Her sleeves stuck to her arms. Her shoes were soggy. The top layers of her skirts were sodden, its hems and those of her underskirts alike were saturated, then coated with specks of grass and mud. Her dress weighed about twice what it should.

Coco looked out into the downpour as she blotted herself. It was difficult to discern anything beyond a blur, as if a chilly, watery curtain had come down. Rain roared outside beyond their alcove, turning the landscape into a smear of watery green, a smudgy tree wavering its limbs, a streak of fence, a huddle of spots she thought to be cows.

If it was murky out there, within the alcove was dimmer still. It was outright dark at the rear, where she heard James rattling the door to the chapel.

"Locked," he said. He made a sound of disbelief. She glanced over her shoulder. As he came out of the darkness, he offered, "I could go for a carriage."

"You'd drown. And so would I when I ran to the street. There's no point." She paused, surprised by the fact: "We're here for a while."

She looked around them, turning, taking stock. They had found cover under the deep overhang of a side portal to All Souls' new chapel, a chapel that, like King's, deserved more the word *cathedral*. The door at the rear of the portal was a massive shadow, set back into a thick, arching stone wall, the outer face of which took the rain and elements, leaving herself and James a wide, deep inside nook. A little room with a gothic arch ceiling and a floor of old flagstone.

Coco handed James's handkerchief back to him. He began to dry his face, while she turned toward the opening and watched the rain sheet. She huffed out her disgust. "I was supposed to meet David half an hour ago. We were to go to a tea garden, then punt back on the Cam."

"I think not."

She laughed wanly. "I think you're right."

She felt him come up behind. A shiver passed through her when something slid over her shoulders. His coat, its lining dry, full of the heat from his body, like the handkerchief against her face, only a giant dose of body heat that enclosed itself around her. She couldn't even murmur the words *thank you*. It was too delicious; it left her speechless. And so much warmer—she hadn't been aware of how cold she was till she felt the warm, dry lining slide over her arms. She pulled his coat up around her, hugging herself under it.

Behind her, he said, "I have a lecture in half an hour."

"The students would need an ark to get to it."

"It might let up."

"It doesn't look it. Not for the moment."

The weather. Two people who had spent the morning exchanging some of the most private of secrets now for some reason couldn't get off this safe topic.

Coco glanced back. And there he was in his shirt sleeves and vest. That ridiculous cream-colored vest strung with a slender chain of gold—not dandyish exactly but certainly more sartorially aware than his donnish friends were likely comfortable with.

Than *she* was comfortable with, she realized: lightning flashed, illuminating the inside of their dry hollow for an instant. And in that space of time, Coco knew a swift, libidinous curiosity for how smooth his dry shirt might feel on her palms, against her nose and cheek. Would his skin be as smooth? Would he smell like his handkerchief? She raised her eyes to his face, then had to contain a sly, unladylike snort. James Stoker was watching her mouth.

She turned away, toward the relative bright light of a gray world gone mad: the wind blowing rain at a visible slant, every human being cleared from view, while close by somewhere water flowed off a gutter, a *whoosh* that splattered onto the steps at the side, bouncing into a puddle below like sprays of great, galumphing swan shot.

Coco jumped when she felt two strong hands take hold of her shoulders. James rubbed his hands up and down her arms, along the outside of his coat sleeves. She closed her eyes. Oh. She sighed, huddling forward into his coat, burying herself in it deeper.

"You look like you're freezing," he said.

She didn't answer. It occurred to her that he was in all likelihood mentally circling her previous rebuffs, cautiously reapproaching from the same direction as that day at her door, egged on by that moment in the turnstile: that stupid turnstile where sexual awareness had passed over her like a dark, visible cloud, dimming healthy self-interest. Right there in full view, with nowhere to hide.

She asked herself, Why was it again that it was so wrong for her to be drawn to him? Why not an affair with the young and robust James Stoker, just for the pleasure of it? It wasn't as if she hadn't done such a thing before. Or even that she didn't intend to do it again.

He pulled on her arm, saying, "The bottom of your skirts are getting wet. Come back here, where it's drier."

And darker. She went willingly.

Then suffered a small comeuppance. He drew her toward the back, but only to the better lit wall near the thick-planked door. There he rotated and settled beside her, his back against the stones, his feet stretched out in front of him. He leaned there at her elbow, six inches away, without so much as brushing her arm—leaving disappointment to settle on her as palpably as a rock lowered onto her chest.

She wanted him. Oh, the silliness of it. Wanting a young swain with gold eyes, gold-streaked hair, and a blessed twenty-four carat gold reputation. Her Majesty's hero. Society's darling. A young man born so late he probably couldn't remember trouser

seams that weren't stitched on a sewing machine or
cloth woven of threads spun on wheels, not mules
and jennies.

Coco remembered suddenly her own contempt
for "old men" who, fancying her, had made her
laugh in her youth. She'd had no pity for them but
was all pity now. Poor fellows.

She and James leaned side by side against the
wall, she huddled in on herself, wrapped into his
coat, he with his straight back braced, his long legs
forward. More silence. Seemingly more strain. Or
the tension was all hers and her imagination. What
was he thinking? Feeling? Her bad tooth gave her
a sudden twinge, and—the last straw—her soul
seemed to sink.

At which point, James Stoker looked over and
down at her and said, "It's not that I can't imagine
it or don't know the logistics."

"What?" She meant, What did you say? She
couldn't have heard correctly.

But she had, and he took her question as asking
for more specifics. He nodded toward the deep
shadows in the opposite corner. "There," he said.
"I would know how to pull you over there and begin at the buttons down the front of that wet dress.
I could make love to you there—or against a tree
or on the ground or in a hut, on rocks on the edge
of a river or in the river up to our hips. I know the
principles involved so long as you aren't shoving
me. But you would. You don't want me to. Am I
wrong?"

"What?" she repeated. Like a simpleton.

"Would you let me? I want to. God help me, I

want to so much I can't stand up without the aid of a wall."

She blinked, shook her head. She couldn't even get the word *no* out.

Though he understood *no* to be the answer. He asked, "Would you lie?"

"P-pardon?" She laughed nervously.

"About whether you'd let me or not? Would you lie to me?"

She kept shaking her head. "No," she said finally, firmly. "I wouldn't lie."

Though she'd done almost nothing else for the last ten minutes, one falsehood after another. And this was the biggest of all. For—when he crossed his arms and settled his head back against the stones with a clunk (as if he could brain himself and thus get the idea out of his head), her reversal of feelings took the breath out of her. As if a trap door had suddenly dropped out from under her feet. Her stomach lifted. Her head grew light.

Aloud, she said, "It—It would be a terrible idea—"

He looked at her.

She laughed again, such a jittery sound. Not the thing to do. He stepped around in front of her, his face puzzled—a man who meant to investigate her peculiarly inappropriate laughter. He braced his arms on the wall on either side of her.

"Don't—" she said.

"I won't do anything you don't want me to."

Oh, yes, a promise sure to be of great help. She said, "We're really wrong for each other, you know. It wouldn't—"

"Oh, yes," he said. "Wrong. All wrong. This is going to feel terrible." He leaned in.

"James—" The first she had ever naturally used his given name voluntarily aloud. Fine timing. She had to turn her face to avoid being kissed—though why she would choose to avoid it was a mystery to her. She wanted him to kiss her. Part of her wanted it horribly, while another part was so wary that her hair all but stood on end.

He backed off an inch, no more, lowering his arms to take hold of the lapels of his coat. He kept her pressed to the wall, his face immediately above her as he snugged his coat up around her, holding onto the lapels, then resting his fists, contracted around the fabric, onto her collar bone.

Coco wet her lips. Yes, very close up, he smelled faintly of citrus and cardamom and something else foreign, Eastern—tamarind, perhaps. The smell, his proximity made her faint; it thrilled her, excited her, and—how strange—made something inside quake with a kind of terror. A strange, sharp ambivalence held her, while her heart leaped in her chest in rhythm to the rain pounding hard on the stoop.

She waited for him to step into his coat, to wrap it around both of them, put them belly to belly. She could imagine it, imagine being trapped further, tighter, closer to him. She could in fact imagine being under him, under his weight, entered . . . dear God. She blinked, lifting her eyes away.

Then he began down the worst path of all: "I am so fascinated by your moods and laughter," he said, "a way you have about you. I know you worry about your age. But something in you, a strength and generosity—" He shook his head. This wasn't adequate. "Something timeless—" He let off again. Then finished, "You will be beautiful when you are ninety-seven, Mrs. Wild. You are incredible."

What luck, she thought, that a novice should stumble into the exact right—wrong, wrong, wrong—words. Exactly right for his purposes; too soothing, too much a nostrum for all that ailed her. Like sweet cloves applied to her worst fears, fed to the bats that fluttered inside her. She let him fold the lapels of his coat up into one of his hands and pull her, nudge her around and into the deeper shadows.

He walked her backward into the most lightless corner, as if an alcove in the pouring rain weren't privacy enough. He put her where the overhead arch came down into splay-wall, cornering into thick stone doorframe. His body became a backlit silhouette, moving in, cutting off all daylight except for a rainy halo of luminescence around him.

She put her hands up, expecting to fend off an onslaught. There in the dark, her hands found the warm tension of that possibility, a tension in his arms and chest, but it was harnessed. For the moment. And at some expense. The quick rhythm of his heart drummed into her palms. The muscles of wall of his chest were hard as if contracted from physical labor. As if his desire had weight and mass and holding it back were as arduous as holding back a boulder that threatened to roll down over both of them.

He did nothing for several measured seconds, while she felt a kind of horrible slide of her will, all defenses on steep, slippery ground. She held the distance—all of a few inches—then didn't. He slowly leaned his weight into her arms till her wrists gave. There were all kinds of opportunities to stop him.

She stopped nothing. Rather she braced herself for a deep, lascivious kiss.

Yet it didn't arrive. She could feel him shaking slightly. He hovered, his face a close shadow, his breath warm and smelling faintly of coffee. She closed her eyes, aware of her own pleasure in him so close. Close without any real contact other than her hands on his chest and the heat of his body surrounding her, protecting her from the coolness of rain.

Then—much worse than a deep, lascivious kiss—he brushed his mouth lightly over hers. Dry, gentle lips. He dragged his mouth along the tender skin of her lips, pressing his nose to her cheek, drawing in deep breathfuls of her.

He murmured, "Tell me, say one word and I'll stop. But surely—surely this much is all right."

No, it wasn't. It wasn't all right at all. And the most amazing part was there was no premeditation to his actions. Nor any self-protection. He kissed her with open tenderness—a young man whose life had been so blessed he didn't understand that some feelings were best kept to oneself.

And, idiot that she was, she didn't say anything. Or certainly not the right anything. Instead, when he opened the coat, pushing it back, and ran both his hands down the front of her body, she called out softly, "Oh. Oh, yes."

The heat in his palms penetrated her skin; it filled her breasts. His warm hands seemed to melt the muscles over her ribs; they warmed her to her

bones, turning her bones to liquid. Without the wall
behind her, she could not have stood. He cupped
her breasts and kissed her open-mouthed, groaning
a release, a long, low, animal sound as he pressed
his hips, at long last, against hers.

What a welcome feeling. Coco let her hands go
up to James's shoulders, wide and solid, up his neck
into his hair. She pulled his head down to her,
opened her mouth, and touched his tongue with
hers, inviting him in. And in he went, his tongue
firm, reaching, then softer, slathering her mouth.

His hands slid to her hips, around to her buttocks,
pulling her into him. He was rigid against her belly.
He pressed himself to her, sliding against her, a
wonderful, primal grind that elicited small gutturals
of pleasure from somewhere down inside her throat.

She muttered these into his mouth as his hands
smoothed down her thighs and scooted fabric up.
And up and up, loading heaps of skirt and petticoat
onto his arms, till his fingers traced where, beneath
the fabric of her drawers, her stockings ended yet
her corset had not begun. Just the thinnest cambric
separating his hand from her flesh. He smoothed his
palm over her thigh, then found the place between
her legs. With a long, satisfied groan that echoed
lewdly—no other word—in their stony sanctuary,
he cupped her there. A man who had found the
place he wanted.

And she wanted him there. Pleasure, such pleasure. Yet as strong as it was, it existed with a perfectly matched counterpoint of anxiety. A real
escalating fear. She could feel James letting loose,
his mind letting go of all else so as to enjoy sexual
sensation. She could feel something reciprocal in

herself. A lover, a lover like this one, one who was kind and admiring, who listened to her and wanted an intimacy from her, expected it guilelessly.

Her worry seemed connected to this: opening her eyes onto the sight of James Stoker in silhouette bent toward her was like staring into the dark substance of every romantic notion she'd ever mocked—and secretly wished existed all the same— these fused, alloyed, and made steely, with every disappointment she'd ever known. There were good reasons to like the human being, James Stoker. And profound reasons to fear the icon he'd become.

Yes, yes, in a minute she should really do something about letting an icon put his hands where James's were, about her own less-than-innocent hands gathering way too much information—beneath his shirt, across his pectorals to his breastbone, she could feel a cushion of chest hair, unexpectedly thick, a very unboyish abundance. It narrowed into a line she followed under his shirt's placket, down into his vest. She was distracted again.

He had began to pull at her drawers, trying to free them from where they were tucked under her corset. She knew the light touch of his fingers as he partially succeeded. Her body shuddered seemingly everywhere.

What finally coalesced her thinking was the combination: his naked touch, precise, pinging along her senses in the pitch black dark of a rainy stoop, and her own fingers coming in contact with his gold watch chain where it drooped over the points of his vest, over the top of the fly of his trousers. She knew a quick, vivid memory of him standing in

Tolly's, chatting up the help as he waited for her tea, looking for all the world like the heroic young knight Victoria thought he was. Prince Charming. A walking fairy tale.

Yet here was no prince. Here, if anything, to put it in terms of the drawings she was doing, was a full-fledged spinning wheel—fascinating, the likes of which she had never encountered before—and she was about to be pricked, so to speak.

"Stop," she murmured. Coco pushed on his chest.

Then another amazing, heretofore-never-seen thing: he didn't pretend he hadn't heard or protest or try to talk her out of the word *stop*. He just stopped. Just like that. He froze.

It was she who found herself talking, trying to explain. She stammered—she actually stammered out, "Y—you—"

"I've offended you," he said quickly, backing his head away. "I'm sorry. I've never—never been quite like this with a European woman, I mean—I—"

"No, no." She laughed, surprised. "You did nothing offensive. It's just you—you're—"

"Me?" His silence became mildly insulted.

"Yes. The Queen's man. The Vice-Chancellor's man. Society's favorite. I can't. You're far too dangerous for me." She pushed him to arm's length, her skirt falling to where their knees met. She tried to explain. "I did all right years ago. The emperor never invited me to the palace, but I did all right. Paris was different then. Even in Paris now it's not the same. And in England, well . . . let's just say I want calm. I'm old. I don't relish turmoil."

"You're only thirty-six."

"Thirty-seven. My birthday was last week."

"Well, happy birthday," he said.

He stood there nonplused, panting. He knew what was happening. She could feel how much he resented it, but he didn't complain further. Coco wasn't very happy about it herself. But at least she was thinking again.

What to say? She would have told him *I shall not see you again, if you insist on touching me,* except even to think the words *I shall not see you again* put a great lump in her throat.

She said instead to the dark, hulking shadow above her, "All right, we like each other. But you want to belong. You do belong. And I don't." Then the most difficult truth to utter: "James, with you I run the risk of believing all the romantic nonsense you represent. I like you too well. But you are somehow too earnest, too unprotected. I don't dare peel myself down to the same level you do. I'm not as innocent—"

"I'm hardly innocent—"

"Then not as brave. I won't let myself fall in love with you."

The words reverberated in their dim, stony shelter for a moment. The rain eventually beat them out. More gently, she said, "If it were just an affair, James, oh—" She finished, "Let us just say that I am no longer silly enough—young enough or inexperienced enough—to allow myself to get involved with you as a woman."

"How can you presume to control such things?"

She made a shrug, the barest forward movement of one shoulder.

"And if I don't agree to such careful categories?"

She pressed her lips together, against her teeth, till they hurt. Then risked that what she did offer was as valuable solace to him as it was to her. She said, "Then I wouldn't see you anymore. Not at all."

He pushed back immediately, an abrupt movement away, openly irritated. No, upset. He said, "You're the only person in all of England I've been able to talk to since I've been back. Really talk to, I mean. You can't take that back." He paced out into the dim light once, his white shirt and pale vest a startling contrast as he walked out of the darkness.

Coco was mesmerized to hear the urgency in his voice, to understand it in his movement, his posture. "No," she murmured. "I don't want to. Please—"

He paced back, returning to the darkness, the cover of the shadowed wall. "I—" He hesitated. He took a breath. His head moved, as if he looked around, as if hunting for safety. "In Africa," he murmured, "I developed a taste for acting on my sexual impulses. Here, I look at a woman and feel like an animal. Grown men talk about their 'baser needs.' Base. As if it were perverted for a man to want to lie naked with a female. The worst part is, even I used to think this. But I was wrong; it's not." He ran his hand back over his head, through his hair, and held it there. "Or is it?" He paused, a man roaming an inner continent, lost. "I honestly don't know anymore."

Coco laughed. "Of course it isn't. Africa changed you," she said. "But that is not so strange.

I suspect it changes most men who go there. You will survive it. You will adapt.''

He took two or three deep, troubled breaths, then he held out one hand. "Coco, honestly—" But he couldn't put his plea into words. He let out a huge sigh, then said simply, "I need a friend." He laughed. "I could use a lover. But a friend, well . . . I absolutely, positively need a friend who understands." He gave another short, humorless laugh, then held out his hand again toward her, a man indicating a preference. "You," he said.

Relief flooded her there in the dark. "Yes," she said. Oh, yes.

They walked from the dark into the gray light of the forward part of their little sanctuary. There Coco sat down with James, the two of them safely within the dry portal, and watched the rain. Slowly she did what was necessary to proceed: she helped cultivate the notion between them, the pretense, that nothing had happened, that they were not lovers. James seemed willing to become party to her lie, since she insisted.

The time went by quickly. They talked of the university mostly, joked about a dean they both knew and the Vice-Chancellor, who had taken a friendly bent toward the Bishop of Swansbridge, an alliance James thought ludicrous. So did she. They made jokes about strange bedfellows. Though basically they talked with pride about the university. James loved it. And Coco was grateful to the institution for admitting her son. David had not come from the most traditional English educational background; up to this point, he'd been schooled mostly in Italy.

As the rain began to let up, James asked, "And David's father? What became of him? Why have you raised David alone?"

She wasn't going to answer at all at first. She was unused to talking to anyone about her life this intimately. Then she thought to lie, to insist that Horace Wild, as the official documents said, was David's father. In the end though, she settled for a vague brand of the truth. "David's father was—" She looked for the right generality. "An important man on his way to becoming more important. He was afraid to acknowledge either our affair or its living outcome." She paused. "In all fairness, though, he tried. His life was . . . complicated; I don't know what else to call it. He couldn't be David's father, not in any productive sense. So I let him off the hook. If I had forced the issue, I would have injured him terribly—not just personally, but socially, professionally. I didn't want the ruin of the father of my child on my conscience."

"He abandoned you?"

"More or less. He struggled against it for a while."

When the rain finally stopped, she was surprised to learn that the better part of the afternoon was gone.

"I've talked too much," James said, as he threw a loose stone into a glassy puddle at the base of the steps. The stone plopped, ringed the surface; when the surface cleared, it showed the reflection of the sun. "It's your fault though: you are marvelous to talk to."

She rocked back an inch, tightening her arms where she had them wrapped around her shins and damp skirts. "Not always. I'm interested."

He looked at her across her knees, that radiant look his handsome face could take on. St. James. With a beatific smile, he insisted, "No, you are a marvel." He meant it. In his fortunate, highly privileged world, she was a miracle to him. He asked, "And how long are you staying in Cambridge?"

She lifted her shoulders slightly. "Till the bee mess is cleaned up."

"Well then. Till the bee mess is cleaned up."

"Speaking of which"—she leaned forward to push herself up—"I'd better be off."

He quickly leaped to his feet and offered his hand. "You're absolutely right. I should go reschedule my lecture, figure out what kind of difficulties I've caused." With hardly a break in thought, he asked, "Dinner tonight?"

She blinked, glancing up as she handed him his coat. "What?"

"Dinner. Will you have dinner with me?" He took his coat, reached his arm back, sliding into it. "The bees have given us only so much time, you know. We should make the most of it."

"No." Don't be silly, she wanted to say. She looked around for her parasol.

"Over there."

"What?"

"Your parasol. It's over there by the door."

"Ah." She went for it.

Behind her, he said, "Breakfast tomorrow, then," as if it were a decided fact. "Tolly's? Seven o'clock?"

Coco stood, blinked, taken aback. Like an idiot,

she repeated, "Tolly's? At seven tomorrow? Again?"

"Marvelous," he said. He stepped down into the wet grass, walking backward. "See you there."

James Stoker trotted off before she could explain that she hadn't agreed. She hadn't agreed to anything, she told herself.

Chapter 11

A week later, James stood in the center of his vast and chaotic laboratory, the largest lab of six in the Cunningham Science Building on Fairfield Street. Scanning the room, he pulled his hair and asked, "Sam"—his assistant—"is there any way to make the room look less disastrous?" Because, in an hour and ten minutes, Coco would walk through the door.

Sam shook his head pathetically. If they cleared off the top of a stool, they could make a place for her to sit. Other than this, it was surely hopeless.

The floor at the far end was stacked with notes and journals and books, many under maps spread out and rolling with pens and nibs. These piles stood about like high and low islands in the flow of looser debris, mostly field equipment under repair and cleaning—coils of rope, pitons, shoulder slings, swami belts, spikes, adzes, pick axes, hammers, an old compass in a frayed leather case, a tarnished sextant minus a lens, an altazimuth missing its circles and microscopes.

The center of the lab was taken up with tables

156

covered in instruments of analysis: several shiny new microscopes (at one of which sat Sam, looking through the eyepiece). Files, tiny picks, gouges, three of the new Bunsen burners, a rack of chemicals—hydrochloric acid to test for lime, sodium hydroxide to test for iron pyrite, others. Calibrated rocks on a hardness scale, from gypsum, the softest, to diamond. The tables were littered with the best, the most modern instruments.

Yet the value of all the rest of the room did not compare in James's mind to what he considered his best spoils from all his climbings and travels of the earth: an oak cabinet of tiny drawers that ran the length of the longest wall of the laboratory— the most organized part of the room—housed tens of thousands of what many would call rocks.

To James, however, these chunks of petrified wood or fossils or flint or quartz were much too individual to be termed merely rocks. To him, they were as particular as individual human faces. There was the sedimentary slice of the cliff side at Atulla, an amazing compression of millennia. Or the granite with the surprising white mica. Or the deep redbrown garnet-rich skarn, hard enough to jolt his arm up his hammer but that sliced as neatly as liverwurst in the lab, making it a charmer for microscopic inspection. Here were pieces of the earth, the planet on which he set his feet, each distinct in its origin. He wanted to know them the way he wanted to know certain people. He was held by them, without questioning the attraction, the way his body was bound to Earth by gravity.

James had collected rocks since he was so small, he couldn't remember when he hadn't. Family stories had his mother having to take rocks from his mouth in order to nurse him, and a variation on the story was that he was eventually lured away from his mother completely, before he could walk, the lure beautiful rocks, usually offered by Phillip Dunne. Dunne, a geologist himself and very successful at luring, had eventually taken young James into his household, all but stealing him from his parents (the family coachman and local milkmaid). James was the closest thing Dunne had to a son, though he had offspring—four daughters, any one of whom, Phillip laughingly suggested, James might marry. (Not so laughingly, James imagined the second oldest, Vivian, would one day be his wife. She was the prettiest, the brightest, the most light-hearted, the least like her mother.)

James bent over a paper-thin slice of rock under Sam's microscope, then, seduced by it, took Sam's pen and added his own notes to the notebook. He scooted a stool over and sat. This particular task was compelling at some moments, off-putting the next. He couldn't explain it other than to say it was part of what stood behind him, at the near end of the lab, from floor to ceiling, from wall to wall, stacked ten feet out: the trunks and straw baskets he'd brought back from Africa, the sum total of the surface samples, borehole plugs, notes, diaries, the geological specimens and data of the whole of his trip. The work of one hundred forty-eight men, all save one dead now, their labors having survived the hands that took them from the earth, labeled them, lovingly wrapped them and packed them, and noted them in a log.

When James opened a trunk sometimes, he had

to stop, go out for a while, come back. It was the dead, he thought. His friends, his associates. He saw them in the rocks, knew them sometimes by their handwriting on tags. It was like having to pick through their bones some days. This was the trouble, he thought, the reason he was behind on the project.

The project, as it were, was massive: to begin with, James was to create maps. From microscopic inspection and chemical analysis, the samples would slowly reveal pictures of Africa, the likes of which no man had yet seen before. If he ever got his data together, he would make geochemical maps of the distribution of each chemical element, geophysical maps—radiometric and magnetic. He and his team would do a groundwater series. A metallogenic map series. Hazard maps, seismological maps. In short, the data and samples, once organized, would make the expedition more valuable, to James at least, than all the gold in the world.

Yet he had barely begun. A month had gone by and he had done next to nothing—only what Sam here had put together. Sam, who would entice him with bright optical images, images under the microscope divorced from the stones in the crates.

"May I come in?"

James looked up, then felt a rush of disorienting embarrassment. Coco. He glanced at his watch. She was actually a few minutes late. Where had the time gone? He smiled and slid off his stool. The sight of her brought a now familiar rush of happiness, a welcome distraction.

Since that rainy day more than a week ago, he and Coco had met everyday for breakfast. Twice

they had met for lunch, once for afternoon tea. Each
time was a pleasure, a bright point in his day. Never
mind that after teatime, he was banished from her
life—on the grounds that beyond three P.M. their
meeting could be construed as romantic, an impression she very strictly wished to discourage. She refused dinner, refused go with him anywhere after
dark or even on an outing that might last into twilight. They were daytime friends.

His triumph today was that she was coming for
a tour of his laboratory. He was more or less sneaking her in, walking her through the geological lab
an hour or two before the building was regularly
open to visitors during term.

"Well," he said. He laughed. "It looks as though
you sneaked yourself in. Did you have no trouble
getting inside the building?"

"I told them you'd sent for me, that I was part
of an experiment."

He blinked. "W-what?"

She laughed. "Teasing. No one stopped me."
She smiled as she ambled forward, wearing that
warm, gentle smile of hers. "I just pretended I belonged here, and in I came."

She was at once so out of place here, yet such a
perfect example of all that was missing in his life.
A beautiful, civilized woman walking among his tables and rocks and gadgetry, her collapsed parasol
tucked under her arm as she ran a gloved hand along
the table's edge, then up a microscope. She had
something tucked up under her other arm as well,
he realized, unexpectedly a long folder as pretty as
any parasol, gros-grained and tied with ribbon.

"What's that?"

"Nothing." She smiled. "I'll show you later." Her smile lingered on him, and he lost track.

He never tired of looking at her, all over, at the shape of her, her way of tilting, strolling, wobble-hipped, her silk-bustled, Paris-chic mien—mauve silk today piped with silver velvet that twisted in places somehow into tiny rosettes, more roses on her small, stylish hat set at an angle atop her thick black chignon, the hat's net just long enough to extend over her eyes, her dark, kohl-lashed eyes peeping from beneath. He could not take his gaze from her.

She picked something up off the table. "What is this?"

He glanced. "Ah." He reached for a hollow reed cut with holes, using the motion to come closer to her. "I wondered where that was. It's a nose flute."

"A nose flute?" Her eyes widened.

"Yes." James put it to his nose and exhaled. The flute made a soft honk, nothing as melodious as the music it could make. "A friend of mine in Africa can play it beautifully," he told her, "on the exhaled air from his humming nose."

He and she held the instrument together, with her laughing and frowning, both, unsure what to make of the flute or its function.

James touched the folder she held under her arm, both hands on her indirectly. "And this?" he asked.

"My drawings. I brought them to show you, I promise. Let's do the tour."

"You draw?"

"Of sorts. Illustrations for magazines and storybooks. Nothing too artistic, but pleasant occupation.

Your lab, Dr. Stoker. Are you going to show me or not?''

James took her around his cluttered laboratory, then through the other labs in the building. Coco was attentive—no, she was *thrilled*. She tried to hide it, but was wide-eyed over the university, the mechanisms and structure for acquiring knowledge. She very quietly bit her lip when confronted with the shelves of the geology library. "All these books, just for geology?" she said.

Coco read. Somewhere along the way, the kitchen assistant had learned to read in French, English, and Italian. She also, surprisingly, knew people in the university. Sam, for instance. He and she said hello as if they hadn't seen each other in a long time, not with great enthusiasm, but with respect and acknowledgment. Similarly, she knew several fellows in chemistry and an older petrographical geologist. Out of politeness, James didn't inquire just how she might have met these men. It seemed indiscreet.

They went from the labs together into town, where they roamed from store to store buying the items for a picnic lunch—bread at a bakery he liked, cheese from a farmer who left fresh goods daily with the local wine merchant, a half-bottle of French wine (Coco knew which one to pick), and apples from a street cart. They took these onto the Backs, where they ate them sitting on the grassy bank of the river Cam. He shucked his coat in the sun and lay back, basking in a glorious spring day, while he watched Coco open up her folder.

"*Et voilà,*" she said.

It was full of line drawings, elaborate renditions

of people and things expressed in fanciful swirls. The women had hair longer than their feet; it covered the pages in curls. The men wore plumed hats, the feathers so detailed that you could see the down coating on each individual barb of the quills, the barbs themselves tendriling like vines.

James sat up onto his elbows, really looking now as she showed him one sketch after another. Her drawings took him aback. They were quite extraordinary: beautiful.

"I used to make drawings for David when he was little," she explained as she got out a fresh piece of paper. "Last year he encouraged me to take some sketches to a publisher. I did, and my drawings came out in a book of French fairy tales a few months ago. Now a London publisher has asked me to do some for a new English translation of *La Belle au bois dormant. The Sleeping Beauty.*" She laughed, perhaps a little self-consciously, but she moved her pencil across the page and was soon absorbed.

James felt both amazed and a little foolish. What had he been thinking? He had not considered that she would have such a talent. "The Sleeping Beauty," he repeated. "She was blessed with many talents too, wasn't she?"

Coco threw him a skeptical look, working all the while with quick stokes of her pencil to line in a shadow. "In different versions of the tale, different blessings."

"What are some of them?"

"Let's see. Beauty, of course." She drew several longer lines that came together rather astonishingly into the rampart of a castle. "Wit, wisdom, grace, riches—"

"Artistic talent?"

She turned her torso to look fully around at him, her laughter this time quite nearly a guffaw. "No."

They smiled at one another; he, leaning back on his forearms, she, sitting twisted around. "Charm," he said. "Lots of charm, of course."

She raised one eyebrow, a rueful smile.

He tilted his head. He liked teasing her. "And style. And the most beautiful dark eyes I have ever seen. I think you should give her big, dark eyes with thick lashes that lay on her cheeks, black lashes that circle her eyes."

She clicked her tongue, shaking her head at him, then turned back to her drawing.

Surprisingly, when she showed him the sketch a few minutes later, it was of him—in a handsomer guise with longer hair and a velvet Tudor flat cap, the brim spilling over with ermine tails.

"Oh, fine." He fell flat on his back, laughing. "Touché."

"No, no." She wagged her pencil at him. "This is a very good idea. Mr. Pease complains that my people and castles should look more English. So you have solved one dilemma. Now if only I could fix the problem of my castles all looking like French battlements."

As it turned out, her castles, actually, were gorgeous. Each rose up out of its forest in a graceful sweep of turrets and crenelations. James sat up to watch over her shoulder. Eventually, he couldn't help himself. He took her tablet from her so as to page through her designs. Her drawings were remarkably imaginative. She was good; better than good.

Which made him, oddly, annoyed.

How dare anyone dismiss her as a plaything.

As they packed up her drawings and cleaned up their sacks and empty bottle, she mentioned she was on her way from here to meet David, trying again for tea in Grantchester. James volunteered to take her by punt. He hadn't manned one in years, but the idea appealed more than saying good-bye.

Thus he found himself standing at the rear of a long flat-bottomed boat, himself and Coco afloat on the Cam in the early afternoon. He'd taken his vest off. It lay with his coat folded on the floor of the punt, while James, his sleeves rolled, pushed a punt pole. Coco sat facing him, lounged back at the front of the boat, her fingers drifting in the water or flicking splashes at families of moorhens.

She was a delight upon the eye. The sun was bright. She could have opened her parasol, but she left it folded and lying across his clothes on the boat floor. The moment she'd stepped in, she'd lifted off her hat and set it into her lap. It sat nestled atop her folder of drawings in her skirts, safely dry. She'd unbuttoned her sleeves enough to pull them back so they didn't get wet. He would have liked for her to dig the pins out of her hair as well and shake it down onto her shoulders, down into the water, if it were long enough. He speculated as to the length of her hair—hip-length, he decided, the stuff of her fantasy drawings, of course. She remained tidy and demure, leaning back, her arms along the gunwales,

her face tilted back to catch the sun on the crown
of her head.

"Tell me about your rise to fame," she said, as
he dug the pole into the river bottom. Her eyes were
closed. She had a dreamy look on her face. "David
says you wrote something that made you very popular in London, while making you gravely suspicious here."

James let out a wounded snort. "I've written a
lot of things, I will have you know. I'm a very well-
respected scholar." But he knew what she meant.
"When I was twenty-three, though, I did write a
general book on the geology of England: *The Englishman's Illustrated Earth Beneath His Feet.*" He
lifted the pole, reached, then stuck the dripping end
forward into the water again. "The book found a
wide readership in a public terribly keen for the natural sciences."

His pride couldn't help but add, "I've won prizes
since for my more arcane work. And the earlier public notice made men, a number of rich men, aware
of me and my work. They have since stepped forward with grants and endowments: even before Africa, Cambridge had been happy to sit me down
with possible benefactors at dinners and functions."
He shrugged. "I'm not sure how, but I seem to have
a knack for bringing in money."

She lifted her head, squinting an eye at him—
they'd turned slightly eastward in a bend in the
river, the overhead sun shifting into her face.
"Yes," she said, "a knack for hard work, risk—
not the least of which was offering yourself up to
Africa—and more congeniality in one quick smile

than most scholars can muster in a lifetime.'' She laid her head back again. ''David mentioned you'd parleyed your notoriety into funds and influence for yourself and everyone connected to you, including the Vice-Chancellor.''

''Well.'' James puffed a little. Good old David. He liked the lad better and better. He didn't know what to say for a moment.

She raised up again, looked up at him this time from under her hand, shielding her eyes. ''What do you think of the Vice-Chancellor?'' she asked.

''Phillip Dunne?''

She nodded.

He answered with a question. ''Do you know Phillip Dunne?''

She made one of her barely perceptible French shrugs. ''Everyone knows the Viscount Dunne.'' Phillip's formal title. He was a peer of the realm and a relative rarity in that his family name happened to be the same as that of the region from whence his title came.

And, of course, she would know him. She was right; everyone did. ''Well,'' James began, ''I—I suppose I think the world of Phillip. He's not perfect, but he's smart and wants the right sort of things.'' Without a pause, he asked then, tit for tat, ''And Nigel Athers? Do you know the Bishop of Swansbridge?''

She continued to smile at him from under her hand, direct, unflinching, calm. ''Yes.''

Yes. He wished, with equal directness, she would tell him things—what the Bishop had to hide, his weaknesses, his faults, how his mind worked, if she knew.

When her lips remained a closed, faintly curved smile, he said, "He's giving Phillip a hard time, I think, though Phillip won't tell me the specifics. He says, 'Just carry on with your work.' But Athers has several times now confronted me over some sort of bible fund, once that night at the ball and two or three times since. I don't know what he wants exactly, but something." He waited, looking at her over the punt pole. "Do you have any ideas?"

She watched him from under her hand, while leaning back on one elbow. "Do you mean, Has Nigel talked to me about this?"

"Am I that transparent?"

"Yes."

"Would you tell me anyway?"

"Tell you what?"

"Whatever Athers has said. What is he thinking?"

There was a long pause, before she spoke. "No," she said, "I wouldn't tell you. If I knew." Another pause. "But I don't."

He scowled, picked the pole up and, reaching forward, plunged it into the river bottom again. "A fine friend *you* are," he muttered.

"Don't be angry." She let out a troubled sound, a distressed *tsk* of her tongue, then said, "James, you yourself have told me things you don't want others to know. Doesn't it relieve you to think that I keep my mouth shut?"

Yes, it did. He counted on it. But he said anyway, "No." He smiled—with boyish charm, he hoped. "I expect you to keep my confidences, while you reveal everyone else's to me."

She laughed, treating his words fully as a joke.

When of course he had meant them half-seriously.

James was suddenly, keenly curious about what Coco might know about Athers. Though, all right, ultimately he liked that she was tight-lipped. It meant, as she said, that he didn't have to worry; he could speak freely.

And he did. Perhaps too freely, he would think later. "Nigel has a very different idea from mine as to England's right to anything and everything in Africa. Including the very souls of the people themselves. And the gold I brought back to the Queen, well, he just can't let it go, can't let it rest."

They floated around a bend under a tree. James had to duck and let the boat drift.

She said, "I saw it. Quite a lot of gold, as I recall."

"Yes, when people stare at it these days, they say, 'How amazing there is so much.' Though I feel a kind of—oh, I don't know—a tension with some people, Athers especially, as if he means to ask, 'Where is the rest?' I expect, any day, to have to fend off Athers and others as to where exactly all that gold came from, where the Wakua live."

"I thought you were lost till the natives sorted you out."

"Very true," he said.

They silently drifted for the duration of one of his pushes. Then she asked, "Do you know?" She wore an amused look on her face.

A low overhanging branch came toward them. James caught it, using it and a spread-legged stance to stop the boat. He held them there against the flow of the river, the little mooring at Grantchester visible in the distance. He lifted the punt pole up, letting its end drip into the water, and looked down at Coco Wild. He said, "When I woke up after weeks of being ill, my watch had stopped."

She stared up at him from her shady bower under the branch, her expression full of interest but no understanding.

He explained, "I lost Greenwich time." When her face remained blank, he said, "I could no longer compute my longitude." He laughed as, for the first time, he found what he next said funny: "And the mirror, object-glass, and other various pieces of my sextant, as well as parts from our new altazimuth theodolite, were hanging from the ears, necks, and belts of various members of the tribe. I'd lost the ability to compute where I was."

After a moment, she said what everyone, he suspected, was thinking: "But you must have had some idea where you were."

"Yes. Somewhere in the central part of the African continent, with no sense of time and no sense of direction." He let out a snort. "Honestly, I was lost, and for the life of me, could not figure out where I was." He sighed before he added, "Though lately I remember the sky."

"The sky?"

"The stars. The night sky was often clear. It was different and beautiful." He looked at her. Her face waited. He told her, "It comes to me now in flashes, like a chess board of positions and movements, sequences that haunt me. And there are books I could look in. . . ." James let the thought trail off.

"You know," she said. "You've figured it out."

"No." He blushed. He felt it; his face heated. "I only suspect. I haven't gone to the books."

"You know!" she insisted. She laughed, delighted. "You know the latitude from the stars and can figure out the rest."

It was apparently easier to deceive himself than her, for he realized she was right—the woman was perceptive. Instead of anxiety though, James felt relief. Huge, huge relief. Good, she knew. Someone knew. He could now talk about it to someone he trusted. He thought he might know where the Wakua lived, give or take a few miles.

She went immediately from her conclusion to the pertinent question. "Why don't you say, then?"

"Because I believe the tribe that saved my life is not so very far, after all, from where we had taken samples."

"And?"

"And what do you know about the current rush for diamonds in Africa?"

She looked bewildered. "I know some huge diamonds have been found. One, the Star of South Africa, I think, weighed a lot—"

"Eighty-three and one half carats. The earl of Dudley paid twenty-five thousand pounds sterling for it."

"That's a lot."

"Indeed. And between the river diggings and the dry digs of southern Africa, there are tens of thousands of Europeans presently pulling diamonds out of African soil. I've seen the holes in the earth. They're caverns. And the machinery and industry of it, God. Horse whims hauling diamonds up by bucket and windlass, the pits themselves strung with so many wire ropes that they look like giant spiderwebs. And now there's talk of steam-winding engines to replace the horses. Do you have any idea what such an invasion does to a tribe, the people who already live there?''

She frowned. She did; she extrapolated immediately to his worst fears. And his dilemma: ''You've found gold,'' she said, ''but you're afraid to tell anyone.'' After a pause, she asked, ''What do you intend to do?''

He said immediately, ''I intend to do a thorough and honorable scholarly thesis on the geology of the regions we covered.'' Then he sighed. ''Which, alas, is going to show that there are untold times more gold up the southeastern tip of the African continent that man has yet to find anywhere else on the face of the earth.''

James let go of the tree limb, planted his pole on the river bottom, then poled the full reach of his body, letting his words sink in, before he said, ''When I publish the findings, the world will know. But—'' He paused. ''But I will buy the Wakua what time I can. There's no point in sending people into their crop lands and hunting grounds with only the vaguest idea of where to look. The place would be dug up everywhere in a matter of weeks.''

He heard her say as he planted the pole again, ''You're considering not telling at all, aren't you?''

He frowned over at her, then away. ''No. That would hardly be the done thing. Disloyal, all that.''

They drifted. The little wood pier came toward them. He was guiding their boat into a gentle bump against the pilings, when she said, as she had once before: ''Africa changed you.''

Over his arm, James settled his gaze on Coco Wild. Her bare head shone. Her eyes, too; they were filled with a kind and worldly light. Her smile was the most beautiful and gentle he'd every known. "So you keep saying."

What he feared, of course, was that she was right. James worried he had gone to Africa an Englishman, then come back something else. There was no doubt that he was having trouble falling back in step. Try as he might, he couldn't see men, the world as he once had. Africa. He tried to deny its effect on him, but it was like trying to deny the largest continent of the earth. He had been enchanted by it, changed by it in ways he had yet to fully discern. He never, never wanted to return. Yet his experiences there somehow blocked the way back to his old English life.

He helped Coco up onto the dock. David was waiting at the top of a wind in the road at a little tea house—he saw them arrive from its window, then met them partway down the gravelly carriageway. James had met the young man three days before, an attractive, quiet youth who was oddly both gentle and formidable, very much like his mother.

James waved at the two of them as he left. For the first time he did not press Coco to have dinner with him, as he had at their every other parting. On any night, under any circumstance, he would have canceled all other plans, if he had thought she'd say yes to dining with him, to spending the evening with him. But she always said no, emphatically no.

He called to her from the river. "I'll see you tomorrow," he said.

She waved back cheerfully. "Tolly's!" She smiled across the distance. "At seven!"

But, in fact, they would not meet at Tolly's, not the next morning, nor ever again.

Chapter 12

The members of the tribe in which I seem to be stranded eat their enemies. That is correct: eat them, as in butcher them, cook them up in a pot, and serve them at a feast. The old woman who told me about this quaint custom confided that, if they should be so lucky as to catch a member of an enemy tribe, I should have a go at the knuckles because they are the best part.

James Stoker
RGS expedition diaries, 1872–1876

James returned to his lab to wrestle the African crates. When he heard approaching steps, he thought it was Coco returned for her parasol, which she'd left in the bottom of the boat.

But the person who entered was a different surprise altogether.

"Phillip!" James cried, astonished, delighted.

Phillip Dunne walked in slowly, staring at the far wall of trunks, the spoils of James's trip to Africa. His eyes ran over the height and width of the stacks, then drifted through the room, lingering over all the new equipment—the toys, as it were, of their mutual profession. Phillip didn't have much time anymore for the actual work of a geologist.

The Vice-Chancellory was supposed to be a part-time position, but it was in fact an on-going, everyday sort of responsibility. Moreover, to become Vice-Chancellor, a man already had to be the head of a college; Phillip had duties at All Souls as well. James helped as he could, but Phillip was not a man to completely relinquish control, even to someone he trusted. Add to this the fact of some family troubles, and it was no wonder Phillip looked soft these days: overworked and overwrought.

He smiled tentatively at James, then pointed toward the trunks and baskets, saying, "All that?"

James smiled. "I didn't leave a thing behind. If someone on the expedition packed it up, it came home."

Phillip stared at the wall of Africa, blinked, then frowned down at a calibration rock on the table beside him. He picked the rock up. Apatite, a medium hardness, the benchmark of a number five. He tapped his fingers on it once, then set it down again.

"What?" James asked. "Something's wrong."

Phillip immediately pressed his lower lip out and shook his head in denial. Then stopped, thought better of it. "Nothing's wrong, exactly. Just a little inconvenience is all." He scratched his forehead, pressed it once, a sure sign of distress. Distractedly, he said, "But I might have to leave it all in your hands. It's Willy"—what he called his wife, Wilhelmina. "Might have to take her to Bath for a few days, the cure. Might, might not. Haven't decided." He waved his hand.

Wilhelmina Dunne "took the cure" at some private spa in Bath periodically, which meant that the laudanum she lived on had gotten so overpowering her husband had to lock her up somewhere just to see if she was alive or merely a twitching body, an electrified puppet. It was one of the saddest pieces of information James possessed about the Dunnes. He hated that he knew of it, that he could do nothing to help, while the best privacy he could give Phillip was to pretend he knew as little as possible.

James frowned down at his microscope. "Sorry," he murmured.

"Right."

The two men were silent.

Then Phillip delivered what, James realized, he'd taken time away from a family crisis to deliver in person: "It's Athers," he said. "He's asked for all the notes and diaries of his own people. I'm hard-pressed to deny him, Jamie."

James glared sharply. "He can have them when I'm finished. There's not that much. But his people orient some of the samples, verify location. I need every observation written, since I have nothing else to go on."

Phillip was shaking his head, before James even had the full explanation out.

Leaving James to bargain with himself. "I'll go over his people's notes first," he said. "Or Sam could get some undergraduates to copy them."

When Phillip's head-shaking didn't stop, James said, "Phillip, for God's sake, I want to put a whole picture together. I can't do it if people start moving around the pieces before I've had a chance to go over everything."

Phillip's expression remained fixed; no leeway, no negotiation. "He wants them now. And two or three Members of Parliament think he should have them. He's preparing what I understand to be an impassioned speech for the House of Lords."

James let out a bitter breath. "Well, I can speak, too—"

"He'd mop the floor with you. Besides being eloquent, Athers has found the moral high ground here. The Church and the families want the diaries of their dead, the last, consoling words about all the souls they were trying to save."

James snorted. He was fairly certain about Nigel's motives. "Athers wants the diaries to look for notes on the whereabouts of the Wakua. He's looking for gold, not notes on African souls."

Phillip shrugged, unimpressed; it was all one to him. Then he said, "It gets worse, James."

James stepped around the table to face his friend, his advisor and superior. What could possibly be worse?

"He wants your notes, too."

"What?"

"He's claiming foul play over that blasted Bible Fund. He says an honest man has nothing to fear. He wants the Crown to impound everything"—he waved his hand behind him—"and your notes in particular. He wants to look into the deaths."

"What—" James felt his face run cold. "The goddamned son-of-a—"

Phillip held up his hand. "I don't want to hear it. He's wrong. He's way out of line. But you're being too possessive, and that's a fact. What you've brought back doesn't belong only to you."

"Someone has to regulate it, or information will be lost. And I was there, damn it. If what I brought back is anyone's, it's mine."

"Too possessive," Phillip muttered again. He shook his head some more. "It's scholarly material. Samples and data, nothing more."

"I could have left it there, saved my own skin, and been home in half the time—" James stopped himself. In what he hoped was a more rational tone, he pleaded, "Phillip, I want to make sense of everything." He held out his arm, toward the trunks and baskets along the wall. "I want to make all the deaths count for something. Many of those men were my friends—"

"I know that. Mine, too." A sincerely compassionate look crossed Phillip's face. "Look, James, I know he's wrong, but the Crown is going to support him, at least on the diaries of his own people. Beat him to it. I want you magnanimously to take all his people's bloody little diaries and notes and dump them on his doorstep."

"No—"

"Yes. I'm telling you to."

"Phillip—"

"Do it. Don't argue." It was the implacable voice of the Vice-Chancellor.

James stood there, frustrated, trying to master his temper.

"Oh, and Sam," Phillip said.

James's assistant at the back looked up with sudden alarm for being included. "Yes, sir?"

"Would you do me a huge favor?" Sam waited. "Run across Silver Street to the florist on Talwadder and send Willy some roses. Those big, pretty ones. Don't put anything fancy on the card. Just say, 'Be well. Love, Phillip.' "

"Yes, sir."

James tried not to balk at seeing his assistant go out the door. It was petty to mind that he should be sent on an errand that Phillip could have done himself on the way home. Should have done himself.

Phillip gave James another moment of his attention, a glimpse of the old astuteness, the old crafty bugger James used to love. He said, "I'm protecting your notes to the end, fella', eh?" He used a rhythm of speech James's father used to use, an old joke between them. Phillip delivered it with a half-smile, as close as he could come these days to a real one. "Athers has no right to those. I'm behind you all the way."

Splendid, James thought, and so effectively, too. He tried to settle himself down, make himself more generous. His friend indeed looked strained. "Phillip," he said.

The Vice-Chancellor looked at him.

"Is there anything I can do?"

He shook his head and muttered, "She's just . . . just not well, you know?"

"I'm really sorry."

"I know." He nodded.

Phillip Dunne turned and wandered out—there was no other word for it. He looked lost. James was suddenly glad Sam had gone for the flowers. Phillip was so preoccupied he couldn't have safely crossed a street.

James watched him leave, then thought, Good. If Phillip was leaving him in charge, well, it was for the best. He'd give Athers the diaries Phillip said he had to give him. Then God help Nigel Athers if he pressed for anything more. Because, unlike Phillip, James would fight him. He would fight them all, if he had to.

Chapter 13

⌒⌒◯〜⌒⌒

*I find that I do not think as I once did.
For instance, we came upon a company
of ostriches today, a cock and four hens.
Mtzuba insisted I try to ride one, which
eventually I could—hilariously. It was
an afternoon's entertainment. When I
tried to explain to him about horses in
terms of the zebras he has seen, he
laughed and laughed for trying to imagine the various national styles of riding
zebras. French* manège, *Spanish saddle,
these terms were meaningless to him. He
is free in a way I can't explain. He rides
his ostriches without the aid of books or
lessons, no equitation or dressage. And,
oddly, I discover I admire him for it.*

James Stoker
RGS expedition diaries, 1872–1876

As James came through Arnold Tuttleworth's wide entrance room, he could see the glow of the dining room in the distance. The house's gas jets had been turned low. The soft radiance of candles illuminated the far room, golden, casting faintly guttering shadows. Within the dining room, beyond its French doors, James could see several people—men like himself in white tie and tails, women in low-cut satin and plumes—gathered near a huge, dark-wood sideboard on which burned two giant, ornate, silver, multistemmed candelabra, their candles dripping, burned halfway down. He was a bit late.

"Still time for a sherry," Tuttleworth said. The man had answered his front door himself. "We're all keen as bells to see you. Been waiting for you, old man."

James smiled and proceeded toward the quiet chatter of a dinner party he was not terribly thrilled to go to. Some duke or other was in town, a long-ago graduate of Trinity, he thought, with not the faintest notion of university needs or funding, or any inclination to learn about or answer to them. James neither knew the man nor cared to. Yet here he was, the resident African explorer. The man had expressed a desire to meet Sir James Stoker while in Cambridge, so meet him he would, since the fellow was cousin to some rich benefactor or other and wealthy in his own right. A mark, as it were, James thought. In the great shell game of money and science.

In fact, he had yet to settle down from Phillip's little revelation. He'd been livid all afternoon. He hardly felt like eating; his stomach was in knots. If he got hold of Nigel Athers in the next twenty-four hours, he would be greatly constrained not to put his fist through the man's face.

Nonetheless, James followed Tuttleworth politely into his dining room. What he had thought was a large sideboard was actually a liquor cabinet. Perfect.

"Sherry, James?"

"Whiskey, if you don't mind." All seemed very civil.

Then James turned, looked down the room, and the floor shifted beneath his feet, a kind of tilt that left him leaning forward, pressed upon his toes: for there, standing down the table, was the Bishop of Swansbridge in person, his hand on one chair, his other holding a glass of sherry.

Anger rose up, so surprising, so primitive that James was taken unaware. Like molten magma, it simply came from the core of him and flowed over his every thought. Before he knew what he'd done, he'd called, "Athers, you sodding son-of-a-bitch—"

The Bishop turned. The room grew silent.

For three pounding seconds of uncertainty, no one was sure what to do. With James red-faced, wanting to throw the glass of whiskey that was pressed into his hand at Athers, wanting to cock his arm and plug him with it.

His name, like music, rang: "James." It came from the side, from just behind the French door.

He swiveled his head. And the floor that had merely tilted before seemed now to drop out from under him. Coco Wild glided toward him, her neck, shoulders, and most of her bosom bare. Full evening dress. She apparently had no problem spending her evenings with Athers (notably minus Mrs. Athers). Or Tuttleworth or Mrs. Tuttleworth-to-be (one-third old Tuttleworth's age), or a dean and his spouse, two assistant deans, the heads of Trinity and King's, and the asinine duke they had all come to court. And here was the explanation of why Coco Wild was suddenly welcome in this company: the duke was traveling in the company of a woman who was clearly not the duchess.

Coco squeezed James's arm. "They just told me you would be here tonight, Dr. Stoker. What a pleasant surprise."

James stood like stone, fused into rock.

He heard Coco tell a joke, something about "bedders" and "gyps." Everyone laughed. She eased James into a chair, then sat down beside him.

Across from them, Tuttleworth cleared his throat. He said, "I thought you and Coco would get along. Sat you beside each other. Didn't know you two were already acquainted. Isn't she, though, the most charming creature, James? Been everywhere. Done everything. One of the most agreeable, most accomplished women. . . ." La la la. James stopped listening. He understood. He was to let her take charge of him. And, oh, wouldn't he just love to.

He kept glancing at her décolleté, where candlelit shadows flickered across ivory breasts mounded above dark purple satin, a purple so dark it was all but black, the color of the skin of plums. The dark sheen of the satin was remarkable against the white of her breasts, breasts that were very round, very full, wider than his hand, crowded onto her small chest. Never mind that every dinner dress here had as low a neckline. Never mind that it was perfectly proper for a woman to display herself thus in the evening. It was a display to James, the way certain birds in mating season fanned their feathers or did a particular dance.

Someone mentioned Phillip. James realized he was being asked to explain Phillip's absence. "Phillip left," he said.

When he offered no further comment, he was amazed to hear Coco fill in the rest. "This afternoon. He followed his wife to Bath, a little family vacation."

He *took* her to Bath, James wanted to say, to sober old Willy up. But the minor inaccuracies weren't the point. The surprise was that she knew of the Dunnes' activities at all. And, while he was at it, James asked himself peevishly, what did she know about "bedders" and "gyps?" Even at Oxford the servants who made the beds and lit the fires in the colleges were not called by these names. The terms were strictly Cambridge expressions. So who the hell had she slept with here? Athers, for certain. Possibly Tuttleworth. Probably everyone here but himself, James thought.

He downed his whiskey over starters—tiny dove breasts stuffed with apples. Dove breasts. He devoured them, then drank down the glass of claret that came with them. And if he found himself feeling sane for even a moment, all he had to do was look down the table at the Bishop—a man ready to call him a liar and murderer if it would get him a map to gold. Athers talked away blithely to the old duke and the ducal companion, a young woman not a day over twenty.

James felt like an animal, a naked man.

Native. Coco had not said the word. He'd never admitted it aloud. But he'd done it, and she knew. *Gone native* was the expression. Been one of them. Run with them on a hunt. Joked with them over their fires. Learned the weight and feel of a long spear, understood its advantages; utter silence and, in close range, great accuracy and damage. James looked down at his white bib-front and vest, at his black trousers; they were a joke. They were ridiculous. He looked at Athers and wanted the limb of a long, heavy hardwood in hand, honed, smoothed, made aerodynamic, the tip tongued with a sharp stone point.

Coco must have sensed some of his mood, for under the table, quite astoundingly, she put her hand over his. She stroked the back of James's hand once, his friend. And, God bless, it felt so good— her hand stroking his where it rested on his thigh— that he could only stare at her: a look he could not keep inside, a look he knew to be burning, open, filled with lust, vivid-bright sexual awareness.

She glanced over at him, away from a conversation, smiling, then blinked, lost her smile, and tried to take her hand away. He caught it under the table, no longer his friend's hand. He gripped the hand of his would-be lover, the woman he wanted above all others. The center of his emotional and erotic interest, the subject of all his fantasies.

This woman smiled at him sweetly and murmured, "If you don't let go of my hand, I'm going to dump this cold, palate-cleansing sorbet they've just brought me directly into your lap. Settle down.'' She raised her eyebrows. ''Cleanse your mind.''

Right. Yes, yes, he needed to, though he couldn't remember why. He let go of her hand, lifting his finger toward a servant. More wine. He pointed to Coco's glass. ''And give her some, too.''

Food came in waves, trays of it. Only God knew what had arrived on James's plate. It could have been lion or boar. Caribou. Biltong. Fish and chips, for all he knew. James ate it.

Miraculously, he eventually did what he was supposed to do. By rote. The duke asked about Africa. James regaled him with tales of natives and jungles, deserts and camels; nothing too original or taxing on the imagination. He then explained how one could boil iron pyrite in sodium hydroxide to determine if it were fool's gold or the real thing—and of course how the chem lab could really use new gas fittings and pipes and a way of valving air into their new Bunsen burners so as to regulate their flow better, the implication being that one could boil more gold, find more gold . . . and, of course, this was expensive. Money and gold. Gold, gold, gold. James was sick of the whole business. What was a geologist doing here?

He had another glass of wine and let go. Who gave a damn, anyway? His eyes found Coco and feasted. Dessert came. Fish and chips again, with ice cream this time. It tasted like vinegar. He forgot to eat it, though he drank the sauterne that came with it, gleefully, while he watched Coco over the rim of his glass. *Coco, Coco, Coco-Nicole,* like the call of a bird somewhere in the high trees.

There beside him, the pretty bird's waist looked

so small, he could have spanned it with his thumbs and fingers. Her bosom—oh, her bosom. Full and high and round, her dress pulled tight across it, shoving it more into view, every seam pulled taut. The fabric of her dress drew straight across her all-but-concave abdomen, then belled out softly across her chair, heaping slightly behind her, up her back. The bustle, James knew, gathered upward into yards of fabric, as if someone had simply unraveled bolts and bolts of inky satin onto her derriere to form the softest, most generous-looking . . . oh, God, he loved the bustles of her dresses. He wanted to plunge his hands into them, lose his arms beneath the yards of layered fabric.

He kept staring. Her dress was round where she was, every seam pulling just enough to acknowledge shape, yet not so much as to seem uncomfortable. He wondered if it was hard to take off, fitting as closely as it did. Did those tight, dropped sleeves have to be peeled down her arms . . . like stockings off her legs?

And under her clothing did the flat plane of her belly rise at all? Did it round softly or descend straight into the rise of her mons? Was the hair between her legs as black and glossy as the hair of her head?

What fine, civilized thinking as someone put eggs, little eggs, on his plate. Plover eggs. What course was this? What was he supposed to do with plover eggs? And why did he have to bother, when Coco was in the room, sitting right beside him? He wanted her. Why not? Who the hell cared what the two of them did in private? He just couldn't remem-

ber the answer anymore to the ringing question
Why not? Why not? Why not?

Meanwhile Coco put her hand to her forehead,
pressing a piece of her hair back. It was damp. The
late April evening was unusually warm, while candles up and down the table made the room outright
hot. And James . . . well, there was no word for him.
He was an inferno tonight. Hot under the collar,
tetchy, difficult, not his usual polite self. Not to
mention as randy as a young bull on his first day
out in the pasture.

She did not have control of the situation. She was
not even sure what the situation was.

She tried not to look at him, because every time
she did, she felt the heat of his regard like a thistle
brushing delicately up her spine. So instead she
laughed at Arnold's stupid jokes, more loudly than
she needed to. She teased Nigel and the duke about
their politics. She baited James; she knew it a dangerous thing. But she couldn't help herself. She
punished him for his rudeness and for his gallantry
both. She mocked him in her mind: Sir James, dining fashionably, succeeding admirably in his
knightly vows, which included, of course, chaste,
unworldly love.

His clean-shaven face, his natty attire, galled her.
While Arnold kept eyeing *her* suspiciously, as if
she'd seduced the young hero. As if she were De-
lilah, Salomé, Eve with a cartload of apples. Coco
felt unhappy, exhausted, tired of being good—tired
of a goodness that brought no peace and won no
credit. Alas, one glance at James's burning stares
and it was hard to imagine that he was anything but
her lover. The fool behaved like her lover. Bloody

hell and *sacre bleu*, she had tried to protect him
from just the sort of speculation that was forming
up and down the table, tried to protect herself from
it. A calm and tranquil life, that was what she fought
to maintain, for her own sake. But where had it
gone? It felt tonight that, for a public dignity and a
private calm, neither of which could she possess,
she was depriving them both.

The whole blessed mess made her head hurt, her
tooth ache. She had done what she had promised
Arnold; she had soothed everyone's nerves, everyone's but her own.

She stood suddenly. Several men, including
James, rose partway. "No, no," she said. "Please
sit. I just need some fresh air. Not feeling well. . . ."

She excused herself with every intention of taking French leave, just the sort of thing that delighted
the English anyway. Let them talk. Let tongues
wag. She would write Arnold a little note, call a
cab, and be gone.

James, however, followed her. "Coco," he
called. The sounds of the dinner party softened as
he closed the dining room doors behind him. As he
came toward her, she stood waiting in the entry hall,
not happy or relieved to see him, a woman waiting
her doom. He said, "Let me take you home."

"No. I've asked for a cab."

"My carriage is right outside. Please. I insist."

"Well, go insist somewhere else. I have had quite
enough." Emphatically, she repeated, "Enough."

He frowned, though it was a dispirited look. They
stared at one another.

A maid brought her wrap, a fur cape.

James took it, held it. After a moment, Coco

turned around and let him place it on her shoulders. He whispered, "Please. Let me take you home."

He wrapped the cape around her, then his arms, enclosing her. When she didn't pull away, he bent his head, put his face into the curve of her neck. When his lips brushed her collarbone, his cheek at her shoulder, pleasure jolted through her so sharply and suddenly she couldn't control a small, convulsing groan.

For just an instant, just a taste, she tilted her head, gave him better access. He pulled her back into his chest and kissed her neck, open-mouthed, wet. She bent her head, and he took his ministrations up her vertebrae to her nape. She let herself slide into the sensation as into a warm pool; she swam in it, in the starchy warmth of him, in the sure heat of his hands—they pressed her cape, flattened her bosom against her ribs. He rubbed her chest, flat-palmed, spread-fingered. Pleasure, oh, the pleasure of his touch.

Pure, limpid pleasure, as clear as glass, undiluted. When had she last really let loose and indulged in it for its own sake? She weighed that glowing possibility against how likely it was to fire in the pan, blow up in their faces. He didn't understand. . . . He didn't partly because she hadn't let him. But there was a solution, an end one way or the other.

To James's enveloping shadow, Coco murmured, "All right. Get your carriage."

She didn't mean for him to think, Yes, I'll sleep with you. She was thinking, Wait. Wait till you see. Wait till you understand how complicated this could become, how difficult it is already, then you will either have full knowledge and be responsible for yourself or you will stop everything and end the torture.

In the carriage, she gave him directions rather than the address. At least this way she wouldn't have to argue or explain all the way home. His little calèche flew, a man with a mission. He said nothing, except the *yah*s and clicking encouragement to the horse. When they pulled up, he looked immediately the wrong way and said, "How funny. Your aunt works directly across the street from the Dunnes' house."

"She lives inside it. She's their cook." She opened the half-gate, leaped from the carriage without help, and went up the front walk.

It took James half a minute to rally, jump from his side of the carriage, tie the reins, and come after her. He was still trying to absorb what she'd said, trying to make it all right.

But something wasn't all right. His heart began to pump hard. He felt . . . frightened, fascinated. Out of his depth. And was not even sure why. He took the front steps two at a time, then stood, agitated, unsure, while Coco hunted for a key in her pocket. They stood at the front door, he realized.

"I thought you said your aunt was the cook. This isn't the servants' entrance."

She frowned up, lips pursed in the moonlit shadows of the stoop. "David didn't like my staying in the servants' quarters, so he had a word with the Viscount—"

"A word with Phillip? A twenty-two-year-old told Phillip Dunne he doesn't like that his mother is staying downstairs with her aunt, the cook?"

"My aunt is quite revered. Besides, I'm not a

servant, and there was plenty of room in the guest quarters. And the family is out of town.''

"They weren't out of town till today.''

"Phillip was.''

It was true. Most of the week he'd been in London. Though James couldn't imagine why this was relevant. He said, "Well, it hardly seems proper—''

She found the key. Clutching it, she told him, "No one in Cambridge but you seems to care particularly which room I sleep in. And, since it makes David happy—''

"David? What's going on here?'' The anger from earlier began to course through James again, thick and hot.

It dawned on him. "Phillip,'' he said incredulously. "You call him Phillip.''

"So do you.'' But she grew wary and still.

James said, "Phillip Dunne is on your damn list.'' Then another possibility shook him even more profoundly. "David. The missing father you've never mentioned. He's David's father.''

She said nothing, only standing there stiffly, brittle—proof enough for him. Her next words were no doubt the literal truth, though James was sure her omissions, all she didn't say, amounted to a lie. She said, "David's father is dead. Phillip, an old friend of Horace's, is kind enough to appease the pride of an admiral's son, who is sensitive about his mother's origins.''

"Phillip. Nigel. Horace. Probably Tuttleworth, the present High Steward of Cambridge and recently drafted into a cabinet post, just your style. It's a tight little group you work in, isn't it? And you've slept with every bloody one of them, haven't you?''

For a moment, he thought she was going to deliver a not entirely undeserved slap across his cheek. She stood rigid, as if forcibly holding her arms down. He watched a faint shiver pass over her from tension, restraint. Then she said simply, ''Good night, Dr. Stoker.''

And turned away. She inserted the key into Phillip's front door. It opened. The house was dark inside, absolutely lightless. No servants, no one. She was through the door, closing it behind her with a click, before it occurred to James that he could have pushed his way in and there would have been little she could have done about it.

Why, though? To what purpose? He spun around on his heels and leaped down the front steps. Fine, he thought. Good. She was leaving sometime soon, anyway; she'd been hinting as much. If he never saw her again, that would be well and enough for him.

But he turned around and saw a dim light come on somewhere. The front parlor. And he suddenly found himself walking around the house into the side grasses. He walked through the dark, down along the parlors, till he stopped and saw her: Coco alone in the dining room, pausing to lean over some flowers. Roses. Fat, pale pink hothouse roses. Phillip had sent the roses to his house—for Coco, as he had sent the same to London a month ago. Willy, poor Willy . . . if she hadn't been on her way to Bath already when these had arrived, she was in the process of being packed off. How else could the family have left so quickly? The roses were never for her. *Be well. Love, Phillip.*

Vice-Chancellors. American financiers. Ministers. Admirals. Bishops. A French prince. The future king of England. Rumored sultans . . . czars . . . emperors . . .

James stood there in the dark, reeling with jealousy and fear, and in an uproar inside. Everything he'd hoped for seemed suddenly locked beyond him, inside that house with Coco, his greeds and hopes and longings. She embodied these. They grew horns and prodded him, becoming more than mere lust: a desiring willfulness, I, ego, the center of himself, a need as basic as the slippery, involuntary contractions of his own blood-filled heart.

She'd locked him out, but here was a man who knew where the servants' entrance to the house was. James shoved tree limbs aside, striding along quickly, cutting over grass, through a hedge, then between the bushes of the rose garden—it was an overgrown tangle of summer shoots, prickly thorns, and bobbing flowers, but he pushed through anyway, which brought him round to the back of the house.

And there she was again. Coco set a gas lamp onto the cook's table in the kitchen, took out a basin, then turned away. At the stove, she put on water to boil, then unbuttoned her sleeves, pulled at combs in her hair, stripped off jewelry. James stood in the dark, invisible. He pushed his hand back through his hair, his mouth suddenly dry. She was going to wash up, unaware he was there.

All wrong, he thought. He should go; this was wrong. Or he should let her know he stood not ten feet away. But he held his breath instead. Coco's hair came down. It was dark, heavy, uniformly straight and sleek, like the shining, uncut hair of a maharani. Or of an odalisque, a concubine, a geisha. Heavy hair, so healthy and clean it slid against itself, a single entity. It poured like liquid down her back, pooling onto her bustle, spilling over it. As she reached for the kettle, he watched it part across her shoulder blades. She tossed her head and the mass of it slipped to the side, out of the way as she turned around. She came back, busying herself with the task of pouring hot water into the basin on the cook's table.

She loosened her dress, pulled the ties of a side-lacing corset. She was about to wash, facing him, facing the darkness out the back servants' entrance.

James stepped up onto the back stoop. He leaned his arms onto either side of the door, making himself known with the banging force of his hands, making himself visible through the door's window-panes.

Coco glanced, then leaped back. She stared at him, startled yet somehow oddly unsurprised. Then—the strangest thing—looking right at him, she lifted her chin in a kind of focused fury, her eyes irate somehow: and peeled her dress off her shoulders. The sleeves fit like skin, like a snake shedding.

James leaned his forehead into the window pane. "Coco," he said, "let me in." He wet his lips. His groin stirred sharply, a feeling accompanied by sudden rushes, filling, the hydraulic events of his body making him erect. His whole body seemed to fill up on the sight of her. He hit the wood frame of the door once with the heels of his hands. "Let me in," he said.

She only stood there, straight-postured, staring right at him as she took her chemise down as well. Bare bosom. Oh, God, she was pretty. Round, full breasts that bobbled with the tiniest of her movements. She lifted a sponge and squeezed water at her neck, bending forward slightly. Water ran between her breasts. They had large dark-pink nipples.

James tried the knob. He pulled on it, rattled it. "Coco, open the bloody door," he called. "Open it." He shoved on the door with his shoulder. It shimmied on its hinges.

She said nothing. She eyed him as she took up a bar of soap and rubbed it over herself, over her neck and shoulders, down over her chest, her palm sliding in circles over her skin. She cupped her bosom. She let the bar slide into the basin, then lathered, rubbing her breasts, pressing them. The tips of her nipples puckered tightly. He watched them shrivel into hard little knobs.

James could barely catch his breath. He threw his full weight against the door. It gave slightly, the sound of splitting wood. He threw his shoulder into it again. And again. Beyond it, inside the kitchen, he heard a small shriek. He didn't care. He beat on the door with his body. Till he heard the fracture of wood. The lock came off the frame, and the door banged open with such force that the knob or key in it, something, chunked solidly into the wall. Plaster flew.

Coco laughed at first. "You—you broke the door," she said, incredulous, aghast. Yet her eyes were wide, bright. She backed up. "James." She laughed again; disbelief, nerves. "What are you doing? Go home."

"What are *you* doing?" he asked. The words came out in a kind of whisper.

She laughed again, lightly. A nerviness in her gave the sound an exhilarated ring, a ripple of laughter that edged into a cackle of delight.

James walked forward, Coco backward. There was no fear on her face, possibly even the trace of a smile. The smile grew, half taunting, half sly; touched with humor. She used her arms ostensibly to cover her breasts, but where her arms pressed them, her bare bosom rose higher, came out everywhere, round, voluptuous, her nipples in view, her fingers spread over herself more like an embrace than a shelter for modesty. She licked her lips and James felt it in his penis, a throb in direct response.

He breathed like a bellows, from the hard work of breaking down doors but also from simply watching her. Coco, the female he wanted . . . so female with her soft shoulders and silky hair and soft, soft bosom. He could feel the churn of his testes, the hot pressure of his penis tenting his trousers like a pole.

And he hadn't even touched her yet. He watched her back up, watched the wall and stove come up behind her, watched her startle as her bare shoulders collided into the corner where the wall met the pan rack hanging over the stove. James trapped her there, the flat of one hand on the wall, his other gripping the stove's edge, while the rasp of his own breathing rivaled the scrooping scrunch of stiff taffeta as his legs stepped into the skirt, crushed it between them. He stopped there, all but up against

her, savoring the moment, knowing he had her
cornered and willing. God bless, her expression . . . sloe-eyed, pupils dilated, lips parted. She
seemed wound as tight as a spring, alive, waiting
for whatever he might do next.

He took her hands away from her chest and let
out a huge, shuddering sigh as his palms found both
her bare breasts. Her skin was unbearably fine-
textured, smooth, sweet to touch. She closed her
eyes and bent her cheek to her own shoulder, moaning out a soft *oh* of pleasure. It was the smallest
sound, but it tumbled him over the edge of any sort
of restraint.

James began to slide his hands over her, along
her bare ribs, down the front of her, pressing between her legs, feeling her through her dress, while
he took her mouth. He kissed her, reaching round
to the back of her dress, and pulled, unhooking
where he found hooks, yanking where he didn't,
getting her out of the damned thing. He penetrated
her mouth with his tongue, while his hands grabbed
fistfuls of bustle. He buried his fingers in the cool,
copious flounces of satin as he pressed her buttocks
forward, bringing her hips tightly against him.

The second their hips met, he felt her push back,
an instant rhythm between them. Her arms came up.
There was no pretense to her, no feints or fluster,
no sighing ignorance or conflict. No difference of
opinion here. The field was level. She opened her
mouth to him. The moment her skirts and crinolette
were loose enough, she stepped out of them. When
he couldn't undo all the strings of her corset, she
helped. He pulled at her chemise, at her drawers; he
couldn't get them off fast enough. "Get rid of

these," he whispered insistently. She helped as he stripped her there by the kitchen stove.

And she liked it. Her breaths came light and quick, her eyes often fluttering closed. But when they were open, they were brightly on him. He maneuvered her till he had his hand between her bare thighs, pressed tight, his finger finding her. He felt inside her. She was silky-wet. And moaning, groaning in his arms. Her knees gave. James had to use the wall and his own body to brace her as he opened his trousers. Then events, and Coco, proceeded from here.

She displayed no distress—or no distress in any negative sense. She knew; she wanted. In fact, with a kind of panic, her hand came down between them, adjusted his erection the last inch, and—there was no other word for it—she took him: standing up onto her toes, pressing the head of his penis down till it was at just the right spot, she curved her hips forward and raised one leg round his waist. Her heel in the small of his back, she helped drive him into her.

"God Almighty," he muttered. His head swam, a blur so exquisite, so delicious. He let out air in sharp syllables. *Hha. Hha. Hha.* As if he might catch something back.

She hung balanced, one arm from his neck, bending him to her. James hooked his arm under her hips and lifted, taking the deepest possible angle with a jerk of movement that hardened his buttocks into ridges. He thrust himself deeply, so deeply. . . .

Coherence itself ebbed. Consciousness seemed in question for an instant, the pleasure became so intense. He withdrew, but before he could bring himself all the way back again so as to re-experience the bliss of that deep entry, she was moving with him, cooing a nonsense chant of low syllables, touching his face with her hands, her hips sliding in a rhythm of their own.

James buried his nose in Coco's hair, in the crook of her neck, and answered her movement, trying to find just a few more deep, rhythmic strokes, heading for the precipice. The wall became necessary for balance. He felt her shiver in his arms. Then it was almost as if she became smaller; her body folded into him as she let out a guttural whimper from her throat, then louder—"*Aah!*" He held on to her.

James couldn't believe it. She went over the edge before he did. He laughed from the surprise of it. Which was perfect. It delayed him, sidetracked him just enough. He braced himself, one straight arm on the stove, one curved under her hips, wedging her into the corner, and mated the way he wanted to. In long, deep businesslike thrusts, no apologies, no restraint. While she called out, clinging to him, quivering.

He felt his gonads tighten to his body, rotating, pressing into the base of his penis, as rapture, hot and slippery, grabbed him. And, from there, only convulsions . . . explosions . . . blinding white heat . . . lava . . . fusion . . . charged vapors . . . melting cinders superheated under pressure . . . the hottest molten matter . . . viscous, rushing, spreading in all directions . . . flowing out in a rolling sheet of pleasure . . . an ecstatic crest that overtook him.

Shuddering, with Coco naked in his arms, James slid along one shoulder down the kitchen wall, the floor coming up at him. Only at the last moment did he think to put his arm out again, like a brake against the side of the stove, to keep from landing full-weight on top of her.

Chapter 14

As Coco recovered, she became aware of
James, lying beside her on the kitchen floor,
digging his fingers through her hair. His fingertips
would glide in against her scalp, along the side of
her head, till they rode the back of her skull. As
they continued on, her hair would tug gently. Sometimes, combing up and out, before he got all the
way to the ends, he would bring a handful of her
hair against his face. Or his gaze would remain fixed
just above her head, his planed features stark in the
elongated shadows of lamplight, while she felt her
hair slide from between his fingers, gravity taking
its weight through his hand.

"What are you doing?" she asked.

He shook his head, then didn't answer precisely.
"This," he said, lifting a handful, "is the most
beautiful hair that has ever existed." He stopped to
touch her cheek, a caress, then let his hand drift to
her breast. "And these"—he cupped and lifted one,
then the other—"are the most gorgeous breasts."

She put her arm over her chest, trying as non-
chalantly as possible to cover herself. Coco was

self-conscious that her breasts were no longer the
plump, pert things they used to be. Her body was
changing: a small betrayal of nature. Those blessings that she had counted upon once, to draw, to
charm, no longer charmed *her*—she was fuller
through the hips than she liked, her skin noticeably
less resilient, her breasts, well . . . not to put too fine
a point on it, they drooped.

James pulled her arm and hand away as he had
before. "The best part about your breasts is how
they move," he said. "They wobble and shudder in
a way that mesmerizes me."

Coco made a pull of her mouth, a skeptical click
of her tongue. "James, they're . . . well, pendulous.
They sag. I'm old."

But the young knight disputed vehemently. He
shook his head. "They are perfect. They are lush.
Mature. Voluptuous. I love them." He laughed—
perhaps nervously, she thought, for having spoken
the word *love*. He smoothed his hand over her, the
flat of his palm down her belly. "And your hips,
your waist, your feet—I adore your feet—"

"My feet?"

"Oh, yes." His fingers circled her ankle. He
drew her foot up across his chest. She emitted a
surprised *ah* as his tug rolled her, bringing her belly
against his scratchy trousers, her pubis against his
hip bone. "What wonderful feet," he said.

She laughed. "You lie."

"I never lie. Look at this instep." He ran his
finger along the top of her foot. "High, elegant.
And this arch. Except for your other foot"—he
grinned—"there was never one more graceful. And
here." He traced the veins along her ankle bone.

"Little, blue threads, cerulean, like light shining from beneath a surface so delicate and white—your skin is translucent." He kissed the tops of her toes.

Coco found herself discomposed in the way she was so often with James. "You—you are such a—" She finished, "such a charmer."

"I never lie," he repeated.

"Everyone lies sometimes."

"Well, maybe once or twice, but not to you. Why should I, when the truth is so wonderful?"

"All right. Poetic license, then. The scientist is a poet."

If she hadn't been on the floor already, his next words would have put her there; they leveled her. "No," he said. "The scientist is in love."

Coco raised up slightly onto her forearm and stared at him. Normally she would have said, *Oh, no,* or teased him, tried to talk him out of his foolish turn of mind. Foolishness, yes; that's what it was. She tried to reduce his declaration in her own mind to nothing but romantic rubbish, the delusions of youth, but her efforts were not successful. She ended up pressing her lips tightly together, then having to hide her face in his shirt, her cheek on his chest.

Love. The word scared her; it thrilled her. It made her feel reckless—afraid of what she herself might do in order to hear him say it again.

He continued. "You are the most beautiful woman I have ever touched."

"Stop." More discomposure. She couldn't let him go on like this. She playfully filliped his shirt stud and made light of what he was saying. "As if you've touched so many as all that.'' She attempted to roll onto her back again.

He held on to her foot. ''Hundreds. I've had hundreds. Well''—he laughed—''four, anyway, counting my two widows in Africa. Do they count? I mean, they were, it was, such a different world there.''

''They count,'' she said. Four, she repeated in her mind. Four women. Coco laughed, dizzily aware of her own past. ''Four,'' she said again. ''Tell me. Name names.'' She mimicked him from a week ago. ''Details, where are the details?''

''Hmm.'' He tapped her captured toes. ''Details. Let's see. There was Greta, the household scullery who made it a point to be every lad's first.''

''That's funny. I knew a Greta like that. And she was a scullery, too.''

''And there was Chi, my nickname for her, since I couldn't pronounce her real name properly. And the one I called Leeta.''

''And the fourth?''

He laughed. ''Ah, her name. Coco, I think.''

''Go on!'' she said. ''*I'm* what makes your fourth?'' She groaned. ''Oh, Lord. A baby. I have seduced a baby.''

''Ha.'' He pulled her foot till her leg lay over him, his other arm around her, his hand patting her bare buttocks. ''I'm as experienced as I need to be, Mrs. Wild,'' he told her. ''I've been busy up till now. And perhaps a little tentative—or, more likely, there was just no one worth the bother. But I have no trouble with any of the concepts here.'' There was joy in his voice. ''I can match you.''

''Good,'' she said. Since she couldn't pull her leg

free, Coco extended it forward, rolling up onto him, sitting astride.

His eyes widened. "Whoa," he said, with more air than voice. It was an expression of appreciation, not restraint.

She pushed his coat back and off his shoulder. "Take this off." He was not sure what she was doing at first, cooperating, turning one way, then the other, to let her have his coat. "You are dressed about as formally as a man can be, while I'm stark naked." She unbuttoned his white piqué vest. "You're right, you're a cad. You took off my every last stitch without even knowing that my aunt is with her daughter in Girton, my maid is in London, and the rest of the staff is with the Dunnes in Bath."

He resisted when she stripped down his trouser braces. "Oh, no—" He grabbed them up, shouldering the left, losing the right.

She wrestled both down again and laughed at him. "For all you knew, anyone might have come in."

"No-o-o." He denied it. "I could see there wasn't anyone around." He rallied to the call of battle. "Oh, no, you don't," he said. He attempted to button his trousers around her busy hands.

"Yes." Gleefully, without the restriction of clothing or inhibition, Coco attacked whatever garment he left undefended.

She had his smooth white shoulder braces off and tangled, his starchy shirtfront half-unbuttoned, and his vest off one arm before he became serious about the game and rolled over onto her. He pressed her flat to the kitchen floor, nestling himself between her legs. It would have been an unqualified win, a shoulder pin, except that his trousers and combination were open and he dropped, semi-erect, directly into the best possible niche of her.

"Aah," she let out. Pleasure, swift and sharp, rose up to pinch the backs of her eyes, while James ground his hips into hers, a slow, astoundingly skilled movement.

He groaned, blissfully smug. "Oh, Lord, Coco," he muttered. "I have wanted you for the longest time—I think, all my life."

When he kissed her, she threw her arms around his neck and drew him to her.

It had been a long time since she had let a man rest where he rested now. And a longer time still since she had felt any hunger for the way a man kissed her mouth, her neck, her shoulder. In fact— perhaps never as this. Oh, dear, she warned herself, don't let young Galahad here, his touch, become important. But James's hands felt so warm and good on her skin, his body so perfectly suited, its movement and breathing and rhythms immediately in tandem with her own—the hunger was there. He was important already without her having any say in the matter. But I am not in love with him, she kept telling herself. Even though he might . . . he just could be . . . it was possible he was in love with her.

A voice inside her cheered, gloated: he loves me. The thought was too wonderful, too horrible to examine any further.

She lay her palms on his cheeks and scanned his fine, angular face. Light from the gas lamp on the table cut across the top of his head; his hair, flopped forward, shadowed his brow. Coco let go of herself. She took James's handsome face between her hands and pulled it to her. Her lover, her friend. She kissed him deeply, open-mouthed.

They were another half hour on the kitchen floor.

Eventually they extinguished the lamp and made their way through the dim house. In the dining room Coco plucked a rose from the vase and put it in her teeth, then danced in circles in front of James, naked up the staircase. She felt happy, so happy. And he . . . oh, he. . . . He seemed like a wonderful discovery at the end of a maze she had had trouble getting through. But here she was, at the right place at last. With James's prowling figure following her up the staircase, his hair a mess, his shirt undone, his vest and coat in his arm. He held both their clothes crumpled against his chest, while never getting far enough away that he couldn't reach out to smooth his hand around her buttocks or run his palm over her stomach. Meanwhile, his gaze followed her every movement, any glimpse of his shadowed features always fixed in the same peaceful look: the ready look of lust fulfilled and more promised.

They went down the corridor to the guestroom all the way at the end of the hall, Coco's room. There, James followed her in, then halted.

"Oh, my," he said. He tossed their clothes onto a chair and went straight across the room to the far window.

Coco leaned back on the door till it latched, watching him reach and pull back a curtain. A three-quarter moon shone through the wide window, providing surprising light. It windowpaned the room in moonlight; it threw his shadow across the bed.

She watched him shed his shirt as he stared out.

He stepped out of his trousers. He stood unbuttoning the front of his combination. At first, she thought he was shy, as he had seemed downstairs, for he didn't face her. He kept looking out the window.

Then he pointed. "Out there," he said. "Across the rose garden, on the other side of the hedge, down the ally that runs along it, there is a cluster of apartments; the mews. See that rooftop? Do you see where I mean?"

Coco came up beside him, pulling his undergarment off his shoulders and down. "Hmm," she said, with less interest than he might want—if James Stoker was handsome with his clothes on, with his clothes off he was wondrous: strong, smooth-skinned. She ran her hand down his back to his haunch. His body had fine hair along it here and there—at the base of his spine, more that curled sparsely and singularly down his long legs. It was blond, silver in the moonlight. Such lust. It felt new, strange. Coco wanted him to turn around so she could see the mat of chest hair she had felt beneath his shirt in the alcove of All Souls' chapel. She felt unsettled and squirming. She wanted to touch him, to look upon him.

He remained turned from her, looking out the window. "That far rooftop is the carriage house. I was born in the flat over it. I lived there till I was nine. After that, this was my bedroom. This very room."

The information should have surprised her, yet she said quite calmly, "You're Jamie," she said. "The industrious young boy who worked for Phillip, whose parents died, whom he took in." She had realized Phillip was his colleague and superior, even his mentor, at the university. She had not known James was the young man whom Phillip had all but adopted.

There were several moonlit rooftops in the direction he indicated, stables, a carriage house, a number of apartments for the outside staff, if Coco remembered correctly.

"From the time I can remember," he said, "I used to come up to the house. Phillip would give me tuppence for hauling rocks around for him, sorting them. Once I was older, I sometimes got to drop them into chemicals or split them or pulverize them in some cases." He paused thoughtfully.

"I should remember, but I've forgotten," Coco said. "How did your parents die?"

"In a carriage accident, of all things. On the way home from my aunt's wedding in Newcastle-upon-Tyne, the public coach overturned. The carriage tongue broke as they were taking a curve. The horses took the bend, while the coach took the ravine." He stared out for a moment without saying anything. "I was staying with the gardener and his family. Phillip sent for me, gave me the news in his study. Then he took me by the hand and walked me up here. My things were already moved in. I was—I don't know, nine, I guess: I became his lab assistant."

"It's funny that we didn't know each other, isn't it?" she asked.

He looked at her over his shoulder. "You only worked here four months, you said." She nodded. "And how old were you?"

"Fifteen."

He laughed. "Well, I was masquerading as a seven-year-old at the time. You just didn't recognize me."

"And you were out there and I was inside."

"And I was more interested in the dogs at the kennel than in pretty girls from the kitchen."

"What a shame," she murmured. "Yet there we were, within a stone's throw of each other. How odd life is sometimes."

He glanced at her again, then turned. He looked her up, then down. "It has its moments, though, doesn't it?" He reached behind him, lifting the curtain higher, letting the moonlight flood up the front of her body. In silhouette, she watched his body change. His penis rose from partially to fully erect, a stiff, upward angle, bold, sleek, beautiful. It was gorgeous. Round-headed, helmet-rimmed.

When he reached for her, Coco backed away, leading him toward her bed. There, she pulled back the covers, climbed in. James stretched out beside her. Ironically, the young man who had fought over his pants in the kitchen lay down beside her, easy in his nakedness.

"A tribe of two," he said. And with these words, he became the man who broke down doors, who stood her hair on end for his open sexuality. He grew happily, darkly erotic.

Any vestigial notions she'd had that the young gallant was other than a straightforward, fully mature—and very free-spirited—male were contradicted. He covered her with his body; he made love like an angel, his hands warm, his mouth and tongue hot, his erection thick and strong when he entered her. In the last seconds, rising up onto his knees, he pushed her legs all but onto her chest and drove into her till the room itself seemed to shimmer, her body alive, electric. Then, with a jolt that began at the center of her, the feeling burst into pure, ringing sensation. She arched like a bow, shivered, then lunged upward, arms, legs, body, and clung to James, his wide shoulders, his strong hips, holding him till she could feel the bed, the real world, again.

Sometime later, when he'd grown quiet yet seemed wakeful, she simply said, "No matter what tribe life drops you into, large or small, I suspect most of its members will see your excellence, your decency."

"Well, I don't know about that—"

"And humility." She shook her head, rolling toward him, smiling in the dark. "You're just plain *good,* James Stoker. Gold yourself. A heart that is pure twenty-four carat weight."

They made love on and off all night, till the sheets became damp, till their bodies were sliding together. In the wee hours, James ended up awake, staring into the canopy, his arms behind his head.

He had more or less put together that Coco had arrived here, a young girl come to work in the house with her aunt. Phillip would have been already five or six years into a marriage that was proving difficult. The very pretty young Coco got pregnant, so Phillip shipped her out. Then what? Where did Phillip fit into this? And why was James lying here in a room in his house, with Phillip out of town, with Phillip's . . . what, who was Coco to Phillip?

James lay there worrying over these and other

vague anxieties, thinking he was alone in his fears.

Then Coco spoke up out of the dark. "Phillip thinks he wants me back," she said.

She let this offhand revelation register before she added, "I won't stop long enough to let him say it. But he sends me flowers. He had the servants open up this room when he heard I was downstairs. He moved my things up here when I was out to breakfast with you one morning." Pause. "And David is delighted. He loves that Phillip is treating me well—after ignoring both of us for a decade. He wants his father's attention. He wants to know his father, which has suddenly loomed as a possibility. Only—"

She sighed before she went on. "Only—well, Phillip is much more unhappy than I'd have expected, and I can see that he thinks I may be a key. A missed boat, something like that."

"Are you?"

She left a dreadful pause, then said finally, "Yes. Very missed. Long past. But David might not be. . . ." She let the thought drift.

He had a hundred questions, but was sure she would answer few or none. So he asked the important one—after he could get it unstuck from his throat. "Um . . . did you love him, do you think?"

"Oh, James." She sighed. "I was a country radish fresh from the backwaters of France. I walked into a proper English house more grand than anything I'd ever entered, and there stood its owner: sophisticated, monied, a viscount. And the Viscount showed an interest in me—real, genuine interest. Love him? I'm not even sure. All I know is, for a time, I thought he was God. I felt as if I were suddenly alive, as if I'd been sleepwalking till the moment he entered my life.''

"Then what?"

She rolled onto her side to look at him. She touched his face. "Then, my dear," she said, "I grew up."

James turned his face into her palm and kissed it, while he tried to make sense of everything here. "And David—"

"Has his own life, his own place. He doesn't need this house or Phillip's money. I've seen to that. And he's a resourceful, resilient young man." There was an odd moment then, a long disjunctive pause: a but. "It's just that David wants the chance to know his father, and I'm afraid to ruin it for him."

"Which means?"

She left another silence that was too long, too full of wrong possibilities. James dangled in it, growing more unhappy by the moment.

"Which means," she said, "that I wish to treat Phillip civilly, fairly, while not giving him the first reason to believe I would ever start up with him again. It means I'm afraid of getting in the way of his and David's building something."

She left several long seconds before she announced, "My maid is in London getting us ship's passage to Italy. The bees and honey are cleaned up. In fact, I was going to see the roof repair through, but I've decided, well—I've decided to leave early and let David see to it. I'm leaving day after tomorrow." She rushed on. "I didn't expect tonight. I'm not sorry it happened, though." She ran her palm down his arm to his hand and squeezed. "But it's still best that I go."

"I don't agree."

"Well, you think about it. I can leave you my address in Italy." She rose up on her elbow and looked at James. "If you were sneakier. If you *liked* conducting an affair as if it were commerce with the enemy. But you." She sighed and touched the backs of her knuckles down James's cheek. "Well, you. You are nicer. So nice. If I were twenty and, say, the daughter of a proper English family, I would set my cap for you. You are all I'd want, no one else. Ever."

James let out a snort. "This is the most insane thing—"

She put her fingers over his mouth. "Go to sleep."

"No, you can't just walk away. We should be together forever, not just for a night."

"I'm glad you think so. Come with me, then."

"With you?"

"To Italy."

The suggestion bewildered him. "Leave my work?" Everything he'd ever built for himself?

"I have money enough for both of us. A house on the Italian Mediterranean, one in London, another in Paris, another in Biarritz. Or we can sell them all and buy something new somewhere else."

"Let you keep me?" he asked, laughing.

She shrugged. "Well . . . yes. I suppose." The notion amused her. "Certainly. Why not?"

"I have a better idea," James said quickly. He tried to sound light, tried to laugh. "You stay here with me."

"Oh, yes." She succeeded in laughing—in that sardonic way she had when she found things that were not funny funny. "Wouldn't that be lovely? We could sneak around under Phillip's nose. He would love us both for that. And do we tell David, or keep it a secret from him, too? And your friends? Your proper English dons? And the Queen herself? Should I mention that Victoria intervened person- ally on her son's behalf when she thought Bertie had sat once too often in my opera box in Paris? She sent an underling, offering me money to refuse him entrance."

He looked back at her. "Did you take it?"

Coco seemed momentarily insulted, then said, "Of course not. But I told him not to come any longer, that a future king should not just *be* above board, he should *look* above board." She snorted. "After which he took up with that horrid actress." A pause. "I'm hoping you'll put my good advice to better use." She waited before she said, "If you want that earldom, now is not the time to take up with a woman who embarrassed the Queen twenty years ago. Nor—if you want Phillip's loyalty."

They were both full of advice that night, though, good advice that was not very much fun to contem- plate acting upon.

In the middle of the night, Coco's tooth woke her up. It ached badly; her jaw was slightly swollen. James found her cloves. They packed half a dozen into her mouth. Then he got her a cool towel, lay it on her cheek, and curled up beside her, holding her, stroking the side of her head.

"You ought to have it out," he counseled.

"I know," she muttered against the towel and her own hand.

He segued into a litany of practical matters.

"Have you found a good man to repair the board-inghouse roof?"

"I think so."

"Would you like me to check on it for you? Help David see the repairs through?"

"Oh, yes, please . . . that would be so nice. And you'll write, of course, tell me everything that happens, keep me up to date in the ongoing battle over maps and Wakua gold. I'll give you my address in San Remo as well as in Paris."

"Yes, yes," he said quietly, nodding. "We'll write."

After a long moment, though, she whispered, "Oh, James, perhaps we shouldn't. We should make a clean break of it, don't you think?"

"No." He pulled her more tightly to him. "I must have some piece of you. I can't give all of you up. You've become my friend, my sweetest, dearest friend. Everyone knows we're on companionable terms, so let that be the case. Maybe a time will come when we can—" He didn't finish the thought.

It should be enough perhaps that they were real, true friends. They trusted each other; they had the other's best interest at heart. Here was a lot, in and of itself.

She asked him what exactly had made him burst out at Athers at Tuttleworth's dinner party.

He told her the latest installment—the fact that Athers was ready to call him a liar and murderer, if he thought it would get him notes that would draw him a map to African gold. James spoke of how worried he was that Phillip, who had the means to stop Athers, was too distracted to care, that he seemed more a hamstring than help.

In the morning, James left out the back. The only way. The only reasonable thing. They used other idiotic words—*practical, adult, responsible.*

Mostly, though, James understood that he simply couldn't have her.

Chapter 15

Whether set into motion by the pique of goddesses or evil fairies, the punishment of gods, or the wisdom of sages, in all versions of the Sleeping Beauty legend fate is the ultimate enemy. Though one can hope to mitigate its effect, no precaution is enough to avert its trouble.

From the Preface to The Sleeping Beauty
DuJauc translation
Pease Press, London, 1877

Ironically, the next day, as Coco was waiting for her train that would take her away from Cambridge, who should arrive on an incoming train one platform over but Phillip Dunne. Neither his wife nor his family was with him. He stepped off the train, looked across the platforms. His eyes met

Coco's and his eyebrows went up. She thought at first he would ignore her.

He didn't. He smiled away his surprise and walked right around, right up to her. "Coco, I've been wanting to talk to you."

While staying two weeks under his roof, Coco had successfully avoided speaking to Phillip more than in passing. But here, in a public train station, she could not now think how to avoid a conversation. She smiled at him politely—distantly, she hoped—and prepared to have to say more than "hello" to him for the first time in a dozen years.

He wore his hair differently, combed straight back, against the way it grew in front. It was thinning. The combination, less hair combed against the growth, made it stand up from his face. The style—perhaps combined with the way he'd always watched a person's face, as if gauging, always gauging, for applause—gave him somehow a look of edgy expectancy, an air of watchful, perpetual startlement.

"Hello, Phillip." She apologized with the rise of one shoulder. "I'm about to go. My train is due any minute."

"How are you?" he asked jovially. "You look wonderful."

"Thank you. I'm fine."

"Are you seeing anyone?"

She angled her head. Talk about right to the point. It was none of his business, but she answered anyway. "No."

Then he took her full attention by saying, "Spoke to Tuttleworth this morning. You were at his dinner party Tuesday night, where you met, I think, a man by the name of James Stoker?'' He laughed as if to put her at ease, a sound that put her on guard. ''Almost impossible to miss him. Handsome fellow, articulate, magnetic—everyone around here loves him.''

''I met him.''

He waited for her to say more.

She said cagily, ''He seemed quite decent. Certainly a good friend of yours. He speaks highly of you.''

''Then you know he's closely associated with me, that I've all but sponsored him at Cambridge, appointed him to committees, seen him into a pretty high position.''

''Well, then, he has much to thank you for.''

''Hell, yes. Supervised him as an undergraduate, was his Director of Studies. All but raised him, too, for that matter.''

She didn't know what to say.

''What did you think of him?'' Phillip asked.

Coco knew less and less how to proceed. What was he looking for? She hesitated before she offered, ''He seemed . . . idealistic. His vision doesn't seem to agree exactly with yours.''

''Ah!'' He held up a finger and gave it a wag. She'd somehow guessed close to the answer the don wanted. His eyebrows went up in mock affront. ''Though I'm deeply offended.''

She laughed, partly because she was meant to, partly because Phillip had always entertained her. ''You're practical, Phillip, which precludes your being terribly idealistic, I'm afraid. But 'practical' has its advantages.''

He chuckled, mollified. He looked around them, at ease suddenly. Phillip liked to watch—when one

spoke to him in public—to see, Coco always imagined, if there was anyone else he knew, anyone he
might like to hide from or for whom he might wish
to abandon her in favor of a more useful association.

Distractedly, while watching a couple at the
newsstand, he said, "I don't know. Someone mentioned that they thought James might have an eye
for you, that—"

"Phillip, honestly. I don't think he's even thirty.
What would he want with a woman my age?"

Much too quickly to be flattering, he said,
"Right," and laughed. "My first thought, too. I
mean, not that you aren't lovely, Coco, but James
is just so—oh, I don't know." He made a face,
puffed cheeks, then let the air go. "*Pfffah*, he's no
paragon, I'll tell you that." Phillip pushed his lips
forward, frowning. He was going to size James up
for her, correct any misconceptions. "Stoker is a
walking chain reaction of money flowing into Cambridge. All right, he's intelligent, a true scholar, but
mostly he's charming: full of the social skills that
in a different lifetime, with less talent and less honesty, would have made him a successful con artist.
Idealistic, ha."

"All right." It was a waste of her breath to say
more, Coco thought.

Yet as they stood there, a train whistling in the
distance, she grew more and more uncomfortable.
It seemed intolerable that Phillip misunderstand a
young man who meant him only good, his ward, his
protégé, his surrogate son, without at least someone
saying something to him.

She said, not only for James's sake, but for Phillip's—who needed all the friends like James Stoker he could get, "I think you distrust him, Phillip, because you've let distance come between the two of you." When she glanced at Phillip Dunne, he was looking at her, attentive. And suddenly she couldn't shut up. She told him, "You've been out of town too much. You've separated yourself from him. You're the practical one: talk to him. Fix it."

"Coco—" he began, but the rushing air of an arriving train, followed quickly by the loud screech of steel and blasts of steam, put a break in the conversation.

Coco signaled her maid. A porter came forward, rolling her trunks and bags on a trolley.

The train rumbled down to the loud vibration of a waiting engine. As her bags were loaded, Phillip said, "Coco, I'd like to see you again. *You're* something I'd like to fix."

She glanced at him. "I don't need fixing, Phillip." She laughed. "I fixed myself years ago. But if you're in the mood, call on David. He'd enjoy any efforts you might wish to make."

He took her arm to help her step up onto the train, then kept hold of her hand. When she turned on the vestibule step, he said, "Don't reach too high, Coco." He paused. "I'm the best you can do."

God, she hoped not. What a curse *that* would be. She stared at him blankly, acknowledging nothing.

He said, "A man like Stoker, well—" He shook his head. "You'd destroy him, you know."

Her chest tightened, as if the air on the platform had grown cold, hard to draw in. A chill spread through her. Yet she kept her eyes level, facing Phillip: facing him down.

After a moment, he turned loose of her hand with a sniff, as if she had injured him. With anger, like a poke with a sharp stick, he said, "Willy's worse. The clinic wouldn't take her. I had to put her in a hospice in Bath."

Coco pressed her lips together, frowning. "Oh, Phillip. Why aren't you in Bath, then?"

He made the smallest shrug. Then he became the man she'd known, the man she'd cared for once. He held his hands out, empty, bereft. His eyes, honest, really meeting hers, glassed when he said, "She has no idea"—he shook his head—"no idea whatsoever I'm there."

"I'm sorry," Coco said. "Oh, Phillip, I am so, so sorry."

He nodded.

She felt taut, helpless as the train pulled out. Through the window glass she saw Phillip. He stood on the platform, rigid, watching as she left, his mouth a thin, stretched seam in his face, the tightly drawn mouth of a man in crisis, fighting tears.

As the train lurched forward, faster and faster, Coco didn't take her seat. Rather she stood, holding onto the luggage rail overhead, maintaining her balance only with difficulty. She felt sad for him. He made her throat tight, her lips tremble. But as the feelings rushed in, he was only an excuse: Phillip was past business. It was safe to feel bad about a man who'd made mistakes and whose wife was now dying. She did feel sorry for him. Yet he was not the reason the muscles of her neck felt strained, stretched till her throat felt narrow, till she couldn't swallow.

She was leaving James, really leaving him and every possibility of him, behind. She dare not write as promised. It was necessary to make a clean break.

Because she had always known what Phillip had put into words: She would destroy her young hero if she let their association continue, if she let James hope. They could not be "friends only," though they had tried to be, because he was in love with her. Moreover, there were high feelings on both sides, feelings that wanted to escalate. He and she had somehow gotten into a heady spin of emotions not easily brought under rein. Too intense, too large. Too impossible. The situation spelled disaster for Sir James Stoker. If she encouraged him, he would eventually do something rash, ruin himself over her.

Because her worst fear was tied inextricably to one of her greatest pleasures in him: Her stalwart knight did not possess the necessary duplicity to remain in contact with an infamous woman. It was not in his nature to live the hypocrisy required.

She stood there swaying, hanging on for dear life as the train clattered into a steadier rhythm—wishing likewise that all she might have said in letters would move as quickly from her mind as the accelerating countryside. There seemed so much all at once that she had intended to say that must now go unspoken, unwritten. She hadn't told James yet about her beautiful garden in Italy, about the funny quirks of her land agent in Biarritz, about how she could become afraid if she were alone in any of her houses when a bad thunderstorm struck. She had wanted to ask what Mtzuba looked like, how he and James had managed to talk.

This sort of minutia rattled through Coco's mind, till Lucia made her sit. Coco turned unstably, gripping the overhead rail, then fell into the plush velvet train seat. Relief. Yes, yes, she told herself as she leaned back, I'll be fine. She closed her eyes. She had always been alone, always gone her own way. It didn't matter that others saw her, at best, in a shady light. It didn't matter that she was leaving behind someone she admired who had miraculously seen her, known her in a way similar to the way she knew herself. She had been fine before she met James; she would be fine again without him.

She sat there, dry-eyed, stoic, bumping along, alternately grieving and reassuring herself. It was not until she fell into a doze that her mind took on the larger aspects of what she was giving up: the sight of his face and smile, his humor ... the feel of his strong, warm body ... his gentle, upright spirit ... his understanding, so rare and generous—oh, God, this. In her sleep she saw again the look in his soft gold eyes, their bewildered tolerance and, where need be, forgiveness ... their welcoming acceptance ... their open, undefended expression of love.

When she awakened, it was with a disoriented jolt. She was befuddled. The train had stopped. Steam hissed in rising cloud-like bursts outside her compartment. London. The day was gone. Lucia, her back to her, stood, reaching overhead to organize hat boxes, to gather up their things. Coco took in a breath, then let it out slowly. Her sternum ached as if a tight band had been wrapped around her chest all the way from Cambridge. The compartment door opened, outside air blew in, and her cheeks felt suddenly wet, cold. Goodness—she madly wiped at her face with her knuckles and the backs of hands, unable to think what else to do. She was unsure how to cope with what had not happened to her since she was seventeen: She'd been crying. Her lashes and under her eyes were damp from it, while salty-dry tracks made her cheeks feel stiff.

Chapter 16

At the end of May, almost a month later, James sat at his desk in the book-lined study of his rooms at All Souls, while on his lap lay his tattered African journal. Its binding had rotted long ago; its cover was blistered, its pages foxed. By the end, he'd held it all together with string. Today, he'd been leafing through it—from the carefully regimented pages, dated and inscribed with locations and landmarks, full of respectable observations about the "natives" and the "primitives," into the undated pages of a man lost. These last became simple notes and were the most interesting of all to James. They dealt with nothing, with everything; the spectrum of human life, large wonders, small events, minutiae, from the conundrum of why the crocodiles didn't eat the hippopotami to the practical matter of the best dart poison for bringing down a warthog. Here was where the Englishman's pages gave way to the pages of simply a member of the tribe of man.

James tried to remember when he'd begun to feel differently about his homeland. He loved England.

He had; he still did. It was the backbone of his existence, but it was also somehow wrong about its authority and rights in the community of the world.

The world was becoming a smaller place. And a lonelier one for James.

He wished Coco were here to talk to about the turmoil of all that lay in his lap here. He missed her. It had been more than three weeks since her departure, and still he had not heard from her. Term was ending, which meant exams, then a week of student celebration, then Congregation and Admission to degrees. After which followed the Queen and an earldom. Her Majesty's birthday, though she was born in May, was to be officially celebrated June twelfth. Oh, happy day.

James dropped his loose-paged journal down onto the desk top. Happy day, indeed. He harrumphed as he milled about through the papers and a few rocks that lay on his desktop, looking for a pen. He could find not a thing with which to write. Just as he could find not a single celebratory feeling within himself. There seemed nothing whatsoever to celebrate, nothing that made him happy.

"Blast and damn," he muttered, as he riffled through the surface debris of his desk. Blast and damn. Never had he been more thriving; never had he felt more miserable.

He didn't wish for a moment to be part of any celebration. A letter from Coco might have made him shout; he wasn't even sure. He was puzzled as to why he hadn't heard from her. Puzzled, annoyed, and hurt. He had no idea where he might contact her. He kept meaning to look up David and ask him for her address, but this seemed to put Coco's son in the middle. In any event, James kept asking himself, Why didn't Coco write on her own? She had *his* address; he'd made sure of that. Why didn't *she* tell him where she was? Didn't she *want* to hear from him?

James didn't know.

He slapped his journal closed, then pivoted in his chair to set the book back up on the shelf. His private journal. Part of what Athers had wanted in his quest for gold. James's own private papers. On second thought, James lifted the journal back down, pulled a few books out from his bookcase, then set the journal behind them, putting the books back.

Stupid. He hated doing things like this. Coco would laugh. Coco would have helped him think it through. She would listen. They would talk. She would have helped him make sense of the idiocy of Athers. Along with the idiocy of Phillip fending off the Bishop with a random, careless swipe when it occurred to him; worse than no help at all.

If she would only send an address, send word . . . let him know where to contact her. . . . Then none of his distresses would feel as burdensome. And his joys, shared with her, would feel tenfold.

James was nine years old when Phillip Dunne and his wife took him officially into the main house. More Phillip, actually. Lady Dunne, the Viscountess Dunne, lived in a cloud of severe headaches and daily laudanum. She spent most of her time in bed. James had inhabited Wilhelmina Dunne's house for ten years and hardly seen her; he hardly knew her. Worse, he suspected no one knew her any better than he did. For this reason alone, he had sympathy for her.

The Dunnes slept in separate rooms. The Viscountess slept on the ground floor. She was afraid of the stairs—sensibly, since she was frequently too incoherent to safely negotiate a staircase. The Dunnes' marriage served them both, no doubt. But James could not see how it was a happy union.

He had always been struck by the labor of it on Phillip's part. Of course, now he understood what drove Phillip a bit better. Though it wasn't all that simple—had a young Phillip indulged in a fling with Coco, then felt horrible about it and thus taken care of Willy out of guilt? Or had he been so miserable in his marriage that he had sought solace with the cook's assistant—continuing to care for his wife out of duty? A little of both, perhaps. In any event, there was no doubt that Phillip was emotionally connected to his ailing wife. When she was happy, his spirits were visibly lighter; he took pleasure in her bright moments.

Thus when Phillip came through Cambridge—another single afternoon on his way somewhere else, back to Bath again—and announced he had rented a house near Monte Carlo for a family holiday, James assumed Willy's "cure" to be going well. Phillip was buoyant. He was sure that the sun, the sea, the air in the South of France was just what she needed. He'd rented "a romantic house with a lovely garden overlooking the sea—Willy will love it."

It was hard for James to imagine Willy working up enough response to anything to be called "love," but he nodded. Then was surprised to hear

himself invited along. "Like old times," Phillip
said. He'd patted James on the back, all but cuffing
his ear.

Perhaps it was what he needed, James thought. A
trip that took him away from perpetually trying to
waylay the postman would certainly do him no
harm.

It was not unusual that James be invited with the
Dunnes on holiday. He was close to the family—
the girls and Phillip, mostly—though he was certainly on as good terms as anyone with Lady
Dunne. He just hadn't gone anywhere with the family in a long, long time. Good, good, he told himself. At the very least, he and Phillip could
reacquaint themselves with each other. Since
James's return, there had been precious few opportunities for the smoky sort of postprandial chats he
and Phillip had once favored, over cigars and
brandy, man-to-man. This would be excellent,
James assured himself.

He arrived in Monte Carlo by train, then hired a
carriage and driver for what turned out to be twenty
minutes' ride straight up to a tiny French village
near the Italian border. To get to the house involved
a further turn west, then a descent. In point of fact,
the house Phillip had rented, though within a hundred yards of the sea, was inaccessible to wheeled
vehicles except by this circuitous route. One all but
had to have a map to get to it. James's driver got
lost twice. From the narrow, winding coastal road
below it, the house looked to be—it was—unap-
proachable.

As James came around to the main door, however, his bags and driver in tow, he glimpsed a winding footpath that led down toward the water. The house was quaintly remote, truly a love nest— or aerie, as it were. It was nestled back loosely in trees atop its own little cliff. Indeed, the perfect place for a man to romance his ailing wife.

James was met at the door by a Frenchwoman, local help hired on the spot. As he came in, he was quite overtaken by the view. Through a wide, un- usually open parlor, then a wall of French doors, the outlook was immediately spectacular: a gor- geous elevated view between trees of the vivid blue Mediterranean in the distance, its beach across the road below.

In fact, James knew within minutes of arriving that the house itself was an extraordinary place, spa- cious, magnificent in every way—breezy, balcon- ied, simply though beautifully furnished, freshly kept. It smelled of sunshine and the fresh herbs that grew wild through the arid hills. Within five minutes of setting his satchel down, however, James also knew that Willy would not "love" it. She was, in fact, not even in residence.

"She wouldn't come," Phillip said.

He turned and, with a pout meant to indicate high dudgeon, handed James a drink, something cloudy and sweet.

He continued, "Then the girls decided to stay behind with her." The outrage in Phillip's face though, was somehow feigned. He wasn't as un- happy as he pretended. James didn't quite under- stand.

Until he happened to look out the window. He

glanced, turned all the way around to be sure, then stopped, nonplused.

Below, through the panes, down on the beach, James saw a petite woman with shining black hair that blew behind her in wisps, stray bits coming out of a chignon in the sea air.

No, it couldn't be. It was his own fanciful imagination.

But it was. To his enormous, delighted—then, come to think of it, pretty damn annoyed—astonishment, there was Coco Wild. Indisputably down by the water, not a hundred yards beyond him, she walked along on the tiny wet stones of the tide.

She held up her dress, picking her way along the stones in her pretty, bare feet. They looked naked, these feet he loved. Exposed. And unusual; she was always unusual. One rarely saw anyone, let alone a well-dressed woman, so near the water. She more or less danced, moving to avoid the tide, as it inched forward, then following it as it receded. Increasingly aggravated, James thought, Where the hell are her shoes? Why is she dancing around there in nothing but her sweet, vulnerable feet, no stockings or slippers? In public. Or almost in public. In full view of Phillip Dunne, at least, who had stepped up beside James.

The two men looked down through the window, shoulder to shoulder, as they watched her together.

Finally, sheepishly, the Vice-Chancellor offered, "You know Mrs. Wild, I believe."

James had no words. For no easily justifiable reason he would liked to have smashed Phillip in the face.

Phillip shrugged, nonchalant. "We go way back,

James.'' He left a pause. "I may as well tell you: we were very close once. I have a son by her.'' He barely let this sink in before he was off, a trip down memory lane. "Never could acknowledge him, you understand. A French rascal. *Mon moutard fran-çais.*'' Phillip uttered French with a strong English accent, but with astonishing ease. "He's splendid—cheerful, pleasant. Handsome devil, too.'' He chortled. "Looks rather like me, I fancy, when I was younger, of course. He's at Cambridge now. It's been a real torture. Seeing him there, well. . . .'' Phillip waved his hand, supposedly waving in understanding.

When James found his voice, he said, "I'll—'' He'd what? Much against what he would have liked—to raise a commotion, demand explanations, particularly of the woman down on the beach—he made himself say the right thing, the decent thing. "I'll, ah, I'll catch the next train back. You should be alone with your—'' Phillip's what? What were these people to each other?

"No, no. David likes you. We talked about it. He wants you here.'' David wanted him here? James felt dull-witted as a cow. What did David have to do with anything? "And James—'' Phillip leveled one of his sincere looks at him, the sort of eye-to-eye candor he was so good at that James was always hard pressed to tell whether it was pretended or not. If he hadn't seen Phillip use it routinely with men he disliked, he might have felt close to Phillip in the next moment.

As it was, he felt merely at a loss, when Phillip added, "*I'd* like you to be here. A friend, all that.''

Phillip went on. "I'm scared, I have to tell you.

My marriage is rot. My wife is in a stupor most of
the time. My career is on the softest ground of its
life. Add to this that my back hurts sometimes so
badly I can't get out of bed." He laughed, looked
down at the beach again. "And Coco—Mrs. Wild,
that is. She's none too pleased with me. I'd—" He
stammered.

James had heard this stammer before, the whole
act under highly manipulative circumstances. But he
gave Phillip credit: one built one's lies on one's
own real experiences. James was damned to call his
friend's speech a lie now.

Phillip said, "I'd be very grateful if you'd stay.
You know, chat me up, cheer me up, join me at
night for a few manly brandies, that sort of thing.
Shore me up while I get to know this son of mine.
High time, all that, I know. But you won't judge
me or make it harder. I know you'll make it better.
Please stay."

James frowned at Phillip. How earnest was this
request? Perhaps more importantly, how selflessly
motivated was its answer? He said, "Phillip, whatever you ask of me, whatever you need, you know
my response: If here is where you want me, I'm
here."

Phillip hit his back once, a solid *thwack* that was
followed by two or three gentler ones. When his
hand remained on James's back for a companionable moment, James thought, Yes, it felt right that
he stay here with Phillip. Phillip was in trouble
somewhere. He needed James.

That is, it felt right till James looked out the window again.

Coco was walking along the water contentedly,

the way she could, a woman who was sufficient unto herself. And unsuspecting, it occurred to James. She didn't know he was here, that he was coming. She couldn't, not walking along as she did, so carefree. And David—James just noticed that David was up ahead of her, running on the beach. "Son-of-a-bitch," James muttered.

"What?" said the man beside him.

James laughed and cranked his head sideways. Very clearly, he enunciated, "You're a son-of-a-bitch, Phillip."

Phillip started, then burst out laughing, taking it all in jolly humor. "I am, aren't I?" he admitted. "The biggest son-of-a-bitch around. Trying to fix it though, James. Trying to fix it."

James could not imagine being dropped into a more awkward situation. If Phillip hadn't been so absolutely desperate for an ally, he'd have been furious with him. As it was, Phillip just made him feel dispirited.

Coco, though, was another matter. She entered the house half an hour later, rounding the edge of the front door, then stopped cold. There was a flash of emotion in her face. Anger, of all things. Oh, fine, James thought, she was angry to see him. He might have been less exasperated with her if she had kicked up a fuss, been fully irate. But she blinked once, pressed her lips together as if to brace herself, then rolled with it. She set down what she'd been carrying—her shoes, stockings, and a sketching pad with her little pocket of pencils—smiled right at him, and came forward. She offered her hand, dropped at the wrist in that infernal Continental summons to kiss a place that was at least an arm away from all places he wanted to put his mouth. "Sir James. What a lovely surprise."

Fine, James thought as he took her fingertips. Two liars.

David came in just after that, quite happy, the only one who seemed to be enjoying himself honestly, without unreadable motives. He seemed a little shy, but he was obviously basking in his father's attention.

Everyone had a sherry, saying positively nothing worth saying, keeping as close as possible to safe ground—while James hung there, waiting for someone to explain to him what the hell was happening. They spoke of the weather, for godssake. The casino in Monte Carlo: should they visit it, or should they not? Did anyone want to go? David's schooling— a safe topic for everyone but James, as it turned out. David had been listed as the first score on his Mays exams, the highest. This mention was the first that Phillip had heard the news. He beamed as he absorbed it, while Coco could not resist exchanging a smile with the father of her clever child.

For James, David's scholastic victory made the afternoon three for three. He would like to have shot Phillip, Coco, and Coco's son now as well. One happy little family. James got up from his chair when a second round of sherry was offered. "Sorry. No, thanks. You must excuse me. I need to unpack and freshen up."

The only happy realization—and one he checked with obsessive care an hour later—was that Coco went upstairs to change her clothes for dinner, while Phillip knocked around in the room next to James's on the ground floor. Wonderful. She and Phillip weren't sharing a bedroom, at least. Not yet.

By dinnertime, James was determined to confront the woman at the first available moment—God, he was so in love with her, it made him dizzy; he wished he could rid himself of the feeling. The combination of roiling churns of desire and possessiveness and jealousy and confusion set his nerves on fire. He was so agitated his brain seemed to jump from question to question, topic to topic, without satisfactory conclusion reached on even one. He was in a state.

Then she didn't come down to dinner as she was supposed to; she had a knack for torture. Phillip, James, and David all stood around downstairs, three men dressed for dinner, waiting, till she finally sent word she'd be late. She'd lost an earring into the piano; she and a maid were looking for it. The gentlemen were to begin dinner without her.

Phillip shrugged. "Typical. She marches to her own rhythm, that one."

"Oh, hell's bells," said David. "Let's eat."

"Into the piano?" James repeated. No one else seemed to find the explanation in any way unusual. He suggested, "We could go up and help her find it."

Phillip rolled his eyes. "If she'd have wanted help, she'd have asked for it—trust me on this, old man. She dresses her own way, at her own pace. She'd just fuss at you."

With this cheerful thought—that Phillip knew Coco's habits and moods when she dressed, while James didn't—they went into the dining room: three Englishmen, in white tie, pulling out chairs to a

Mediterranean table that overlooked the curving
French coast. They began on starters, some concoc-
tion of fresh minced olives, garlic, and other bits
slathered onto hot bread, while claret flowed every
time a glass was emptied so much as a swallow.

By the second refilling of his glass, James found
that his exasperation was sufficiently lubricated that
instead of waiting to ask Coco, he began to blurt
questions at Phillip. "And how is it that Willy
ended up—where?"

"She's in Cambridge."

"Indeed. In Cambridge, while you ended up here
with David and . . ." My own sweet Coco, he
wanted to say, though with effort he was able to get
out, "Mrs. Wild?"

"Well." Phillip glanced at James while heaping
the olive stuff onto a round of bread. "I stomped
off when I realized Willy wouldn't come, not unless
I kidnaped her and dragged her here. Then I ran
into David." Phillip grew sheepish. His son's
watching him from down the table made him honest. "Well, no. Truth is, I went over to St. John's
and watched for him," he admitted. "I'd done it
once or twice before, hoping to run into him, you
know? Anyway, there he was. And this time he saw
me. We ended up saying hello, and suddenly I found
myself asking him if he'd come here with me."

He gestured with the bread, an offhand movement
meant to diminish the importance of the event. He
continued, "He said he couldn't because he'd promised to meet his mother. Except, as we talked, it
turned out he was meeting her in San Remo, not
fifteen miles away." Phillip laughed. What a coincidence. "*Voilà*, as the French say. David came

with me, then took the train this morning to San Remo, where he talked his mother into making a kind of a peace treaty visit. She and I, well—'' He looked down for a heartbeat, then over at David, a level look. ''We didn't part on the best of terms years ago. I hate to say it, James, but I haven't always done right by the two of them.''

''Ah.'' James nodded. A wonderful explanation. If he hadn't known that Coco had been planning to spend the summer in San Remo, that she owned a house there, had lived there—spent every summer there—for the last several years. It seemed impossible that Phillip didn't know these things as well, that he hadn't perfectly well known she was fifteen miles away when he'd rented this house in the first place.

The conversation wandered into what Phillip was trying to get through the House of Lords, a unifying university financial structure. ''I need Athers's support on the commission, you see,'' he said, ''as we try to legislate a portion of each college's revenues to. . . .''

Blah, blah, blah. Phillip said more. James simply didn't have the interest any longer. He seemed to have left his political ambition in Africa.

He felt vaguely competitive, some of the old desire to win trying to nurse itself alive, when Phillip wagged his finger and said, ''Now, just because the Bishop got the better of us in that round involving his people's diaries, James, doesn't mean this old bowler here is giving away more runs these days for fewer wickets.''

Cricket. Phillip was keen for cricket. James supposed, in this comfortable, sporting way, Phillip was about to edge into what he'd referred to earlier as his career's new "soft ground."

But Coco finally appeared.

And what an appearance it was. She came through the double dining room doors, a vision in a garnet-red dress that V-ed down at her breasts and pinched tight at her waist. Her hair was swept up, showing off her long, elegant neck. She glided into the room, a swan of a woman. "Good evening. Sorry I'm late."

Even her son was affected. As all three gentlemen rose from their chairs, David said, "Gosh, Coco, you look smashing." He almost never called his mother by other than her given name, which rankled James tonight. As if she'd protected the illusions of clients. The word haunted him. *Clients. Just call me Coco, darling, when the clients are about.* Smiling with open pride, her darling glanced at James now and asked, "Doesn't she?"

Before James could say anything, however, Phillip chimed in. "Coco, you are without a doubt still the most gorgeous woman ever to look upon the Mediterranean. More beautiful than Helen of Troy."

The live, legendary woman settled onto the chair across the table from James, air shushing through sliding, scrunching silk that had a life of its own—it finally rustled to a standstill about twenty seconds after she did.

Lord, all the same, chagrined or not, to James the woman was the most beautiful on earth. And when she put herself together just so, she became more than earthly: ethereal, otherworldly in her loveliness. Tonight yards and yards of dark red satin, black hair up, her white throat dotted with the blood-red garnets from the night of the ball, giant, gorgeous droplets, the largest sitting in the delicate recess between her clavicles. She wore more garnet drops at her ears.

James became aware that he was staring at her. "Ah," he said, trying to smile, "the lost earring is found." Oh, his friend, his lover. His smile became natural. Never mind his anger. Seeing her felt wonderful. Despite himself, he felt his chest flood with warmth.

She touched an earring, holding her ear as she turned her attention on him, eyeing him. Their gazes held for a moment—she was still irritated, he realized—while the rest of the room may as well have evaporated, taking the air itself with it. Who cared; who needed air? James thought. He'd just breathe Coco for a while. God, she was just something . . . everything.

He wanted her beside him. He didn't want her ever to leave his side again. And he especially wanted her beside him tonight, upstairs in his bedroom. Friendship stank; it reeked without the rest.

Chairs scooted. As James sat again, he started asking himself questions like, Why was she angry with him? And how angry? The damn woman guarded her feelings so closely, it was hard to know. Angry enough to throw him out if he slipped upstairs into her room tonight? Would she make a fuss? Would she be willing to come downstairs to his? And, How bad would it be for Phillip to understand his interest here? How competitive, exactly, were he and the man who'd sponsored him, half-raised him, and now directed much of his work and most of his career?

He realized Phillip remained standing. Phillip had lifted his wineglass. Contemplating it, then looking over its edge at Coco, the married man of the group offered a highly inappropriate toast: "To the most self-possessed—and prepossessing—woman I have ever known."

Known. To James's jealous mind, the last word seemed to carry a biblical nuance of meaning. He scowled down into a plate of roast beef as it was set before him. His blood in the pit of his stomach began to thump, an unpleasant knock.

He heard Coco, across from him, murmur, "Sit down, Phillip."

Phillip held on to the edge of the table for a wobbly moment—he was tipsy, James realized—then shuffled into his chair.

James felt a kind of inebriation himself as he lifted his gaze, looking for Coco's face, but getting only as far as her breasts—their globular swell in unison above the satin neckline of her dress, their regress back. He could hear the rhythm of her breathing, like music playing to a perfectly synchronized ballet. He could not distinguish a word of conversation; exchanged murmurs blended into a vaguely irritating hum. Yet he could quite distinctly hear the gentle indrawn rush of air down Coco's windpipe, then the soft hiss of air rushing out. Slow and rhythmic to the rise and fall of her pale bosom straining against the dark red neckline.

Across from him, Coco felt his interest in a soft flush that spread over her skin. She couldn't seem to regain her balance, not since the shock of setting eyes on him this afternoon. James's arrival, his presence, churned up a commotion inside her. She'd been in a state all afternoon. And, now, just look at this dress! What had she been thinking? She had paced and raged upstairs, telling herself she wasn't even going to come down to dinner. Why should she after going to such painful lengths to separate herself and James, only to have him undo it all by showing up not even a month later? It was outrageous, unfair. Well, I'll show him, she'd thought. I'll wear a dress that looks like exactly what I am. A red, low-cut dress—a savvy, experienced, expensive dress that'll set him on his ear. How dare he come here. He'll be sorry he did.

Fool. She may as well have dressed to seduce him. She may as well have put on a coating of hard cherry candy, because James Stoker looked for all the world as if he could eat her dress right off her skin.

Meanwhile, she didn't know which galled her more—the nerve-jangling surprise of James or the relentless annoyance of Phillip, who yammered away, saying all manner of things meant to impress her.

Phillip's renewed pursuit after all these years should have been flattering; it was boring. Next to James's ardor, it was lukewarm at best. James, oh, James. He was at it again, staring, wanting, like the night at Tuttleworth's.

Oh, why did it have to feel so wonderful to see him—when it should only have felt maddening? Coco wanted credit, wanted all she had tried to do to count for something. *I did this for you,* she wanted to tell him. *I separated us, held us apart, sacrificed my happiness and quite nearly my sanity. And here you are again.* She would have screamed it at him. Only her resentment was watered down, confused and muddied by the sight of him. Why couldn't she rally a clean, undiluted anger? And why for goodnessake couldn't he keep off his face what was going on in his randy young mind?

If eyes could have left prints like fingers, then her mouth and throat and bosom would have been reddened, all but abraded, from the graze of James's lingering glances. They slid over her; they slid away while he tried to keep them under control—it was marvelous how he couldn't. Marvelous, frustrating— and pitiable because what he wanted was madness.

Lord, she must leave. She should have left already. She should have left the instant she realized he was here. She should leave now, stand up and go.

Yet she sat there, feeling lost, ready to shatter, as delicate as a thin thread of glass.

Phillip meanwhile dominated the conversation. God knew what David made of the evening. Coco picked at her food. James ate hardly at all, pushing potatoes around on his plate, alternately glancing in her direction, glowering in Phillip's.

It was Phillip who inadvertently put an end to the torture. He suddenly rose to his feet, again lifting his glass, and said, "To the mother of my son." He cleared his throat. "Who, once upon a time, I wronged and wronged and who, if she'll let me, I'll make right. Willy doesn't want me any-more, *bella*—"

Dear God, his pet name for her years ago. Coco

stared up at him, near-frozen with dread. The man was drunk.

He said, "It will be a simple matter to get a divorce. I'll be good to her, take care of her, do right." He laughed hollowly. "She won't even know I'm gone. Then I'll marry you, Coco. I'm asking, here in front of our son and my friend. Let me do what I should have done twenty-two years ago—"

Across the table, James stood so abruptly his thighs caught the edge of the table. It lifted a fraction, clinking glassware, then thudded with a scoot back onto the floor. "Excuse me," he said over the noise. "I meant to go earlier. I was thinking of going to Monte Carlo, the new casino—" He stammered, "I—I've been wanting to, ah, see it." He blinked, made a press of his mouth. "I don't belong here. The three of you just cozy up to each other and let me know the outcome later. I'll help you celebrate whatever it is."

And with that he was out the dining room doorway, the click of his heels diminishing through the parlor.

Phillip looked stupefied as footfalls echoed in taps down the steps into the foyer. He scowled. "Something's up with that young fellow." He looked at Coco, narrowing his eyes. "I don't trust him. He's hiding something. I can feel it."

The front door slammed. James had left.

Coco swallowed, trying to find her calm. It took the greatest of self-control simply to lay her napkin into her plate, then reach for the arms of her chair. "Excuse me," she said, as she slid back.

With as much dignity as she could muster, she got up and ran after James.

On the path at the side of the house, Coco stopped, breathless. She listened, yet she heard only the sound of her own heart beating over a din of emotion, over her own jumbled thoughts. She turned around once slowly, hoping for a glimpse, a sound, a sign. Nothing. Just *tha-thump, tha-thump,* as if her heart were trying to leave her chest.

James had been swallowed up into the night. Coco herself stood in perfect darkness, the sort one found only far from large towns, away from other houses, from other human beings—lightless, still, silent. She called his name softly. No answer. She could find no clue, no indication as to which direction he'd gone. She stood there for a time, bewildered. Please God, don't let him be near but quiet on purpose; don't let him not want to speak to me.

I need to speak to him. I need to.

Though, if she did, what would she say?

Go away? I'm not safe for you? I'm not good for you? Or, Come close? I've missed you so badly.

A kind of panic took hold. Coco put her hands into her hair, holding her head. If she had never met anyone whom she admired so much as James, anyone who seemed so radiantly and purely good that she was in awe . . . if she had never known his honesty, his fearless interest, never known his openhearted understanding, never felt his warm hands and strong body . . . well, then she would have never been the wiser: She would not have believed someone as fine as James Stoker existed.

But she knew now. And the knowledge was awful. Nothing could be worse than knowing he existed but living without him.

Hang his reputation. She wasn't the good one, the decent one. For godssake, she wasn't his mother. Let him take care of himself. She wanted him. She hated him for being here, for undoing all the good she had tried to do him, but she wanted him anyway. Where was he?

In the end, she walked all the way down to the water, calling his name, all to no purpose. A carriage rolled by down on the main road. A small animal, either a cat or a rabbit, took fright in front of her path on the way back up. Other than these events, no one, nothing.

She didn't have the slightest notion where James was, not then nor for most of the night. It was hours later when she finally heard him straggle in, at which point the sun had already lit her bedroom with the first rays of daybreak.

Chapter 17

The next morning—almost noon, actually, since everyone had slept in or at least kept to their rooms—Phillip walked from between the open French doors of the parlor out onto the balconied terrace, where, up before everyone, Coco sat curled onto a chaise longue in the sun, where she was drinking tea.

He greeted her with, "Did you succeed in calming James down last night?"

"No," she said. "I wasn't able to find him."

"Well, I appreciate your trying," he said. As if she'd gone after James especially for him. "He's as tight lately as the string of a fiddle. Don't know what's gotten into the lad."

Coco looked at Phillip over her teacup. She would simply have told him at this point about herself and "the lad"—if only she had known what exactly there was to tell. She felt absolutely up in the air as to what was happening between James and herself. Nothing. That was the pity of it. Nothing was happening, except he had dropped in front of her again, as if from out of the sky, and barely spoken two words to her.

251

At the far end of the terrace, a maid came out carrying a platter, one of the staff's many trips from the kitchen. Food kept coming through the far French doors. The whole south wall of the inside parlor opened up, a wall of glass-panes that swung out and hooked back to back. The far sets of doors had become a thoroughfare for an elaborate lunch being set out on a table covered in bright table linens, green and blue patterns with scrolling yellows and splashes of purple. Through the French doors beside her a balmy breeze passed through the house and out across the terrace.

Coco focused on the breeze where it touched her face and neck, on her tea and the view: ignoring Phillip as much as possible. (Coward that she was, she did not wish to begin her day by debating Phillip's conscience or, God forbid, his ridiculous proposal of marriage.) The vista toward the sea was a sheltered, rather spectacular one: an azure-blue Mediterranean at the end of a short tunnel of trees. Determinedly, however, Phillip came around to settle himself against the balustrade beside her, putting himself between Coco and the view. "I really mean it this time," he murmured. He was about to say something further, but stifled it.

Out the far French doors, behind a boy carrying a plate stacked with roasted hens, came "the lad" himself. James looked at the table, apparently with some expectation of finding them there, then spotted Coco and Phillip down near the other end of the balcony. He headed intrepidly toward them.

"Phillip." James's demeanor was stiff and business-like. "I have to talk to you." He gave a passing look to Coco, a befuddled moment as if still unsure what to make of her presence here. Then he moved into what he wanted to say to Phillip as if off a list.

"First of all," he said, "I need your help and full support. I've told you and anyone else who's asked that I don't know where I was exactly in Africa, and I don't—or didn't. But I do now. There are landmarks in my notes, a savannah, the bend in a river, a pattern of hills. And I remember the sky. With the help of a star atlas I could say, I think, precisely where the Wakua live. And that's the issue: I want your help in protecting the information until we can protect the Wakua themselves."

"Protect the Wakua? From what?" Phillip stood slightly, alert. "What are you talking about?"

"Gold. I know where an awful lot is."

Phillip blinked and went around the end of Coco's chaise. "You know where that tribe gets all its gold?"

"More or less. But I won't turn the information over to Athers. I won't even turn it over to you, Phillip. I'll fight you both if I have to. I want to go to friendly quarters in the House of Lords, get guarantees, treaties set in motion. I want the Wakua and their lands protected, a ten-mile belt around them that is inviolate. No one can bother them. I won't lead a pack of greedy Englishmen into the lands of a tribe who saved my life. It isn't right; I don't care what anyone says.

"Moreover," he continued, "the Wakua sent a sizable friendship offering. They deserve to be treated well; they expect it."

Phillip looked alarmed, askance. "If their 'offering,' as you call it, is any indication, my boy, there looks to be a *lot* of gold. Surely it's enough for everyone, including the Wakua tribe.''

"That's not the point. It's all around them. It's under them.''

"*They* mine it.''

"In relative small quantities. We'd come in with machines and in droves.'' James set his jaw. "Look,'' he said, "we have all that I brought back. It's worth a fortune. If we must have more, there's gold elsewhere than right around the Wakua. I can show you where it is.''

Phillip's frown deepened. "How much more are we talking about, and how much of it is on their land?'' After asking the question, though, he came to the answer without help: "They sit on the richest deposits. They sit on the best.''

James nodded. "But there's more over a vast, very rich area. Let me do the geological studies at my speed. I'll map out the metals first. We'll know exactly what's where. We'll get the Crown's cooperation and our international agreements. *Then* everyone can go in.''

Going in, yes. They were at last in agreement. Phillip said, "Right-o.'' He was keen, ready to lay plans. "You'll lead the expedition. We'll—''

"No.'' James blinked, shook his head. "No,'' he said, quiet all at once.

"No?'' It took a few seconds for Phillip to understand. "You don't want to go yourself?''

"No.''

After a moment, Phillip accepted the certainty in James's voice. He said, "All right, we'll get someone else. James.'' His tone was straight-from-the-shoulder, gratified. "It's good you've told me.''

Only then did it occur to him: "God, if Athers gets the notes, he wouldn't waste a minute getting up an expedition of his own and going straight to the richest veins."

"It's not in veins."

Phillip turned, waited, unsure what James was saying.

"It's detrital," James said, "in reefs: thick, conglomerate beds of continuous gold, Phillip. There's never before been a known auriferous formation like it, nothing anywhere else on the face of the earth. And there's plenty. It goes well beyond the Wakua's little plot of land."

There was a moment of appreciative silence before the Vice-Chancellor said in a low voice, "My God." Then more brightly, "James, my boy, we have something here of great importance, and you're right to have been worried." James's face looked watchful; Phillip's voice was solemn. "I'm flattered as hell you've trusted me. You've done the right thing, you'll see." With the top of his fist, he sent, full-armed, a sideways swipe at James's shoulder, a manly plug of camaraderie.

As Phillip turned he happened to catch a glance of who else had been trusted. Coco met his scrutiny, saw there a flicker of troubled awareness. Then he either dismissed or hid his apprehension. His face became unreadable. To James he said, "You may count on my help. You do what you need to do, tell me how I can assist—"

"Fight Athers," James said quickly. "Keep him off my back. Let him take us into the courts, if he wants to. Hire lawyers to oppose him. He has no right to my notes and less grounds still to make accusations.''

Phillip scowled, bowing his head. ''Don't like it,'' he muttered. But after a moment of contemplation, with a grim sigh, he nodded.

''You'll do it?'' James asked, his tone surprised, pleased, and pitifully relieved.

''Yes.'' Phillip nodded again. ''Like old times, James. You and me against them.''

''Oh, marvelous,'' said James with enthusiasm. ''Bloody marvelous, honest to God. If you only knew how worried I've been.'' Then glancing past the Vice-Chancellor, James finally looked at Coco, eye to eye, his full attention.

She felt the prickle of anticipation up her spine.

He cleared his throat. ''And there's another thing I have to tell you.'' When no one said anything, he announced, ''It's Coco.''

Her heart squeezed slightly. She set her teacup into its saucer, then set both down onto her lap.

Phillip cast another backward look toward her, another mystified glance. ''Mrs. Wild?''—ostensibly a corroborative question, though it had the ring of correction: of a parent coaching a polite form of address.

''Indeed, Mrs. Wild—''

Whatever he might have said further, however, became abruptly truncated.

''Sir. I'm terribly sorry to intrude.''

All three of them turned their attention toward the doorway.

A servant stood in the opening, a gauzy curtain from inside blowing out to lap at his back. ''A telegram just arrived for you,' '' he said. He offered a

silver tray toward Phillip. On it lay a yellow tele-
graph envelope. Phillip took it.

Frowning, he turned it over in his hand once, then
opened it while he offered his usual sort of banter.
Who the hell knew he was here? he asked rhetori-
cally, with a kind of jocular peevishness. Drat his
clerk and amanuensis for telling someone. Never a
dull moment, never a real holiday. Not unless he
left James up there. James was the only one he
could dependably send to bat, his best wicket, all
that.

Then his face blanched.

Coco spoke first. "What is it?" she asked.

He looked up. His expression was that of a man
the second before he was mowed down by, say, an
omnibus: in the instant of recognition that he would
be ploughed under and dragged down the street.
"It's Willy," he said. "She's fallen down the staircase. She, um—" He choked for a moment on the
words. "Um, ah—" He muttered, "broke her
neck."

"Is she—" Even Coco hesitated.

"Yes. She's, um—she's not well. Worse. Much
worse." Phillip scowled down at the telegram,
shaking his head. "You see, she's dead." He stared
at the message in his hand as if he could say something to it, have it respond. He glanced up. "The
girls, um, they—" Again his voice broke. "They
want me to come back and help."

A voice said, "I'll go with you." David. He'd
been standing in the doorway, having come up behind the servant. He walked out now, straight over
to Phillip, and lay his hand on his back. "I'll take

you back to Cambridge, Father. I'll help you," he said.

Coco, James, and Phillip looked at him, all three struck dumb.

Phillip found words first. "Would you?" he said, his voice thick. "Oh, would you, please?" Offer accepted. To James, he said, "Ah—James, my boy, see that Coco gets her tickets and train, and—" He waved his hand. He had no idea what he was saying. "You know, gets back, all that."

James shook his head. "No, Phillip. I'll come with you. David can see to his mother."

Standing, Coco interrupted. "No one needs to take care of me. I can get where I need to go on my own. Phillip, can I do anything?"

He shook his head vehemently. "No, no. You two have your holiday. The house is rented. I'll have David all to my—um, that is, David's help. He'll be a wonderful consoling presence. I really would like him to come with me." He looked at them and added, "Willy's at peace now; she won't mind." He blinked, too tumbled by events to dissemble. He said sincerely, "And I would like the girls to meet him."

Phillip's bottom lip began to tremble. He put his hand against his chin to stop it. When this didn't work exactly, he bit his lips together. Turning, he said, "Excuse me. I, ah, I'll just go."

David followed. "I'll throw your things in with mine, into the duffle. We can make the one-oh-five train."

As if on cue, distantly up the hillside, bells began to toll—the village church announcing the noon hour.

And, indeed, by twelve-thirty, Phillip and David were out the door. Coco was stunned to see the front door close behind them, to turn around and face the wide white open-air parlor, its back line of French doors opened into a balconied view of the sea. It seemed even more unreal when James entered the vista. He walked from behind her, moving in his lanky, straight-shouldered way, through the parlor out onto the balcony, where he placed his hands on the marble banister and looked down. He stood near the table where lunch waited, two servants watching over it, swishing insects away with fans.

Unable to think what else to do, Coco went out and sat. A moment later, without a word, James joined her. A maid brought the courses, which were too many and too much, since two of the people for whom they'd been prepared were on their way to the train station. Coco and James stared at a feast of little herbed hens, fresh bread, ratatouille, mesclun . . . oh, more; there was so much. Then, across the table, she finally grew brave enough to find James's eyes. He and she stared, wide-eyed, at one another.

Coco said, "I don't know what to do." She added, "For Phillip, that is."

James offered, "We could follow them to Cambridge and see if we can be of help."

"I don't think we could."

"Nor do I."

Awful, excusing questions came to mind. What could they do, after all? Wouldn't they just be in the way? Phillip was pulling his family together, shoring up, as he called it, "fixing" what could be fixed. Nothing; she and James could do nothing.

And wouldn't it be a waste, since the house was rented, not to stay in it at least a few days?

What a horrid woman, she chastised herself. The man who had rented the house was facing one of the worst times of his life, and all she could think was, How convenient. Thank God he was gone. And, my, oh, my, look who remained.

Her conscience gave her one additional pinch before she silenced it. It said, You liked yourself best when you left James, when you put neither his reputation nor his integrity at risk. If he loves you publically, he becomes less than a hero in the world's eye; if he pretends he doesn't, he becomes less in his own. One way or another, you tarnish his armor. You won't love yourself for it, and you as well will almost assuredly be hurt. There are no happy endings anywhere to be found in this mess.

To which Coco responded by reaching across her plate to tear the drumstick off a roast chicken.

As if they hadn't the slightest idea what to do, she and James began to work their way through a Provençal meal—set out on a vast terrace balcony at the rear of a remote house on the edge of a town so small it was not on the map. The sea gusts picked up. The curtains blew along the length of the terrace, a dancing flurry darting in and out between wide-open doors, out into the Mediterranean air, the hems all but touching the edge of their table.

But it was only a matter of time. For half an hour she and James talked. They settled the mystery of where he'd disappeared to last night. (He'd headed up toward the village for a pint, not an easy thing to find in a small French town, as she had been walking down to the beach.) They spoke of her property matters. (She had met with both her French and Italian estate agents in the past week.) They discussed the seasoning of the food (a lot of oregano, but good), the quality of the wine (middling). Nothing significant. They squirmed in their chairs. They picked over everything and ate very little. They got up. They wandered the terrace. They wandered inside, through the rooms of the house.

There, they grew silent as James followed closer and closer. Then, as they passed into a hallway, he cut her off, turned her, and backed her up against the wall. Her head hit backward with the force in which he pressed a full, sexual kiss onto her mouth, his tongue going immediately, feverishly deep inside. He half-pinned her to the wall, half-pulled her to him. Her back braced her balance there, while he tucked her by the buttocks into his hips so severely she would have gone over backward without something solid behind her. She slid her fingers up and into his hair, cupping the base of his skull, clinging for a moment. Oh, yes. From here, she let her hands slide all over him, as if making sure every piece of him was still exactly as she'd last known it.

They kissed like this, touching each other everywhere in their dark corner of the hallway, while dishes clatters and feet padded somewhere beyond—their lunch being cleaned up.

In the end, it wasn't even a matter for discussion. James backed off. He stared into her face, inches away, frowning, examining her intentions. He must have seen them, for he abruptly let go and marched down the hall.

In a quick speech, he sent all the servants away with three days' pay and the understanding that they

would return on the fourth to clean everything up.
Afterward, he and Coco went upstairs to another
breezy, cool room, her bedroom—or rather, the music room. It had been her split-second choice when
she'd arrived, the most distant room from Phillip's
that still had a bed—though, in this case, a small
daybed.

Thus from one end to the other of the large music
room that faced out toward another wide terrace
with another idyllic view, James and Coco scattered
each other's clothes. He hung her corset on a small
harp in the corner, her chemise on the piano stool,
her stockings on a music stand. His trousers, braces
still attached, lay eventually over the foot rail of the
daybed. His shirt was thrown on the floor. His gentleman's combination swayed from a terrace door
handle. While Coco and James themselves ended up
on the terrace balcony, making love in the sun on
the cushions of an iron loveseat: James sitting, leaning back, Coco astride him, naked, hands gripping
his shoulders, her body arching as he lifted her by
the buttocks.

He entered her, uttering a delicious love-muddle
of words. ''Oh, Coco, I adore you I love you can
you arch forward till *oophhh* yes the nipples of your
breasts touch my chest yes there there am I doing
this *oophhh* too hard *oophhh* I've missed you
oophhh I love *oophhh* I *oophhh* oh God need
you . . .''

She wanted to laugh. She wanted to shout for joy.
She smiled down into his face as her body rose
toward climax. Oh, this is worth it, she thought. I
won't regret a minute of it. She held his face in her
palms, watching his amber wolf-eyes, fixed on her,

focused, unflinching, as direct and warm as the sun on her back. It became a kind of game, staring into these eyes as she felt his fingers dig into her backside; he parted her buttock slightly as he lifted and drove into her. They joined, riveted to each other's gazes.

And, oh, the pleasure. The deep, warm pleasure of James. James, whose face she caressed, James's smooth cheekbones, perfect under her fingers; James's jawbone hard against the pad of her palm, the skin of his jaw gritty, the friction of a recent shave of a stiff-growing beard.

He watched her reactions, penetrating her body with what became sharp, hard spasms. His eyes never strayed from hers as he tightened his grip on her, as the muscles of his shoulder hardened, bunching up under her hands ... as, lower, her body opened, welcomed the thrust of his hips, shuddered with the pleasure of his strong, rigid member, the strength in his driving buttocks.

She let go before he did. Her vision blurred. She no longer saw him as she called out, giving herself up to shivers that quickly amplified into pulsing contractions, pleasure beyond thought or control. She became aware of only the most basic throbs of stimulus. James pulling her against him with sudden force ... James kissing her mouth violently ... the two of them careening over an edge into someplace else ... a place where, for an instant, they were no longer separate, but rather united in sensation ... one mind, one body, one glowing moment so strong it seemed capable of briefly alloying souls.

* * *

In the middle of the night as Coco lay draped over James, half asleep, he murmured into her hair, "Coco?"

"Hmm."

"Are you awake?"

She muttered softly, laughing, "All right, I can be awake, if you want."

When he said nothing immediately for several seconds, she pushed back from his chest and tried to find his face in her own shadow on the pillow. "What?" she asked.

"Well, I'm half afraid to broach the question, but—" He paused, then broached it: "Does today mean you're not going to marry Phillip?"

She knocked him lightly in the chest. "Oh, a nice thing to say after what we've done from one end of the house to the other."

"Right. Of course. I knew. Still, Phillip meant his offer, I think, and David would like it—"

"And I wouldn't. Oh, James, don't put too much stock in the drunken rambling of a middle-aged man whose life has come to a crossroads. I don't."

"Nonetheless, I think he'd do it."

She rolled off him onto her back, looking up into the dark. "My dear, if I had a ha'penny for every time Phillip Dunne had said he would make an honest woman of me, well, ha!" She laughed outright. "I *do* have a ha'penny for every time he's said it, and I'm a rich woman from it, I will tell you."

James wasn't comforted. He lifted up onto his elbow, rolling up onto his side. "He's asked before?"

Coco lay in his shadow up against him. "Certainly," she said. "Years ago, he offered regularly, at least once a month." She sighed. "I'd believe him. I'd wait at the house, while he was supposed to set things in motion. Then he would return saying Willy was not feeling well; now was a bad time to burden her. Or it was too close to the holidays; after the holidays he'd 'give her the bad news.' There was always a reason. For two years I waited in England. For five or six years more, he visited in Paris, saying much the same thing. But no matter what he said, he kept having babies with Willy. I was slow, but eventually caught on: if I wanted holidays and any sort of regular care and attention myself, I had to make my life elsewhere. So I did."

Realizing that James might take the story as a threat, an ultimatum—and, above all, not wanting to hear any excuses why he couldn't marry her— Coco said quickly, "And now, of course, marriage is ridiculous."

"Ridiculous?"

"Certainly. I've grown used to an independent life. I don't ask anyone's leave to do anything. Moreover, I could never turn my property and fortunes over to someone else. No, thank you. I've raised my child, given him a name. There is nothing to motivate me ever to marry again."

James's silhouette nodded, but he said nothing.

Coco worried she had overstated her case. What if he were thinking he'd *like* to marry her? Would she like to marry him? She loved him, there was no doubt. Then she had to sigh. "Oh, my poor tarnished knight. What am I doing to you?"

He let out a surprised laugh. "Nothing."

She wished it were true. She willed it to be true. She said a little bleakly, "We're going to lie, aren't we? I mean, you weren't thinking you *wanted* to marry me, were you?''

''Hmm?'' His voice in the dark had become distant, as if he were lost in thought.

''Were you thinking we should marry?''

He didn't answer for a moment, then, a man called rudely back to earth, he mumbled out, ''Um, ah, I wasn't—I—''

She cut in quickly. ''That's fine. I just wanted to know in which direction we were going to compromise you. So,'' she said, ''we'll be surreptitious, live one way, act as if we live another. We'll trade a little piece of your honesty for our time together.''

He snorted. ''My honesty, my God. As if it were so shining.'' He jostled her good-naturedly. ''Come now, you can't think a man gets to the ripe old age of twenty-nine without having told a tale or two.''

''You never lie. You told me so.''

''I was lying when I said that. I tell huge lies. I once told my mother I was down the street, when in fact I'd taken the train to London, spent the day there. I was eight.'' He laughed.

Coco wanted to cry. *This* was James's idea of a falsehood. A lie to his mother regarding his whereabouts when he was a child. And he still carried it with him, remembered doing it, because in his mind it was noteworthy. ''Oh, dear,'' she murmured.

Defensively, he insisted, ''Coco, I can tell lies with the best of them.''

Tell them, yes, but could he live one? ''Fine,'' she said. So an illicit love affair was what it would be.

As decisions went, it couldn't have been too bad

a one, she reasoned later, because they certainly took to it with enthusiasm.

They spent the next three days glutting on fruit, leftover game hens, some salt cod they found in the kitchen, and each other. It was an existence so lovely for Coco, it seemed more magic than reality. They ate, drank wine, laughed, talked, and made love. They swam at night naked in the cold Mediterranean till their teeth chattered. They snuggled under a blanket till they were as cozy as puppies piled up by the hearth. They went to bed late, then slept past noon, entwined.

Three magic days. They became the most ridiculously happy ones Coco could remember living in the entirety of her life. Perfect days, or almost. Because, in the back of her mind, she had begun to count them. Three magic days, four, five. . . . How long would they last? In reality, she told herself, there were no forevers. *Happily ever after* was a phrase strictly out of fairy tales.

Chapter 18

❦❦

"How are we going to manage this?" Coco asked, as she watched James dress on the morning of the fourth day. The servants were due in at noon. His train left at two-twenty-five, taking him back toward the Channel, then another train to Cambridge where he had to be day after tomorrow for congregation and commencement.

"I don't know," he said distractedly. He was re-buttoning the fly of his trousers. Talking about departures and train schedules, he'd buttoned it wrong on the first attempt.

She lay back on the bed, watching his agitation, full of sympathy for it, but uncertain how to put him at ease.

She might have told him that the standard way now was for him to buy her a house . . . oh, in Ely or Royston, somewhere near him though not so near as to be obvious, to establish her there. Except that she was loathe to think of herself and James as "standard"—and neither did she want to be the one who defined where they departed from the usual expectation. This left her silenced, unsure of herself in a way to which she was unaccustomed.

His fly still gaping by two buttons, James stopped and pushed his hands back through his hair. "You should come with me," he said.

She laughed. "Ah, my dear, the first rule of illicit goings-on: We don't arrive together. And I most definitely don't move into an all men's college with you. People would catch on to us right away if we did that."

He looked at her. "Coco, I need you." He blinked, frowned, searching for words, then said with utter sincerity, "I can't be happy without you near me."

Sentiments like this one, out of James's mouth, stopped her cold. With anyone else, she would have made fun of the romantic idiocy of it. But with him, the way his eyes fixed on her, something softened inside; the core of her chest grew warm, liquid. So instead of bringing him back to earth as she should have, she smiled foolishly over the bed's foot rail and said, "I'll buy this house. We can stay here." She laughed so he would know she meant it as a joke.

He didn't move. His hands remained upon his head, elbows in the air, his hair askew, while he simply looked at her. As if he might really be mulling the idea over.

Not likely, she thought. Yet what a picture: the captain of the cricket team. Or, no, James didn't care for cricket, she'd discovered: a rower, a crew member of a victorious eight in the Mays, the Bumps race, the Head of the River, an All Souls fellow with double firsts to his credit, exuding all the fresh-faced, creamy English charm of a Canta-brigian—while standing there with his fly partly open, his trouser braces dangling at his knees, the shirttail of his generous bespoke shirt hanging out of his tweedy, well-tailored trousers—seduced, un-done, contemplating throwing over his upperclass friends and future for the sake of his shady lady love. An outrageous image that he manifested ex-tremely well with his bewildered expression, his blond hair disheveled, and his clothes askew; his handsome self in disarray, looking besieged and overwhelmed.

Coco stared, though in the end had to avert her eyes. She picked up his vest where it lay on the bed beside her. Light summer worsted, heavier on one side for a watch in its pocket. "Here," she said, holding out the waistcoat. "You're going to miss your train."

James took the vest. As he slipped it on, he said, "If we bought this house"—she blinked up at him—"or one like it here, I'd still hardly ever be able to get to it. Between terms perhaps. For longer during the summer." He threw her a frustrated frown. "Coco, I want you with me. I want my life to include you in a regular way."

Oh, yes. Oh, no; if only she could have kept the voice inside her from cheering every time he said things like this. Coco pulled the sheet around her hips for modesty. All right, she thought, was buying a house here all that crazy? Why not? "Don't go back to Cambridge. Let me buy the house. Truly. Stay here."

She caught a glimpse of his expression, a frown that furrowed into a quick scowl, then he bent away.

On one knee as he looked under the bed, he asked, "Have you seen my shoes?"

"Under the piano. Oh, James, really: stay here. Don't go back." It seemed like such a bright idea all at once. "There are good universities in France. Apply to one."

"I don't speak French." He threw her an impatient look over the edge of the bed. "Nor do I speak Italian. I'm English. Besides"—he dragged his shoes from under the piano—"*you* heard Phillip. I can go back to Cambridge"—he balanced, pulling on one short boot, then the other—"do the most interesting work of my life, and do it all honorably in a way that is good for everyone."

"And there's your earldom to consider, which should be right around the corner now, yes?"

He shrugged, a not entirely honest gesture. The honor mattered to him, she was sure, not to mention the property that undoubtedly went with it. Scholars did not in general grow rich, but James Stoker would.

Coco picked up her dressing gown from the bed and slid it onto her arms as she stood. She used it as a kind of curtain to hide the childish plummet of disappointment she felt. Genuinely childish. One didn't ask a lover to give up such fine earthly rewards. Of course, he should have his earldom, the satisfaction and prestige of work well done.

As she tied the gown, another idea occurred to her. "Well, I'll buy a house near Cambridge, a house like this one."

James grimaced over his own arm as he stuck it into the sleeve of his suit coat. "Of course, it would have to be very, very tall to get as good a view of the Mediterranean.'' He was saying they shouldn't try to find again exactly what they'd had here.

"All right, a little English cottage. Some roses in front, some honeysuckle in back over an arching trellis.'' She laughed. "Maybe a little tributary with moorhens and coots. Or a pond with a swan.'' She was being silly, trying to make him laugh.

He paused long enough for a labored smile. But he was thinking about it; he didn't dismiss the idea outright.

Coco's spirits took wing. Yes. The idea grew in her imagination. She said, "We could find a place in the countryside. A sweet little place of our own close enough for you to ride to it, for me to take the train from London. I could stay a week here and there, sometimes just for the weekend. You could drive to it after your last lecture or meeting.'' Oh, yes. She said brightly, "You could even arrange your schedule so you have Fridays or Mondays free and—''

"Coco, I couldn't do that. I can't take off days and days from my work and still make adequate progress.''

"Well, we could find a house that was at least close enough so you could come for dinner, spend the night occasionally midweek.'' She teased, "You eat dinner, don't you?''

"Sometimes.''

He was serious. Sometimes his work kept him from eating a regular meal. She frowned.

He added quickly, "But it's still a good plan. The best either of us has come up with.'' He reached toward her, took her hands, and drew her to him. "And we'll buy it together,'' he added. "We'll neither one keep the other. It will belong to both of us. Our own cottage retreat out somewhere so remote no one will know, no one can bother us.''

A hideaway in the English countryside wasn't a perfect solution, but what else could they do? ''Yes. Our own private place. It will be the sweetest house. An oasis.''

He smiled back. ''Absolutely. It's what we'll do. Can you come up in three days, after Commencement, to start looking?''

''Yes.'' She laughed—laughter that started out light, sophisticated, vaguely cynical that became a hard, full-bellied cackle. A guffaw of delight.

Coco took the train back to San Remo that afternoon, where she closed up her house. She would stay in London till she and James had made their arrangements. She, the cook, and Lucia sealed up rooms and covered furniture with Coco humming to herself, daydreaming of England again. England, lovely, green England. Why had she ever thought Italy was prettier?

She boarded the train again the next day, in high spirits as she headed north. Her plans were to not even stop in London for the time being; she went straight to Cambridge. She'd stay with David, provided the honey was cleaned up. She'd find a hotel or another boardinghouse, if not. Lucia would stop in London and take care of opening the house there, making it habitable and comfortable again. Coco would go back and forth as need be.

She arrived in Cambridge only two days behind James, where she hired a carriage and headed toward her boardinghouse between the university town and Grantchester. It was a glorious ride. Cambridgeshire was in the full, summer flower of early June; beautiful. David was waiting for her when she arrived. He waved from a second-story window.

Coco stepped out of the hired carriage, waving at him overhead. The sun was high and warm, the sky was a bright, cloudless blue. What a day, she thought.

She didn't even see Phillip till he was lifting her bag from the boot.

An hour earlier, while Coco was still on the train clattering along toward Cambridge, James had walked into his rooms at All Souls, glanced at his front parlor, then thought, Well, where the hell was Nowles, and why hadn't he put away the books James had used last night?

It took a moment more for James to understand what had happened. He frowned as he set down a case of rocks he'd been carrying. He hadn't used so many books as all that, he thought. And Nowles had cleaned them up, hadn't he? Were these there this morning? It was such a mess that James himself began to pick them up.

Indeed, books lay everywhere. Books and papers. And Nowles had nothing to do with the matter. James's rooms had been ransacked. As if someone had gone through every bookcase, looking for something. The drawers to James's desk at the back of the room gaped open. Everything on his desktop was in a chaos other than his own making; he didn't recognize the order. The place was upside down.

"Ah. There you are."

James startled, then turned.

His legs crossed, a book in his lap, Phillip Dunne sat on James's sofa. He sat at an arm, where James himself usually sat while instructing and occasionally grilling undergraduates in geology during a supervision.

In Phillip's lap lay James's African journal.

James scowled at the book. "Yes. Here I am. And here *you* are. Who the hell did this?" He looked at the mess again, waiting as if Phillip might have a reasonable explanation.

Phillip cleared his throat, a small *ahem*. "I did, actually." Before James could demand to know why, the Vice-Chancellor raised one eyebrow, a superior arch that challenged James to say differently. "I needed to read your journal. You said I could, so I helped myself."

"Yes, but I rather thought you'd ask for it politely. Then I'd get it for you." James allowed himself to cast his eyes around the office again. "My God, Phillip," was all he could say. His file cabinet was dumped out onto the floor. Next to this scatter of paper lay his records of examinations, his supervision appointments, his lecture notes for next week.

There was more here than a simple search for some travel notes.

"Why did you do this?" he asked.

"Athers."

"That's a bit of a stretch, Phillip. You turned the room inside out, not Nigel."

Phillip defended quickly, "He wants these." He tapped the tattered binding in his lap. "He's rabid, James. It's the gold." He cleared his throat again. "I've been told we'll be facing a court demand by the end of the week for your journal, logs, every last piece of bumfodder involved with the expedition. It will be served on you, and you'll have no choice but to hand these all over. I needed to see what they said.'' He paused, then added, ''James, he's claiming you helped your fellow expedition members along to their deaths, that you have gold tucked away of your own, that you did a heinous thing for gold and glory.''

James didn't know what to say for a moment. He frowned. ''Then you're here to try to decide if there is merit to the accusation? To decide if I would murder a hundred and forty-seven of my friends and colleagues?'' He felt compelled to add, ''I didn't, you know. Nor can I believe anyone, let alone you, would think I could.''

Phillip shook his head. ''I know, I know. It's terrible. I don't believe you would hurt anyone, not intentionally.''

Whatever that meant; small relief. ''Phillip, you can't be so frightened of the truth here. We have to stand on what we know and on our righteous indignation if anyone, Nigel or otherwise, says differently. We can appeal to the Crown—''

''And the first thing it would want is to have a look at your African notes.''

''Fine.''

''Not fine. James, James, James.'' Phillip stood, clucking his tongue, shaking his head wistfully, as if speaking to a dull child. He sighed. ''I've glanced through them, old boy.'' His eyes became direct. He blew air out through his compressed lips, before he said, ''There are things here''—he held up papers, loose pages he had come away with in his hand—"that make you look bad: concocting poison with the natives, maunderings about England and your Englishness. Can't have it. Can't have my man looking—well, like he's running with the lost boys, spearing things, playing savage."

Ah. James began to understand his crime.

"Nigel is right to want these," Phillip continued, "if he means to impugn you. These make you look bad. Can't have it, James." He paused before he said, with no give, no latitude for negotiation, "I want them now. I'm taking them. I'm going to hide them, bury them, if I have to."

James took the words as they were no doubt meant: as a veiled threat to disavow him, to hand him over—to *help* Athers—if he didn't do as he was told. He would look jolly English and valiant, or he would be labeled suspect, a traitor. Investigated as a fraud and possibly a murderer.

James went to the sofa where Phillip had left the rest of his journal. He closed the rest of his notes into their rotting binder, making neat his poor, loose, vulnerable pages. He had to use both hands to hold them all intact; Phillip had not been kind to them. James slid the bundle to him so he could redo the ties; he tied up Africa: his two years with his friends, his year and a half alone, the only Englishman, only white man to be found in a hundred miles or more, the whole experience tied together with string. He lifted it up, offering the slightly neater package to Phillip.

It was actually, physically hard to let it go as Phillip took it.

A span of silence opened as the two men faced each other.

Then Phillip asked, "Are you sleeping with her?"

"What?"

"Coco. Kelnicker said he saw you coming out of Tolly's a month ago with a black-haired woman. Tuttleworth thinks you fancy her. And I keep remembering your bolting from the table the night I asked her to marry me." With hardly a pause, he added, "I could if I wanted to, you know. I hardly give a damn anymore. I mean, I'll do my best, but if I go under, I go under. But you—" He let the thought linger, unfinished. "Are you?" he asked again. Then couldn't resist saying, "It would be so stupid, you know, for a man with your ambitions."

James blinked, staring at Phillip. He could hardly believe he was hearing these words from a man who for years had conducted a clandestine affair with the same woman, an affair so well managed that no one had even suspected, not even James. Phillip's righteous posture didn't make James feel angry so much as worn, frayed at the edges. He said wearily, "Right. No, I'm not her lover." What did Phillip expect? Honesty, for godssake?

Phillip nodded. He believed him. Well Phillip should: James had never lied to him before.

Lying here was of course the right thing to do. Yet it felt strange doing so—sad, oddly destructive. Like striking a flint to dry grass, dead grass, watching it ignite. The expedient of the lie admitted their friendship was over. Or a piece of it, anyway. And like a grass fire, James feared, once the pretense began, it would be all but impossible to contain.

Chapter 19

~~~⌒⊙C~~~

"**W**-why are you here?" Coco managed to say, as Phillip took her bag from the carriage.

"Just dropped in on David," Phillip explained. "I'm seeing a lot of him, and I can't tell you how much I enjoy his company, Coco. You did a damn fine job with our son."

"Th-thank you." She frowned as she followed him inside.

Despite his reputed bad back, he carried her heavy bag with a bounce to his step. He dumped it at the foot of the stairs, and immediately turning around, said, "We can get that upstairs later. Come have tea with me, will you?"

"I—ah—"

"Only for a minute. David and I are off to the cricket match." He wiggled his eyebrows with enthusiasm. "Front row seats in the pavilion at Fenner's." He took her elbow.

Coco found herself being guided into the boardinghouse's small eating common. Several young men held down a table by the unlit fireplace, stragglers from elevenses tea. Phillip waved at them, calling them by name while he escorted her toward the interior pass-through window that opened into the kitchen. There, he ordered them both tea, then leaned on the counter, waiting for it.

He purely beamed at her for several seconds, before he said, "I've been dying to talk to you. Been thinking of you."

Coco tried to be positive, supportive of an old friend who'd recently lost his wife. Though she couldn't say that Phillip looked bereaved. In fact, he seemed in fine feather, able to take some of the old pleasure in life she remembered.

Then he added, "You and me and David."

She was set back by the juxtaposition, but was determined, in the short amount of time before his cricket game, not to nitpick her way into an argument. Besides, why begrudge a new widower his good spirit?

David, she told herself. David was making him happier. Or a combination of David and the weight of Wilhelmina Dunne lifted finally from her husband's shoulders. David had helped Phillip with the funeral arrangements. Lady Dunne had been buried in London four days ago. Whatever sort of grieving Phillip was doing, he was doing it while putting a very good face to the world.

He shifted on his feet, toward her slightly, saying, "You know, I've been thinking. He shouldn't be David Wild. He should be David Dunne. He *is* David Dunne. Always has been. And if you and I got together, no one would even think twice—"

"Whatever you and David want to do, do it. But leave me out of it." Coco tried not to sound as annoyed and severe as she was beginning to feel. "So far as I'm concerned," she said, "Horace is David's legal father today, just as he was when David was six."

"Except that he wasn't. And isn't. Some things should be set right, Coco—"

"And some things can't be." She held his eyes a moment, pressed her lips, then gave up. Pointless. She had never won a dispute with Phillip. He always thought he knew all the answers.

Nonetheless, he stood quietly for a moment, leaning on the counter till a tray bumped his elbow. He jumped, then took it. He carried their tea and accoutrements to a table with Coco following, with Coco wishing she were somewhere, anywhere else.

He set the tray down, pulled out a chair for her. As he set her chair in from behind her, he leaned over her shoulder and murmured, "No matter what you think, no matter how late I am with it, I want to square myself with David. Let me sign the papers."

She glanced up at him as he came round the table. "What papers?"

He sat. "I want to admit in writing that I am David's father."

"Well, do so, then."

"No, the official papers. I want my name amended to his birth certificate. I want the Home Secretary notified."

"Horace's name is already on the birth certificate."

"He lied." He clattered the teapot onto the table with a blithe *thunk*. As if aligning himself with the truth at this late date was a great asset.

Coco tilted her head, contemplating him with a narrow look. "Yes, happily, he did," she said. "Horace was willing to lie for us, when you weren't willing to tell the truth. He gave David a name."

"The wrong one. Which I now wish to fix. And it isn't up to David. *You* have to say I'm the one."

"I won't do that to Horace."

"Horace is dead."

Coco let out a snort. "Yes, he is. For almost three years now. But it's another death, isn't it, that's making it suddenly convenient to be David's father?" She lost all patience. "I'm sorry, Phillip. Put it in writing for David, if you like, but he knows you're his father. You don't need to do more. Meanwhile, live with what's left. I'm not unwinding anything so as to tidy up your loose ends." She leaned forward slightly, lowering her voice and spoke in a vehement tone. "Leave me out of your plans. Stop inviting me, waylaying me. David wants your attention. I don't."

She scooted back, about to stand, to leave, but Phillip stopped her by reaching across the table.

He lay his hand over her arm, a gesture of restraint without any force. "All right," he said. "I deserve no less. I'm sorry. Don't go." He faced her with a contrite expression—yet it was indulgent, too, solicitous in a way that was not flattering. He said, "I can see you're still angry with me two decades later."

She heaved a breath. "Oh, Phillip, honestly. Get this through your head: I'm not angry. I'm not anything with you—not anything but finished. Over. Done with. I've moved on."

"Yes, yes, I have too, of course. You don't need to worry about me."

As if she would. "Good," she said.

"I'm back in the game," he continued. He smiled slightly, though she could only see part of his face. He'd glanced away, watching the doorway, perhaps; watching across the room to see who was coming and going in the hallway.

"Good," she said again. She scooted forward on her chair, reaching for the sugar. In an effort to put the conversation back on a friendly tenor, she added, "And with first-rate seats at Fenner's, too." A cricket match always put him in good humor. She calmed herself by spooning sugar into her tea, one scoop, two. Where was David? When did they leave for this blast-and-damn cricket match?

Phillip muttered, "Yes, good seats at Fenner's. But that wasn't the game I was talking about. My term as Vice-Chancellor is over in the autumn. There was mention of a cabinet position for me."

"Well, good for you," Coco said genuinely. "That's lovely." To be a queen's minister was something he'd always wanted.

"Was," he repeated. "But I hear now that they're favoring a certain young knight instead."

Oh, dear. James.

"And the Royal Geographical Society wants him on their board of advisors, which makes me sick to my stomach since I gave up that board so as to compete for the presidency of the society next spring, but Ranshaw took early leave. Kilmoore, the vice-president, stepped in, and he won't leave for years. So I have nothing there. You see," he smiled, "I could marry you easily. I have nothing to lose."

His face grew stern. Rigid, in fact. "Unlike that bastard Stoker, who is not so slowly collecting everything I ever wanted. The Queen intends to make him an earl, did you hear that? I suggested a title, and Her Majesty suggested one higher than my own. Can you believe? The son of my old coachman, going into dinner ahead of me?" He scowled, then raised one smug eyebrow. "But that's the game I'm in again. He won't get any of this, because I have taken care of him. God, what a burr in my side he's become."

"Pardon?" Coco stopped, halting her spoon in mid-motion on the gritty bottom of her teacup.

"Nigel is right. James is as daft as a loon. And his own African journal hangs him out to dry." He tested a quick, triumphant smile on her.

Coco wet her lips, cleared her throat. "Phillip, I don't think you have something quite straight." Her heart began to pound strangely, noticeably so that she wanted to put her hand over it. She didn't. Instead she shook her head tolerantly, making small, slow circles with her spoon in the cup. "James is—"

"A liar and a possible murderer. His notes admit as much."

"Excuse me?"

"His African journal."

"You've read it, then?"

"Yes. He betrayed us, Coco."

"Us?"

"England."

She blinked, stared at him. The urge to shove from the table, to get up and leave again, was there. She restrained herself. Her heart kicked with sudden vigor in her chest. Her blood leaped through her veins in surges she could feel at her wrists, at her neck.

James would arrive momentarily, she realized. Why had they agreed to meet here? It seemed stupid now. She and James had debated how much to hide their affair from those closest to them. But neither of them had anticipated Phillip's being a familiar of the place. Even David she had imagined would be at the library or the chemistry lab most of the time. Yet here she was, trying to figure out how to keep everyone from colliding with full knowledge of hers and James's affair. While trying to figure out just what Phillip was on about.

It had been a long time since she had coddled a man along in earnest. She didn't do it anymore. But she attempted to remember how. She smiled with interest, saying, "He won't just let you take his notes, you know."

"He has already." Phillip raised his brow and smiled broadly. "And I left him with three star atlases. I don't think I'll have to play him along very far before he gives me the exact area of the gold. Then he's gone. He'll be lucky to escape jail once we're through with him."

"Jail?" Her breath lurched in her lungs, while she tried to smile outwardly with wonder and appreciation.

Phillip leaned closer. Coco knew what was coming and smiled with utter sincerity at this point: years ago, Phillip had enjoyed confiding his shenanigans to her. It was a matter pride with him, wanting someone to know that certain incidental events hadn't just occurred, but rather had been masterminded.

He raised his finger, waving it back and forth in mock sternness. "It's all very murky, you see. His notes. He made poisons with those people. Poisons strong enough to kill regiments of Englishmen."

"Really?" she said.

"Really. He's as good as out." Phillip looked pleased to announce this. Then wonder and delight passed across his features. "But wait. He tells you things, too, doesn't he? Like the day on the balcony in France. He said everything right in front of you. Ha!" He laughed. Phillip tilted his head sideways, studying her. "What *are* the two of you to each other? He says you're not lovers. Are you?"

This part was long-practiced and easy to do. Coco kept her face fixed. Other than the faint remnants of her smile, she met his question deadpan, without a word or indication one way or another.

He laughed harder, a man who'd expected as much. "Tight-lipped Coco," he said. "We could always count on your silence. No one keeps a secret like the Queen of Pillow Diplomacy." As his laughter died, he sent her a gleam, a kind of rictus really. "So would you like to know more? A little peek as to how?"

She raised her brow.

He asked, "You wouldn't tell him, would you?"

Again she gave him a look of stoney evenness. In all her years, the "Queen of Pillow Diplomacy" had never told one man another's secret. He knew she hadn't. He'd counted on it at one point.

He and Nigel had known about each other. They had each told her things they shouldn't have. There had been a kind of intimacy that had come from the fact. She had become an odd connection between the two men, part of their rivalry, wherein they both told—and knew they each did—like two chess masters confiding blow-by-blow to a third party whom they tried to impress with their grander, bolder, clever strategies.

So there was an old pattern at work when Phillip said, "His pages talk a lot about his friends the Wakua. As if they were just like us, Coco. When they're not. They're simple-minded and dirty. He dusted himself in ash, you know, to be like them— naked but for ashes. He hunted with them, learned their customs, acted like them." He made a sound down his nose, a grunt. "Protect them indeed. Honestly. Protect those black-skinned bastards from what, I ask you? From English gentlemen, scientists, and missionaries? Quite the opposite, I should think. We need the protection. Cannibals, the lot of them, you know. As soon eat you as look at you. I read it in his journal."

Phillip eyed her a moment, as if to see if he had her coming along with him. Apparently she wasn't as good at pretending to be sympathetic as she used to be. Because he sat back, his face bluff. His expression said, Hang her and anyone else who didn't agree with him; full tilt ahead. He blustered, "Add to this the fact that he took the Bible Fund."

Coco blinked. She couldn't have heard correctly. "Now, wait one—"

"There's no use defending him. He did it. Your sterling young knight embezzled twenty-eight quid. On top of everything else, he's a small-time, petty swindler."

Twenty-eight quid was more than many Englishmen saw in a year of wages. Though, granted, to Phillip it would seem very little. Still, her mouth remained open; no words would come out. She was purely dumbstruck.

He leaned toward her across the table, defending against what he took to be her reservations. "Coco. He's developed his own point of view, his own side. I can't let him get away with it. If I don't level him, he'll level me." He pushed his lower lip out and scowled in a way that asked for sympathy. "You know, his returning as he did wasn't exactly ideal for me."

"What do you mean?"

"Well—" He started to say something, then stopped himself. He chose to say instead, "Let's just say I had my plans made in one direction, then he came back and I had to reorganize rather quickly and seriously."

"Phillip, you are sounding, well, almost larcenous. You're alarming me."

He sat back, waving her alarm away. "Look, I'm going to make some sort of excuse for Stoker regarding the Bible Fund. It's a pittance. But I want him out of the way for a while. Athers has all but accused James of wrongdoing in the deaths of his friends, suggested events didn't happen quite as our James has said. And James's journal is an indictment: he went native, his sympathies converted. He made poisons. Our people died. He gained fame by bringing home a king's ransom of gold that his friends gave him for helping to kill everyone, gold he can replace by simply going back. What a story.

It has everything. Treachery, tragedy; greed and glory.''

"Everything but plausibility. Phillip, I don't think James's journal says these things.''

"Ah, but they do." He smiled. Their old game: Coco's playing devil's advocate, so he could show how clever he was. He leaned toward her again, confiding, sotto voce, "After about the first year and a half, James's notes aren't dated. He lost track of the day, the year; he just wrote. It will be a fairly easy matter to slip these undated pages behind dated ones. It's quite amusing, actually, what a difference it makes to simply change the order of events.''

Coco was trying to smile, but she was open-mouthed. Her jaw wouldn't close.

Seeing her distress, perhaps, Phillip said reasonably, "Coco, my plan isn't to ruin him, just to clip his holier-than-thou wings a little, so I can proceed. Rest assured, I don't think the charges of murder will hold in the end. Who's to say? James was the only one there. But these charges will certainly cast some doubt and keep him occupied for a while, so I can go down and stake out my gold.''

Coco was completely dismayed. Phillip had never seemed so . . . venal. He'd always had money. She could make sense of nothing that he was telling her.

He was about to say something further, but he spotted someone at the door and suddenly stood.

From behind her, David's voice asked, "Are we going, then?''

"Right-o.'' Phillip pushed his chair in, looking across the table at Coco. "Well, I'm glad to see you again, my dear. And we should definitely have dinner some night. Sometime when you're free, let me know. I'll take you somewhere nice, someplace posh that suits you.''

She wanted to say no, but she didn't. She eyed James's former sponsor and friend, a man who had something more tucked up his sleeve for James. A very nasty something, something that involved Bible Funds and a sudden unexplained thirst for money.

In her silence, Phillip's face took on a slow, faint smile. ''Dinner then, sometime?''

She said nothing, but stared at Phillip, not taking her eyes from him; which was a kind of admission. She didn't say no this time.

David came around the table to kiss her cheek. ''Off to Fenner's. See you later.''

Coco said something perfunctory. Right, dear. Take care. See you later. Mostly, though, she was inside herself, trying to figure out what to do.

The first thing she thought was, She and James could never meet here. It wasn't nearly far enough away from Cambridge. Then, Well, at least they'd been lucky. James was running late.

Except there was only one road here, and Phillip and David would pass him on the roadway. James in his little open calèche.

The man and this very calèche trotted up the drive not five minutes later. Coco came to the front doorway as, with a soft *whoa*, James halted his bay. He looped the reins, then leaped down, smiling across the courtyard as he came toward her.

And, despite herself, her dismay was relieved. James charged her, his face radiant with pleasure. ''Ah, me loov'ly,'' he said, imitating an accent he did sometimes. His father's, she thought. He scooped her up, lifting her right off the ground, grabbing her up into his arms. He felt strong, sturdy; he made her feel slight, a piece of paper, a drawing of a woman. "Are we off, then, to look for sweet little cottages? I've heard of two without tenants, both within ten miles."

"And an agent in London responded to a wire I sent," she said. "If it's not one of your two, I have a third."

Laughing, he half-carried her to the carriage, lifting her, turning, kissing her. It made her dizzy. "Dear God, woman," he said between attacks, "it's been the two longest days of my life. I've missed you."

He lifted her up into the carriage. Strong, clever James. A remarkable fellow, she thought. He was fully capable of handling his own affairs. He had for years without her. Moreover, Phillip was a grandiose, transparent lunatic beside him. James could see what Phillip was about a mile off. She needn't worry for him. She leaned across as from the other side of the carriage he mounted the seat beside her. Before he could sit all the way down, she'd cupped the back of his hatless head, pulled his face to her, and kissed him soundly on the mouth.

He was caught off guard for only a moment, then accepted it, relished her forwardness. After which, he asked, "What was that for?"

"Because I wanted to. And for being so handsome and smart and just plain good, Dr. Stoker, Sir James, Knight of the Order of the Bath."

He picked up the reins, glancing sideways at her. As he clicked to the horse, his smile held both an ease and candor that were just right, just so; they matched a feeling inside her. He and she so easily fell in step, it seemed, as if they had always been lovers.

Always. What a concept! Coco felt daring even letting her mind form the word.

Chapter 20

In the Volsunga Saga *version, the beauty
is a strong and powerful daughter of
Odin who is put to sleep—made alone
and vulnerable because she helps a war-
rior who had been destined to die on the
battlefield.*

From the Preface to The Sleeping Beauty
DuJauc translation
Pease Press, London, 1877

The white, steep-roofed cottage had two gray
stone chimneys, one sprouting right in the
middle of the roof where two portions of it came
together, the other originating at the ground and
funneling up the center of an outside wall to become
a narrow cubic stack above the gable. Behind the
house was a weedy patch of dirt that had been a
vegetable garden, or so a scarecrow in the middle

of it attested, a whimsical figure at the end of whose one remaining arm was a glass mug, precariously full of rainwater, Her Majesty's seal on it assuring that it was exactly one imperial pint.

Coco stood at a split-rail fence, looking at this dollhouse of a cottage six miles from the nearest village and ten miles from Cambridge. The house was in need of only slight repair that James kept insisting he could do. "Nothing to it." The Renaissance man. He could mend roofs, replace glass panes in windows, and set in a new front step. He remarked three times in praise of the house's situation. It sat in the middle of its own twenty acres, English countryside spreading out in every direction without a hedgerow in sight, the land green, verdant, rolling, nothing but the occasional tree and a distant line of willows that marked the Granta River a mile off. James loved the house.

Coco hated it.

"Come inside," he said. "Inside it's lovely and in quite good shape."

It was, in fact, most suitable. The agent had given James the key. They were allowed to browse at their leisure. The front parlor was small but would be sunny in the morning. James suggested she do her sketching here. She could set her easel so it faced the window, put her drawers of papers, pencils, pens, and inks to the right. They could set up a little tea table to the side; he would bring her minted tea the way they made it in Morocco. He himself, if he brought work home, would do it with a cup coffee (the way the Dutch made it in South Africa) while reading in the chair beside her, or, if he needed to, take to the kitchen table. The kitchen was large and accommodating. There was only one bedroom, but it was spacious and it came with a large bed and wardrobe in place.

"It's perfect," James said.

"It's drafty in back. We would freeze in the winter."

James looked at her with an expression of mild concern, as if to say he had not known she could be so difficult. Well, now was a good time for him to find out, she thought. Difficult, snide, hard to please. And tense for no reason.

"Well, it is," Coco asserted.

As fine a distraction as James was, she couldn't quite let go of her conversation with Phillip. It left her edgy. Phillip, Phillip, Phillip. The stupid cottage reminded her of him. Of him and others. Other houses, other promises, other clandestine unions, the disrespectful intentions of men that these secret places had always implied. Little castles with a hundred years of thorns, places to lock her away, to put her to sleep until, princes that they were (and one or two had been, literally), they arrived and bestowed their kisses. Ha, she thought. Not anymore. Not for me.

Yet here she was. And she couldn't rise up on her own and walk away, because it was a simple fact: if James Stoker could be in her life, no matter how she had to arrange it, her life was better, warmer, more blessed for his presence in it. So stop this carping, she told herself. Stop resenting what cannot be changed or improved upon. And stop, above all else, wishing Sir Knight here would stand up and tell the world he loves you. Drawing fairy tales could be fun; believing in them, letting them define one's expectation, was purely dangerous.

She made herself enumerate the real and significant losses James could sustain, if he declared himself for her. If he damaged his place in the hierarchy at Cambridge, he would lose access to the best endowments and grants, the best equipment, and the immediate worldwide comradery of the best minds in his field. Moreover, the title he was about to acquire would not only add to his stature, it should add to his income, allowing him to pursue his vocation without worry for his needs and comforts for the rest of his life.

Coco watched her privileged, rising young star of a lover walk around the little house. He opened every window to look out from it, swinging sashes, sticking his head out, muttering things like, "Well, how quaint," or "How lovely."

Phillip, too, had loved the view from their hideaway, a field of cows, as she recalled. Phillip, who intended to "take care" of James, "keep him occupied." Which was none of her business. There was nothing she could do about it. She couldn't say; she never said. She dare not even mention it to James, for what was there to mention?

That Phillip was no longer his friend? James knew this. That Phillip believed he could cause James trouble with James's own journal? James could simply explain, couldn't he? Say it had been turned around? Sir James Stoker was believable. He would always write down the truth, kindly, compassionately, and the truth about what James Stoker thought would never condemn anyone, let alone the good Dr. Stoker himself. So what was there to report? Nothing. She would say nothing.

"Honestly," James said, as if she had only been joking so far, "what do you think of the place?" He turned toward her, his face asking her to please him, to let him have this little house because he liked it so well.

"I truly despise it. I'm sorry."

"Why?"

"It's paltry. It's thorny and closed off. I can't breathe here."

He looked amazed by her definite opinion. It was amazing of course, since it was based less on the house and more on the fact that Phillip would have liked it and that she didn't know what to do about Phillip.

"You can't breathe?" James laughed at her. "Well, that doesn't sound very good." He reached, tried to take her hand. She turned away. He ended up catching her by the waist, drawing her backward into his arms. "I suppose that means you don't want it then, right?"

"Right." She couldn't keep herself from going on a bit. She felt so discontent. "It's small and ugly. Limited. A narrow place. I want a larger house for us." I want the whole of the world.

Above her head, James sighed. "All right." His tone once more though was worried and puzzled. Then he took her hand, lifting her fingers over her shoulder, and kissed her knuckles, one by one. "What's wrong?" he asked.

"Nothing." She tried to pull her hand away.

He kissed the crook of her neck as she squirmed. "What?" he said. "What? Tell me."

She shook her head, trying to push away.

"Then I'll tell *you*," he said. "Everything's

right. We're together. We'll be together forever. And it makes me so happy to think so. I'll live anywhere with you. I'll sleep under the same roof as often as I can. And my work is going so very well.''

When she had nothing further to say, he filled up the silence. "I began day before yesterday with the samples and resource maps. It's exciting. I'm beginning to lay out the geology of an area of Africa never before charted. Meanwhile, Phillip and I have reached a truce of sorts. I glanced through a star atlas today, and I'm going to be able to keep him off my back. Oh, Coco.'' He tucked her up against him, resting his chin lightly on the crown of her head. "I've been drawing the night sky as I remember it from the time when I was lost—and I wasn't so lost! When I opened the atlas today, almost all the patterns in the southern skies that I remember were there. And they have names.'' He began to recite these softly, as if murmuring poetry into her hair: "Hydra, the sea serpent, Centaurus, Orion, Eridanus with its bright star, Archernar. These dovetail into familiar constellations low in the sky, Gemini, Taurus, Virgo. . . .''

He went on, so pleased with himself and these names, his spirits high while Coco's sank to a nadir. The Phillip she had spoken to an hour ago was not a man pacified by a truce, not of any sort. She asked, "You don't trust him, do you?''

"Who?''

"Phillip.''

"No.''

"Good.'' Then don't take him at face value, she thought. Don't imagine everything is going ''so very well'' or that you can "keep him off your back."

Coco clenched and unclenched her fists as James's recitation continued—more star names from his memory that ultimately degenerated into hums and mumbling kisses down the vertebra of her neck. She felt a shiver pass down her spine, part arousal, part horrible presentiment slithering over her. Phillip meant to destroy James somehow. He couldn't, of course. Not her James. Clever James.

So clever. Golden, shining. She wished she could show him off. Childish, but true. Silly. Jejune. Yet he was the finest man, and he was hers. She wished the world could know. He turned her around in his arms and went to kiss her mouth, and somehow it felt . . . harrowing. She struggled free.

"Coco, what? What for godssake is wrong?"

"Nothing."

"No, something is bothering you. Is it me?"

"No. Of course not."

She went to move away from him, but he took hold of her skirt. She gave up. She let him pull her to the bed, lay her down on it. The covers smelled musty. She let him lift clothes, move her around to where he seemed to want her. At one point, he stopped and said, "Could you be just a little less accommodating? You're making me feel as if I need to leave a ten pound note on the dresser when I'm finished."

She let out a small, insulted sound—"*Aahchh*"—and pounded her fists on his chest, a dual thump that reverberated into her arms. His chest was as solid as a brick wall.

She meant to hit him again, but he caught her

wrists, laughing. "There you go. You are alive, after all." He pinned her arms out, her legs open.

"Ah!" she called. "You have no respect for your elders."

"None at all." He reached between their bodies and cupped her through her skirts, then lifted fabric, pushing it out of the way. Till his hand touched silk knickers, nothing but thin silk between his hand and her body. He ran his nail lightly over the fabric, at the tenderest spot.

Her mind swam down into the sensation. Ho, Lord. She wet her lips, closed her eyes. *Ooh la la.*

He groaned softly in her ear and murmured, "Tell me, tell me. I'm going to do this forever until you do." He added, "Or as long as I can stand it. Ooh, Coco, you are so-o-o-o sweet here." He let out a rueful laugh. "I want you. Again. Some more."

Doing what he was doing forever might not have be so bad. It was fairly high on her list of divine pleasures. He was gentle, warm, sure. And so delicate, so precise. He knew exactly where to put his attention, not too hard, maddeningly right.

"Tell me," he murmured. "Tell me tell me tell me," chanting in a whisper. "Why are you—so—oh, God, you're going to kill me. You are so warm here and, well"—he made a kind of choking sound—"and, well, you're rather, um, wet. Ooh, just right."

Ready was the word. She was ready for him. "Now," she told him. "Now." Coco found herself trying to climb upward, wrap herself around him.

"Not now. Tell me first—"

"No. Now."

"What a demanding shrew—"

"An ogress," she said with a faint laugh. *"Now."*

James opened his trousers, while she fumbled at her drawers. A second later, he eased himself into her. Then the damn man held back. He held to a slow, irregular rhythm, pausing, torturing both of them, marking time while letting out grunts from effort. But waiting. He was going to try to maintain his game.

She thrust herself upward, hard against him, taking him by surprise. He caught his breath, exclaimed softly, convulsed. It was over moments later.

After which—perfectly absurd—Coco burst into tears. She could neither understand them nor stop them, and the more she fought them, the stronger they came.

She hadn't broken down like this since she was seventeen, since she had packed her bags, grabbed up her infant son, and left Phillip and London, the last place he'd tucked her away. She prided herself on the fact: she rarely cried. And when she did, it was a sniffle, a little weep, nothing more.

Till James. She sobbed like a baby as he stroked her hair and cooed to her. "There, there, it's all right," he said, bewildered now to the point of alarm. "We'll make love a thousand times more," he promised, "and every single time"—he let out a snort—"will be better than *that*. That wasn't very graceful, was it?" He laughed. "Of course, even graceless, it was good. Oh, sweet Coco, what is wrong?"

Tired, confused, at wits' end, she mimicked him.

"What's wrong, what's wrong," she repeated, then said: "What's wrong is I want to parade you down the street, show you to my sisters and my son and every friend or enemy I have ever made. What is wrong is that I think my own wish itself is silly and girlish and hysterical. I hate myself for wanting it, but I want it all the same. And I know the private part of us is perfect and is the most important thing. But I want the public part. I want, I want. . . ." And she cried some more.

"Aah," he said, and petted her head. Then she cried all the harder because he said, "Oh, sweet Coco, I wish I could. I will think on it. What can we do?"

Nothing. They could do nothing.

They dressed, ascended into his carriage, and dutifully went to look at the two other houses available to rent. James wasn't fond of either; Coco hated them both. The estate agent of the last one suggested another house for tomorrow. A larger more dignified home that "would require a servant or two."

At which point James winked at her and patted her hand. "We'll pay a cook and a gardener. They'll be our audience. We'll spoon and flirt in front of them, and they will tell the neighbors what lovebirds the Mr. and Mrs. James—let's see— Peach, a peach of a couple, the perfect couple. Oh, that James and Nicole Peach." He talked quickly, purposefully trying to entertain a laugh out of her. "No, Peach-Pitt," he said with a serious air. "Hyphenated, you see, because they're so posh. And he's Armand, not James. Arm, for short. Mr. and Mrs. Arm Peach-Pitt."

Coco laughed, taken aback by this unsuspected side to James's humor—a ridiculous side.

He continued, "Who never entertain because they are too wrapped up in each other. And you be Edith. It has a nice snobbish ring. More English than Nicole. Let's be English and proper. Edith Peach-Pitt. Dame Edith. She's been knighted, you see. You can wear my Order of the Bath from time to time. *Just* my Order of the Bath draped over you, nothing more. And I'll bring my oar from when I was Head of the River. Arm went to Cambridge and took a first in rowing—"

Coco chimed in. "Though he's as dumb as a wooden spoon. Oh, yes." She took to the game. "He was a fellow commoner, you know, one of those noble blokes who gets to eat at High Table because his family has a lot of money."

"Right. A rowing scholar and his dame for the servants to gossip over. In fact, if the house is nice enough, let's be a duke and duchess. . . ."

James's scenario went on. It became a lengthy joke as he and Coco rode along. Just as it would seem they had quieted into silence, one of them would think of something more to add.

They laughed and laughed, taking turns, revising, making up, trading around fictional pieces of themselves. They leaned, shoulder to shoulder, heads together. Coco laughed till tears ran down her cheeks.

A good distraction from really crying, this laughter James could wrench from her—he had from the first moment been so good at it, in all circumstances. And there was no doubt that she would have cried without this gift of his, for when they got near Grantchester, and she asked to be let off where no one could see her, she was indeed stabbed again by the pity of their predicament. She would have cried indeed, but didn't, because James's joke, his silly, inventive game said he understood so well.

Because it said her dear, sweet, hapless—helpless—lover wanted so badly to help what couldn't much be helped.

James thought it great fun, with Coco, to ridicule that to which he himself aspired. He would happily give up his dignity, if it would stop her from feeling bad. Moreover, he was happy to acknowledge that worldly success had its ludicrous side—not that its being ludicrous kept James from aspiring to it. Nor did he believe Coco wanted him to achieve less. Would she, he asked himself, be as interested in a coachman's son as she was in a muckety-muck at her beloved Cambridge (where she knew all about not just gyps and bedders, but of firsts and fellow-commoners and the wood spoons given out for "lasts")? He was a knight and scholar and soon to be more; would she want less?

He wouldn't.

James liked the idea of the earldom that he was within days of having. Yes, it seemed vaguely comic, if not raving mad, to make him a member of the nobility, but he nonetheless liked the idea of membership. He let himself imagine what it would be like. A little estate somewhere, not too grand, green and rolling, like the land around Cambridge or the little cottage. And maybe a butler. Yes, a butler would be nice.

Actually, a butler was unnecessary and a bit silly to contemplate, when Nowles alone sufficed perfectly. But it was slightly absurd to hang an oar with names on it on one's bedroom wall, yet James had one of those from his Bumping Race days, and James loved it.

Meanwhile, the next day, he enjoyed the surge of power and privilege (and private humor) that rushed through him when the estate agent addressed him, "*Sir* Armand"—it had been irresistible—"do you think Dame Edith will be much longer?"

"No, no. I'm sure she'll be right along shortly." He tapped his hat against his leg, pacing in the gravel drive as he waited for the mysteriously delayed Coco.

He and she had agreed to meet at the larger rental house that the agent wished to show them—Coco had been adamant they never meet at her boarding-house again. Something about not wanting to involve David. Her reason didn't matter; whatever she wanted that James could deliver was hers for the asking.

He had a bracelet for her in his pocket. A celebration present. He couldn't wait to give it to her, see it on her. He checked his watch. Yes, a tad late she was. Well, twenty-five minutes late, actually. A tad more than a tad. He cajoled the agent a little longer, then said finally, "You know, I think I'll just go see what's keeping her. She and I can meet you here at another time. When would be convenient?"

"I can wait, if you prefer." The owners of the house, Lord and Lady Somebody-or-Other, while traveling in Greece, had decided to live there. The agent was keen to see the house rented.

"Fine," James said. "I shouldn't be more than

half an hour. I expect she's just delayed at home.''

Rain broke through an overcast sky just as James pulled out into the main road. He didn't let the sprinkle stop him, however, from racing his little vehicle over the ever wetter roadway. He probably should have pulled over and put the top up on his carriage, when it became a thorough cloudburst, but he didn't do that either. And paid for it: the leather of his pride and joy grew blotchy, dark, and damp. When he finally stopped before Coco's boarding-house, water sloshed forward onto his feet in a small wave that rolled forward, then receded like an ebb tide over the floorboards.

It was a testament to how preoccupied he was that, soaking wet, he popped his umbrella before he hopped down from the carriage and picked his way through the downpour. Inside, he and his umbrella dripping puddles in the set stairway, James asked a young man in the common parlor if Mrs. Wild was in.

"Not presently. She left, let's see—" He consulted his watch. "About two hours ago."

Well. James stood there, perplexed; he scratched his head and wondered where to look next.

Point in fact, he decided to trot the extra mile or two back into Cambridge so he could change his clothes, get his mackintosh, and dry the carriage off. If this were all that was in his mind, though, he might have asked himself, why, then, was it that he drove right past his rooms at All Souls, where he could have found or done these things, and toward the house where Coco had once stayed?

It was just an inkling, a little jealous ping that he told himself he should put to rest, just a feeling that took him across town, then turned him round the corner of Chesterton onto Blayney Street, Phillip's street.

It was an intuition that, alas, paid off: for, lo, what he saw made him yank the reins. His horse whinnied in protest as wheels sloshed up rain in the street. Water slapped on the floor bottom, back and forth, then subsided into a gentle lap. All went quiet. All but for the patter of water hitting him, the seat, *ker-plunk*ing into the pool on the floor of his carriage, tapping on the stones of the street.

Everywhere rain. Everywhere but under Phillip's front overhang, under which stood a dry-as-you-please Coco Wild, her hand raised. She was hailing a hansom that had pulled to the curb in front of the house.

As James saw her get in, he gave a violent shake to the reins in his hands, with the sudden intension of cutting the vehicle off. James's own carriage, however, took a moment too long to gain momentum, and Coco, running late, apparently paid the driver to make up for lost time. The cab leaped forward as if banshees were after it.

James chased her tailwind all the way out of town. Had he tried, he realized, he might have caught up, might have pulled alongside. But in the end something perverse made him hold back, made him follow—where he could privately rehearse irate speeches. What was she up to? And Phillip? Why Phillip, of all people?

The rain had let up slightly by the time James followed Coco's cab up into the driveway of the appointed house—a mere hour and ten minutes late.

The agent was just closing the front door behind himself.

As Coco was paying the driver, James descended his carriage and yelled out the gentle words, "Have something important to say to Phillip, did we? So important you had to leave me stranded, worried, chasing after you?"

Startled, she spun around as the hansom rolled off. She was left standing alone in the drive, a light rain covering her.

James continued, walking toward her, wet gravel crunching underfoot with a kind of grating satisfaction. *Scrunch, scrunch, scrunch.* "What the hell were you doing at Phillip's? Did you decide to get engaged today after all?"

"I—I wasn't at Phillip's—"

"I saw you. Coco—" He paused, considered the wisdom of his words, then launched into them anyway. "Coco, I'm not accusing you of being promiscuous, but you are, well ... without false restraint. I have always liked that about you. But this—you can't slip off secretly to see Phillip without making me feel—" Livid. Ready to roar, hit someone, something. Jealous to the point of seeing goblins in his bed.

Her mouth twisted up, a sideways pucker. "You're accusing me of—"

"I'm accusing you of nothing. I'm only saying you have to help me with my—well, it's my problem. I'm uneasy with the fact that you've known a lot of secret arrangements." How many? he might have asked, for instance. How many men could she manage at once? What was her quota, the maximum that she'd juggled? And was she juggling now, for godssake?

Phillip. Anyone but Phillip. Phillip who took his journals and threatened to hand him over to Athers and a court of inquiry. Oh, the horrible thoughts that ran through James's mind as rain sprinkled down on him, the drive, and Coco.

He watched the feathers of her hat bead with rain, watched her face—she had the oddest combination of warring emotions on it, both angry and crestfallen. The brim of her hat protected her eyes, her unyielding, furious eyes, while the rain made her cheeks and chin wet as if someone had thrown water into her face.

Her back had grown rigid. She stood very straight, met his regard, staring him down.

The famous—the mythically infamous—Coco Wild, in her stylish hat and her dress from Worth, the epitome of a woman with a past . . . a past that could rise up before him in an instant, shared as it was with his archrivals, Phillip, a bishop, not to mention an admiral, emperors, kings. God knew who else. Her lovers were legion, legend, men higher, grander, more impressive than himself. A knight and a scholar. Ha, a nothing. If her lovers weren't worth a fortune, she wouldn't have them. They all gave her houses—wasn't that the gossip?

"Do you want this house?" he asked. Did he want her that much? Would he buy her if he had to? Was she worth it, if he could?

"Wh-what?" she asked. Under the brim of her hat, her eyes blinked. She hadn't regained her balance from his previous questions. She was angry, but she was also shaken, fearful.

He stepped toe to toe with her. "The house," he said. He jerked his head toward it. She glanced over her shoulder, then turned her back on him. She slowly rotated to see what he meant.

Like a figurine atop a music box. She walked a step toward the entrance, a petite woman in dark blue-green taffeta and black velvet. Coco Wild had always seemed to James somehow too small, too demure and well dressed to have such a roundly questionable ability to draw princes to her. *La Belle au bois dormant.* The Sleeping Beauty in the Woods. They came; they mired themselves in the thorny bramble of her reputation and her oddly potent power wielded from the bedchamber. Her forest slew some, while others fled with scrapes and scratches. Yet here she stood, looking more like a fairy than some lethal femme fatale.

She glanced back at him. "I'll go in and look at it. And James—" The sweet, innocent face of a wronged princess held his regard over her shoulder. "I was visiting my aunt. She was very attached to Lady Dunne. She's grieving; she couldn't stop crying this morning."

If it were possible for a man to shrink from six feet to an inch in a moment, to stand no taller than the toe of her shoe, James did so. He'd had no idea he'd thought these things: that his own imagination could conjure up apprehensions that were so powerfully real.

And wrong. "Oh, Coco, I'm so—" God, where to begin? What a mistake.

"Let's go inside," she said. She led the way.

James shoved his hand back into his wet hair and

followed. The estate agent, waiting at the door, stared at the two of them, fascinated.

James's face ran hot, cold. His head vaguely dizzy from what he'd just done, he went up the steps into a classical portico of Ionic columns. The front entrance was high, heavy double doors, artfully carved and polished.

Inside, the floors were marble; the twenty-foot ceiling was coffered. The house wasn't huge, but it was immediately fine at first glance. Well furnished, rich, well kept. Sixteen rooms, if James recalled correctly. He could afford to rent it for a while, though he couldn't afford to buy it.

Which might describe precisely what his limits were with Coco

He was quiet. What an error, he kept thinking regretfully. What a leap *that* conclusion had been.

But had it? His horrible misjudgment made him aware of his own fears. And perhaps reality. Why had he ever thought Coco could be happy with a man who subsisted off his Fellowship dividend, while praying for a permanently endowed chair? He needed the earldom, he thought. To compete with the princes and emperors and sultans.

A few feet in front of James, the agent chatted with Coco about the advantages of the modern venting in the parlor's fireplace, "forced air," or some such. James fell back and rubbed his temples.

He'd been standing to the side for some minutes, when Coco touched his arm. "It's all right," she said. "Besides, I *did* end up talking to Phillip. I rather went there thinking I would."

James snapped his head around to her, frowning, squinting. "You *what?*"

"Well, I *could* have been there just to visit my aunt. Why did you make such an awful assumption? And I was talking to Phillip, nothing more."

"Why?" His original anger rolled over with a kind of infuriated groan, not quite dead. It rose up, coming to life again like a wounded beast recovering with a stagger from a stunningly harsh blow. "What the hell were you talking to him about?" He made himself lower his voice, a vociferous hush. "And why the hell did you lie to me just now?"

"I didn't lie. Don't be angry. I went to see my aunt."

The agent stood just beyond in the next doorway, rapt, eagerly listening, trying to catch the gist of the argument.

James frowned and jerked his head. "Let's look at the blessed house."

She whispered at his shoulder, "You're taking everything wrong."

Fine. They walked behind the agent, while James tried to think how else to "take everything" as the man led them into a library-study.

The room was dark, a few books, a lot of crystal decanters full of amber liquids set out across a section of shelves, brandy and such. The estate agent went to the window and reached for the drapery pull.

Coco must have indicated somehow not to bother. The man put his arms down, leaving the room dark, though he looked uneasy. James, meanwhile, found himself absorbed with getting as close as he could to Coco so he could mutter down at the top of her hat, "So what am I *supposed* to think? If I'm not reacting properly, what is the right behavior here?"

She glanced up and around, her face appearing out from under the short brim. Her mouth had a troubled set to it. "James," she said. She made a sound—frustration, fretfulness—then nothing more. She followed the agent into a large dining room that gave way into a ballroom with two fireplaces, one at each end.

The house was absurd, James thought. It was for a couple, a family who had gatherings and friends in. Country balls and hunts and shooting matches out back.

"And the balcony overhead can hold up to a fifteen-piece orchestra," the agent was saying.

Coco turned suddenly, speaking over the poor fellow's head. "Oh, James," she said, "you're seething. I can feel it. When you're angry, you're like a steaming pot. You fill up the room. We must talk. I have so much to say to you." She paused. "I think I do at least."

"You think? You're not sure? How long did you talk to Phillip? Were you sure about talking to him?"

"Stop it."

"I waited for you."

"I had to see him. I had to ask."

"Ask what? If he could give you the public marriage you want? You could be Lord and Lady Peach-Pitt. The Viscountess Peach-Pitt. He can do it, you know. He's stepping down in October from his duties at Cambridge. Retiring, he says."

"No, he's not."

James was taken aback. "You discussed Phillip's retirement with him?" Splendid. She and Phillip were planning Phillip's future together. "You talked him out of it?"

Coco stared at James, her eyes boldfaced beneath the velvet brim, as if she might chew him out. Then frowning, her expression crumpled, and she spun around. She walked briskly toward the next doorway. The agent had to run to catch up with her. He was all eyes, all ears, a wiry little man having an exciting day.

She went through the next doorway, muttering, "Oh, James." She hit the doorframe with her gloved hand as she passed through, a smack. As if James were somehow at fault, as if she would really like to thwack him.

The agent trotted along in her wake, offering, "Would you like to see the back garden, madam?"

"No," James called to him. The fellow turned. "We'll take it," James said.

"You want the house?"

"Yes. So could you leave? You can bring us the lease tomorrow."

A grin spread across the man's face. They hadn't even discussed amount or terms. "Certainly," he said. "Tomorrow at noon, say. I'll have all the papers."

"Fine. Now get out."

He hesitated. "Sir Armand," he said a little uncomfortably. "Madam here seems to think your name is James. Not that I care. But there is the little matter of deposits, monies in advance, good faith, you see—"

"That's no problem." James reached into his pocket and pulled out his notecase to see what he had. Twenty-six pounds. He could live a month on it, though it wasn't enough here, he was sure. He tossed the whole notecase at the man. "I'll give you the rest tomorrow. Now do you mind?"

"No. Of course not." The estate agent bowed, smiling unctuously as he pocketed the leather fold of bills. When he took his hand out of his pocket, he was offering the key.

James took it, then stared at the fellow till he began backing.away. "You can see yourself out, can't you?" James asked.

"Certainly."

The front door clicked distantly as James turned toward Coco.

She pressed her lips together as she lifted off her hat. She yanked off her gloves, scowling down at them as if they were alive, as if she might pluck them like chickens, pull the nap off their velvet cuffs. Her mouth remained pursed with a kind of irritation. Irritation, frustration, a sadness, too, somehow, and an overwrought brand of . . . exasperation that seemed, for the life of James, on the verge of tears again. So many emotions played across her face that some of his own anger eased. Her emotions, as they could sometimes, puzzled him. They seemed complicated.

As she set her things down on a stack of trays—they had somehow ended up in a servant's back passage—she said, "How are you doing with Phillip?"

"Swimmingly. Why?"

She swung around, away, shaking her head. "Oh," was all she said. She walked down the passageway to the first available door, turning to push through it. James followed. It opened into a small mud room, the sort of back entrance that servants or the master of the house entered after riding or working outside, coming in wet and dirty.

It was cluttered with galoshes, sinks, rags, garden implements, a mackintosh on one of several hooks, the rest empty but for a straw hat at the end. Coco went over to a sink, placing her hands on its rim, and stared out the window over it. She stayed like that for more than a full minute. At which point, for something to do, to make him feel less helpless, less lost, James went over to her and turned her around.

What a surprise. The bold, confronting woman who had led him a merry chase through Cambridge-shire, then through this blasted house with an estate agent in tow, this woman pressed her mouth so tightly that her lips went white. Her chin quivered. Her eyes, as they found his, were glassy with the struggle against crying.

She said, "Phillip is not your friend."

"I know that." When she offered nothing more, he tried to reassure her. "But I'm doing all right with him. Really."

"No, you're not."

"I'm not?"

"No." She touched his face, just a brush of her cupped palm. She tried to smile, didn't quite make it. "And it's none of my business. In fact—" She laughed hollowly. "It's the very antithesis of my business."

A cold feeling settled into James's chest. "What do you know, Coco? Tell me. What did Phillip say?"

She didn't speak at first. She sighed, let out a

larger breath, all the while looking into James's face; she sighed again. Then said, "Oh, James. I do love you so very much." She left a brief pause, her face wincing as if she were about to take a blow, then launched into it. "You're a lamb to the slaughter, I'm afraid. He is setting you up."

James shook his head no at first. But the idea, as improbable as it was, did not ring false. It was like finding he'd been standing on a ledge all along, looking down into a Himalayan drop, but recognizing immediately that that far thing below, distant but clear, was the ground. Reality. The truth. She didn't have to tell him twice. "How?"

Very calmly, she said, "Well, the key problem seems to be that he has doctored the financial records of the expedition. You are about to take the blame for a sizable amount of finagled monies."

James squinted and leaned back against a potting table. "What?" Yet even this shock was short lived. He let out a dismal laugh as he realized: "A Bible Fund is part of it."

"Ah," she said. "Then you know something of what is going on."

"What else?" The cold feeling had descended into his stomach. He wanted to wretch.

He could remember all the times that Phillip Dunne had gone after an enemy. Phillip was fearsome, sometimes irrational. He was always brutally competitive, without conscience or remorse. And now Phillip's focused venom, his aggression, was somehow turned on James himself. James had seen it many times, yet always believed it was for someone else—though at the back of his mind he had perhaps always been wary, always feared that like a loaded gun, it could be pointed anywhere. But why at him now?

"Because of you?" he asked.

"I would say yes—me, and other things he envies about you. Except envy alone doesn't seem to explain it. He's fought over power and preferments before. Granted, you're especially bothersome to him, but you have also been especially valued, at least at one time. So I can't say why. But I asked him how and when and where. And he told me. Because—" She laughed again, a hysterical edge to her humor now. "Because he believed I was incapable of interceding." She snorted. "But he is wrong. James, there's more: he has altered your journal."

"My journal? How could he?"

"He's changed the order of it. He's made your friendship with the Wakua and how much you admire them appear earlier, along with some page or other about England not being as stalwart and glorious as she thinks. Oh, and he's moved forward a notation you made about poisons you'd adapted for Mtzuba. These notes all now come while every Englishman is still alive. Phillip is building a story of how you conspired with the Wakua to kill your friends."

"And what exactly would make me do that?"

"For gold and money."

"I brought the gold home—"

"According to Phillip, it was a rich expedition in money alone. If you got rid of everyone before supplies were laid in at Cape Town, there was almost ten thousand pounds available—"

"Ten thousand pounds!" James heaved himself

forward. "We couldn't get enough money to hire merchant solders when the Crown refused a military escort. We had to piece together—"

Coco help up her hand. "You don't have to explain to me."

"I do if you believe him."

"I don't. But Nigel will. It gets worse."

James took air deeply into his lungs, trying to settle himself. "Go on."

"Besides this, Phillip wants to go back into Africa with Nigel. He'll go himself once he knows where to look. He won't protect the Wakua. He wants their gold. He wants the thick deposits you've told him about. He waxes rhapsodic about them. Oh, and James—" She looked down.

"There can't be more."

"No. Not exactly." She paused, then said, "He's called the Home Office, the Home Secretary is sending someone. There's to be an investigation, during which time, well, your name has been struck from the Honors List. That part hasn't happened yet, but it will this afternoon."

James spotted a stool in the corner. He pulled it forward, sat, and tried to think what to do next. Purely and simply, what he wanted to do was be sick. Ah, his earldom. Watching it slip away was more of a blow than he'd thought.

Coco stood there by the sink, one elbow braced on it, waiting respectfully.

At last, James stood. "Can you wait here?" he asked.

"What are you going to do?"

"I'm going to the Bishop. I'm going to tell him the whole story. If I can get hold of my bloody journal, I'm going to show him the proper order of it, then trust in his intuition for the truth. Nigel is zealous, but not stupid.''

"It's going to be a little harder than that. You *did* actually doctor some of the expedition's accounts: some examples Phillip showed to the, ah, new Chairman of the Financial Board. He showed you how the ledger system worked, how to write something in one night, yes?''

James frowned, thinking, then remembered with a sinking sense of doom. "O-o-oh,'' he groaned, "yes. The night he got the college dividends confused with contributions to the expedition. I showed him. Oh, God, I showed him. I crossed out the figures he had and wrote in what he seemed to be saying.''

There was a moment of silence then, as if they both stood at a graveside, which in a sense they possibly did. James's wonderful rise in the world of academia and English peerage was a serious, if not fatal, arrest.

After a minute, he turned to her and said, "Um . . . Coco?''

She looked up at him, her expression troubled, inward, but calm. Filled with love, he might have said.

Yet he had to ask. "Why would Phillip hand so much information over to you? I mean, this wasn't just a casual conversation you had with him, was it?''

"No.'' When she took his lack of response to be an accusation—and it was—she said, "I didn't sleep with him, if that's what you're thinking.''

"Then why did he tell you?''

Her plump bottom lip rolled up, meeting her pretty top lip in a tight line. "Well . . . I let him think that I was going to."

"Oh, good. That relieves me. What could possibly have made him think that?"

Her brow drew down, but she didn't answer.

So he helped her. "Could it have been . . . oh, let me think . . . that he had his hand up your dress?"

"No." Her expression stiffened.

Good. Let her be angry. "What, then? What would make a man think he had your trust so much?"

But Coco had stopped being quite so loquacious all of a sudden. She made a truly nasty face at him and said, "I'm not used to having to account for myself to a man. You're not my ponce, you know."

"No, I'm not." He shouldn't have said it. He knew that *after* it had come out. "So what do you know about ponces, Coco?"

She didn't answer, but rather crossed her arms. A tooth appeared at the her lip; it bit the side edge.

After they had stared at each other for a long, uncomfortable minute, she said, "You're under a lot of strain, James. You'd better go. I'll wait here." She laughed in that cynical way she had that sounded as brittle as glass. "Since we seem to have rented the house." As extra momentum, she added, "Phillip thought it fascinating that the Wakua eat their enemies. He said, and I quote, 'Well, well, so maybe Stoker will understand when I have his balls for dinner.' I'd go spoon them out of the soup, if I were you."

James nodded once and stood, the stool scraping as he rose. "I'll be back, then."

He left, but he felt horrible. It was a toss-up whether to go after Phillip or simply crawl off somewhere and hide. James's stomach was churning. His heart felt like he'd swallowed Coco's bitterness into it. It *galumphed* in his chest, swollen, leaden. What had he said? What had he done? He regretted how he'd behaved—yet he didn't. He felt angry, possessive, outraged at the injustice of what was happened, and furious over how he'd found out.

And ashamed. Ashamed that he couldn't be more grateful to Coco for finding out for him, for telling him, because he knew it had cost her to do so. It was just that he couldn't bear the thought that Phillip might have touched her. Not anywhere. Not on her fingertips. Not her toes. Coco was his. It was stupid and primitive to feel this way, but James did. She was not for anyone else. Only *he* knew her best. Only *he* was special to her. And she was his, only his alone.

Chapter 21

J ames did not bother trying to get any university records. He was sure Phillip had them. He went to All Souls instead, where he picked up the account ledgers for the college. Next, James wired the Royal Geographical Society and asked if he could inspect their books as well. Barney Kilmoore there wired him back within the hour. Of course, he said, the Society's contributions, though sometimes anonymous, were always open for inspection as to how the money had been allocated and to whom it had gone. Then, only then—and knowing Phillip was safely gone to a meeting with the High Steward—James went to Phillip's house, where he let himself in the back door.

A servant stopped him in the front hall, but James said, as he had truthfully on a number of other occasions, that Phillip had sent him to pick up something. After which James went boldly into Phillip's study.

It was ridiculously easy to find Phillip's bank records. Top drawer, a folder at the back, exactly as he kept the same sort of records at All Souls, exactly as were organized the records of the Financial Board. Phillip's bills, most of them for Willy, and the viscounty estate records were right beside these along with a letter from a creditor. It was a polite notice regarding a delinquent account, nothing that seemed repetitive or harrying. James took everything out, then sat down at Phillip's desk for a look.

The next part was not as easy. On first glance all looked well. It was an hour of sorting through papers before James noticed a side-entry in All Souls' records that corresponded in amount to a deposit four years later into Phillip's bank in London. It was because of the amount that James noticed the entry at all: twenty-eight pounds, two shillings. All Souls had it down as a donation to the missionaries for Bibles.

After this, he realized, there were other matching figures. An entry in All Souls four years ago, a deposit much later of the exact same amount into Phillip's bank. All the matching entries were inserted, lost in among what looked to be a correction to a far-reaching accounting error. Whether there was an error or not was hard to sort out in an hour, but one thing was certain: the majority of these "corrections" were contributions to James's expedition, monies attributed to the pockets of dead men.

The amounts weren't much, in fact, visibly little, only about thirty pounds a month. It made no sense, but there they were, and remarkably consistent.

It was enough. James packed up the books and papers. He was missing the middle link, the accounts of the university through which all had flowed—the university had managed the expedition's income and disbursements. But he trusted in two things: find Phillip, and he'd find these records (with, alas, James's own hand having adjusted some of the "errors"). And once found, these records would show similar manipulations, but of a much larger order—something that would add up to ten thousand pounds.

James loaded himself and the stack of papers and account books into his carriage and *hi-yah*ed his horse. All the while, his heart pounded so hard it made his chest reverberate. Phillip. Phillip, whom he had trusted, his idol at one time, who'd given him an education at his knee, then at his side, given him a profession he loved as well as a step up every time he'd turned around. Why?

James meant to find out. He and Nigel Athers. Because that was where he was taking the records: to Swansbridge, where stood the ancient cathedral, its offices with Father Menlow in back, and, within walking distance, the manor home of the Bishop of Swansbridge himself.

When James got there, however, there were already a number of carriages in the Bishop's long, rounding drive. Some sort of social tea, James thought at first. Mrs. Athers was keen for the society of her countryside neighbors. Then James recognized the only carriage he would know anywhere: his father used to drive one almost exactly like it. Phillip's old brougham was at the far end of the line of vehicles.

Inside, as James handed his hat to the butler, he could hear voices. He knew immediately the sounds of Tuttleworth and Teddy Lamott, two voices together that became those of the High Stewart and

his Deputy, respectively. Odd. Their official capac-
ity was mostly ceremonial, derived from when the
Senate's Steward judged university members once
privileged to be tried under the Chancellor's juris-
diction rather than the ordinary courts.

James walked into the room, and the eyes of a
dozen men turned toward him. Besides Teddy and
Tuttleworth, there was Nigel Athers, of course, also
two fellows from All Souls, another member of the
Financial Board, a few others, all Regent's House
and Council of the Senate men, plus three men he
didn't know. Stiffly, they all stepped back to admit
James into their midst—he had every right to be
here, if the meeting was official: it boded badly that
he hadn't been invited. Awkwardly, he was intro-
duced to the three men he didn't know, two from
the London Home Office and the local constable.

As these men parted, James spotted Phillip and
the room grew hushed. The Vice-Chancellor sat in
an overstuffed leather chair next to one from which
Nigel Athers rose. Both men, Phillip sitting, Nigel
standing beside him, seemed stalled as to what to
do about James's arrival, like a prisoner suddenly
shown up to help hammer up the gallows. Because
that's what this was. The What-to-do-about-James-
Stoker meeting.

James only now realized what he must look like.
Damp, spottily dry in places from all the rain he'd
taken today. Rumpled, uncombed, unpressed.
Standing there with a stack of ledger books and accounting sheets, some of which he'd filched from
the house of the most senior member of the university administration, who now rose to his feet.

Phillip did not look disappointed. He came to his

feet looking anticipatory—in fact, almost glad, with a very small but very triumphant smile on his lips.

"James," he said. "We were just talking about you. What have you got there? Let's see." It was possible he'd recognized the spines of the All Souls' ledgers.

Boldly, Teddy interjected himself. "Jamie," he said, "Frankly, I'm bloody glad to see you, have to say. Only fair. You should know we're drawing up a warrant for your arrest."

Phillip threw him an annoyed glare. "Lamott, let me handle this."

"Right-o. Just want Jamie to know my part in it. Tuttleworth and I are here to protect the university's interests." Tuttleworth was a barrister, it occurred to James. "But I want you to know, old man, I don't believe for a moment the charges of murder and don't believe for a minute you did any of that disgusting business with those devils." He was serious. He shook his head, looking so sad. "Still, the money, James. Why the money?"

"I didn't take any money."

Athers came forward. "Dr. Stoker, this is actually a closed meeting. I am sorry to say—"

James held out the All Souls ledger with Phillip's bank records sitting on top. "Nigel," he said. "Before anyone says anything more, perhaps someone should have a look at these."

Phillip tried to take them. "Where did you get those?" James evaded him, his reflexes quicker, younger. "They're mine," Phillip protested mildly. "Oh, James, this thieving streak in you disappoints—"

"They're his bank records—" James got out, before Phillip interrupted.

His voice was slightly shriller than it should have been. "Oh, James. Now this. Breaking into my house, taking things." He gave Athers what was supposed to pass for a forbearing look, but for once he was a little off balance. The sight of his own books was surprising enough for his face to be pale.

James pushed his advantage. "Also here are All Souls' financial records. There are entries, I believe, attributed to the expedition that in fact went into Phillip's bank account. The dates aren't the same. But the amounts themselves match exactly."

"We don't care about All Souls," Phillip said irritably. "We have the university records." He frowned, the Vice-Chancellor with serious concerns. "Huge amounts, James. With your handwriting shifting hundreds of pounds at a time—into your account somewhere, which you've probably hidden. Explain that."

James explained of his own choosing in his own order. "Phillip appointed me to the Financial Board immediately, which gave him an excuse to talk to me about what I knew regarding the expedition's finances. What a relief, I imagine, to discover I knew almost nothing beyond what the geology teams had in their pockets. But Nigel proved hardheaded about the Bible Fund, and Phillip started to need someone to blame."

Phillip looked about briefly, assessing, smiling. "Oh, James, Africa has made you devious." When no one rushed to support the remark—in fact, everyone looked bewildered, not sure what to believe—he took a frustrated breath. "You can't trust him.'' He glanced, throwing a scowl around the room. ''He fouled himself, made himself filthy. His mind is sharp, as treacherous as the dart from a blow gun—''

''Be quiet, Phillip,'' Nigel said.

''The Bible Fund,'' James continued. He knew this first part to be true: ''It was the first embezzlement, I think, a fund Phillip invented.'' Then James invented a little himself, a calculated risk. ''You see, Phillip had debt, large debt, and it was mounting. When a bill collector from Bath offered to settle for a few shillings on the pound, with the help of All Souls, Phillip did: he settled up for twenty-eight pounds, two shillings—''

''That's a lie!'' Phillip said. ''I paid every bill. I had to, or they wouldn't take her in the next time, and I knew there'd be a next time. There always was. I *had* to.''

All eyes in the room turned on him. He hadn't admitted anything, yet he had.

''Had to what?'' James asked.

''Well, I, ah—'' Phillip floundered. But he was angry. He wanted to explain something.

''It has to do with Willy, doesn't it?'' James deduced.

His head jerked. It could have been a nod, a single, terse affirmation, or simply a spasm of tension. Phillip released it in a laugh, not very convincingly, shaking his head as if to deny the whole business. ''This is impossible. What a story.'' But his brow rose as if his scalp rippled. He was fairly appalled to hear so many of his pieces brought to light. ''You're trying to blame me, James, old boy, when we all know I come from old money. By Jeeves, I run a house almost as large as All Souls itself, with fourteen servants, three carriages, and a stableful of horses. I could buy and sell your little Financial Board. While you''—he lifted his finger—''you killed godfearing Englishmen. It's all in your journal, which I found, James, and have turned over—''

''After you rearranged it. He took my journal. It's binding was loose. He undid it, then put its pages into a more implicating order.''

Phillip stared at him. He looked deflated. Then he said, just like that, from nowhere, ''My God, she's your mistress.'' He was quiet, as if he himself had a little trouble absorbing the concept. Then softer, he said, ''Coco told you. I can't believe it.''

''No—''

Phillip found his voice. ''Oh, yes. No one else knew. Jesus, she's good. She is really good. But then, the old saw: a whore who likes her work usually is.''

Anger flashed before James's eyes, so swift and strong the room blared white. He knew the quick, primitive desire to smash Phillip, bloody him. It took a moment to control the urge. No, James told himself. Don't let yourself be baited. Don't give yourself away.

You've won.

He said, ''I found out when I inspected the books, Phillip.''

''And your journal? How did you know that?''

Ha, the bastard had admitted it, all of it. ''I found out on my own.'' James knew the heady rush of expanding triumph. ''Why, Phillip? What about Willy? Her expenses can't have been that much.''

Phillip snorted, the bitterness of a man who got no sympathy. "No, but they were eternal." He closed his eyes, reached both his hands back onto his own shoulders, squeezing, rubbing, while he made a pained face. "And we never really planned for them," he said. "In fact, outwardly we kept planning for them never to come again. She'd come home, feel better. We'd celebrate, spend more money. But those damn clinic bills and doctor bills and hospitals and the laudanum itself. The expense of it all just kept coming.

"And the house. Do you know what it takes to maintain a three-hundred-fifty-year-old structure halfway decently? And, James"—he glanced up, a brief look of bewildered regret—"I didn't expect anyone would walk out of that expedition again, not after word came of mass graves and a jungle illness. I didn't think it would matter." He went on. "I *had* to, you see." He lifted his head, looked around at the men, all sitting or standing in the same state: stunned. Then he looked directly at James again. "You know, she went through three different clinics just last year alone, then ended up in the hospital for nine weeks when we thought she would die of pneumonia.

"She was never a huge expense, just a constant one, a slow leak I couldn't stem, no matter what I did. The total built up. So I found a new kind of income. Then you came back. I thought it still wouldn't matter. I mean, it was too buried. But Nigel found one of the places I doctored, the stupid Bible Fund—"

"Phillip, the Bible Fund wasn't even thirty pounds."

"Exactly. Who would miss twenty-eight quid? Of course, after a while, I'd done it all over the place. Then I thought if I got the gold, I could put it back. I always meant to put it back, James. Willy and I were just a little strapped for the time being. Only I couldn't seem to get ahead. And then it got so easy . . . and there were things we wanted, that people of our station had a right to expect, that Willy expected. . . . And an expedition of a hundred forty-eight men sponsored by three different organizations, well, there were a lot of places to tuck away a lot of money."

"Phillip, you should have said something. I could have helped. I could have lent you a little."

"You? Saint James? Ask you to cover for my larceny?" Phillip laughed. "Well, I did ask, in a way, but you wouldn't, would you?"

He left an ugly silence filled with true enmity, then with a snort asked, "So what did you promise her, James? Not marriage, I hope. Because if you did and you intend to follow through, you should let these gentlemen know. I mean, I think they'd overlook a little discreet adventuring, since we've, most all of us, been there. In fact"—he laughed— "a few of us have been *exactly* where you have." Before James could react, Phillip had looked at the Bishop and said, "What do you think, Nigel? When you were in James's place—well, Coco's place, to be technical—did you think she was worth giving up a promising career?" He held his hands out, answering his own question. "Well, of course not. You didn't do it. Neither did I. But did we miss something, do you think? Has James got a point here?"

The room had grown silent, so silent no one drew breath. A dozen men, all educated, relatively worldly, and every single one, save Phillip, awe-struck by the hideousness of crudity so flippant no one could respond.

"Oh, that's right," Phillip said. "Mrs. Athers is in the solarium watering her plants. We'll pretend you don't know the lovely Mrs. Wild. So what about you, Tuttleworth? You ever know a woman who could make the old poker stiff as fast as Coco?"

Deathly silence.

James was so utterly appalled he couldn't even be furious with Phillip. The man had apparently decided to go out in a blaze of shame: a keen desire to alienate everyone permanently.

"What about anyone else?" he asked, looking around. If they had all been staring at any man but the Viscount Dunne, Vice-Chancellor, Provost, scholar, good Samaritan, anyone else, anyone but the man they had all known and respected for decades, he would have been knocked down, had a roomful of men on top of him, James first. "Who else here has shagged Coco?" he asked. "What do you think? How good is she?"

Tuttleworth came forward. "Phillip"—he cleared his throat—"that is, Lord Dunne, I am relieving you of the duties and office of the Vice-Chancellory." To James, he said, "Dr. Stoker, as Deputy Vice-Chancellor you become here and now the acting administrative head of the university. You become also the acting Provost of All Souls and the ex officio chairman of the Council of the Senate and the General Board. Lord Dunne, should you prove innocent of the charges against you, your positions will be reinstated.''

The constable took Phillip's arm. "I'm afraid I have to take him.''

Tuttleworth interceded. "No. The Chancellor can't try him as he once could, but we can hold him till his arraignment. You draw up the warrant, but he is a gentleman and a scholar, sir, and was the head of our institution. We will be responsible for him.'' Tuttleworth was sacrificing the necessary ground, then closing ranks. To Phillip, "Sorry, Phillip, but you must confine yourself to your home until further notice. Ted will take you, then stay with you.''

Teddy acknowledged with a nod, and at last they all in unison moved, a general dispersion that followed Ted and Phillip toward the door.

James rubbed the back of his head. It was over. He closed his eyes. And all in all, it had gone much easier, quicker, and cleaner than he'd had any right to expect.

Someone on his way out of the room patted him on the back once, a bit of man-to-man reassurance, while James stood there. He realized he was shaking and tried to control it.

He followed at the rear as they all escorted Teddy, Phillip, and Tuttleworth out. Like everyone, apparently, he felt the need of movement and fresh air. The rest of them would go back in. There was much to discuss. How best to handle the scandal that was sure to become public. How to manage the smoothest possible transition as power shifted. How to keep the university on an even keel while one of its highest members sank to the bottom like a stone. Fresh air, yes, James thought.

Nigel held his front door open while men filed through. It was twilight. Tuttleworth's carriage was pulling up in front of the portico. James was just about to step outside, when Nigel stopped him by simply saying his name in a lowered tone.

"James." He spoke nothing further for a moment, folding his hands over the bottom of his waistcoat, steepling his index fingers. Then he asked, "How deeply involved *are* you with Mrs. Wild?"

The others, already on the front stoop, turned with interest.

James had to push down a nasty tantrum, a spate of resentment into which he could have lost everything he had gained. After all, Nigel only asked for the same damn lie he'd already spoken to Phillip. Only now he had to tell it to the Bishop. With witnesses. He was supposed to say, We aren't involved at all. That was what he and Coco had agreed he'd say. They would live the truth—in a secret house where no one would know—but speak this lie to the world. She expected it. They had both expected it.

Yet it wouldn't come out.

"You're not involved, are you?" Nigel asked.

James tried to answer, but still no words. They'd agreed, he kept telling himself. Just say it. He was going to.

Perhaps the bewilderment on his face made Nigel compassionate. He patted James's back and said, "No, you aren't involved at all. Of course not. I shouldn't have asked."

Whatever reprieve James might have felt was lost when Teddy, a few steps ahead of them, chimed in cheerfully with, "Really?" He looked from James to Nigel and back to James again, searching the silence for what shift was afoot. Then he lowered his voice to a quasi-confidential tone and asked, "So the path is clear to her, then?" He awaited James's answer, his face, bright, intent.

Dear God. The shaking inside James increased. His mouth was dry. His tongue felt fat, sluggish with all it wouldn't speak.

Teddy's eagerness faltered for a moment. "I mean, James," he murmured, "if I thought for a minute she meant something to you, well—"

Damn him. Teddy wasn't playing. Unlike Phillip, he wasn't manipulating. Unlike Nigel, he wasn't asking for hypocrisy. He was genuinely asking if Coco meant something to James; he would stay away, if she did.

Teddy said, "You see, I'd like to send her, oh, just some flowers, you know? God, I think she's gorgeous. And regal, the way she carries herself—"

James got out, "She's too old for you, Ted." Never mind that Teddy was a year older than James himself.

Teddy laughed—James's expression couldn't have been too cordial. "Heh, heh, heh," he said uncomfortably. "Just interested. I've always been interested in her. You know that; who isn't? Don't get cross—"

James took a step toward him.

But another voice stopped him. "Let me help you out here, James, since you seem to be confused."

James turned to face Phillip, and something in the man's expression made James's head grow light. His vision blurred.

Phillip stood before the open door of Tuttleworth's carriage. Smiling, he said to Teddy, "What the new Vice-Chancellor here means to say is that the good Mrs. Wild means nothing to him. She can't. Circumstances don't allow it." He laughed. "Have at it—"

James saw white. It was as if electricity snapped along his muscles, innervating his limbs in a way that shocked him as much as anyone else.

His strength amazed him. He ascended into the air in a leap to fall on Phillip, who collided back against the carriage, half into it, taken completely by surprise. Rage roiled so hard through James's veins, he couldn't see. He was barely aware he was striking Phillip but for the impact of his fists against against bone and flesh, the jar up his arms, in his elbows, at his shoulders. They slid somehow to the flagstones. He had Phillip by the shirtfront, shaking him. "You rotten, sodding son of a—"

"James!" "Stop!" Voices called. Arms, hands tried to grip and pull James off the man beneath him. He'd straddled Phillip, who held his forearms over his face and bellowed like an animal, caterwauling. James was loathe to give up the satisfaction of breaking flesh and bone, of blood. He wanted more.

He was dimly aware of being lifted forcefully off Phillip, of the others helping Dunne to his feet. His mouth bled. His nose was broken.

Good. James sat huddled on the doorstep, his arms wrapped around his chest, breathing like a bellows, trying to catch his breath, his sanity.

Nigel clapped the carriage door shut. "Get him out of here," he said, then turned to James. "Are you all right?" he asked.

James nodded, staring at the flagstones. He wasn't of course. He wasn't all right at all. He was ashamed, outraged, stunned by his own behavior—and frightened. He was so scared somewhere and to such a degree, he couldn't even make sense of it.

Then Nigel drew a crystal clear picture of the worst that could possibly have come to be.

The Bishop of Swansbridge, of all people, sat down beside James there on the front doorstep. They sat shoulder to shoulder. Nigel murmured, "I know what you're going through." He paused, then said, "And I am so, so sorry." He left a space of silence before he told James gently, oh, so gently. "But you know Phillip is right. You can't go to her. We need you, James."

James bowed his head over his crossed arms, clutching himself across his chest, rubbing his own arms.

Nigel continued in a reasonable voice, the tone of a man of the cloth consoling the bereaved. "There is going to be a horrible mess over what Phillip has done, and we must count on you to pull us through it. Don't abdicate. We need your sterling reputation—your sterling character, for that matter. We need a leader. An unsullied one behind whom we can all rally. You can't afford to be smeared or even put in a shady light, not while you are taking us through what is going to be a very bad time. James—" He paused, waiting until James had raised his eyes and looked at him. "You can't go to her. You can't afford her anymore."

Coco waited, but James did not arrive that night as he had said. She wandered the house of strangers. Her house. But it wasn't. It was the house of a family, of an affluent English couple who entertained and had friends and children and responsibilities to the community.

She liked it. She touched the loom of the lady of the house, a big wood frame on which were interwoven the beginning warp and woof of what might have become an amateurish tapestry—the woman was a weaver. It amused Coco when she found, beside a basket of carding equipment, a small spinning wheel. She rummaged through a writing desk, where she found paper and made a few sketches of the thing.

A spinning wheel was a piece of folk craft now, archaic since the advent of spinning mules and jennies, new machines that made yarns a hundred times stronger and faster. Nonetheless, archaic or not, Coco was superstitiously careful not to touch the spindle. Ha, ha, ha, she thought. Wouldn't James laugh?

The spindle didn't look sharp or dangerous. It was blunt, dumb wood. She couldn't imagine how it could prick a person's finger.

When James still hadn't come or sent word by midnight, Coco fell asleep with her drawings in her lap. Drawings not just of the wheel, but of the fragile-looking writing desk with its neat cubbies filled with vellum envelopes, announcement cards, rose-scented papers, drawings she had made for no

other particular reason than the desk struck her as
pretty.

When the estate agent arrived the next day with
all the rental papers, she delayed him. Her "husband" had been called away on business. Then she
asked him for a ride back into Cambridge. She left
a note on the house's door.

> *Gone back to Cambridge, my sweet. I'll be at*
> *the boardinghouse. Hope you're all right.*
> *Come to me soon.*

But James didn't.

The next day she went into Cambridge, to the
offices of the geology faculty. There, she was going
to ask if Dr. Stoker was lecturing today—she just
wanted to see him, stand at the back of the hall,
perhaps, assure herself that he was healthy and
whole. Instead, though, she overheard a man, a secretary of some sort, worrying to a passing proctor
as to whether "Dr. Stoker would want his tea in the
Vice-Chancellor's offices or in the combination
room of the Regent House, as the old Vice-
Chancellor usually did."

Well. He'd done it. Good for him. Coco stopped
long enough to ask, "Did Dr. Stoker mention anything about moving from the Provost's lodge of All
Souls?"

It was an impertinent question. It received its deserved alarmed stares and silence.

She smiled, then thought to flip open her little
drawing pad, removing its pencil. "I'm from *The
Ladies' Gazette*, you see. Will there be any sort of
official welcome? Will the new Vice-Chancellor

live on university grounds, or will he be moving into a house in town, like the last?''

The two men frowned at each other, then the smaller one mumbled, ''I shouldn't think there will be much celebration, given the turmoil the good Dr. Stoker must untangle. And he is only the acting Vice-Chancellor until the election in October. Though, of course''—he smiled sanctimoniously— ''we fully expect him to succeed to the position.''

Right, as James would say. That was that. Coco understood what had happened.

Outside, walking home, she cried a bit, but then wiped her face. Stop. This was what was always going to be; it was inevitable. Sir James Stoker, soon to be Earl of What-not, had undoubtedly done what he thought he must. Never mind that she had believed he was stronger, believed that together they could overcome any circumstance that might threaten them. Never mind that she'd allowed her-self to put her faith in him.

See? said her old cynical self. See? A darling young man, a great fling, but hardly true love. Which didn't exist after all, except in fairy tales and nursery fables. A real sort of life for herself and James had always been impossible. Don't mind. You are used to going your own way alone. Get beyond this. Get rid of him. Carry on.

So Coco tried to: At the boardinghouse, she wrote a quick letter to the estate agent, saying she and Sir Armand would not be taking the house after all; please keep the money as a token of their regret.

Then she packed herself up, kissed David good-bye, promised to write, and took her sad self to London.

* * *

James had walked back into the Bishop's house that night ostensibly with great power, dreams fulfilled. Yet he could not fight an expanding sense of disillusionment. Hang them all, he thought. He'd see Coco, of course. No one could tell him not to. Meeting her would be difficult, delicate, but it could be done surely. Up till now they had made only the smallest effort to keep their relationship to themselves. They would do better. They would be secretive; private, covert, downright clandestine if need be. Oh, yes, he looked forward to that. Sneaking around yet more carefully.

Disillusionment became outright gloom, however, when another subject came up. Phillip had told the others that James knew where the Wakua gold was—information that was judged to be "the perfect distraction." The others discussed "getting up an expedition," "making the news public." To a man, everyone expected James to lead the way to gold and glory.

Everyone did *not* think that they should protect the Wakua, whom by the end of that night every member of Council, save James, had called children or worse. The Wakua were to be bought off with baubles, so they could get on with the business of going in, tearing out, digging up their land and homes.

At one point, Athers told James, "You can't honestly expect to deprive poor Englishmen of a chance for wealth so as to protect a tribe of primitives who don't know what they have in the first place."

"But they *aren't* primitive. The gold they sent— did you see, besides how much, the way it was worked? The art in it, the skill? They have their own way.''

Athers shrugged. ''Survival of the fittest way, James. Survival of the fittest.''

Except without the Wakua, James himself would not have survived, and there was the matter of one hundred forty-seven Englishmen who hadn't. He didn't say these words, however. They didn't change the fact that if Athers took in an expedition with rifles and mining equipment, the Wakua would be no match.

It was midnight before James left Athers's house. When he did, he departed, angry, baffled, unhappy—feeling like a tart himself: gussied up, bent to the will of others, and holding a fiver for his trouble.

He'd simply been too unsettled and exhausted to face Coco. She would be disappointed in him, he thought. He was disappointed in himself and the world at large. So he went to his rooms at All Souls.

There he'd lain in bed, tired, but finding sleep elusive. Tomorrow he'd tell Coco; he'd see her. He'd explain how things had become rather precarious. He'd tell her that for a while he and she would have to be much more careful. They would have to live one way, but act as if they lived another.

Their existence would become, just for the time being, a kind of . . . hypocrisy.

Jesus God, he thought, closing his eyes.

And, oh, yes, he would have to tell her that—there was no help for it—he would also be a great deal busier. Which proved so very, very true: In the morning the authorities came to take Phillip to London, and all hell broke loose. James didn't get away that day or the following one, either.

Chapter 22

A week later, Coco lay back in a barber chair, able to hear a dental engine through the bone of her jaw. The sound faded in and out, while above her head she watched the pulleys of the dental machinery. Her tooth had broken, and the dentist was having to cut it in half to get it out. It didn't hurt too much. But the drilling and the sight of the wheels and the little rubber belts, all vibrating in her head, surprised her every time she rallied to consciousness.

She watched the wheels come into focus now, mesmerized. She was fascinated because, until today, she had never seen such an apparatus. The little belts made it clatter along, spinning, humming, thrumming in her head.

She blearily watched the wheels spin, then suddenly—spinning wheels! A spinning wheel! And she had already been nicked by it. She could taste the blood. Coco began to laugh as the rubber facepiece came down again to settle over her nose and mouth. She inhaled, still laughing, as she sank down into inkiness once more, drifting on a sweetish, rubbery smell that came through the mask and tubing.

She dreamed of liquid sleep supplied in small iron cylinders. Values and tubes. Or perhaps she was not dreaming. Perhaps she was floating up into wakefulness again. The close-fitting face-piece was over her nose and mouth. She could see the India rubber bag above expand and contract as she breathed, hear the sound of the dentist pumping the little handball. Then she was suddenly talking to James.

She told him, "Well, I hope you're happy." Her tone, though, said she didn't mean it; she hoped he was miserable.

As if to please her, his face appeared around the wheels and belts, and her wish came true: his eyes had dark circles beneath them. His hair was askew. Misery was conveniently written all over his features.

She smiled at the sight. "It serves you right," she said. "Have your fame and glory and title and money—"

She stopped listing all that he had traded her for because, articulated, none of it sounded as appropriately unappealing as it should. Shoving at the dentist, she tried to see her apparition better. To James the Dream she announced, "Well, just take all the things that you want and enjoy them. Me, I'm having what is rotten removed. I don't keep what can hurt me. I'm strong. I have it out and move on."

She felt sad all at once, though, strong or not. She consoled herself, thinking: losing a tooth did not rationally make a huge difference, and neither would losing James. Ultimately she'd remain intact.

He had made his decisions. They were bad ones from her perspective, but they weren't her decisions. Leave him to them.

She must have said something like this, because the dream disputed with her. He'd been busy. He hadn't been able to see her—

Right. For a whole week. There wasn't pencil and paper in Cambridge, so he couldn't have written a line. The twenty-minute walk would have killed him. The five-minute carriage ride would have exhausted his horse.

Stupid dream. He still disputed. He was trying. He was fighting. Life was hard.

Oh, please. She held up her hand that rather flopped on her wrist.

The dentist's voice tried to soothe someone, possibly move them. Her, she presumed. "No, no, it's all right," she told him. "I'm fine. Really. I have my integrity. I did what I thought I should do. I told him, so he could save himself. I had to. I'd do it again. Then he betrayed me, because, you see, he had plans of his own, plans and schemes and ideas, a life with a trajectory of its own: it surpassed me."

The dream James argued with sputters and indecipherable words.

She said merely, wisely, "You made your choice. Now go lie in it." This wasn't quite right. "Your bed, that is. Me, I have a perfectly good life to which I have returned. I don't need you to kiss it to life for me." She began to laugh again. "I have a castle in Paris, another in Italy. And I can cut through the brambles all by myself, thank you very much. I shall go to Vienna and dance in the New

Year. I can wake myself up.'' She said this perhaps in French. She wasn't sure.

But an English voice said most clearly, ''I don't see how you can take the moral high ground here. There's the university, others to consider. It wasn't just for myself that I didn't go straight away to you—'' The voice—it was James's again—stammered, then continued. ''Besides I wouldn't have been half so upset or confused if you hadn't slept with half the men in the room.''

She laughed a dreaming laugh, cackling and giggling. ''Laughing gas,'' she explained. Though the dentist had told her that laughing gas didn't make a person laugh. ''Never mind,'' she said. Then she told Dream James, ''I won't dispute your accusation, only its banality. We know what I've done; we know what I've been. But I never hurt anyone. I never did anything anyone didn't want me to, and before you I never betrayed anyone's secrets, neither their simplest nor their darkest. I know lawyers, kings, and lawmakers who can't say the same. As to what I was a decade ago, I liked what I did and was good at it. If that is dishonorable, well, then, shoot me.''

No one shot her. That was the beauty of dreams.

Though her imagined James argued some more. With less conviction, he said, ''You slept with men for money.''

''Not precisely. I slept with men I liked, then let them give me money. Wives do the same.'' She said, ''Women don't have many ways to accrue wealth, Dr. Stoker. In the tradition of geishas and concubines, a courtesan in Paris a decade ago was

not such a bad thing. Perhaps you are too prudish—
too English—to understand.''

There was a long pause, the sort in dreams that
meant one had triumphed totally, the villain van-
quished at one's feet.

But then James's meek voice asked, ''And
love?''

''Ah, love is a different matter.'' She said dream-
ily, ''I was in love once. It was fun. But also a
torture. It was compelling, I'll say that. I'm glad to
have had it and glad to be done with it.''

Exactly. That's what she'd tell him. Those words.
If she could remember them. If she ever saw him
again. Though they were just the sort of words she'd
never think of or dare speak to the real James. But
in dreams—ah, in dreams, here was where one was
always at one's most clear-sighted and eloquent.

The dental wheel kept spinning, the noise loud,
then soft. Much like something similar happening
inside Coco's head. Her brain buzzed while doing
slow, floating somersaults inside her skull. Her jaw
ached slightly in the way that foretold a bad time
later, though it wasn't bad now. Her tongue checked
once in a lull of drilling and found a hole at the
back of her jaw that was the size of a crater.

The tooth was out. Overhead the spinning wheel
slowed to a soft, whir, softer, softer, like the hymn
of a little choir in the distance. An untold number
of minutes later, perhaps hours, the dentist helped
her to her wobbly feet.

''Will you be all right?'' he asked.

''Oh, I'll be grand. You watch. I'll be tip-top.''

She took two steps and dropped right into the
arms of—it was her fantasy James.

"Coco?" he said.

The room faded around him. It became nothing but chest, warm, hard James-chest that smelled spicy the way his clothes could . . . of cardamom . . . cinnamon . . . lemons and honey. If James ever made her tea as he'd promised, she would ask him to make Dinka tea the way they fixed it in the Mountains of the Moon. What lovely English words, she thought. *Dinka. Moon mountains.*

What a lovely chest. "Mmm," she said. Yes. She could have stayed here against James's chest, against his warmth redolent in that strange way of Africa and Englishness. She could have stayed a moon's age, stayed forever.

The next thing she knew though, she was on a couch, with the dentist telling someone that she was fine and that everything had gone well enough. "I added a dash of ether at the end. It works slower, but lasts longer. She kept coming around and talking. Anyway, the ether was the trick, though it takes longer to wear off."

She heard these words while sinking into couch cushions.

Then she was standing, insisting on a cab all to herself.

People were moving her, she didn't care where. She was holding something. At one point, she opened her fist and wondered, What strange thing was this that lay on her palm? Then she recognized it: the better part of her tooth. She squeezed her eyes shut, wrapped her hand around its brittle edges. The extracted tooth was sharp in places. Good. Out. Done.

She was back on the couch. David was mysteriously there. "What are you doing here?" she asked, as he put his arm under her.

"I brought you, remember? I've been waiting out here to take you home."

Oh, yes. She patted his neck.

Her son, her sturdy, handsome son, picked her up into his arms and carted her bodily out into the sunshine. She blinked as she was loaded into her own brougham, then David climbed in afterward.

Mistakenly, her phantom James tried to get in too, but, ha, David was so clever. No more illbehaving dreams. He blocked the dream's way. "You leave her alone," he said. "You and Phillip have done quite enough, I think."

"Indeed," she added from the back. Then, "Wait." She stretched her arm out. "Here," she said. She dropped her tooth into the dream's hand.

He took it as if not certain what to do with her gift, then stepped away, looking suitably dismayed. Oh, the vengeful joy of dreams. She had to remember to have more like this. James looked terrible. Thin and prosperous and abjectly discontent. Good, good, good, she thought. He misses me. He is lost without me. Perfect. Oh, this is perfect!

As the carriage door closed, he called to her. "What do you want of me? What for godssake do you want?"

She laughed uproariously at this, because an idiot knew the answer. "The fairy tale," she told him. "I want the fairy tale ending of course. If you can't give it to me, then go away."

The carriage lurched forward, and she swayed against David. At some point, her jaw began to hurt, really hurt, and her tongue found a specific place, the hole where her tooth had been: a soft, mushy pit that ran deeply into her jaw, huge and tasting of metal. It felt like a cavern. Yes, indeed. The tooth was gone. She missed it. She was sad. She would never be the same.

But she could get along without it; that was fact.

Part 3

The Thorny Forest on Fire

In Africa, in some of the denser jungle, a man can step off the footpath and suddenly lose his way completely. The path is presumably there, a few paces away. Yet it could take hours to find it again. Or he might not find it at all; this is always a possibility. The way he meant to go can disappear like a piece of sunlight behind a turn in the trees. There, but vanished. Frustratingly, invisibly close, but no longer an option. Ultimately, he may have to make a new way; his journey may take a day longer, a week longer, a year longer. Or forever: He may never get to where he'd been going in the first place.

From the Earl of Bromwyck's
African Travels
Pease Press, London, 1878

Chapter 23

Well, *she* was certainly jolly. Hardly the Coco James had expected to find. He had bullied his way into the dentist's surgery—heroically, he had thought at the time. Though now he accepted that guilt and worry had driven him into London. He had feared that by ignoring Coco he might have destroyed her. James had imagined finding her crushed, distraught.

Well. So much for *that* whimsy.

Meanwhile, here he was, King of the World, Head of Everything. A man of substantial success. Michaelmas Term, it looked like, was going to bring a permanently endowed chair, one being created *ad hominem* for James. He would have his own lifetime Professorial Fellowship, one of less than a hundred in all the university. There was no higher that he could go, not academically, not administratively, not even socially, so far as he knew, unless Queen Victoria decided to marry him.

Only a little exaggeration of his possibilities these days: the Queen herself was vocally unhappy over James's name having been scratched from the list of her annual birthday honors. Her birthday was past, but she'd let it be known that she intended to do something about what she saw as injustice.

He had it all, James thought.

And all anyone expected in return—aside from a lifetime of commitment to knowledge, teaching, and the running of the establishment that supported both—was for James to announce today that reefs of gold, as if poured along one side of the continent, had been revealed in samples brought back heroically from Africa. *You are the perfect one to say, James. People will be so enamored of you, your discovery, and the possibilities, they will forget all about our disgrace.*

Right, James thought. Let's forget about disgrace.

Thus he stared out the window of an administrative office, awaiting the arrival of two reporters from the London *Times*. In the room beyond, several men privately thought they knew what James would be telling the reporters in half an hour.

James himself, though, wasn't so sure.

He stood by the window, looking out onto the Backs. The trees had begun to change color, but the grass was still rich and green as it rolled down to the Cam. Distantly two punters poled slowly on the river. His eyes glazed then. He saw nothing. Just the glare off the glass of the window. And Coco. He could see her in his mind's eye.

Coco listened to the orchestra warm up from high overhead in her opera box, where she sat with Jay Levanthal and his friends—already a breach, since mainly such boxes were occupied by families or, in the case of single individuals, women sat with women and men sat with men. For a woman to sit in a London opera box with four gentlemen, none of them husbands, brothers, or fathers, was risqué. But such was Coco's life. The risqué Parisian *belle* with the house on the Bois. It was an old notion, as antiquated as the Second Empire, but she carried the freedom of her ruin inside her. She didn't *want* to live it down. She liked what it wrought.

She sat back in a dress that rustled when she moved, leisurely spreading the ivory ribs of a silk fan. Jay chattered at her now and then. He would woo her if she'd let him; so would two or three of his friends. They might have enjoyed the excitement of her accepting one of them, yet she couldn't help feel that—like herself—they counted on her to refuse, to maintain the status quo. They were all happy to be exactly as they were. Content. Making the same plays for each other as they had for a dozen years. Flirting safely. Stirring gossip when they got bored.

It was a lovely evening, a good evening for gossip. The Alhambra Theatre was packed. Within five minutes, the orchestra would strike up into the opening overture of the newest operetta by Strauss. *Die Fledermaus*, a production that had opened in Vienna already, and closed in short order. Still, London was keen. The waltz from the second act was becoming quite popular; it was melodious enough to draw in by droves the people who would dance to it the most, high society.

Across the vast space, between her box and those boxes that rounded their way along the opposite wall, Coco could see the heads of the several Members of Parliament she happened to know as well as a banker or two. The far box that sat nearest the stage held a Queen's minister. Coco raised her opera glasses and, with an ironic laugh, realized that sitting beside him was the Chancellor of the University of Cambridge. She couldn't resist scanning every member of this box, yet would not admit to herself who she really looked for.

Coming upon the rosy-nosed face of Tuttleworth, she lowered her small binocular glass instantly and sighed in disgust. Of course, it was not Tuttleworth she had hoped to see. Of course. What an imbecile she was! But then she sat back again, thinking, Well, at least my tooth doesn't hurt.

The orchestra stopped its whining and dissonance all at once. The gaslights lowered, dimming, dimming. In the silence the audience seemed to hold its breath as one. A light, the spotlight that normally was focused on the stage, swung wildly up suddenly into the high dome of the room.

And there in the spotlight a black drape of some sort was whisked off a contraption and with a swoop—as the bass drum in the orchestra pit suddenly rolled into a rapid chest-vibrating rhythm—a bat, indeed, a four- or five-foot bat cruised down in a rapid descent over the audience. Women shrieked, then laughed, thrilled. The bat. *Die Fledermaus,* indeed. A mechanical *fledermaus,* with widespread black wings, soared over everyone's heads on a network of wires operated somewhere by a puppeteer.

Coco began to laugh. It was too good. It was just too strange. The mechanical bat flew within feet of her box. She felt the wind in her face off its kitelike wings. Oh, if James could only see. James. James,

James, James. He would die in his tracks. He would be immobilized.

Actually, what he would do was nearly crawl up the back of a doorman who had just informed him that he must take his seat or return to the lobby.

James had already been at the Alhambra for nearly ten minutes and had no intention of returning to the lobby, where he'd scanned the faces of those who hadn't found their seats; he had prayed to find Coco before the operetta began. When the very last people had straggled into the theatre itself, however, he still hadn't seen her. So he had gone in the central doors and stood at the rear, trying to recognize the back of her beautiful dark head. That was when the lights had dimmed.

He knew she had an opera box in Paris and would not have been surprised to learn she had one at Covent Garden, but now here, he reasoned. She hadn't been in England that long to have established herself at all the theatres. Thus, he was looking in the orchestra seats, trying to spot her while trying to talk the doorman out of grabbing him by the collar, since he didn't have a seat to take, when out of nowhere a bat—a bloody sodding bat as big as he was!—cut down through the air and came straight for him.

It was a nightmare come to life. James screamed. No other word for it. The hero let out a wail and attacked the doorman who had grabbed his coat. No one but no one was going to stop James from evading a bat that big.

He half-climbed, knocked down, half-walked over the doorman, only to find himself running down the aisle in the direction of the stage. All the while, trying to make shorter work of his ordeal, he began to call, "Coco! Coco, for godssake, where are you? Lucia said you were here, but where? Where?"

He heard, he thought, distantly from the other side of the theatre and above, the sound of his name. A tentative, disbelieving sort of voice, just once. "James?"

The bat swooped again. It wasn't real. James distinguished this much, at least. Yet somehow that seemed an insignificant fact, since it seemed to be after him. "Unfortunate," he muttered to a man with more eyebrows than hair. "So unfortunate. Pardon. But you see, I simply *must* get to the other side." James slid into the row.

The man resisted when James tried to climb over him. He grabbed James's trouser leg.

James simply slapped him down. "So sorry. I say, there, most unfortunate." He then proceeded to scramble over the knees of the man's neighbor, over shoulders and arms when necessary, making a dash through the entire line of seated people.

Two women stood, making a fuss. Honestly, if they would only be quiet. . . . But then the wrong people were quiet: the orchestra drizzled instrument by instrument to a stop. The lights came up.

And the bat came down, narrowly missing James's head. He thought his heart would stop.

"James?" It was Coco's voice.

He looked up. "Coco? Where are you?"

"Here."

She was in a box near the front of the far side, if he could just get past about ten more people.

Someone else said his name, not nearly so nicely as Coco. "Stoker," they said with surprise. Then another voice, "It's Sir James Stoker." Oh, fine.

Whispers, disapproval. Oh, and this was only the beginning. Just wait.

But it did hurt to hear them. "Stoker? What the devil is James Stoker doing here?" Like a little thorn that caught, then let go. "Making a fool of himself, it seems." A bramble that slowed him, but didn't deter him.

It would be a full scale forest by the end, he knew. Lit by his own hand into a full conflagration. Oh, the damage he had done himself today.

"Coco," he called, still several people from the aisle. He wanted nothing so much as to look up at her while standing with some sort of dignity. "Coco, I have to talk to you."

Using a wobbling, evasive head and shoulder for balance, James caught sight of her as she rose, stepped forward to the rail overhead, and looked down. Oh, God, she was radiant. Why had he let her go? How could he possibly have thought anything was better than the relief of knowing she existed, knowing she was there? His reverie was interrupted, though, when the bat dived at him again. He yelped and clambered over the last few people. Up the aisle all six of the theatre's doormen now—like a wigged, stockinged, red velvet, gold-braided army—were coming toward him.

Meanwhile, Coco stared down, unable to believe her ears or eyes. James. As if she'd conjured him up. James being harried by a puppeteer. "Oh, James," she said again. What in all the world was he doing here? Looking down, she asked, "Are you all right?"

"No," he said. "No." In the aisle at last, he held out his arms. "Aside from the bat," he said, "I can't sleep. My lectures, when I get to them, are nonsense. I haven't gotten to my rocks or notes or anything that matters to me in weeks." He took a breath. Everyone about had grown noticeably quieter. "All I do is think of you," he continued, "while I walk around feeling as if I just swallowed my heart, as if it were beating inside my stomach. Here." He reached into his pocket, withdrew something, then heaved his arm back. He threw whatever it was up to her.

It was small, whizzing by, then landing with a little tap. Jay picked it up and handed it to Coco.

She stared at it in her palm: it was a tooth. Someone's disgusting tooth.

Wait. It was *her* disgusting tooth. The disgusting tooth she had given to her Nitrous Oxide James, which the real James below had just tossed up into her opera box.

She bit the edge of her lip and looked down over the rail again. Had he really been there? What had she said? Awful things. Like the truth. Like what she really thought. Except that she didn't remember telling him that she loved him, which was the truth as well. "Oh, James," she said. "Where have you been?"

"I don't know where I've been. Asleep. African sleeping sickness. But I'm awake now," he yelled up at her, "and I want to put it back."

"Put what back?" The vast auditorium had grown absolutely attentive.

"Your tooth," he called up. "Please. Let's put it back as it was."

Any child could see there was no putting back what she held in her hand. "You can't."

"No," he agreed. For a moment her James looked more cheerless than she could even imagine seeing. But then James the Stalwart, the relentless man who'd crawled through jungles and ridden thirsty on a desert and battled bats, was about to proceed—

When the mechanical bat took another plunge at him. He ducked, waved his hands for a frantic moment. "Coco!" he called over the next foray. As if she might save him, but by then a doorman had his arm.

James ducked the bat once more, then, on rising, his arm simply came out. Straight from the shoulder. That was James. Nothing devious. He simply and straightforwardly decked the fellow.

She laughed; she wanted to weep.

"Coco!" James called again.

"Watch out!"

Five more liveried doormen took hold of him at once. They all but lifted him, while he yelled, "Coco—" He faltered, an *oof* as they grappled. "I want—" he said. The bat hit him, a misguidance on its puppeteer's part, she thought. It ran into the back of James's shoulder. He leaped as if the devil had found him. "Jesus," he said loudly. Then he spoke very quickly from here: "Coco, I want you to marry me. I don't give a—a—a flying bat what anyone says. I love you. I'm unhappy without you. No one is as—as—as real as you are to me. I am connected to you somehow, the way I'm connected to myself.''

Now the place hushed. Coco rose slightly onto her toes, her fan dropping to dangle from her wrist. She rested her belly against the railing, leaning slightly, as if she could get closer. She couldn't have heard correctly.

''I love you,'' he said again. Someone cheered in the front circle. The largest doorman, who had James by the scruff of the neck, let go. The others seemed perplexed. Cautiously, romantics that they were, they turned him loose. ''Your fairytale ending,'' James called up again. ''I want to give it to you. Marry me. Become Mrs. James Stoker.'' He laughed. ''Dame Nicole. Or Dame Edith, if you prefer. I want to wake up beside you forever. And if there is anyone who doesn't like that, he or she can go jump in the Thames.''

There were people who wouldn't like it, of course. And a lot of them were sitting right here in the room. Reality was reality. But Coco herself felt as if she could have flown out over the box rail, done a swoop with the bat around the room, then landed gently beside the handsome wonder of a man who stood beneath her box, waiting for her response.

Since she was too practical a woman to try flying, however, she lifted her skirt, spun around, started to weave through the two rows of chairs, then remembered: ''Excuse me,'' she said as she shoved Jay out of the way to rush back to the box rail. She leaned over out into the air, bending in half to get as close as she dare to James thirty feet below her. She called down to him, ''Yes! I'm saying yes! You wait right there!'' She turned again. This time Jay had the presence of mind to get out of her way. He moved himself and two chairs quickly, making her exit clean as she broke between the red, gold-fringed curtains and let herself out a black velvet door.

She ran the full length of the upper lobby, then descended the side staircase at a gallop down into the main lodge. Hardly anyone was there. She heard the orchestra strike up the overture again.

No James. Till she came level with the mahogany bar-kiosk. At which point James Stoker walked out the center doorways, two doormen behind him, both stone-faced, one holding a fistful of his collar rather like a bouncer removing a disturbance from a posh brothel. She laughed.

James smiled at her. They let him go when they saw her, then closed the doors to the main auditorium.

Alone. Or almost alone. The man at the kiosk. Two ladies exiting the powder room. It was quiet, just rich swaying music playing softly beyond. Coco walked up to him, stopping three feet short of rushing into James's arms: just for the simple pleasure of looking at him. ''Oh, you are a fine-looking sight, James Stoker,'' she said.

And a sheepish one. He looked down. ''I have to tell you what I've done.''

''What?''

''I've almost certainly lost my job,'' he said. ''You see, I took all the tags from the bore samples this morning.''

''You did what?''

''I removed the tags that identified where all the

gold samples came from, then mixed everything up. There will be no figuring out where the gold is.'' He shrugged, smiling, delighted with himself. ''Other than somewhere in the south of the African continent.''

''But you told Phillip where the gold came from—''

''Ah.'' He shook his head, a mock apology. ''Didn't really trust Phillip. So I told him a longitude and latitude that should put anyone who attempts to go to it into the hottest, wettest part of Africa that any man has ever attempted to visit. Not been there myself frankly, but I suspect there's more mosquitoes there than gold.''

Coco started to laugh. ''You told Phillip the wrong place?''

''I'm afraid so.''

''Do you know the right one?''

James's smile crinkled up, sweet at the edges as it so often could be, then his expression, the smiling timber-wolf eyes, became somehow sly. ''Perhaps. But I'm not telling if I do. And I'm never going back.'' He made a more serious face. ''Look. After I confused things immeasurably in the geology lab, I packed up all my own notes and took them. As I see it, the notes at the very least are mine. They're going to run me out, almost certainly. But I don't care. Ruling over the whole mess wasn't nearly as interesting as I'd thought, anyway. I was forever fighting to steal a moment for my rocks or lectures or readings.

''In any regard, I told several fellows at All Souls what I did. They were appalled but said I could stay.'' He shook his head. ''They said they'd back me, but it's going to be ugly, I think. *I* think I've behaved more heroically than ever before in my life, but this time, alas, no one will cheer. I've essentially robbed people of gold. Gold that wasn't theirs, but still they won't see it that way. And they'll find it anyway, of course, eventually. They know it's there somewhere.''

He smiled broadly then, holding out his arms, turning once before her eyes as if putting himself on display: *Look at me.* "I am so happy with myself though, I can't tell you.'' He came around to face her. "I have given Mtzuba and his family another year, maybe two, maybe three, maybe a decade. Enough time for his child to learn to walk and his wife perhaps to have another before their way of living is turned upside down.

"And I decided to spare All Souls. I moved my things out. I've left. Every possession I could carry is now in boxes at the train station. Not so many boxes as all that. And my carriage will arrive on a car tomorrow.'' He rolled his eyes and smiled at this point, mugging with his handsome face. "Can I stay with you?'' he asked. "Just for a while. Till I can figure out a way to make ends meet again.''

She laughed. "You want me to *keep* you?''

"Yes. If you would.''

"Well, I don't know. . . .'' She sauntered toward him now, opening her fan, circling him as she looked him up, then down. "Yes. I think you'd do nicely. Can you entertain? Are you polite and well mannered, presentable to the Grand People?''

He laughed. "Probably not. I have developed some rude habits.'' He wiggled his brow. "I go naked sometimes.''

Quite suddenly, James rushed her then, grabbing her round the waist, swinging her up, spinning her. The room went round and round, with James at the center. "Where's your wrap?" he asked.

"Where's yours?"

"Forgot it."

"We'll share mine."

"Wonderful. I don't own much, I should warn you. Some clothes, my books and rocks, and a carriage with nothing to pull it. That's what I bring. And this. Ta-*dah*," he announced, setting her down as he pulled a box from inside his coat like a magician. A very tiny velvet box, the sort that held rings. "It used to be a bracelet, one I didn't get a chance to give you. The jeweler exchanged it for this, though, when I added my pocket watch and—"

"You traded your pocket watch?"

"Yes. And the horses for my carriage."

"Your horses!"

"Yes, yes," he said, as if horses were bothersome details. "You see, I wanted to offer you something grand, something ridiculously beyond my means. Just once. Something that seemed as unrealistically wonderful for me to have as you."

"Oh, James, that is so unnecess—" She broke off.

Inside the box was a wide, simple wedding band set with diamonds. If you could call a band of pea-sized, back-to-back diamonds simple. When she could catch her breath, Coco said, "James, this is so foolish."

He was disappointed. "No, it isn't."

She looked up at him, dismayed. "You sold your horses?" she repeated again.

"You have some. We'll hitch your horse to my carriage. A marriage made in heaven." Furrowing his sincere, well-meaning face, he said, "Coco, I saw it. I had to have it for you. I want to marry you tonight. I want you to put it on and never take it off again."

As it turned out, they couldn't marry that night. There was no one to do the job so late. But they could start the honeymoon—which they did. In her carriage on the way home, and then upstairs in her room in her house in London, the house where he had first arrived and asked how to court her in what seemed an age ago now.

Chapter 24

❧

Though given many great blessings—beauty, wit, grace, wisdom—the Princess conquers what was to be her ruin with the best gift of all: serene endurance.

From the Preface to The Sleeping Beauty
DuJauc translation
Pease Press, London, 1877

Indeed, a further scandal ensued, with the London *Times* somehow getting the inside details of all Sir James Stoker did and why. Few people were understanding. James was removed from committees, from boards, from the Council itself, and all but thrown in jail "for vandalizing university property"—for rearranging and unlabeling the rocks he himself had carried up the length of the African continent. Needless to say, he did not get his professorial chair.

In the end, he resigned his lectureship early—it was difficult nigh unto impossible to teach anything, whether in supervision or in the readings, partly because of his own distracted state, partly for the impassioned feelings everyone seemed to have, one way or another, about what he'd done. Moreover, what part of his work he himself had not destroyed was taken away. By the end of the year he had retired to London, completely severed from the town in which he'd been born and the university life he loved. James did what he could: he applied for posts at several other universities and awaited word.

It was a hard time for him, but it was not without its consolations. He and Coco settled into a quiet married life, the rhythm of which suited them both. Privately, the worst that befell them was his nursing Coco through what they both thought was the grippe just before the New Year. She held down no food for days, was weak and tired. She missed her menses—and laughed over the notion of being pregnant. Then her menses came, or so they thought. In fact, much to their surprise, she miscarried a child.

She recovered quickly. The pregnancy, obviously from their time in France, had barely started. Coco joked over her narrow escape. James was happy if she was happy. The idea of the lost baby made him oddly sober about the notion of never having children, more so than he would have expected, but he was content when he saw Coco's health bloom again in her face. She resumed doing her sketches, finishing all but the last for Mr. Pease. She began to look for a castle, planning a day trip so as to make drawings. It was with some relief that the New Year began without fanfare. Eighteen hundred seventy-seven promised to be a better, more uneventful year.

Until an emissary from the Queen knocked at their London door. A scolding at least, James supposed. It was due. And indeed it was a kind of scolding that Victoria sent. But the means of it was quite shocking.

> *Sir James,*
>
> *We take great exception to your recent behavior. Our differences, however, do not annul the fact that you have been of great and heroic service to us in ways we had always intended to acknowledge. You are a man of integrity, even if I do not think you are a man of perfect wisdom. Please accept the enclosed documents as they signify as tangibly as we are able to express our most gracious thanks for your service to us.*
>
> *HRH Queen Victoria*

Three weeks later, Coco said, "My lord, it *is* a castle."

She and James stood in a carriage drive, frazzled and dusty beside their laden coach-and-eight. Their footman and driver came to stand beside them. "My lord," she whispered again. The sight before her took her breath away.

The windows of Bromwyck Castle looked down at them like hundreds of sleepy eyes, blinking, startled awake. It was a trick of the light, of course, only morning sunlight flashing off glass—off all the many diamond-shaped quarrels set between the crisscrossed cames of latticed windows. There were three floors of these tall, graceful windows, like the twinkling regard of a group of shy but curious medieval ladies, huddled together in their steeple headdresses—blue turrets limned a roofline that was delicately dotted with an uncountable number of chimneys, the whole crowned with a central dome that rose to a single glorious spire.

"Did you think she had done something like this?" Coco asked.

"No," James admitted. "Though wait: we haven't seen the inside. There may yet be a joke here."

But it was no joke. Inside they lifted sheets and cover-clothes from highboys and velvet sofas and chests full of silver. All old and splendid, the accumulations of the very elegant old home of a favored earl, recently deceased with no issue, not a relative in sight: and the Home Office had searched for nigh onto twenty-eight years.

The old line had died out; long live the new.

Meeting up with James in the buttery after a quick look around, Coco asked, "How was the upstairs?"

"Old. And buried in an inch of dust."

She laughed ironically. "Yes. On the main floor, too. Enough dust and cobwebs for the place to have been asleep for a century." She wiped her hand along a shelf and came away with a powdery layer of grime.

Then felt arms come around her. James wrapped his arm round the front of her waist and pulled her

back into him. "At least you have your English castle for your next drawings. It is perfect."

"Indeed." Coco laughed in response, while he
nuzzled her neck. "Well, she certainly must be
pleased with you," she said finally. "Secretly. She
can't be that angry."

By *she,* Coco meant Victoria the Queen. Her "attached" had been letters of patent. She had bestowed upon James the Earldom of Bromwyck,
complete with an entailment of the present, somewhat rundown estate. It was a solidly built stone
castle that suffered mostly from decades of neglect,
but the estate also included farmlands that, run
properly, they were hoping, might finance repairs as
well as remodeling or building into the main house
a geology laboratory. If a university wouldn't have
him, James would simply branch out on his own.
He would gather his own specimens, do his own
work, and write about it wherever he could find
print. And the English countryside seemed the perfect place for his pursuit—more space than in London, less criticism, less visibility.

Coco felt the hooks at the back of her dress yield-
ing to her husband's fingers. She turned in his arms.
"Oh, you are wicked."

"Yes. Whenever I get the chance. Where are the
others?"

"Unloading the coach."

"Good." He tried to turn her around again.

But, brazen creature that she was, Coco pressed
forward, settling her hands over James's trousers,
unavoidably rubbing a bit of dust there, over his
fine, thick erection. He had the most perfect penis
she had ever known, as Coco considered herself

something of a connoisseur. His was a cock if ever there was one. It grew straight and full, as hard as the rocks he explored. She explored him, up, then down, delicately tracing the tip through his trousers with her nail. She liked to push him to wits' end. She liked him best absolutely wild.

Which he knew. He laughed, panting, letting himself go as he knocked the breath out of her, taking her backward into a tea cabinet. He was careful with her, yet not so careful that something, a glass, didn't break inside the cupboard as he propped her buttocks on the ledge of the cabinet's small counter. His hands went at the neckline and the hems of her dress at the same time. He touched her, making her head swim, her body hot at its core.

Yet she had wanted to tell him something. "James—"

He was beyond sense. He only wanted her mouth. He chased her face with his as she tried to speak, all the while sliding her drawers down over her hips. Coco would have waited till afterward, if it hadn't mattered so much: she said, "Don't pull out." When he made love to her these days, he withdrew just before he climaxed. "Don't leave me," she said. Then so there could be no mistake, she took hold of his cheeks, made him look at her, the eyes inches away, and whispered quite distinctly, "Stay inside me. Leave yourself, leave parts of yourself in me."

He pushed her legs up, while through his teeth he said, "I'll leave a child in you, Coco." They both jolted as he entered her in a strong thrust of that magnificent penis of his. He went deeply into her body, till his face before her dimmed. Dear

Lord, there was nothing like him.

"Yes," she said. "Yes." She closed her eyes. "I—I want—I want you to." She laughed as they took up their rhythm. They were so good at this.

Each knew where the other wanted to be, where their own pleasure lay. They maximized both in angle and stroke. Till Coco was panting for air and laughing, a woman who laughed a lot—she could barely contain herself now, partly from joy, partly from the worried-amazed startlement she could sense in James. She explained in huffs, "I'm—I'm not feeling as—as old as I once did. Give me a child, James. Make a baby in me."

He smiled then. Whenever she slit her eyes enough to see, he was watching her, smiling at her slyly, a small, relatively gentle expression, given that he roughly ploughed himself into her—in, then away, in, then away, elegantly smooth, broad, hard, lengthy, and as hot as an iron from a fire. Her last thought, before she herself went to cinders was, Make a baby, James.

And, bracing his hands on the cupboard doors that had begun to clank to their rhythm, James did just that.

Several months after he and Coco had moved in at Bromwyck, Oxford University (publicly appalled, but secretly delighted with the stink James had caused at Cambridge) offered the marginally respectable new earl a guest lectureship in geology. By the time the baby arrived—young Samuel, named after James's father—James was happily arguing over whether Oxford could publish his papers on Africa and whether or not he'd speak of the continent's gold in his lecture Hilary term.

For Coco, an English countess with suddenly a proper English home, complete with a proper little English earl to raise, it was all a strange and wondrous second life. She wrote to David, "Please come. I know you are annoyed with James, but my life is so happy: I would have been embarrassed to ask for so much in my fondest prayers."

David did finally visit, though he reserved judgment. James was able to woo him slightly, but not much. David sided to a degree with those from Cambridge who were put out with Coco's husband. Neither did David like that James hadn't treated his mother perfectly at every turn; and he hated what had befallen his father at what he saw partially as James's hands. Still he arrived and was pleasant for the gathering James arranged in honor of the two joint events that autumn, Samuel's baptism and the publication of Coco's drawings in *The Sleeping Beauty*.

To celebrate, the Stokers opened Bromwyck Castle up to their new neighbors—and, surprisingly, a great many who were invited actually came. It amused Coco in particular that the vicar and his wife of the nearby village of Wyckerley arrived with flowers for her and a toy, a lovely little duck on a push stick, for Samuel. A country vicar, of all things, sat down comfortably and amiably in her parlor. Coco couldn't decide if he and his wife were simply too remote out here to know who she was and of James's scandal, or just too naive to appreciate it. Or—a distinct possibility—too generous to mention any awareness they had. In all events, that afternoon, a vicar, his wife, and a host of new neighbors seemed astonishingly willing to be friendly, possibly even supportive.

The only blemish was that David left immediately after, a day earlier than planned. He didn't explain. Coco supposed he was jealous. She reminded herself to visit him soon in Cambridge. She could see how the sudden new direction her life had taken could be shocking, difficult for him to embrace. She must make sure he saw a place in it for himself.

James, on the other hand, had not a complaint in the world. Lying in bed the night of their successful party, he read his wife's book for the first of many times to his son, who promptly fell asleep nestled into the folds of his father's nightshirt. Then, before James could carry the little fellow to his cradle, Papa himself dozed off, Coco's book collapsing open onto his chest.

Coco discovered her husband and son just so, asleep together. Never, she thought, were there two more lovely sleeping beauties, not in all the kingdoms of the earth. She was so taken by the sight, she flipped open her sketch pad and began to draw them.

After she had finished, looking at her work, she thought, Well, yes, there had been another little sleeping prince in a kingdom long ago. She took her pencil and wrote across her drawing:

David,

Samuel so reminds me of you. How I wish you had had a father like James. Though fathers, mothers, we can all be so obtuse. Perhaps what a child really needs is a brother. Please come see us often. When it comes to chemistry, cricket, and bees, Samuel will be relying on you.

A thousand kisses,
Coco

While James dreamed of stars.

Star maps . . . black African skies twinkling with patterns of light . . . a celestial landscape so precise . . . as clear in his mind as the position of trees or bends in the road on the way home from London. He dreamed of Mtzuba playing his nose flute and having a son or daughter as fine as Samuel. In James's dream he told Mtzuba, I am happy. I am not where I thought I was going, but I like it here. I have found my way home.

Author's Note

The literary convention of "Oxbridge" is usually used to fictionalize the atmosphere of England's two most prestigious institutions of higher learning, Oxford and Cambridge. I have used here a different convention, however. All Souls College does not exist at Cambridge; there is a college, though, at Oxford by this name. For the purposes of this book, I combined the two universities in this manner a great deal, marrying elements of Oxford and Cambridge into one fictional "Cambridge" within these pages that does not exist in reality. As to the nastier elements of embezzlement and personal betrayal, the reader will please realize that I made them up entirely. Though I don't doubt that anywhere there are human beings one can find larceny and misuse, my impression after one blissful summer at the University of Cambridge was that less of these vices thrived there than usual, not more.

As to the town itself, many may recognize it as Cambridge with not a trace of Oxford and only the smallest degree of fictionalization. I allowed myself to use the real town strictly for the selfish pleasures of walking to Grantchester again and punting the Cam and smelling the lavender by King's and the honeysuckle just after Clare Bridge.

Judith Ivory